Panverse Two

Five Original Novellas of Fantasy and Science Fiction

Panverse Two

Five Original Novellas of Fantasy and Science Fiction

Edited by Dario Ciriello

PANVERSE

Panverse Publishing

These stories are works of fiction. All of the characters, organizations, and events portrayed in the stories contained in this anthology are either fictitious or are used fictitiously.

Published by Panverse Publishing, 2207 Holbrook Dr., Concord, CA 94519

Cover Artwork, "Fire Dance," by Susan McGivergan
Cover and interior layout by Dmitri Sled

Visit Panverse Publishing online at www.panversepublishing.com

Printed in the United States of America

ISBN 978-0-615-37736-0

Acknowledgements

In these days when hot lead is a memory and even the word *typesetting* seems quaint, anyone could be forgiven to thinking that producing a book is easy. It is—but producing a book that is both aesthetically pleasing and contains something of value is as hard as ever. I therefore want to express my heartfelt gratitude to the many people without whom this anthology wouldn't have been possible.

Thanks first of all to our authors, all five of whom trusted me with their creations; to artist Susan McGivergan for channeling one of the *Fiereste* in her gorgeous cover artwork; and to the intrepid Dmitri Sled, for his outstanding layout work on both the cover and interior of this volume.

Thanks also go to the many superb editors and anthologists in the SF and Fantasy fields, all of whom have delighted readers over the years and blazed a bright trail for Young Turks such as myself to follow.

A huge thanks to my very dear friend Bryta Schulz, for being there when the world went to hell and the Nazgûl rode hard at our heels.

Finally, my unbounded gratitude as always goes to my wife Linda, whose patient and amused forebearance in the face of my dreams and eccentricities brings even the stars within reach.

Contents

Introduction

When we launched Panverse One, a year ago, I felt like a castaway throwing a message-bearing bottle into the ocean. With luck, fair winds and steady currents would deliver it to a shore where people understood the message. I believed there were readers out there who enjoyed the novella form as much as I did, and who missed the all-novella, original, unthemed anthologies of decades past. If I was right—and it was a big *if*—there might be a market for the Panverse series.

Wind and currents both proved favorable, and Panverse One was well-received and reviewed, especially given the fact that both I and most of the authors were barely known, and that the title was only available online.

And so I'm thrilled and delighted to bring you Panverse Two. As with our first volume, some of our authors will be new to many readers. But from the first paragraph the reader knows with certainty that each of these authors has traveled to strange realms and times, and brought back tales and truths wondrous, fearful, and unique.

Welcome to Panverse Two.

A Clash of Eagles
Alan Smale

The 33rd Legion had begun to leak men as if from a slow wound, soon after they'd broken camp and marched away from the *Mare Chesapica*. Now, two weeks inland, Praetor Gaius Publius Marcellinus was down fifty-eight soldiers, and this out of a legion where his so-called centuries had only been seventy men strong to begin with.

They had cleared villages and taken slaves, but had yet to be engaged by the enemy in a real fight. Their losses were solely due to harassing actions; the lone arrow flying out of the trees, the blade from behind, and more often than not, the unexplained disappearance. It was hard enough to march into an empty continent on the wrong side of a giant ocean, blaze a trail broad enough for eight cohorts, tramp twenty miles along it each day and build a marching-camp the size of a small town every night, without having to risk being picked off by cowardly savages whenever a few twigs'-worth of cover separated you from your mates.

It was a slow bloodletting, of course. At this rate of attrition his legion would have time to walk twice around the world before the savages got them all. But morale was suffering. Marcellinus was their Praetor. It was his job to stop things like this happening.

And, since his cohorts were filled with the superstitious dreck of

Roman provinces from Aethiopia to Scythia to Magyar to Hispania and back around, the night-camp was alive with rumors. Man-bears were hiding behind trees, huge hawks were swooping in from the air to pick off the valiant Roman infantry one by one. Giant rodents, even, burrowed up from beneath them. It seemed that in the wilderness of a foot-soldier's imagination no animal was allowed to be normally proportioned. Superstition was strong at the best of times in a rabble like this, and the further away from Urbs Roma he took them, the worse they got.

Marcellinus wasn't exactly happy himself. Nobody in his right mind could feel comfortable with two months of ocean separating him from the Imperium. Romans were not natural sailors, and the trans-*Atlanticus* voyage had been a puking nightmare, the way the big Roman troop transports rolled on a heavy swell. But however far afield his duties took him, Marcellinus wasn't about to start believing in giant hawks.

Which left the natives. They were everywhere, of course; on the fleet's arrival the shores of the Bay had been crowded with dirty villages of cringing fishermen so spineless the Romans had started calling them "braves" in mockery. They'd already had to slaughter at least half of them. Many of the remainder had fled. Others were now roped to the heavy carts that made up the Legion's supply train.

Now, though, they'd left behind the fisher-folk and the berry-pickers. The villages they passed might be empty, but the woods around them were not. Hiding behind the tree-trunks of inland Nova Hesperia was a different breed of redskin altogether.

"I am supposed to ravish you now," said Marcellinus, "but I shall not."

The young *Powhatani* brave gaped, so startled that the necklace of seashells on his chest rattled and the feathers nearly fell out of his hair.

"Not *you*," said Marcellinus, exasperated. "You're here to translate. Tell *her* that."

The *Powhatani* word-slave—they called him 'Fuscus' because he was brown—only now saw the squaw sitting on the blanket on the floor of the Praetor's tent headquarters. Fuscus eyed her warily, but didn't seem upset on her behalf. Why would he be? She wasn't of his tribe.

He babbled at her, and she replied, rather haughtily for one of her smallness and unpromising situation. Compared to the mellifluous flow of patrician Latin, their primitive *Algon-Quian* tongue sounded like baby-talk and twigs snapping.

Her eyes narrowed. The expression she turned on Marcellinus was contemptuous.

Perhaps she had misunderstood; *Algon-Quian* had an ungodly wide range of dialects. Marcellinus turned to the word-slave. "She understands? She is my prisoner. I should brutalize—use?—use her, then give her to my men. Custom… demands it. Yet I shall not do that. I show her mercy. Yes?" Here he knew he was on safe ground; 'mercy' was one of the first words Fuscus had learned, and it was still one of his favorites.

The woman spat out a couple of words, steel in her sneer. Marcellinus sighed. "Now you're supposed to tell me what she said."

Fuscus cleared his throat nervously. "She say, 'Disgust.' And that Roman are wild hog." Alert to Marcellinus's irritation, he took a step back. "*She* say it, sir. Not me."

"Ask her what she was doing in the road in front of my army," said the Praetor.

Such was the height of the 33rd Legion's superstition that it had taken just one lone woman to bring them to a halt. Faced with twenty braves, or a thousand, his soldiers would have charged and hacked them into bloody dog-meat. But at the sight of a solitary woman standing calmly in their path with flames leaping up from a fire behind her, they'd slowed to a ragged stand-easy and looked back over their shoulders for orders. Marcellinus would have to thicken their spines somehow before they reached the lands of the mound-builders and their—Norse-alleged—city of gold.

"She from West further, sir. Over hills. Hear tell of Roman, come to see for herself. She chieftain, daughter of chieftain. She ask you, go home where you come."

"I see," said Marcellinus.

The woman struggled to her feet with some difficulty. The two guards who stood in the doorway of the Praetorium tent looked at Marcellinus hopefully, but he shook his head at them, allowing her impertinence.

"She ask what you want."

Marcellinus looked at her. "We want your land. Your country. Your gold and spices. Whatever you have is now ours."

She looked at Fuscus blankly and spoke. He translated, "She say you cannot take the ground. Cannot take sky. It here always."

Marcellinus stepped closer. Well-nourished compared with the savages, he towered over her. The squaw's eyes widened but she stood as tall as she could. Given that the Romans in their plated metal armor and plumed helmets must have appeared utterly alien to her, her courage was considerable.

Her forehead was flat and her hair muddy, but her cheekbones were set higher than those of the coastal tribes and her bronze skin was better cared for. Most telling of all she stood straight and calm, with a dignity their local captives lacked. She was the dusk, the evening star; she was Nova Hesperia, the giant unopened continent of it. And he, Marcellinus, was a bully and past his prime, and he knew it.

He made his decision. "What's her name?"

"She calls her, *Sisika*," said the brave.

"Well, if Sisika really is *daughter of chieftain*, the tribes to the West will know her. Yes?"

"Yes," said Fuscus.

"Then say this to her: *Sisika*, I set you free. You will run ahead of my army and tell all the tribes of the *Haudenosaunii*, tell the *Iroqua*, tell whoever else might lay in our path that the Romans are coming." He struck his steel chest plate with his fist, making an impressive clang. "She will tell the tribes we are mighty and shall not be stopped. We will pass through their lands, and onward to the West."

The *Powhatani* quacked and popped at Sisika, relaying Marcellinus's message. He continued: "If the tribes allow us passage we will spare them. But if they resist, if any more of my men die in these cowardly sneak-attacks, we will kill every man, woman and child, every deer and bird, and the land will be silent and broken after our passing. She must tell them this, or their blood will be on her head." Marcellinus jabbed a finger towards her, and she flinched. "On *you*, Sisika. We will wipe them from the earth because of *you*."

As Fuscus finished his translation, Marcellinus held the squaw's gaze, stern and unblinking. She stared back. Her deep brown eyes were very disconcerting.

She babbled like a woman trying to mimic bird-tweets through a mouthful of moss. Marcellinus waited. One of his soldiers languidly drew his *pugio*, short dagger, and poked the *Powhatani* from behind. The word-slave yelped and said, "Sisika will do this, tell tribes Praetor-words."

She had certainly said more than that. "And... ?"

"And, but, land of *Iroqua*, very savage, very hurt. Men of harsh."

"And?"

"And once past *Iroqua*, west, is then great city, people of eagle and thunder-bird. These will fall on you and... burn, cut off your hair, laugh."

The city the Norsemen told of. Marcellinus felt a quickening of interest. Now he was getting somewhere. "This Great City has gold?" He showed Sisika the ring on his finger, the plate on his table, the small statues of his *lares*, household gods. "Gold?"

Sisika reached for one of the statues, and Marcellinus had to slap her hand away. Her eyes flared, and for a frozen moment he thought the squaw might actually hit him back, guaranteeing her instant execution. Instead she turned to Fuscus and spoke.

"She ask who these toy persons are."

"They are not toys. Ask her about the gold."

Fuscus tried again, pointing anew to the various objects, but the answer was clear in the squaw's demeanor. She didn't understand gold's significance. She had never seen it before.

Fuscus looked nervous. "She say no gold."

Marcellinus sighed. "All right. Enough. Get them out of here."

He turned as his guards manhandled the primitives out of his tent. "Well, so much for that. What d'you think?"

"That your soft heart will be the death of you." Behind him sat Aelfric, tribune of the Fourth and Fifth Cohorts, gruff and mustachioed, his arms folded.

"Likely enough," said Marcellinus.

Aelfric gestured after the native woman. "Why let her go? Really?"

"You don't see Vestilia in her?" Vestilia was Marcellinus's daughter. The army, and his long absences on searing campaigns against the Ayyubid and Khwarezmian Sultanates and then deep into Sindh and Bengal, had cost Marcellinus his wife. Only his own arrogance and neglect had cost him the respect of his daughter.

"You see Vestilia in all women." Aelfric shrugged. "Not bad, to send the squaw on ahead, though the *Iroqua* will probably do for her before she gets twenty miles."

"She made it here. She can make it back."

"Perhaps."

Marcellinus walked to the tent door. "Did Sigurdsson return yet?"

"None of the scouts did. I'll bring 'em to you right away when they do."

"Hmm."

"Don't fret," said his tribune dismissively, walking past him out of the tent. "Our Norsemen can rip the arse out of any 'men of harsh' *this* sorry land might throw at 'em."

Strictly speaking, they weren't yet Roma's Norsemen. The Imperator Hadrianus III had shut down the Viking raids on the coasts of Britannia, gobbling up Scand for the Imperium and acquiring every Dane and Geat and Sami clear up to Ultima Thule, but these days a nation had to live loyally within the Pax Romana for two hundred years before its people were granted full citizenship.

It was 1245 years since Augustus Caesar had recast the bloody Roman Republic into an Imperium. It was a full one thousand nine hundred and seventy-one years since the founding of Roma, *Ab Urbe Condita*, and it would be the year 2100 by that reckoning before every new Scand child would enter the world a Roman citizen.

The Norse didn't care a fig about the delay, though. A pragmatic race, they had already carved themselves out a critical role. Roma needed its navy now as never before, and the well-traveled Norsemen were just the people to help them run it.

After decades of stagnation and even retreat under a succession of weak Imperators, Hadrianus III had grasped the nettle. Right out of the gate the man thought big: he had vowed at his coronation that by the dawn of the third millennium A.U.C. the power of Roma would encircle the globe. Only thirty-five years of age at the time, he had figured that if he set the wheels moving quickly enough and remained popular enough to die of old age, he might leave as his legacy a world where the sun never set on the Roman Imperium.

Candidly, Marcellinus thought the man was cracked. Roma had reined in its expansion in the first place because of the high cost of defeating the Khazars and Eastern sultanates. And now Hadrianus was trying to expand the Imperium even further into the East at precisely the moment when the Mongols and Turkics were swooping westward into Kara Khitai and southward towards the Chin Dynasty. Leave the buggers to it, that's what Marcellinus thought: let the nomadic Mongol Khan swallow all that and try to administer it. Roma should hold its current line in India, which Temujinus—or Chinggis, or however he wanted to be addressed this week—had shown no ambitions towards. Eventually the Mongol Khanate would overreach itself and crumble, and that would be Roma's moment to march eastward again. In the meantime, the real estate from Hispania to the Himalaya and from the barren northern ice to the fetid jungles of Aethiopia Interior should surely be enough Imperium for anyone.

But of course it wasn't, and so here they were, pushing on beyond the sunset into Nova Hesperia. Because clearly if your territorial ambitions were stalled in one direction, it was only logical to spearhead an attack in the other. As if controlling two frontiers at the same time hadn't been a nightmare for the Imperium ever since the first Nero had tried to conquer the barbarians beyond the Danube while simultaneously holding the Parthians at bay.

"Imperators," as Marcellinus might say over dinner, "have no sense of history."

And, "Soldiers," as his First Tribune Lucius Domitius Corbulo would regularly chide him in response, back in the days when they had still gotten along, "have no grasp of economics."

Corbulo would remind Marcellinus that if popularity cost money, keeping your army loyal cost even more. Bread, circuses, and bribes: big money. And if you were an Imperator spending cash faster than you were raising it in taxes, then you needed somewhere to invade so you could steal some more.

Which brought Marcellinus full circle, back to the Norse.

His officers awaited him in the open air outside his Praetorium: Lucius Domitius Corbulo, sitting off to one side looking bored; Aelfric, tapping his foot; Tribune Marcus Tullius, solid, earnest, sunburned and blond; Gnaeus Fabius, the magistrate and junior tribune Hadrianus had assigned to the 33rd Legion at the last minute either to get him out from underfoot or to spy on Marcellinus (most likely both); and Leogild, his Visigoth quartermaster. Nearby, Marcellinus's Praetorian guards stood bunched around the savages, Sisika and Fuscus.

Sisika's eyes were wide. When they had frog-marched her into the Praetorium the *castra* had been little more than an outline, a large square ditch and embankment surrounding virgin meadowland. In the intervening hour the camp had sprung up all around them to become a living community of wooden buildings and goat-skin tents as familiar to Marcellinus as his hometown, and as foreign to Sisika as the surface of the Moon.

Fuscus, who witnessed this transformation every night, had now adopted an even more noticeable air of condescension towards her. It was a dynamic Marcellinus often saw amongst slaves and captives, this petty jockeying among the have-nothings for small scraps of perceived status. He smacked the word-slave over the head and pointed down the lane towards the slave-quarters, and Fuscus cringed obsequiously and set off at a trot.

To his guards, the Praetor said: "Safe conduct for this one, out of the camp. No interference. Understood?"

Leogild assessed the squaw, up and down. Sisika's hair was still matted and her knees skinned, but her light brown skin was clear and uncreased, almost glowing in the evening light. She was easily the least ugly savage they'd come across since landing on the shores of Nova Hesperia. He cleared his throat. "Couldn't the men have a go with her first, boss? Send her on her way proper-like?"

"That is hardly what 'safe conduct' means," said Marcellinus.

"They'll be disappointed," said the Visigoth.

"They can have the next hundred women we snare. This one has a job to do. I'm sending her out with an ultimatum to the villages ahead: get out of our way or perish." He turned back to his guards. "Two of you, escort her to the Northgate. Nobody meddles with her."

Sisika looked back at him with those disconcerting brown eyes. His soldiers watched her go, unhappily.

Corbulo eyed her legs as she walked by. "We make agreements with barbarians now?"

"This is a new land," said the Praetor. "We try things, and we see what works. Worst case, we've only lost one squaw."

"Whatever will get us to the gold more quickly," said Gnaeus Fabius.

Too many expectations of gold. "And home, more quickly," said Marcellinus.

It was quite the walk Sisika had to make down the Cardo, as the camp's main street was known, hemmed in close by a long silent gauntlet of ogling soldiers. Marcellinus noted that she walked with her chin up and showed little fear. Maybe she really was 'daughter of chieftain'.

"Cut off your hair, eh?" murmured Aelfric. "A dire threat. I'll wager you didn't see that one coming."

"Perhaps they could arrange me a manicure as well," said Marcellinus.

Twenty yards shy of the Northgate Sisika came level with the wooden shrine housing the golden eagle standard of the Legion. Her mouth dropped open and she turned to stare at it; the Aquila, wings upraised, lightning bolts around its feet, glowered back at her with its beady raptor gaze. The *aquiliferi* honor guard stepped forward instantly, hands on sword hilts; orders or no orders, if Sisika had disrespected the Aquila its guards would have cut her down where she stood. But Sisika knelt, bowing so deeply her forehead touched the road.

Tribune Corbulo stood to watch. "She's left it a little late to curry favor."

Marcellinus had seen eagles here, wheeling high in the dusk skies. And Sisika had mentioned them. "Maybe the Aquila is sacred to her, too. She honors the bird, not us."

Sisika stood and walked on through the Northgate. If she ran, she waited until she was out of sight.

Marcellinus wished he hadn't asked her name.

Corbulo tutted. "A wasted opportunity to raise morale, Gaius. It'll be trouble, and we need no more of that."

"One woman," said the Praetor.

"Still bad tactics, with the troops as fractious as they are."

"Discipline's a problem," added Gnaeus Fabius, who rarely passed up an opportunity to suck up to Corbulo, or state the obvious.

"An even worse problem, if the redskins keep picking us off."

Marcellinus looked around him. "I did not request a discussion on this topic, gentlemen."

"God knows what we'd all have caught off her," said Aelfric loudly, glancing around at the other tribunes. "I doubt these people ever bathe. A good commander safeguards his men's health as well as his own."

"And the men bless you for it, sir," said Leogild to Marcellinus, straightfaced.

Marcellinus sighed. "Don't we have a convenient festival coming up? Where do we stand on wine?"

"We'll be out of corn and cheese first," said the quartermaster. "Wine's not yet an issue."

The other officers looked at each other. None of them had any clearer idea of the date than Marcellinus did.

"Let's call it Easter," said Aelfric. "That's a moveable feast anyway." Aelfric's Fifth were mostly Northern auxiliaries, and many of the Legion's worshippers of the Christ-Risen served in that cohort.

"Tomorrow, not today," warned Corbulo. "Let them walk off this disappointment first."

"Of course," said Marcellinus, who'd had no intention of fueling his legionaries with extra liquor tonight. "All right. Get out there and make it known that the squaw was a chieftain's daughter that I sent out to calm the way ahead, and that I'm not setting any new precedents with this. And then remind them that tomorrow's Easter."

"Most of them won't know what that is," said Fabius.

"Or care," said Marcus Tullius, scratching under his helmet.

"Tell 'em it's the Christ-Risen feast of double wine rations," said Aelfric. "They'll understand *that*."

"Dismissed," said Marcellinus, and Leogild and most of his tribunes—Corbulo, Fabius, Tullius—saluted and set off through the camp in various directions to brief their centurions.

Naturally, Aelfric dallied. "So, Praetor. Even when you were younger. Would you have raped her?" He raised his hands. "Nothing implied. I'm just making conversation."

Marcellinus looked at him. It was an impertinent question, but that was Aelfric's way. Britons were very direct. "You don't have daughters, do you, Aelfric?"

"No."

"Ask me again when you do."

The Norse were a smart people who mostly understood the massive advantages of being important to the Imperium and the terrible costs of being an irritant. But every race contained its bad apples. And so the Imperator Hadrianus had issued an edict allowing no quarter to Norse pirates, those renegade few who refused to come to heel.

A year ago, a Roman navy warship had intercepted a Norse longship approaching the north coast of Hibernia. An innocent Norse vessel sailing home from Vinlandia had naught to fear from a Roman inspection; this longship had tried to use its greater maneuverability to escape and when that failed had tried to bluff the Roman captain, badly.

After a brief but fierce engagement the Romans boarded the vessel to find it stuffed with gold plate, jewelry and bizarre statues from an as-yet unknown culture, along with large quantities of lapis lazuli and a few bags of spice. Alas, Roman efficiency had slammed into Viking berserker battle-ardor with such completeness that there was nobody left alive on the longship capable of testifying where they had acquired such a lucrative cargo.

Despite this inconvenience, Hadrianus was badly in need of revenue and not one to pass up such an opportunity. It was at this point he had raised the priority of the conquest of Nova Hesperia.

There was no reason to suspect that the equatorial regions of the Evening Continent should be any richer than those of famine-stricken Aethiopia. Logically, then, the gold must have originated around the same latitude as Roma.

Hadrianus sent scouting parties into Nova Hesperia. Those who returned brought back tales of a large city of mounds, longhouses, and at least ten thousand people, in the plains far beyond the mountains. Admittedly they hadn't brought any gold back with them, but then again, the savages hadn't allowed them within the boundaries of the city.

Very well; Hadrianus could spare a legion to throw at a high-risk, high-return venture. Now all he needed was the right Praetor to lead it.

By dawn the next day the Legion had folded tents and were on the trail again, heading West in as straight a line as they could manage. Which, being Romans, was pretty damned straight.

For a while, Marcellinus's tactic seemed to be working. The harassing actions that the primitives had been running against the Legion's advanced corps of engineers and its flanks and stragglers stopped. Freeing one squaw had apparently earned the Fighting 33rd a clear path all the way to the mountains. Even the grumpy Domitius Corbulo had to agree it was well done. The miles fell away under the military sandals of the Legion; day by day they left the sea further behind, and the interior of the giant land opened up around them. They covered two hundred miles without a single death, and the daily march became so routine that the centurions began to grumble that the men were getting soft.

True to his word, Marcellinus left the villages unscathed. Usually the savages deserted them and hid out in the wilds till the army had passed; sometimes they sat sullenly outside their scrappy, insect-ridden hovels with their heads bowed. Good enough. They might be untouched by civilization, but at least they comprehended a threat when they heard it.

Truth be told, Marcellinus felt a little sorry for them. He hadn't asked to be sent here, and these folks hadn't asked to have a Roman legion trampling their pastoral quiet. The redskins had so little to begin with. His far ancestors might have been painted men very much like these, long before all the marble buildings and the metal-smithing and the law-making. Less than farmers, their tiny patches of sickly corn were so pitiful that even Leogild didn't think them worth requisitioning; as far as Marcellinus could tell, the inland savages really survived by trapping coneys and picking berries. Marcellinus could be ruthless when necessary, but there was no glory in waging war against beggars. The true enemy lay ahead, in the Great City that the Norse scouts had reported and Sisika had now confirmed.

Soon enough, the terrain creased around them and rose up into a series of rolling ridges and craggy mountains that Fuscus, in his broken tongue, called *Appalachia*. The peaks were neither as classically sculpted as the Alps of Europa, nor as grand and tall as the ranges of the Himalaya, but they had a hazy comeliness to them that reminded

Marcellinus of parts of northern Italia. Despite the rigors of getting the Legion through such a trackless wilderness, Marcellinus thought it a land of some charm. Then again, he got to ride a horse up the interminable hills.

They had only a couple of dozen horses, and only the Praetor and his tribunes, scouts, and dispatch riders got to ride them. They were much too valuable to put to work hauling the supply wagons, and besides, they had slaves for that; to their surprise the Hesperian shores had proved to be devoid of beasts of burden, aside from the *Powhatani* themselves.

Marcellinus felt the odd twinge of guilt about resting easy in the saddle, but he genuinely needed to preserve his strength. At night in *castra* his men might drink their watered wine and gossip over games of knucklebones with no further cares, but Marcellinus spent those hours meeting with his quartermaster about supplies, his tribunes and armorers about their battle-readiness, his centurions on matters of discipline, and a hundred and one other things. There was never a lazy evening for a Praetor. Technically Marcellinus might have left some of these details to others, but with his authority over the Legion as precarious as it now seemed, it behooved him to keep himself involved with all aspects of legionary logistics. If Marcellinus could be everywhere at once, no one could talk about him behind his back.

The men noted his diligence and didn't seem to begrudge him the ride. Their job was the hike; his was to keep enough blood flowing to his brain and heart that he could look after his men and keep them as comfortable as possible, not waste the sweat they were donating to the enterprise, and be trusted not to spend their lives in vain when the crunch came.

Around noon Marcellinus found himself riding near Marcus Tullius, who hailed from Etruria. "What d'you think, Tully? Long views, and enough land for anyone, once we get rid of some of these damned trees."

Tullius made a sour face. "Over that whore of an ocean? It's too far from Roma. Nobody is going to want to come and farm this crap."

"Some men might prize a bit of separation from the capital. Independent sorts, regulation-weary?"

"Ex-convicts, maybe. But they won't be growing olives or grapes on these slopes. Bad soil, worse sun. You've seen what passes for corn here? Even the Norse can't make a go of it, and they can farm Graenlandia."

"Well, only with cattle," said Marcellinus. "They don't grow crops there."

"Either way. No, if the redskins have gold, we want it; if not we just kill the bastards off. Hack ourselves a bloody road right across the continent and use it to go and stab the slant-eyes in the back."

"That might be quite a distance," Marcellinus murmured, and didn't raise the issue of natural beauty again.

Whatever their scenic glory, the Legion found the high ridges heavy going, and their average daily march dropped from twenty-two miles to nearer twelve. On one ignominious day when they had to ford several streams and backtrack twice in search of a route the baggage carts could negotiate, they only advanced by seven. Finding areas broad and flat enough to host a full *castra* added to the challenge, and Marcellinus sorely missed the guidance of Thorkell Sigurdsson and his other Norse scouts, still conspicuous by their absence.

His men grumbled, and even Leogild's sunny Visigoth humor began to cloud over. Each day took them further from the coast and stretched their supply lines even thinner; battle was ahead, a city to be sacked, spoils to be had—but how far? Marcellinus heard the discontent and shared it, but all he could do was show a resolute face and push on.

Then came the ambush, and everything changed.

Imperators come and go. In Marcellinus's time he'd seen nine and served four, and he would not have donned the Imperial purple himself for a million sesterces. He would sooner have lived as a beggar in a shack than be Imperator of Roma, and everyone knew it, so he had survived many a bloody Imperial transition to become one of the most senior legates in the army. His problem with Hadrianus III was the Imperator's ambition, not his own.

Gaius Publius Marcellinus was that rare thing, a Roman who was actually born in Urbs Roma. His family had been military for four generations and he was born with a brass spoon in his mouth, rather than silver; nonetheless his *gens* was reasonably well-to-do and the young Gaius wanted for little, except common sense.

One night on the way home from his tutor's he had wandered into the slums of Subura. There he'd been set upon by a gang of young thugs, beaten up, his tunic ripped, his books scattered. In fact he had been lucky; Subura gangs sometimes killed or gelded their victims just for the joy of watching the rich suffer. That evening, the young Marcellinus was saved from worse damage only by his tender years. Several hours after the beating, a waterboy and a prostitute had discovered him and carried his bleeding body out.

His distraught mother's slaves had had to banish her from the room so they could bandage Marcellinus's wounds; the poor woman had had to worry through quite enough of her husband's campaigns against the Magyars without having her son's body slashed and pummeled on her own doorstep. Once the slaves let her back in she fell upon Marcellinus moaning "We'll leave the Urbs, we'll live in Campania, you must never go near the Subura again, they know you there now." And he had looked at her as if she were crazy, and from the side of his battered mouth had said in a clear, piping voice: "Of course they do. And that's why I must go back. They mustn't win. *They'll* take orders from *me*."

So went the story his father told their friends, anyway. But the slaves corroborated it.

Soon, Marcellinus was leading a life of relative gentility by day and masterminding one of the busiest gangs in the Subura by night. Marcellinus's gang were not murderers and emasculators, though, but thieves who broke into the villas of rich merchants to liberate their valuables. His parents did not consider this such a fine story to regale their dinner guests with; when his father finally searched his sleeping room and found a collection of silver cups and jewelry that certainly should not have been there, he gave young Gaius a whipping that put the Subura-boys' beating to shame. A week later, long before the stripes on his back and legs healed, Gaius Marcellinus found himself delivered ahead of schedule to boot camp in the army of Titus Augustus, his first and favorite Imperator.

And, as before, he'd never looked back.

By contrast, Lucius Domitius Corbulo was a member of an old patrician family and a distant descendant of that Gnaeus Domitius Corbulo who had served as a Consul under Caligula, commanded the armies of Germania Inferior under Claudius, and been appointed Governor of Asia under Nero. One day he would make the leap from army to politics, and perhaps end up a Consul himself. Perhaps it was predictable, then, that Corbulo was the most alert to their place in history. More than any other Roman present he felt the full sweep of Roman power. But Corbulo was also alert to money, and sought riches as well as glory.

When Hadrianus had called upon Marcellinus to lead the 33rd into the new land across the *Atlanticus*, Marcellinus had chosen Corbulo to be his First Tribune. Corbulo had served under him in his Sindh campaign, and Marcellinus knew him as a man of breeding, spotless record, and endless anecdote. If Marcellinus had to dine with someone for months on end, he wanted him by all means not to be tedious. Later, he came to marvel that tediousness was the worst sin he had dreaded in the man.

So what did it say about Marcellinus that, despite everything, he now spent more time with Aelfric the Briton and Sigurdsson the Norse scout than he did with the Romans among his tribunes? Nowadays he even got on better with the bluff working-class centurions and their men than he did with Corbulo, Fabius, and Tully.

The answer was that Roma had grown effete under its most recent Imperators, and this batch of tribunes bore testimony to that. After Titus Augustus, whose assassination Marcellinus had barely survived, things had spiraled from bad into worse during the reigns of Vespasianus II, Arcadius Victor, and now Hadrianus III. For the values Marcellinus prized he now had to seek out plebeians and foreigners, just as in his errant youth he'd felt more comfortable with the street boys than the youths of the gymnasium.

Once more, Marcellinus was blazing his own social trail, navigating by the seat of his tunic. And, once again, this would come at a high cost.

The ambush came as no surprise. The Legion was ready for it. Craving it, in fact.

They marched down a long sweeping valley, narrow and high-sided. Below them the plains opened up; they had conquered the *Appalachia*, and an enemy might suppose that high spirits would make them careless. But the Fighting 33rd were career soldiers to a man, and this was such an obvious site for an ambush that there really had to be one.

They had been sighting *Iroqua* all day, a fleeting glimpse of a redskin behind a tree here, a feather seen over a rock there. Once the trend was clear Marcellinus had passed the order down through his centurions that the men were to ignore the natives until actively engaged. That way, the redskins might assume they'd gone unnoticed. As the *Iroqua* tried to lull the Romans into a false sense of security, Marcellinus was sanguine that he had instead tricked them into overconfidence.

As his cohorts tromped downhill, eagerly awaiting the onslaught and whistling like longshoremen, Marcellinus felt that surge of energy he loved, the spark that ran like lightning through well-trained men on the verge of combat. Today, at least, his Legion was behind him to the last man.

Sure enough, where the way was narrow and the crags around them tall, the redskins attacked.

Predictable. And yet not.

Suddenly the air was full of darting shapes that whirled above them as if the laws of nature and commonsense had ceased to apply.

Briefly, Marcellinus feared he had lost his mind. He seemed to be assaulted by a swarm of giant moths, and for several dangerous seconds he couldn't even bring them into focus. Then the shapes resolved and he realized they were further away than he'd thought. The moths became men, harnessed to rigid triangular wings.

Each pilot was spread-eagled beneath his wing, lying prone, steering left and right by tugging at a stiff cord that passed under his chest and extended from wingtip to wingtip. Yet control of these crude aerial vehicles required only part of their energy; each also held a bow and could reach across himself to pull arrows from a streamlined quiver strapped to his thigh, to rain down death upon Marcellinus's troops. Each aviator wore a mask bearing the powerful hooked beak of a falcon.

Had this been a circus display, Marcellinus might have laughed for joy. Men in flight! Yet these wings were not for sport; their intent was deadly serious. Marcellinus was caught flat-footed. Behind the beat of the battle, he mentally lunged to catch up. The archers of his First Cohort, the cream of his military crop, capable of recognizing an enemy no matter what direction it came from, laconically pumped arrows into the air. But they were below the thrust of the attack and so were forced to fire back over the mass of the Legion. If they weren't careful there was a real risk that their arrows might fall among their own fellows.

As the *Iroqua* swooped over the densely packed line of the Legion, their own deadly projectiles rarely failed to find a mark. These were arrows that needed only to wound. Poison-tipped for sure; legionary after legionary toppled to the ground like a cut-string puppet moments after suffering no more than the shallowest nick.

Behind Marcellinus, the Third Cohort broke in panic. Legionaries milled, unable to evade the soaring enemies without trampling their comrades. Such a loss of discipline was unacceptable; where was Corbulo? Marcellinus recovered himself, left the First under the control of his senior centurion Pollius Scapax, and ran uphill into the ranks of the Third.

Marcellinus thought Corbulo was down and wounded until he reached his tribune's side. Corbulo was watching the wings whirl over his head with something like terror, his hand thrown up as if to ward off a curse.

Marcellinus applied his foot to Corbulo's ribs. "Up, man! Must your men see you trembling and afraid?"

"What?" Corbulo's eyes searched for him, as if the tribune were drunk or in darkness.

"Men in kites! You're not so daunted by that?"

"Kites?" said Corbulo in a daze, but of course he was too young to remember the party-tricks that Vespasianus II, the Imperator-before-last, had imported from the Chin twenty years ago and sent twirling gaily over the Palatine Hill in the lamplight.

"Aye, kites," said the Praetor. "And aboard them, just men."

"Men!" said Corbulo. "Of course, I see it now," and rose to his feet. Rushing into a group of his archers, he marshaled them to shoot long at the *Iroqua* who stood on the crag-tops waiting to launch. A fusillade of arrows knocked a good half dozen of the savages off their perches, while several more leaped off the crags, consigning themselves to the air. At least one crashed to earth immediately, a victim of the treacherous winds swirling up the valley.

Marcellinus leaned back to study the flying braves. It was the Praetor's job to think strategically, but he was hard pressed to devise a strategy against an enemy that soared out of reach.

Now, he saw smoke. A flaming arrow had embedded in the canvas of one of the supply train carts and was setting a merry blaze. Provisions were at risk.

Marcellinus grabbed up a pilum from a fallen soldier and ran to launch it upward at the nearest *Iroqua*. The javelin drifted lazily behind the wing and dropped back to earth; Marcellinus had badly underestimated the flying brave's height and speed.

"Lead with your bows!" he shouted. "Fire ahead of them! *Well* ahead!"

Across the Legion the wave of superstitious terror was ending. The men had found themselves an enemy they could fight. It became a game now, though a deadly one; the more practiced *Iroqua* slew three Romans for every wing the legionaries sent tumbling into the rocks.

Marcellinus took a bow from a man of the Third who had fallen to his knees, cradling his arm. Nocking an arrow, he swung it upward and let fly. And then he did it again. His second arrow pierced an *Iroqua's* stomach, and he savored the redskin's scream as he plummeted into the ground.

The bow was not Marcellinus's favored weapon. But no man could say the Praetor was not flexible, in a pinch.

When the final tally came in, the Legion had lost two hundred and fifty men in the skirmish. In return the Romans had shot down several dozen of the wings. Perhaps a couple of dozen more of the *Iroqua* had fallen out of the sky due to overzealousness, or misjudged the canyon walls, forging their own disasters.

Marcellinus loathed the loss of even a single legionary out here beyond the edge of the world, where they could not be replaced. Yet the deaths of their comrades brought such fire and fury to his men that, considered as a whole, his Legion might well be the stronger for it.

"Cowards and skulkers, shooting their poison arrows from on high! We can hardly clamber into the air and meet them blade to blade!"

Side by side they rode at the head of the Legion, Praetor Gaius Publius Marcellinus and First Tribune Lucius Domitius Corbulo, as they had in happier times out East. Corbulo had advanced to the vanguard of the Legion, with the alleged aim of helping Marcellinus select a site for the night-camp.

"Aye," said Marcellinus, tactfully. Corbulo was obviously not taking his momentary lapse of reason on the battlefield well.

Corbulo skewered him with a glance, and Marcellinus added, "As cowardly as picking off our legionaries when they step out of their marching-line to fetch firewood or take a crap."

"Worse. What kind of man hides in the air?"

"The flying itself is not without risk," Marcellinus pointed out. "Merely learning the skill must present its hazards. Plenty of opportunities to tumble out of the sky onto your head."

"The basic trick looked simple enough," Corbulo grumbled. "Those men were not warriors."

Marcellinus doubted the simplicity of it. The skills of these aerial redskins must take a lifetime's learning. More ominously, the flyers must be supported by their community while honing their talents. On the shores of the *Mare Chesapica* it had been every redskin's chore to trap his own fish. Here, though, they were no longer scrabbling farmers and part-time warriors, but specialists. It was the beginnings of civilization.

"But there'll be no next time," said Corbulo, shaking Marcellinus out of his reverie. "It's a trick that only works once. You know how the wind rises, on meeting a steep slope? Their kites ride on that. But the mountains are behind us now, and I see no terrain ahead where they'd have that advantage."

Marcellinus glanced sidelong at his first tribune. "No more element of surprise."

"No more surprises," Corbulo agreed.

And yet Marcellinus almost regretted that he would never see such a thing again. If the aerial *Iroqua* had not been deadly enemies, he could have watched them all day. Idly, he imagined himself jumping off the Palatine Hill and circling over the glitter and marble of the Roman Forum before alighting in front of the new Curia building where the Senate met. Now *that* would be a triumph!

He wished he'd opened his eyes even wider, to take it all in.

Domitius Corbulo checked back over his shoulder. "And speaking of surprises… a word in your ear about Aelfric."

"Aelfric?" said Marcellinus, startled.

"He presumes too much. And you allow too much."

"Is that so?"

"Yes. Have a care, Marcellinus. Your friends should be good Romans, not Norse, Britons, or any other bloody savages. You'll be chumming it up with Fuscus next."

"Last I heard, Britannia was still solidly part of the Imperium."

Corbulo gave a laugh so short it was almost a cough. "Well then, you've never been there. I was stationed up in Caledonia, did you know, at the Wall of Antoninus? Three years."

"That's a long time," said Marcellinus.

"Dismal bloody weather, and a complete mess politically. You wouldn't believe so many client-kings and bizarre religions would fit onto such a small pair of islands. I could write you a list of the odd things they believe. It's one of the few regions left in the Imperium where they still have genuine shamans, you know. The Hibernians are the worst: mystics and moaners. They'd wail as soon as talk."

"Somehow Aelfric never struck me as the wailing type," said Marcellinus.

Corbulo would not be distracted from his theme. "Britons are all natural plotters and counter-plotters, it's in their blood. And they mask it with congeniality. They'll worm their way inside your thoughts, get you talking, though they're quiet ones themselves. Before you know it, you've told 'em secrets they can use against you."

That brought Marcellinus up short. He had certainly discussed many things with Aelfric that it would never have occurred to him to tell Corbulo. About his wife and Vestilia, his doubts that they'd find gold, and probably a dozen other topics that he probably shouldn't have confided to a tribune. All because he felt comfortable with the man. What did he really know of Aelfric's motivations?

"I see I'm not wrong," said Corbulo. "And what do you know of him, in return? Do you even know where he was born? I do. Eboracum. He's a Brigante."

The Brigantes were a Celtic *gens* with an ancient heritage in the north of Britannia, one of the last tribes to fall to Roma during the conquest. But that was a long time ago.

Marcellinus frowned. "He's really a Celt? Isn't 'Aelfric' a Saxon name?"

"Celt, Saxon, they're all mixed up together now. But either way,

Aelfric is too familiar by far. Ponder on it, that's all I ask."

"I'll take care," said Marcellinus. He paused. "Thank you."

Corbulo smiled.

The *castra* was a roving town that recreated itself daily in its own image. They rebuilt it identically every afternoon, occupied it for one night only, then abandoned it the next morning; civilization on the march through Nova Hesperia.

Again tonight they selected the site and leveled the ground, measuring and marking with a knotted rope where the streets would be laid out. Up went the ramparts, earthworks six feet high around the perimeter. Down came any trees unfortunate enough to be located within the square, their wood used for construction. Up went the tents, down went the latrines. And, finally, up went the four temples obligatory for feeding the Legion's superstitions: the Mithraic temple, the shrine to Cybele, the open-air altar and prayer rail of the Christ-Risen, and the small but rather forbidding statue of Jupiter Imperator, which had more presence than any of the real-life Imperators Marcellinus had met.

The *castra* was square, with streets constructed on a grid pattern. Its alignment was as constant as its arrangement, with the wide main street called the Cardo aligned north-south so that the evening and morning light would shine down the long cross-streets, named for the cohorts and centuries that lived along them. The rank and file lived one contubernium—eight men—to a tent. Marcellinus's own Praetorium tent formed the center of the camp, with the latrines, the field hospital, the stables and the armory arrayed around the rim, and open areas at the corners for the supply carts, wagons and horses, and slaves.

The camp was their home from home. Whatever skies the Legion slept under, the streets that surrounded them were always the same. By now, the layout of the *castra* was more familiar to the legionaries than the streets of the towns and villages they grew up in.

"You didn't tell me about the wings," said Marcellinus.

Fuscus gulped, but carefully. The Praetor's pugio was at his throat, and the word-slave was rammed painfully back against the wooden walls of the cart he'd spent the day helping to haul across his own country.

"Is not know," Fuscus whimpered.

"Oh? 'People of Eagle and Thunder-Bird will drop on you'? Words chosen carefully. Aren't you a clever rascal, Fuscus? 'Man of smart,' no?" He pushed the blade a little harder.

"No! I stupid man!"

"That's right," said the Praetor. "So, what next? How soon comes the next surprise from your people?"

"Mercy!" said the red man, his eyes full of tears. "Mercy!"

Aelfric ambled over. "Not to stand up for the little weasel, but Fuscus is quite likely further from his birthplace now than he's ever been before. I doubt he knows much more about this place than we do."

Marcellinus glared at him for the interruption, but he recognized the truth when he heard it. Anything Fuscus knew was probably based on hearsay, tales told over a campfire. And he'd established long ago that the little runt knew nothing substantive about the Great City. But it had been worth a try.

The Praetor dropped his word-slave on the ground, giving him a kick for good measure. "All right, Fuscus. One more chance. One!"

"You do know there's no gold ahead, right?" said Aelfric quietly as they walked away. "Fool's gold, maybe. A coppery mirage or two."

"Hush," said Marcellinus, though the men nearby were hard at work getting the *castra* situated. "Such talk is treasonous."

He was only half joking. Few of his common legionaries gave a fig for the lofty ideals of global conquest, or would be indefinitely content to molest and slaughter barbarians. Today's battle with the flying men had been a novelty. But by now they were marching on half-rations across a largely uninteresting and seemingly endless plain, interspersed with forestland that would be equally boring if not for the danger of being picked off and slaughtered by savages.

Aelfric tutted. "You still cling to the hope that these simpletons are hiding cities of gold? You know better. You had to show that squaw what gold was. She'd never seen it before."

"The gold is just over the horizon," said Marcellinus, with a straight face.

"It always is."

"Maybe we'll find them something else worth the effort," said Marcellinus.

"'Course you will," said Aelfric. "That's your job. But you might want to plan ahead for what that'll be."

"Hmm," said the Praetor. "You're a real bearer of sunshine tonight."

"One more word," said Aelfric. "Corbulo."

Marcellinus sighed.

"The centurions are reporting rumors of him freezing up during the ambush. Panicking. Not giving timely orders in the heat of battle."

"I hear rumors about giant rodents, too," said Marcellinus carefully.

"Oh, I didn't say I gave them any credence," said Aelfric. "I mean, a veteran like Corbulo? It's surely nonsense. But I thought you should know."

"Right," said Marcellinus.

Up the Cardo they saw Leogild and Corbulo step out of their respective side streets and head towards the Praetorium tent. "Speak of the devil," said Aelfric.

"He feels the same way about you," said Marcellinus.

"Does he, now?" said Aelfric thoughtfully, and Marcellinus kicked himself. Once again, he'd spoken too freely.

He nodded to Aelfric and walked on, vowing it would be the last time he'd make that mistake.

Once his meetings with his quartermaster and tribunes were over, Gaius Marcellinus liked to walk the camp. A Praetor should never be a stranger to his men, not if he wanted to keep his command and his neck intact.

At dusk the *castra* was alive with sound, movement and purpose as the men set their campfires to cook their fry-bread and soup and corn hash. Given a cool night and an area with enough free wood they might build a larger bonfire and sit around it telling stories and bawdy jokes over their wine-and-water, but tonight they were too battle-weary for that additional luxury.

Marcellinus strolled among the tents, past the cook-pots and the knucklebone games. Around him, men were sharpening blades, polishing armor, tightening a strap here and loosening another there, hammering a new sole or strap onto a sandal, lancing a boil or a blister, and trying to rinse stiff sweat-stains out of their tunics. Some were writing letters that they would not be able to send for months, to sweethearts who had probably already forgotten them. Having lost one wife, several mistresses and a daughter, Marcellinus was under no illusions about the constancy of women.

It seemed that even more men than usual were paying their respects at the temples. True, soldiers had died today, but surely there were other ways to honor their sacrifices than to, well, sacrifice. What had Seneca said? "Religion is recognized by the common people as true, by the wise as false, and by the rulers as useful"? Well, in that case perhaps their piety was useful in calming their unease. However, Marcellinus almost envied them their ability to believe. Life on the road could be lonely for a man without a personal God.

As he wandered Marcellinus was generally greeted with a nod, a joke, or a comment on the weather. His presence in the lanes of the *castra* was commonplace. Rarely did he hear a complaint; most men knew better than to trouble their Praetor with trivial matters. He spared some words for the sycophants and operators, little as he enjoyed the company of either; broke up a couple of squabbles before they turned into brawls; and reminded himself of the names of some of his more seasoned centurions. He did not, however, intrude on two men fist-fighting over the attentions of one of the *signiferi* of the Seventh Cohort, a duplicitous lad with smooth skin and improbably long eyelashes. Nobody would thank Marcellinus for getting in the middle of *that*.

He took particular care to compliment tonight's sentries of the watch, who would get only a few hours' sleep. He also spent a while gossiping with the *aquiliferi* honor guard, which was easy enough to do; not only were they veterans of a similar age to himself, with similar memories of old campaigns and bygone Imperators, but also these were men who would give their lives for the Aquila. Their loyalty to the Legion was absolute: they *were* the Fighting 33rd.

All in an evening's rounds.

Marcellinus liked the masculine society of the *castra*. He did not miss Roma, and rarely yearned for its comforts. However, deep within the pitiless interior of Nova Hesperia, he found that he did miss the *Mare Chesapica*, a bay so wide it almost counted as a sea. He had enjoyed the slightly ridiculous sight of the immense Roman troop transports wallowing in the deep waters of the bay as the square-rigged Viking longships danced around them, tiny by comparison. (The longships had guided the mighty vessels of Roma down the then-chill coastline of the new continent, like sprightly mice leading a lion on a leash.) He had liked watching the gulls floating on the breeze and the herons wading the marshlands, liked walking the small sandy beaches that had proven quite pleasant once they'd cleared the savages away and cleaned up the sand. It was not at all like the Campania coast in southern Italia where he had furloughed between campaigns—the land around the *Chesapica* was too flat for true beauty—but it had its appeal nonetheless.

More particularly, their time in the bay had marked the optimistic beginnings of their expedition, before their energy got sapped by the endless marching and their numbers depleted by cowardly foes. Back then they had been able to hope that this whole campaign might be easy.

And, back then, Marcellinus had still felt the authority of Roma on his shoulders, guiding his actions.

Roma had never lost its savagery: a bit of muscle and the willingness to shed blood were crucial in keeping an Imperium strong. Kindness to your own, brutality to those who opposed you; those were the ways of Roma. The Imperium was the greatest civilizing force in the world, and must remain so even if it had to hack off a few heads from time to time. But here in the heartland of Nova Hesperia they were far away from all that, so far from the Forum in Urbs Roma that they might as well have been at the bottom of the sea or—why not?—high in the air.

The further they marched, the less Marcellinus felt Roma's power. Nova Hesperia owned a different power, something forceful and primal. The natives might be weak, but the land itself was strong, and Marcellinus had not yet come to terms with it. In his heart of hearts, it daunted him.

Here, for the first time in his life, Praetor Gaius Marcellinus felt like he might be the only law.

And with this thought, his sixth sense for danger suddenly came alive.

He was strolling down a lane occupied by auxiliaries. Around him a blur of provincial languages filled the air: German, Magyar, Nubian. Yet despite the comfortable low babble of conversation, the men nearest him were too alert by far. These were men on the verge of action, maybe about to rush him.

Suddenly, Marcellinus was in the lion's den. For a moment he was a young man back in the Subura, forced to live by his wits.

Was he sure?

He did not look around him again. The men might interpret that as weakness, seeking help. Marcellinus did not need help. He stopped walking, and placed his hand on the hilt of his gladius.

Auxiliaries glanced about, estimating spaces and angles, checking for their centurion, who was conspicuously absent. Yes, his instincts were correct.

Marcellinus said: "The punishment for laying a hand on your commanding officer is death. I'm sure I don't need to remind you."

All heads turned towards him.

"However, that death need not be immediate. I could have you whipped till your limbs fall off and the skin peels from your bones."

He knew they were listening intently. They all understood Latin. It was a condition of service. How many of them were in on this? And who might they crown as the Legion's new prelate, once he was dead?

He pushed the thought aside. "If you have a grievance against me, make it known now. Otherwise—"

To his left, someone moved. Marcellinus spun and stamped down hard on him, and the man howled in Magyar. Leaving his gladius sheathed, Marcellinus grabbed the man's wrist and twisted his arm up and around in a full circle behind his back; the Magyar came up halfway off the ground and hung there, helpless.

Marcellinus looked not at his potential assailant, but at the other men that surrounded him. He did not blink. This was the moment of truth. It was time for them to decide.

The auxiliaries showed their decision by shuffling back away from him, dropping their gaze, keeping their hands clearly visible. All right, then. To the soldier whose arm he still held in an iron grip Marcellinus said, "When I release you, fall and stay down, or I'll kill you." He let go, and the man immediately toppled to a supine position, clutching his arm.

Looking down on the soldier, Marcellinus had a sudden distracting memory of Vestilia as a baby, when his wife had first laid his daughter on the ground before him for his approval. Had he not picked her up, Vestilia would have been left out to die. A time-honored Roman tradition.

"I meant you no harm," said the auxiliary. "I swear it."

Marcellinus doubted this was true, but any further action against the man would be pointless. "Then up you come, soldier," he said, and lent the Magyar an arm, pulling him to his feet. "In future, be more careful." He looked around at the others. "Without discipline, we'll never get out of this country alive. Think on that."

He turned and walked away, without looking back.

Rounding the lane's end, he glanced casually up at the *signifer*. Third century, Fifth Auxiliaries. Aelfric's cohort.

A minor incident, but a harbinger of worse to come. He could no longer assume that merely doing the right thing would be sufficient to ensure his men's loyalty. For the first time, Marcellinus understood his Imperator's desperation for gold.

His men also felt the waning power of Roma. The further west they went, the more his Legion threatened to degenerate into a mob. Marcellinus could imagine another thousand miles ahead of them, and another. How far could they march before all order would be lost?

Of course, they'd probably starve first.

A week later they found the remains of one of their Norse scouts tied to a tree, carefully positioned in the path of their relentless advance.

Thorkell Sigurdsson would march no more. His thighs were blackened stumps; his legs had been burned off completely to above the knee. His face was intact but hideously distorted. He had received a haircut clear through to the bone; his scalp had been hacked away, revealing the grey-white of his skull.

The wreckage of the scout was an essay in torture and barbarism. It was an act of appalling atrocity, and judging by the decaying state of the body had happened several days earlier. The Romans might not know exactly the route they would take, but the *Iroqua* did.

Once more the Legion had come to a halt. The standard-bearer looked like he might throw up at any moment. His eyes skittered around nervously.

Marcellinus did not fear an ambush. They stood in a meadow with the trees well separated and little undergrowth, and they could see for hundreds of yards in each direction. The *Iroqua* had arranged their violent tableau with care, and would allow time for the lesson to sink in.

Very well. But the lesson his men learned might not be the one the *Iroqua* had intended.

"Bring me my tribunes," said Marcellinus. "Then have the cohorts march past this spot. Parade order, half speed, no chatter."

Pollius Scapax nodded. "Helmets?"

Helmets-off would have been the standard mark of respect, but this was enemy territory. "On," said Marcellinus. "Sigurdsson would understand."

Flanked by an honor guard of tribunes, and holding the Legion's golden eagle standard in his own hands, Marcellinus stood to attention by Thorkell Sigurdsson's side for the whole hour it took for the Legion to march past. On each of the three thousand faces, legionaries and auxiliaries alike, he saw the same expression: not fear, not revulsion, but respect tinged with a steely determination.

Towards the rear of the army came the baggage carts, hauled by their redskin slaves. Marcellinus stared hard-faced as the savages trudged by with their shoulders to the wheel, but none of them showed disrespect to the dead man. Most, in fact, looked quite nauseated at the spectacle.

"That man," said Marcellinus. "Fuscus. Fetch him."

Pollius Scapax strode into the baggage train, cuffing redskins aside until he reached the word-slave. He hacked through the cord that bound Fuscus to the cart, and hauled him out unceremoniously. The five braves that remained tethered to the vehicle leaned into their task even more grimly.

Marcellinus drew his gladius and whacked Fuscus on the back of his thighs with the flat of the blade, driving the word-slave to his knees. Fuscus bit off a scream as he found himself face to face with Sigurdsson, but cried out in earnest when Marcellinus struck his bare shoulders another blow.

"This is what your people do? The cowardly maiming of captives?"

Fuscus gaped at the ruined Norseman. "Is not!"

"We don't need you any more, *verpa*. Know why? Because there will be no more talking to your people. Only killing."

"Marcellinus, man, let him be. His kind didn't do this."

Marcellinus whirled, and the point of his gladius stopped inches from Aelfric's throat. "What?"

Aelfric took a slow step back from the blade. "Look, Fuscus here, he's coastal. His *Powhatani* are crab-eaters and berry-pickers. The savages hereabouts are of a different stripe."

"*Iroqua*," said Fuscus. "Men of hurt. Many take…."

"More war-like," Aelfric interrupted. "The savages we're seeing around here are painted odd, and they move different. They're real hunters and killers." He gestured at Sigurdsson's body. "If the *Iroqua* got their hands on Fuscus, they'd probably do this to *him*."

The Praetor looked down. Fuscus was groveling so hard that he was practically tunneling into the ground.

Marcellinus had sent Sisika alone into this area. The miserable word-slave hadn't warned him he would be signing the woman's death warrant. He seized Fuscus by his topknot and dragged the man up onto his knees.

"Look, spare him," said Aelfric. "God knows we might need—"

Marcellinus slit the word-slave's throat. He died quickly, gurgling, his eyes bulging almost out of his head as he drowned on his own blood.

"Never mind," said Aelfric.

"Something you wanted to say?" said Marcellinus coldly, sword still unsheathed.

Aelfric shrugged. "Me? No. We don't need him. There'll be no more talking to his kind."

"That's right."

The atmosphere over the glade remained icy as the last echelons of the Legion straggled past. At the end, Corbulo cleared his throat, stood easy, and broke silence. "Good. The men are fired up now. I pity the poor red bastards we encounter next. The men will wipe 'em out like cockroaches."

Marcellinus nodded tautly. Corbulo and his other tribunes saluted him and the hideous remains of Sigurdsson once more, and rode on forward to rejoin their cohorts.

The Praetor looked down again at the mutilated body of his Norseman, and for the first time on this campaign felt genuinely exhausted. Not just in his body, because physical weariness was a constant aspect of commanding a legion, but also in his soul.

Yet again, Aelfric had presumed to stay behind. "They knew the path we'd take," said the Briton. "They arranged him here, right in our way. You bloody Romans and your straight lines."

"For gods' sake, we *want* to be predictable," said Marcellinus. "We know where we're going. So do they. We *want* to fight them. Let the scum try and stop us. And in case you've forgotten, you're a Roman too."

"I wonder what became of the other scouts," said Aelfric moodily.

Enslaved, perhaps. Or cooked and eaten. Marcellinus would rather not know.

For a moment he felt dazed. Could these savages really not distinguish between soldiers and scouts? Did they intuit nothing of civilized conduct? How could a war even take place without scouts to guide the armies together?

"Cowards," he said. "An entire landmass of bloody cowards." Corbulo was right after all.

The Praetor and his tribune were off the back of the Legion now, guarded only by senior centurion Scapax and two *contubernia* of trusted soldiers. Normally it would be untenable for a legion commander to be this exposed, but the undergrowth was sparse and the sightlines long. A quarter-mile away, and despite the recent passage of his army, Marcellinus saw a pair of white-tailed deer meandering through the trees. This was very different terrain from the dense woods that lined the coast of the *Chesapica*.

The sandals of thousands of marching Romans and the wheels of dozens of baggage carts had beaten quite a furrow into the meadow floor. Marcellinus looked down thoughtfully, then stepped onto undisturbed ground.

"Praetor," said Scapax. "We must advance and rejoin the Legion."

Scapax might well worry; by law he faced summary execution if his Praetor came to harm while under his protection. Marcellinus didn't think it too likely to happen today. Squatting, he slipped his fingers into the rough grass on the forest floor and probed the loam beneath. His hand came up streaked with charcoal and ash.

"They make this," he said. "D'you see?"

"Let's go," said Aelfric.

"The redskins. They burn away the undergrowth with care, so the deer and elk can graze, and they can see clear to shoot them from afar with bow and arrow. And the trees here; chestnuts, hickory nuts. It's..." Words suddenly failed him at the magnitude of what he was saying. "This is a park, not a forest. It only *looks* natural. They *tend* this. Our dusky savages practice land husbandry."

The centurion came to Marcellinus's side. "Now, sir, if you please."

Behind the trees, Marcellinus saw something gliding high and straight on the breeze. He squinted at it, pretty sure it was a hawk and not a man.

"Don't make me order the good centurion to carry you," said Aelfric mildly.

Marcellinus turned on him. "You forget yourself! Why didn't you leave with the other tribunes?"

At his tone, Aelfric quickly stood to attention. "Sorry, sir."

"You and I, Tribune, we're not friends."

"No, Praetor."

"Your place is with your cohorts."

"Yes, Praetor."

"Then get back to them!"

"Yes, sir." Aelfric made haste to depart.

Straightening, Marcellinus walked back and placed his hand on the shoulder of his maimed scout, looking at Sigurdsson's eyes rather than his injuries. "Thank you, my friend. Watch the road for us till we return."

Only then did Marcellinus allow his guards to pace him back into the protection of the Legion.

"I heard the speech you made for Sigurdsson earlier this evening," said Isleifur Bjarnason. "A pretty thing it was. Excellent and rousing. You'll really take the time to grind the redskins' bones?"

Marcellinus whirled. He had dismissed his guards for the night and had believed himself alone. Yet there sat another of his long-missing Norse scouts, on the same blanket Sisika had occupied. His long flaxen hair was filthy and pulled back into a long braid and his clothes were darkened with dirt and green smears, indicating a deal of time spent concealed in foliage.

The Praetor recovered his composure quickly, as if men crept up on him every day. "I've done it before."

"I thank you for the tribute, on his behalf," said Bjarnason. "Thorkell was a good man. But much as it pains me to say it, the loss of one good Norseman doesn't justify a massacre."

Marcellinus held the man's gaze for several moments, then turned and poured wine and water for them both. If Bjarnason had intended to kill him, he'd be dead already. "I'm surprised no one told me you'd returned to camp."

"I haven't. Leastways, not officially." He grinned. "A poor scout I'd be if I couldn't find a path through a *castra* unseen."

"Such undue stealthiness could get you killed."

"Perhaps. But I'm no use to you here. If I'm to be of service I need to be out feeling the lay of the land. Learning to think as the redskins do."

Marcellinus eyed him. "This territory appeals? Perhaps you're thinking you've served Roma long enough?"

"The scenery's to my taste, I'll admit. I sojourned in Vinlandia awhile, did you know? And Graenlandia before that. I like the spaces empty, and the skies big."

"Then why are you here in my tent?"

"Because I still work for you, Praetor. I wouldn't want to leave the impression that I'd deserted. And, to advise you." Marcellinus raised his eyebrows. "To tell you my impressions, rather," amended the Norseman quickly.

"You have the floor," said Marcellinus ironically, and sat in his chair.

Bjarnason sipped his wine. He must have grown unused to it during his long sojourn in the woods; it was the first time Marcellinus had seen a Viking sip anything. "Very well, then. They're a powerful people, the *Iroqua*. Warriors the like of which I've not seen before, in Europa or beyond. Bloodier than we Norse. We generally leave people alive, but they kill for sport. I'm keeping my wits about me, I don't mind telling you. I don't sleep much."

"And these are the people I shouldn't massacre?"

"Nay," said Bjarnason, "I don't give a shit about the *Iroqua*. They're just one tribe of many, and you'll be out of their territory in a few more days anyway. The people you shouldn't kill are the next lot, the *Cahokiani*. Great builders, they are: longhouses, thatched roofs. Not the equals of the Norse great halls, but they could be, with a tad more practice. And they build mounds of earth, too, wide and tall. And riverine harbors and irrigation canals. They're like no people you've seen yet."

"Do they have gold?" said Marcellinus automatically, and almost laughed at himself for the question.

The Norseman shook his head. "Furs and pretty shells. Aside from that it's mostly stone and bone, wood and feathers. Especially feathers. For they're flyers as well as runners and swimmers, you see."

"We saw what their wings could do in *Appalachia*. It's a fancy trick, but not one that leaves much of a dent on Roman steel."

"You've not seen the best of what they can throw into the air," said Bjarnason quietly. "You haven't seen anything yet."

"But we can beat them," said Marcellinus, and it wasn't a question.

"Oh aye, handily, should you choose to. But maybe you should consider the advantages of trade over pillage." Bjarnason grinned. "And when a Norseman says that, you should probably listen."

"We don't need any shells."

Bjarnason put the wine-cup down and stretched. "I haven't been inside their big city. Can't even get close. There's no cover in the last stages, and I'll not get far trying to disguise myself as one of them. So I suppose they might have gold if it was well-hidden." The Norseman leaned forward. "But these people have more than that, Praetor. They know this land, and they know the air above it. The air! Gods' sakes! And they don't think the way we do. I can't really explain it, because I only speak a few words of their lingo. But there are virtues to them. There are virtues.

"You've seen it yourself, I know; I heard you trying to persuade that clod Aelfric, back there by Thorkell's corpse. The *Cahokiani* husband the land even more so than the *Iroqua*, they live almost *inside* the land. And that's how they fly, you know. They've tamed the air because they have an understanding of it that we lack."

Marcellinus drained his cup. "Tell me something I can use, Isleifur Bjarnason."

"You've only seen the small wings," said the Viking. "Wait till you see the larger. In their language, they call them Thunder-Birds. If the little birds are like sparrows, the Thunder-Birds are like... well, eagles."

"Eagles."

"Flying through the air, quick as ballista bolts."

"The bigger they are, the larger the hole they'll make in the ground when we shoot them down. They're a gimmick. There's little strategic value to them."

"Well," said the Norseman. "That may be so, and it may be not."

"You do realize that I should arrest you?" said Marcellinus bluntly. "Fraternizing with the enemy, pleading their case with me, breaking in here by night?"

Bjarnason grinned. "I'm at my Praetor's disposal."

"Yes, till you turn renegade on me. I haven't forgotten what good pirates you people make."

Bjarnason looked pained. "Damn it, now... sir. That's the Danes. The Danes were never anything but trouble. I'm a Geat, one of the true Scands."

"Then go, Geat, and spy some more."

The Norseman shuffled backward, and now Marcellinus saw the fabric of the tent hanging loose where Bjarnason had uprooted a tent peg or two and crawled under it to gain ingress.

"Oh, and if it's nationalities we're talking, I wouldn't put as much stock in Aelfric as you seem to. He's a Briton first, a Roman only in name. You've got to keep both eyes on the Britons. They're not like us."

"Us?" murmured Marcellinus.

"Aye. Romans and Norse, we're solid stock, hard dreamers with a vision and the guts to make it stick. Both out to claim the world for ourselves. Oh, the Norse bow to the stronger," he ducked his head in deference, "but if it wasn't you Romans, it'd be us out there, carving an empire."

"You're something of a free thinker," said Marcellinus dryly.

"It's true. If Roma had fallen to the Visigoths and Vandals and all—and that was a closer-run thing than people like to suppose, these days—you can wager it'd have been we Norse sweeping up and building an Imperium now. Who'd have gainsaid us? The bloody Mongols, eventually. But certainly not the Gauls or the Parthians or the Britons. Stay-at-homes with mud on their faces, the lot of 'em, no soldiers, and no sailors either."

Marcellinus shook his head. "Is there a point to this polemic?"

"Yes. Watch out for Aelfric."

"Don't worry," said Marcellinus. "I've already received sufficient warnings on that score."

"Right, then." And with a flourish, the Norseman wriggled backward through the tiny gap between the tent canvas and the ground, and was gone.

"Anyone else like to put in an appearance?" said Marcellinus to the goatskin walls of his Praetorium, but if any further spies were present, they remained mute. He went to bed.

The *Iroqua* war party hit them two days later in the early afternoon, rising like ghosts from the long grasses to fling their spears and fire their arrows into the side of Fabius's Seventh Cohort, howling like banshees all the while. Though they had been on the march for six hours without a break the Seventh responded instantly, bursting out of their marching-line to hammer the redskins with Roman steel. The assault turned into a running battle amid the trees of hickory and beech, and if the *Iroqua* were surprised at the turn of speed a fully-armored legionary could attain, their surprise did not generally last long.

Throughout the Legion, Roman discipline prevailed. The cohorts behind and in front of the Seventh came to order, the nearer groups dashing into the fray while the centuries further out hunkered down in a defensive posture. Sure enough, two more *Iroqua* bands burst out from behind the trees, one assaulting Marcellinus and the Roman standards at the head of the Legion, the other aiming to destroy the baggage train and, perhaps, capture the Romans' redskin slaves for their own.

Neither attempt succeeded. The elite troops of Pollius Scapax mowed down the forward band of savages with surgical skill and utter ruthlessness, and Marcellinus bloodied his gladius in combat for the first time on this campaign, cutting down four braves and crippling another. Meanwhile in the rear the terrified *Powhatani* and other *Algon-Quian* slaves corralled the wagons and aided the stragglers of the Sixth in holding off the ululating *Iroqua* until the massed line of the Fourth slammed into the barbarians, slaughtering them to a man.

Other smaller bands of painted barbarians appeared helter-skelter amid the trees, and the Fifth and Second were next to engage in a running fight in the meadows. This ended with the remains of the redskin war parties encircled by Romans. Some twenty of the savages tried to escape by climbing into a tree; the Romans set the tree ablaze and made them choose between death by fire and death by steel. Dozens of others, trapped on the ground, threw aside their slings and bows.

If by surrendering they expected to be spared to join their Eastern brethren in the slave line, the *Iroqua* were sorely disappointed. The Legion needed no more slaves, and Marcellinus would not have trusted a warrior in the role as readily as a fisherman. Slavery was an economic contract between thinking beings. These *Iroqua* were feral creatures who would never knuckle under.

After mourning Thorkell Sigurdsson so recently the men were not inclined to award their captives easy deaths, and Marcellinus would hardly insist upon such a thing. He withdrew to secure the front of the legionary line, and left his troops to their revenge. The screams of the braves troubled him little enough. He hoped the gruesome sounds would travel far enough to deter any further redskin foolishness.

A landscape designed to render wildlife visible also allowed the enemy fewer places to hide. When, later in the afternoon, a cleanup crew from the Fifth stormed into a ravine and flushed out several dozen redskin squaws and young girls, Marcellinus again made no attempt to halt the inevitable. Such scenes were not to his taste, but he understood the paradox that occasionally permitting the most reprehensible of behaviors improved loyalty and discipline in the long run.

They had marched sixteen miles that day, and it would have to be enough. Marcellinus sent in his tribunes to declare a temporary halt to festivities, and his men cheerfully yielded and threw up the *castra* then and there in the clearing. Camp had never been set so quickly.

To inaugurate the *castra*, the Fifth paraded their bound and hobbled *Iroqua* prisoners along the Cardo behind their banner. It was their own homegrown triumph, here in the wilderness. They then generously donated the survivors to the pleasure of the rest of the Legion. The ensuing celebrations, of course, would leave all the *Iroqua* dead.

Marcellinus drank his sour wine unwatered as he walked through the camp, taking care not to look into the faces of the revelers or their victims. It was critical that he be seen out and about, to confer his consent on the festivities. The clamor and the blood made his head hurt. But his profession required mental flexibility. He had, after all, told his men they could have the next hundred women.

The braves had started this, damn them. Let them suffer Roman vengeance.

He stood it as long as he could, and then withdrew. On his way back to his Praetorium he met Domitius Corbulo. His First Tribune looked grey and seemed to stagger. The look he gave Marcellinus was haunted.

At least his patrician colleague had not yet lost his humanity either. The two men clasped forearms, leaned on each other for a somber moment, and parted without speaking a word.

That night Marcellinus dreamed of feasting on a lush array of larks' tongues, honeyed dormice, oyster and mussel pasties, figs and quinces, followed by the main courses: boar's ribs, boiled teals, roasted fowls with asparagus, and fattened lampreys, all flavored with cinnamon and pepper, cardamom and cloves. In his life he had experienced such banquets only at the Imperator's court, and had rarely enjoyed them due to the social stress of such occasions and the precarious whims of his hosts.

Gluttony punctuated by purging in the vomitorium, glad-handed by senators and preening acolytes, had never been Marcellinus's forte. Yet in his dream he gorged on course after course, washing it all down with Caecuban and Falernian sweet wines, till he awoke to a blue and still Hesperian dawn with tears still wet on his cheeks, wondering if he was losing his mind.

"I see you've divorced the Briton," said Corbulo, dismounting to walk beside him. "A worthy decision."

Gaius Publius Marcellinus was leading his horse, allowing it to walk unencumbered for a while. For his own part, it felt good to shake the stiffness out of his legs, and the brisk exercise was helping to shift the fog from his thoughts.

He missed Aelfric's easy companionship, but was not about to confess it. "You were right," he said shortly. "It's easy for a man to grow careless."

The views in *Appalachia* had often been stunning. Here in the lowlands the tedium of marching had taken over again. By now Marcellinus heartily endorsed Tully's conviction that no Roman would want to farm here. The land had become ungodly flat. His eyes ached for want of a hill or even a hummock. He had never known a terrain like it. Like all learned men Marcellinus knew that the earth was round like a ball, but even for him it was easy to imagine the world petering off into an increasingly featureless desert as they marched out of reality altogether.

"Killing Fuscus," said his tribune. "Another worthy simplification. Easier not to hear his lying tongue at all than risk being misled by it."

With uncanny precision Corbulo had just congratulated Marcellinus on the second matter that was troubling him. He could not dispel the uneasy feeling that cutting down the word-slave had been as bad an error as that of the unnamed Roman captain who had slaughtered the Norse pirates to a man. Information was always valuable. And in the Praetor's personal experience, his acting in anger had rarely produced laudable results.

"Thank you," he said. "But if your third step will be to commend me on last night's morale-raising sport with the *Iroqua* women, you should stop now."

Corbulo winced. "No. Certainly you were right to allow it. But it was not something to celebrate. Let's leave that behind us."

They hiked in silence. Marcellinus recognized that an olive branch was being offered, a bid to return to their former camaraderie, but could not find the words to respond. Corbulo's moment of failure still hung in the air, surely the cause of the remaining awkwardness between them. *Everything's all right, Domitius Corbulo,* he wanted to say, *and I think no worse of you.* But that would admit the possibility that another man might have. Corbulo had ambitions, and a persistent rumor about him panicking on the battlefield could be deadly to his career, sinking his chances of one day getting his own legion or advancing in politics. Somehow the thing must be dealt with without being acknowledged.

Unexpectedly, Corbulo himself raised the topic. He turned to Marcellinus and said:

"I apologize for my dithering, back at the ambush. Thank you for plucking me upright. It was well done."

Marcellinus recovered quickly from his surprise and waved his hand dismissively. "We were all startled." He leaned over. "I hope my sandal print in your ribs is not causing you too much anguish."

Corbulo laughed. "Always better to be beaten up by a friend."

Beaten up veered a little close to Marcellinus's most painful childhood memories, but he swallowed and said easily enough, "I would never mention it to another soul, you know."

"And I thank you for that," was all Corbulo said, but he felt the man's spirits lift.

If only Marcellinus's own mood could be elevated so easily. "Well, then. I should ride again."

"We each have times when we doubt," said his First Tribune quietly. "But we need to stick together and get the job done. Whether or not there's gold here, we can make this work for Hadrianus, you and I. In the conquest and annexation of such a vast area we can cover ourselves in glory. Let us not be enemies, Gaius. And let us not forget who rules this world."

"I never shall," said Marcellinus. "Count on it."

It was not Marcellinus's habit to brood, but that night sleep would not come. Dark images and invisible fears coursed through him, banishing rest.

Finally he could stand it no longer. And so he dressed in a simple dark tunic and walked out beyond the *castra* into the relentlessly forested hills.

It was a risk, but a calculated one. Since repelling the *Iroqua* assault they had seen no signs of redskin activity, suffered no sneak attacks, passed no villages. They appeared to be passing through a sparsely populated area.

If he was truly destined to master Nova Hesperia, Land of the Evening, he needed to visit it alone, by night.

The nights here were far from silent. The din of the crickets baffled his ears and rendered him all but deaf. A stealthy redskin could be at his throat before he knew it. This, above all, led Marcellinus to dispense with caution and trust to the gods, although whether he was relying on the *lares* and *penates* of his own people or to unknown elementals of a Hesperian hue, he did not know.

Fearlessly he roamed the forest, equally aware of the feel of the earth beneath his feet and the silhouettes of the tree branches against the sky. Occasionally he reached out to touch the bark of a tree, or knelt to sift the loam of the land between his fingers.

Marcellinus walked for many hours, and saw no redskins, came across no signs of human life at all. He was neither consumed by a man-bear nor set upon by giant rodents. He was observed by a rather large owl, and interrogated briefly in the softest of night-hoots, but he chose not to respond.

If Sigurdsson could meld with the land, so could he. A Praetor must understand the terrain.

He returned changed, his confidence restored. He felt himself healed of the damage caused by his several rages at Aelfric and Fuscus, and the far more extensive wounds to his psyche caused by his Legion's brutality towards their *Iroqua* captives. In accepting the land he had regained his inner peace and flexibility, just as in his youth he had subdued the harsher human landscape of Subura.

Although he had not been keeping a good account of his direction other than by awareness of the Moon's location, his unnamed gods did not abandon him. Or perhaps he merely followed his nose back to camp. In either event he regained the *castra* well before dawn, passed into it with a nod and a wink to his astounded sentries of the watch, and captured an hour's sleep before rising refreshed into a new day.

If the gods of Nova Hesperia had planned to kill him, they would have done so. Fate still smiled upon Gaius Publius Marcellinus.

He would survive this. He might even win.

As the month of Julius gave way to Augustus, the heat soared. The sky became white with humidity, and the air felt like a damp sponge against their skin. The shade of the few remaining stands of trees offered little relief. The moisture invaded the fabric of the tents and wouldn't come out; by night the *castra* reeked like a barnyard.

And the occasional downpours just made it all worse. The rain came down in giant sheets of choking drops that did not freshen the air, merely sat rancid overnight and then boiled off the soil in the morning sun in great mists.

Marcellinus had not known the air could hold so much liquid. Beneath his armor his tunic was permanently wet, and would not dry out at night. His crotch felt like a fouled bird's nest.

Bengal had sometimes been like this. But at least they'd had a cooling monsoon every afternoon and dryer air by night. Here in Nova Hesperia, so far from the sea, the wind had forgotten how to blow. The soldiers were surly and the horses spooked at nothing, their ears flat back against their heads.

The redskins were still out there. Marcellinus lost nine legionaries, picked off while collecting firewood or stalking the white-tailed deer. Forbidding his men to hunt was futile, yet all too often they themselves became the prey.

And the heat and damp played with men's tempers. Marcellinus lost an additional seven soldiers to violence when a brawl turned murderous and he had to execute the culprits. Once more he cursed the ill mix of the men given him to command: raw Nubians, Magyar mercenaries, veteran Teutons and Italians, a mixed bag of races and languages that turned his centurions into diplomats who spent as much time coaxing their men not to kill each other as they did in maintaining their battle-readiness.

His feelings of isolation grew. Urbs Roma became a marbled dream. And, just as his legion eroded further into squalor and ill temper, the barbarians around them seemed to grow ever more civilized.

Though they saw few redskins, they passed plenty of evidence of their activities. The tents and lean-tos of the East had now given way to firmer structures of wood and wattle-and-daub. In some areas the remains of broad tree stumps showed that the savages had torn down the forests for farmland. Though Marcellinus was no lover of trees for trees' sake, he was surprised at how much of an effect this had on him.

The Romans became the beneficiaries of the increased cultivation of the land; they swarmed the maize like locusts, leaving only stalks behind them. Deer would still appear startlingly close to the Legion's path, and die quickly in a hail of arrows. The soldiers often had to pull fifteen or twenty arrows out of a downed buck before they could skin and dress it for the fire.

Despite living off the land as much as they were able, the redskin maize provided a light and paltry yield compared to the robust corn of Europa. Leogild's baggage carts continued to grow lighter as the victuals dwindled. Three thousand men on the march ate a great deal.

As long damp day followed long damp day, Marcellinus saw more and more evidence of how the red men were taming the land. And more than once, he could have sworn he saw a savage aviator fly by, banking and swooping behind the trees.

In his dreams they wheeled over him in a giant flock, and he awoke with his ears still full of the beating of their wings.

Now they started coming across the mounds; small conical earth-works in the clearings by the abandoned villages. In the days that followed, the number of villages and the size of the mounds both showed a marked increase.

"This is more like it," said Marcellinus as they rode past a mound fifteen feet tall.

"Piles of earth?" said Corbulo.

"Yes, just piles of earth, patted down nice and neat. We could put one up in an hour that would put this one to shame. But these people aren't Romans. For them to build a mound like this is a triumph of effort and organization. And these are just the beginning. Ahead, there are cities of these things."

"Ah, *big* piles of earth," said Corbulo. "You should have said so sooner."

"Support me, Lucius," said Marcellinus quietly. "Your sarcasm grows wearying."

"Of course. Sorry."

Leogild cleared his throat. "We should talk about supplies."

"Supplies, always supplies." Corbulo put his hand up to his temple, as if deafened by the Visigoth.

Leogild eyed him. "Fine. You don't want to eat, that's more for everyone else."

Up till then they'd scavenged from the fields and forests as they'd gone by. Now the tended forests were giving way to plains, and fields of tall, well-tended wheat were replacing the patches of sickly corn. The cornfields were separated by stands of nut trees; by now, nobody doubted that the barbarians had transformed the landscape around them. But reaping the new bounty would take time.

"We march on," said Marcellinus. "Let's travel light and get this done. Once we've taken the City, an organized harvest from these fields will feed us to bursting and allow us enough grain to march back to the *Chesapica* on full rations."

Corbulo looked relieved; he had obviously feared a delay in reaching their goal.

"Give the orders that any redskin farmers who don't flee are not to be harassed. The crops are to be left undisturbed."

"Four days, I'll give you," said Leogild. "After that, I'll counsel a day to restock the wagons before going on."

"Agreed," said the Praetor.

On they went. The stillness of the air was uncanny, and the utter absence of any breeze was stifling. Marcellinus rarely saw a face that was not dripping with sweat, or passed a soldier who did not reek. Much more of this and the leather and wool would rot on their bodies.

In Europa such an epic trek could have taken them from Urbs Roma almost as far as Parisi, in Gaul; but in Europa the way would be well signed and the rivers already bridged. Nova Hesperia was a giant land, with no roads at all aside from the one they were creating. This was going to be one hell of a province for a consul to administer one day.

To Marcellinus it felt as if the past weeks had carried the Legion on a long march through time. First, the poverty-wracked fisher-gatherers of the *Powhatani* by the giant bay of the *Chesapica*, at the mercy of the tide and the berry plant. Next, the woodland husbandry of the *Iroqua*, savage to invaders but gentle to the land, cultivating their meadows, burning their undergrowth, shooting their deer. Now, here in the alluvial bottom-lands of deepest Nova Hesperia, the *Cahokiani* farmed their fields and lived in stout wooden huts that represented a giant leap forward from the animal-skin tents and lean-to shacks on the coast. Such settled and well-ordered agriculture was essential to support the Great City they sought, and judging by the increasing size of the *Cahokiani* settlements they passed, that City could not be far ahead.

"Damn it, man," said centurion Pollius Scapax. "If you're not sure you're within bow range, hold your fire."

"Yes, sir," said the soldier thus chastened. "Thought I had him, sir."

"Arrows don't grow on trees, you know." An old Legion joke.

"No sir. Sorry sir."

Their enemy was no longer invisible, yet the armed barbarians in the road ahead did not engage them; instead, they withdrew before the approaching Roman army. From a distance Marcellinus could see they were warriors in full regalia, feathers in their hair and javelins and bows in their hands. They looked very different from the earlier redskins; no one could confuse the *Cahokiani* with the fishing tribes of the shore, the flying tribes of the mountains, or the warrior bands of the woodlands. These were men of much grander aspect than the previous collections of savages.

Never had Marcellinus seen men so practiced in running backwards. Yet their appearance of retreat was obviously a ruse; they were luring the Romans toward a place where they would stand and do battle. Fair enough. Since Marcellinus could no longer safely send his scouts forward to locate the enemy for himself, he welcomed the assistance. Let the *Cahokiani* choose the battlefield; this land was all flat anyway. Aside from the mounds there was no high ground for the savages to launch their wings from, and few natural features aside from the stands of trees and the occasional creek. Little opportunity for a trap or an ambush.

Unless the savages planned to retreat right through their own City and out the other side, they would eventually have to stop dancing backwards and form a battle line. Then, with their metal swords and armor and professional battle discipline, the Romans would march right over them and massacre them without breaking step, and irrigate the *Cahokiani* fields with their own blood.

Marcellinus checked the sun. It was a little more than an hour after noon. And, mercy of mercies, the wind was picking up after their many days of marching through stagnant air. A wise general might call a halt now to build a formidable *castra* for the night, stepping up to battle fresh in the dawn. But the rank and file would never stand for that. He could feel their turbulent energy, pent up over these long weeks of marching. Calming it would be impossible.

So be it. They'd only marched twelve miles today. Still enough freshness in those hard Roman legs to carry them up and over a half-naked foe armed with sticks. They might even sleep in the Great City tonight.

Another stand of tall hickory trees stood in their path, and tribune Corbulo, riding ahead of him in the vanguard, steered the Legion around it in a broad rightward curve. A series of long huts with thatched roofs now bordered the redskin road; the troops stayed wary, shields at the ready in case of a sudden fusillade of arrows, but none came. Corbulo sent in his incendiary-men to fire the huts, which went up in a fast popping blaze.

And now a corresponding crackle of excitement flooded the Legion, the men in the lead raising a ruckus, shouting "Roma!" and fanning out efficiently into battle formation. Marcellinus spurred his mount forward and was soon by Corbulo's side, where he took in the scene with a broad sweeping glance.

He looked out across a plain studded with hundreds of earthworks; cones, ridge mounds, and platform mounds, arranged in well-ordered lines. Set around them in a more haphazard pattern was a swarm of long huts with walls of reed matting and thatched roofs, along with larger wooden structures that must be granaries and lodges. The *Cahokiani* obviously did not believe in urban planning or a grid pattern, or even in streets. But a mile or more away, across what looked like a giant plaza, Marcellinus saw a stockade fifteen feet tall, built of giant logs, extending hundreds of yards in each direction. And within the stockade....

"Jupiter!" Marcellinus swore. "Hold! Hold!"

"What?" Domitius Corbulo paused, contemptuous. "It's a lump. We'll slaughter 'em, then kick it down."

"It's further away than you think," said Marcellinus. "*Look* at it. It must be over a hundred feet high, and acres wide."

Within the stockade sat an immense two-level platform mound, constructed entirely of earth. Its sides angled up steeply like a pyramid to a first plateau, with a long thatched hut on one corner, and then up again to a final flat crest. The mound was topped with a huge wooden structure that must have been eighty feet long and two or three stories tall.

How long must it have taken to construct such a massive pyramid, even using slave labor? The legion dug a six-foot earthen ridge around the *castra* each night, but that was the work of hundreds of tough men at the peak of fitness. This thing had to be fifteen acres in area and as tall as the Palatine Hill in Roma. They must have spent lifetimes building it up to its current height and girth. And on wet foundations such an earthwork must be hell's own job to stabilize. How could one even engineer it?

This was no scaled-up version of a fishing camp or nomad's village. This truly was a Great City, complete with suburbs, urbs, and citadel. From the sheer number of houses and mounds, and the expanse of corn that stretched beyond and behind them as far as he could see, Marcellinus reckoned it must hold over twenty thousand people. After their trek across the most desolate and unpromising territory he had ever seen, the Great City had a grandeur for which he was not prepared.

In that moment Marcellinus radically revised his assessment of their enemy. Savage, yes—yet in the scope of their organization, as civilized as many a Roman province.

And here they came: row upon row of redskins pouring out from the palisade and hurrying in like ants from the outer regions of their City. Around Marcellinus his legionaries were similarly arraying themselves for battle, as they must, since their enemy could charge at any time. He became aware that nearby him Corbulo was shouting the order to advance.

"Wait," said Marcellinus. "Deploy and hold. We don't advance yet."

Corbulo turned, stiff-necked. "What?"

"There's more here than meets the eye. Look at the terrain; the braves can use the huts and mounds to good effect. Advancing, we'll take attacks from the flanks as well as the front."

Thirty years of soldiering had lent Marcellinus a powerful intuition. He had not become a Praetor for nothing, and his gut told him now to keep his distance from that master mound.

"We wait?" said Corbulo in contempt, just as Aelfric rode up from behind and cursed in his own tongue at the stupendous sight before them. "No, we must charge immediately while they're still forming up. Frontal assault, wedge formation. We've come a thousand miles for this."

"Yes, and so we can wait ten minutes more." In the ranks his centurions were in the thick of preparations, running back and forth bellowing at their men. Despite never having received a formal command, his Legion was already deployed in an admirably straight north-south triple line. The banners of the cohorts flapped in the growing breeze, the *signiferi* of individual centuries were displayed proudly, and at the line's center he saw the golden Aquila raised high.

Despite the stress of the moment a lump came to Marcellinus's throat. They'd endured a grueling trek, with hunger, discomfort and danger; dissent and discord had never been far away, yet his men had risen to the occasion in double-quick time. The *Legio XXXIII Hesperia* was ready for battle. And yet, and yet....

"Wings ho!" someone cried. And so there were, a dozen or more, leaping off the top of the master mound and circling out over the assembling barbarian horde like moths, before gliding back to land behind the palisade.

"They can't reach us," said Fabius. "That mound isn't so high, and they've no updrafts to sustain them. Showy enough, but no threat."

Corbulo nodded. "These red bastards don't like to fight unless they hold the advantage of stealth, darkness, or altitude. There's no honor in 'em. Burn a captive, drop a rock, poison a scratch, hack at a soldier squatting under a tree—that's their game. We kill them all now."

"Tribune. Attend me."

Corbulo turned on him. "*You* told the men the redskins are cowards! They cower in defeat. Look at Fuscus!"

"The *Powhatani*, yes. Even the *Iroqua*. Perhaps not the *Cahokiani*." Marcellinus strode forward and clamped his hand onto Corbulo's arm. "I gave you an order, Tribune. Obey me."

Corbulo's hand dropped to the hilt of his gladius. "Not today, I think."

Their eyes met. Looking deep into Corbulo's soul, Marcellinus saw many things: fear, resentment, and above all, Corbulo's desperate and enduring need to redeem himself.

It was the same wild look that he had seen in Corbulo's eye during the ambush in *Appalachia*. Corbulo was suffering that same panic now. His nerve was cracking, and as a result he was lashing out at Marcellinus.

Corbulo broke eye contact, but dropped his voice. "I know you, Gaius. You're looking for an excuse to avoid slaughter. But it's too late. The men will revolt and kill us both if we don't attack *now*."

"The men will do as I order. They respect prudence."

"Prudence?" said Domitius Corbulo, reverting to a voice loud enough to carry into the nearest troops. "Prudence says we wipe out the savages, take their gold and their women, and, yes, grind the bones of the men to pave the temple to Jupiter Imperator that we'll build on that sandcastle of theirs. As *you* said yourself, just the other night. Did you lose your stomach for the fight, Gaius Marcellinus? Forget so soon how these savages mutilated your Norse catamite? Or have you made deals by night, and now favor the red men?"

"What?" Marcellinus shook his head, overwhelmed at this knot of bizarre accusations. But Corbulo's gladius was now unsheathed, and *that* was something Marcellinus could understand.

Legionaries might take advantage of the chaos on the battlefield to scrag an unpopular centurion. It happened all the time. But for a tribune to challenge a legate's authority a few hundred yards from the enemy's gate was unthinkable.

"I'm relieving you of your command," said Marcellinus.

Corbulo grinned. "I think not."

Suddenly, all around Marcellinus was movement; Gnaeus Fabius seized a pilum and stepped up to stand with Corbulo, and flanking the two mutineers came four swarthy auxiliaries, mercenaries from east of the Danube, Magyars perhaps, or Bulgars. Too late, Marcellinus saw that this little scene was not as impromptu as it had appeared. He dropped back several paces to open up space around him, his adrenaline surging.

The pilum of Fabius was the first danger, with its reach so much longer than a sword's. The javelin was capable of ending a fight in a single well-aimed throw, but could be cumbersome as a hand-to-hand weapon. A better fighter than Fabius might have charged in and pinned Marcellinus to ready him for the dispatch, but apparently Fabius's magistracy had not primed him for such martial boldness; instead he launched the pilum at Marcellinus from a distance of fifteen feet. The Praetor took a single step to the right as it flew by, and remained on balance.

Hands free, no shield within reach, Marcellinus unsheathed his gladius with his right hand and his pugio with his left, and stood fast as the six men charged him.

But here was Aelfric, arriving beside him quicker than a thought, so nimble that if the Briton had been a party to the treachery Marcellinus would have been on his knees with a blade through his kidney before he could have parried. With a strange howl that was neither a berserker yell nor a cry of abandon, Aelfric hurled himself into the fray at his commander's side.

Marcellinus cut down the first two mercenaries with swift slices to the gut. They were hardly the first young hotheads to fatally misjudge his speed. The paid help from Roma's provinces were generally not skilled gladiatorial fighters; on the battlefield they relied on numbers and ferocity rather than virtuosity with weapons, and Marcellinus had been training daily in swordplay since he was a child.

The third and fourth auxiliaries backed away rapidly once they saw the fight was not as simple as they'd hoped, and stepped apart to encircle him.

Meanwhile Aelfric's gladius clashed with Corbulo's; the two men slashed and parried, swung and ducked, and Aelfric staggered back. Faced with the choice between two opponents Marcellinus chose the third, darting between the two Magyars to lunge at Domitius Corbulo's flank. Corbulo spun to face him, startled, and Marcellinus drove the pugio up under his breastplate and deep into his ribs, leaning back to slice his gladius across his tribune's gut. As Corbulo reeled like a drunkard, swinging his blade wildly, Marcellinus dropped to one knee, allowing Aelfric to leap over his sword arm and slam bodily into the nearest of the mercenaries, bowling him over.

The unexpected trade in opponents made short work of the insurrection. Corbulo screamed like a banshee as his entrails tumbled out into the dirt, a cry that turned into a guttural bubbling as Marcellinus tugged his dagger free and severed the man's windpipe. Beside him Aelfric had handily slain the third mercenary. The fourth raised his sword over them with a yell and was almost casually decapitated by Pollius Scapax, arriving better late than not at all.

Left alone in his mutiny in a matter of seconds, Gnaeus Fabius stood stupidly before them, his gladius pointing at the ground. He looked around for reinforcements, but the men near him stood mute. Praetor Gaius Marcellinus calmly cleaned his two blades on the grass at his feet while holding his second tribune's gaze.

Pollius Scapax strode the ten paces that separated them. Fabius raised his sword but didn't have the courage to swing it at the centurion. Gently, almost kindly, Scapax reached forward and seized the tribune's gladius at the hilt, turned it towards Fabius's own belly, and kicked his knees from behind. As Gnaeus Fabius fell onto his own sword, Scapax ripped off the man's cape and plumed helmet and threw them aside, demoting him from the rank of tribune and the ranks of the living in the same moment.

Marcellinus sheathed his pugio. The closest legionaries swiveled their heads almost comically back and forth between Marcellinus, Scapax, and the assembled swath of the redskin nation behind them. Marcellinus realized that two entire armies had come to a halt, waiting for the leadership battle to be decided.

He was not surprised that none but Aelfric had come to his aid. To most of the men Marcellinus and Corbulo were of a muchness: patricians, Roma's natural masters, representatives of the ruling class. Their lot would be largely the same whichever man wore the Praetor's crest. Unless they were paid or coerced, they had naught to gain and all to lose by picking a side.

Scapax approached, his gladius still unsheathed but reversed so the point pushed up against his own breast. "I was not close by when I might have served you, Praetor," he said gruffly. "And so I offer you my life. But I'd rather expend it killing some of *them* for you, than follow Fabius to hell right away, if you'll give me leave."

"Of course," said Marcellinus calmly. "Think nothing of it. I relished the chance to clean house."

"My thanks."

"In addition, I find myself short of field lieutenants. I will take the Second and Third; assume the tribuneship of the First, if you please."

Scapax's eyes glinted. "Very good, sir."

He saluted, and Marcellinus returned the salute. His new tribune turned and marched to his command.

To Aelfric he said, "My apologies and thanks. We'll drink wine tonight."

"As my Praetor requests." Aelfric grinned and strategically stepped aside.

Considering there were perhaps ten thousand men present, the stillness of the afternoon was impressive. If not for the palpable tension in the air, Marcellinus could have closed his eyes and thought himself alone in the sunshine. As it was, he felt his army extending out from him in all directions like a drawn bow, arrow nocked and at the ready, bowstring tight, arm muscles a-quiver.

The Praetor slowed his breathing and studied the battlefield. His Legion was deployed uniformly, presenting an even front a thousand yards long. The redskin horde was by no means so well distributed; the northern end of their line was thicker, holding thousands more than the southern end that stood between him and the master mound. Would they deliberately expend more troops defending their population center than their sacred hill? Was it just an accident of formation? Or was the nearer end of their line guarded by something he couldn't yet see?

Not the wings, certainly. Though impressive, their master mound did not approximate to a mountain. Pilots who leaped from its top barely had time to loop back around before they were on the ground again.

A hidden pit? All the soil that went into the mounds had to come from somewhere. Had the *Cahokiani* concealed their borrow pits, in the hopes of enticing their enemies to charge headlong into them?

Perhaps. But in that case all Marcellinus had to do to minimize his losses was to have the Legion walk rather than run. And Marcellinus still didn't like the looks of the mounds and longhouses that stood between his army and the palisade; he wasn't about to rush pell-mell into those in any case.

He turned his attention to the enemy line. At last, Marcellinus could see the *Cahokiani* clearly. In their garb they were a mixed bunch, some wearing only breechcloths and swirling tattoos, others decked out in what might be tunics, with wooden mats hanging down over their chests and stomachs as the simplest of armors. Here and there were men wearing a woven sash, a kilt bearing geometric patterns, moccasins of deerskin, or a collar of what might have been rabbit. Hanging from many ears he saw pendulous adornments of antler and bone.

The *Cahokiani* had no flags, standards or symbols, and little organization. Nowhere was this more apparent than in their array of weaponry: wooden bows, probably crafted of hickory, and clubs and axes too, but also a variety of other tools hurriedly pressed into service; hafted hoes, mattocks, and some men who clutched nothing more deadly than a rock or a knife.

He faced a mass of nobles and commoners, farmers and traders, warriors and weavers all mixed together, and a style of fighting the Romans had outgrown a millennium and a half ago. The Romans were heavily outnumbered, but they had metal blades and armor and intense discipline on their side. Marcellinus's sympathies lay with his foes.

Yet he still felt his instinctive unease at these creatures with their almost intimate stares, waiting as calmly as if they went toe to toe with a Roman army once a week. In the mountains, people not so different from these had assaulted them from above. What was about to happen here?

Isleifur Bjarnason's voice echoed in his head. "They have more... You haven't seen anything yet...."

Corbulo had been quite right; now that Marcellinus had seen the Great City for himself, he would have given anything to avoid this battle. But such a thing was impossible.

They already knew the redskins did not understand the civilized conduct of war. Their sneak attacks, their use of poison arrows, the torture and murder of his scout, and their use of the cowardly flying machines all provided adequate testimony on that score. Marcellinus could easily ride out between the armies under a flag of truce to try to parley, only to perish in a hail of arrows for his pains. Besides, no leader or chieftain was evident in the massed line of savages that faced him. He saw no one to negotiate with, even if he'd still had a word-slave at his disposal.

It was a testament to the steadiness of his centurions that none of his cohorts had yet erupted into a charge; a truce or treaty would be quite untenable to his men, nor did the opposing army appear ambivalent. They were past the point of no return, and Marcellinus could not halt this battle any more than he could hold back the tide.

Very well then.

Praetor Gaius Publius Marcellinus raised his gladius high and gave the signals to his *aquilifer* and *signiferi* while shouting aloud: "Advance in steps, covering! Burn all buildings, secure high ground! Arrows in rotation once in range, maintain formation till melee. Forward the Legion, for Roma, the Imperator, and the Fighting 33rd!"

Marcellinus dropped his arm. His sword rent the air. With a roar the Legion surged forward, but tightly, masterfully, and in control.

Across the plaza the red men raised up their bows, their axes, their hoes. Marcellinus was sure they roared just as loudly as his own men, but thankfully he could not hear them.

The Legion had methodically advanced a quarter of the distance separating them from the redskins when the nearest longhouses burst into flame. Marcellinus had given the order to fire them in passing so the enemy could not use them as cover, but these ignitions were not of Roman doing. The thatched houses went up in a series of giant *whumphs*, burning with an intense red-white flare. What had the savages put in them, to blaze so fiercely?

Yet there was no real explosion and no scattering of burning debris. Not a single Roman was harmed by the incendiaries. Nor were they accompanied by an ambush: no redskins tumbled out from behind a mound or inside a hut. The Legion marched forward steadily, its front line replenishing itself, inexorably closing the distance to the foe that waited on the other side of the *Cahokiani* plaza.

The redskins adopted no formation except the simple line, and still Marcellinus saw no leaders, no orders given. The savages seemed content to watch the Romans closing in.

Up the Roman line to the North, Marcellinus saw the front ranks of the Fourth drop to one knee. Auxiliaries less encumbered by shields and armor, and with fewer huts and mounds to navigate around, the Fourth had advanced more swiftly than the other cohorts and were now within arrow range.

His attention was pulled back by cries of surprise from the men close by him. He followed their gaze and pointing fingers, and his eyes widened.

From the summit of the master mound, the *Cahokiani* were shooting bodies into the air. Clearly a ballista or onager of considerable power ran up the far side of the giant mound. Marcellinus's first thought—that they were lobbing diseased cattle carcasses, as one might heft over a city wall to break a siege—was incorrect; these were humans that were being catapulted aloft, with incredible heft and force. At the greatest altitude of their arc they unfurled broad wings in a sudden stroke to become the now familiar fixed-wing flying craft. In minutes, the air was alive with them.

They dived low and fast over the cohorts like winged demons, each pilot feathered and bird-masked and with an arrow nocked. They flew barely thirty feet above the Roman helmets, but so swift and agile that it would take a lucky pilum indeed to bring one down. Legionaries flung themselves right and left, breaking formation to avoid the flight paths of the wings, but even as Marcellinus drew breath to bellow a harsh command he heard his centurions' voices booming across the battlefield: "Raise up your shields!" "Maintain formation!" "Stand firm, damn you!"

Discipline reestablished, the Legion lunged forward again. The front lines of the Fourth and Sixth Auxiliaries discharged a volley of arrows into the enemy line, advanced a dozen paces, and dropped to one knee; the men behind marched through to become the new front rank, firing their own swath of arrows into the massed bodies of the savages. A wave of redskins stumbled and fell, the Roman arrows scraping off the whole front layer of the barbarian army.

Now Marcellinus saw the purpose of the brightly burning huts. As the wings flew overhead, loosing many an arrow into a Roman breastplate, their paths inevitably took them over the burning long-houses where their pilots expertly rode the hot, rising air up into the skies to recover their altitude. Again and again Marcellinus watched the human moths pass above the white fire and arc up into the sky, their skill even more dazzling than the flames. Three of the wings crossed paths a thousand feet above him, an incredible height with no strategic value, surely just an exhilarating distraction. But as Marcellinus watched them he experienced another dizzying mental leap: the redskin pilots were using their very patterns of flight to signal to their comrades. From their aerial vantage point the battle was laid out beneath them like a map. The wings were the ultimate surveillance tools; scouts in the sky.

These people were not neophytes at war. The *Cahokiani* were a tribe—a nation—that had faced large-scale armed assault before, from the savage *Iroqua*, perhaps, or from even fiercer tribes that the Romans had not yet encountered.

And the aviators were not all men. Here came a woman, circling over him. Lone and unarmed, ribbons streaming out behind her in the air, her job was surely to find the Praetor and loop over his position, perhaps marking him out for attack.

A flaming arrow hit a hut that had so far remained unexploded and it lit up like a torch. Greek fire, thought Marcellinus; these people had independently discovered Greek fire, hundreds of years after the secret was lost on the Roman side of the *Atlanticus*. He made a note to keep some of their apothecaries and armorers—or perhaps their priests—alive at the end of this day, in addition to a handful of the pilots.

The infantry at Marcellinus's end of the line were now within bow range of the enemy. This time the redskins loosed a salvo of arrows first, a ragged torrent of sticks that scattered harmlessly off the tall Roman shields. The men of the First and Third cohorts jeered, drew, and sent a focused wave of metal-tipped death into the midst of the *Cahokiani*....

And then the world changed again, with a titanic roar. Marcellinus's gaze was wrenched skyward once more, and all of a sudden he became aware of his own labored breathing and the sweat that trickled down his forehead, the smell of thousands of men in armor, the screams of the wounded, the strong breeze from the west. And of the massive, incredible shape that soared unsupported through the low skies towards them, spreading the broadest of shadows across the Roman army.

"Jupiter!" he shouted, though he was a man who seldom cursed, and then, more reverently: "Thunder-Bird." Because now everything made sense.

Above them loomed a startling creation of sticks and skins, as if the longest of the *Cahokiani* longhouses had unfurled itself and taken flight. It did not flap like a bird, rather it rocked on the breeze like a gull hovering over a cliff top. Mesmerized, Marcellinus noted how the Thunder-Bird swung steadily on the very air, how the dozen redskins who hung beneath it steered it with concerted leans and pulls and heavy shoves against the rudder bars they clutched, steering the giant craft in a smooth arc. The aerial leviathan flew south of him and then turned, the flying-men using the warm air from the farthest of the burning huts to raise the craft's nose. Even as tiny motes of ash defied the pull of the ground, buoyed on the rising tide of warm air, so steering this Thunder-Bird over the heat that radiated from below allowed it to ascend ever higher.

And here came a second Thunder-Bird, rising from behind the master mound in a thrumming whoosh that was surely caused by the passage of the air over the giant wing and the vibrating of the skins stretched between the wooden poles.

Bitter laughter bubbled in Marcellinus's throat at the audacity of it. This was why the *Cahokiani* had built their giant mounds. It was not merely a conceit to put themselves closer to their gods, nor for their privileged classes to look down upon their people from on high. It was to train their pilots. Why go to the trouble of building a mound in the featureless flatness of the bottomlands, if not to throw yourself off it? Lining the far side of the mound must be the ballista to end all ballistas, used both to fling the insanely courageous braves in their tiny single-man wings to suicidal heights, and to launch these behemoths of the air.

What Marcellinus wouldn't have given for a ballista of his own! One good shot might bring a behemoth down. Then again, the iron bolt might pass right through the wing, leaving a neat hole but not affecting its aerial progress in the slightest.

These beasts had not been fabricated purely for the joy of riding the winds. Marcellinus saw the row of sacks hanging beneath the wings of the first Thunder-Bird even as the braves began releasing them, to fall into the infantry of his First and Second Cohorts.

A burning thunderclap rippled towards the Praetor, blowing him backward. The screams of his men merged into a single agonized wail as the new Greek fire of Nova Hesperia rained down across entire centuries of his men. Those not directly smitten by the deadly flaring liquid fell to the ground once they trod in it with their sandaled feet, there to roll in torment. Through the bright afterimages that dazed his eyes, Marcellinus saw the red, flaming weals on his soldiers' bodies as they frantically tugged their armor away from their flesh. Men who splashed water from their canteens onto their burning skin howled anew; the water did not quench the fire but just spread it further.

The second Thunder-Bird lumbered over them now, directed and shepherded by the smaller wings, sparrows looping around eagles. Marcellinus viewed its trajectory carefully, but the crew of this Bird were saving its firebombs for cohorts further up the line; as he watched, it shed Greek fire into the square formations of the Fourth and Fifth Cohorts. By now his centurions had already called their infantry into the defensive *testudo* formation, their solid metal shields interlocked above them in the tortoise-like structure that gave the formation its name. But huge and terrifying gouts of liquid poured over them, the fire splashed and dripped between the shields, and the shell of the tortoise splintered quickly as the soldiers flung their bodies back and forth in the same terrible dance as their comrades in the First and Second.

In a single pass the two Thunder-Birds had rendered a thousand Romans ineffective. All the formations Marcellinus could see had fallen apart. And clearly audible above the screams of the Romans came the battle-cries of the *Cahokiani* as they sprinted across the hundred short yards that separated the armies, their clubs and hoes raised high above their heads.

Marcellinus bellowed, ripping his voice hoarse with commands to the troops around him to fall in and regain fighting formation. He ordered his Romans to set pila and march forward, and his Teutons and Scythians to ready axes and gladii for the melee, but his words were swept away in the din.

The two armies crashed together. Marcellinus felt the visceral shock as Roman met barbarian. The exultation of combat filled him, and the surge of simple ecstasy threatened to explode his heart. With battle joined, no doubts remained, no fears of fiery torture or flint-tipped death, no visions of his lost Vestilia or regrets at the man he had become; even the memory of his tribunes' treachery was swept aside. Marcellinus had dedicated his life to moments like these. It was time to fight.

In his nose was the smell of battle, the blood and mud and dust; in his ears the warrior roars, the din of steel upon wood, flint upon steel, the screams of the wounded, and the pounding of his own pulse. The frenzy around him became a series of sharp images: a redskin baying as he held aloft a curly-headed Roman scalp, the sickening crunch as a pilum cleaved a path between ribs to a living heart, a Roman sandal skidding in blood, a plumed helmet banged aside by an axe-head, the skull beneath smashed open in the backswing. Everywhere naked flesh slammed willingly into leather and steel plate, the howl and hullabaloo of the redskins fit to deafen Jove and echo across the world, as the people of the Great City of Nova Hesperia showed themselves no simple savages after all but true warriors, less armored and drilled than the soldiers of the Imperium but with a berserker strength the equal of any Roman, be he Germanic or Celt or native Italian patrician.

In every battle there came a moment for Gaius Marcellinus when his opponents elevated themselves in his mind from dispensable human jetsam to worthy opponents fit to be honored in the Mithraic mystery rites. At that moment tears came to Marcellinus's eyes, threatening his vision just when he needed to see clearest. Often he would strike his own face to drive away the treacherous teardrops before they could be his undoing. For always in battle came the factor of fortune or capricious gods, when despite his skill and speed an enemy might get in a lucky strike. In that instant life or limb could be forfeit and he might become a cripple or a carcass, his remaining moments just a coda of decrepitude and regret.

Such a moment came now in the midst of the slicing and hacking, as his legionaries went down in droves under the war axes of the *Cahokiani*. Marcellinus dispatched a tattooed dervish armed only with a hoe who seemed nonetheless to be moving with preternatural speed; he took a fearful blow to his shield and at the same time planted his gladius into the man's face and saw him fall, cheek and throat gashed to the bone. With a fluid motion Marcellinus tugged the sword free and spun to meet the next threat, then froze in mid-swing. For it was a woman who attacked him now, fierce and howling yet large-breasted and unarmored, ridiculously vulnerable. As he paused, her club struck him full on the helmet; he dropped to a knee to absorb the pain, his ears ringing, and sliced through the woman's thigh. As she fell he threw himself forward, his shield grinding her head into the muck.

She stopped moving. Marcellinus, his tears flowing in earnest now, spared himself not a moment to wonder whether she was dead or merely unconscious but hurled himself at the next of them. Knowing that that one short moment of hesitation could have been his last added even more vigor to his arm.

Fury and pain drenched the air, and for a while it all became a blur. Then, miraculously, Marcellinus stood alone and unassailed, surrounded by corpses. A Thunder-Bird roared over him and he leapt up with his gladius outstretched, as if he could actually have slashed it from the sky. Whirling, he got his bearings.

The melee still raged, though far more men had fallen than remained fighting. Yet only a stretch of mud separated Marcellinus from the palisade of the *Cahokiani*. Somehow he had fought his way through the barbarian army and out the other side.

A quarter mile north, the new Thunder-Bird disgorged its bellyful of fire. Close by, yet another Bird creaked in the air, flying in the opposite direction.

Marcellinus cast his shield aside and ran, the thud of each sandal-fall sending a bang of pain up his spine and into his head.

The master mound grew before his eyes. The gates of the palisade were open. The *Cahokiani* guards at the gate backed up and made no move to prevent him from running on through. Marcellinus heard a new cacophony in his ears and realized it was his own voice screaming out the names of Roma, Titus Augustus, and Vestilia; in addition to his land and his daughter, he was invoking the name of an Imperator long dead.

Now Marcellinus was on the mound, and he pounded up it with all the energy and determination he could muster. It wasn't enough. The earthwork was enormous, and after the travails of battle, a sprint to the top of it was beyond him.

At the first plateau, where the steep incline leveled out, he stopped and bent over, panting. Sweat poured into his eyes. He was quite alone, and the hot fire of combat had drained from his blood to leave him bereft and empty. Far above him at the mound's crest he could still see the top of the giant unmarked wooden building—a palace? Temple? Marshalling yard for the wings? Below him was the palisade and beyond that, the battlefield he had left behind.

Feeling ridiculous in his plumed helmet, Marcellinus tipped it off onto the ground and stood bare-headed, almost steaming.

A Thunder-Bird roared over him. Its wingspan was immense, its shadow dwarfed him. Now, that was bravery indeed. Putting yourself under one of those things and allowing whatever devil's machinery lurked behind the master mound to hurl you into the sky was not the act of a coward.

Down in the plaza some areas of fighting still raged, a last desperate effort by his few remaining centuries to take as many barbarians to hell with them as they could. One of the fiercest pockets of resistance marked where the Fourth Cohort had been; Marcellinus hoped Aelfric was still fighting, and would die well. Such pockets aside, the battlefield was a morass of downed Romans, leather and steel doused in blood. From this elevation it was clear beyond doubt that Marcellinus's army was destroyed. The 33rd Hesperian Legion was no more.

From the fringes of the killing ground, some Romans fled eastward. Marcellinus did not begrudge them their escape. For him, there could be no future that way. Even if he were to catch up with the fragments of his Legion, they'd probably kill him. And then on the terrible march back to the *Chesapica*, the *Iroqua* would kill *them*.

For hundreds of years the Roman army had mown down primitives in droves. The Thunder-Birds and firebombs of the *Cahokiani* marked the end of that. The discipline and rigidity that had proved such an asset to the Imperium in Europa and Asia had become a liability when faced with aerial bombardment; the *testudo* was not tight enough, the soldiers' armor too thin, their heavy military sandals insufficient protection from liquid fire.

The Roman Aquila was earthbound, while the People of the Eagle soared. Tactics effective in two dimensions were found wanting in three. They would need to scrap the classic Roman tight formations and re-think them from scratch.

Not that Marcellinus would return to Urbs Roma to advise his Imperator on it; Roma was now forever beyond his reach.

His mad goal had been to climb to the top of the mound, slaughter everyone he found, and destroy the launching system that threw the human birds aloft. But success in that endeavor seemed unlikely, and it was too late anyway. Marcellinus laid his gladius and pugio on the ground by his feet, and sat.

"Fool's gold," he said aloud. Wherever the Vikings had gotten their plunder, it wasn't here. Truly information was worth more than gold; if they'd left even one Norseman alive on that longship to tell the tale, his three thousand Romans might still be alive. Or, if Marcellinus himself had really paid attention to the one useful thing that Fuscus and Isleifur Bjarnason had both tried to tell him....

Let it be.

The wind tousled his hair. Looking along the line of the master mound to his left, he now saw a great brown river. Marcellinus had spent his life studying terrain, and felt sure that the continent of Nova Hesperia stretched a distance at least as far to the west as his Legion had already marched from the east. This was too great a land for even the Imperium to swallow. Yet here he was, Praetor of a doomed Legion, stranded in the center of it.

Several of the one-man wings had crashed or been shot down during the battle. Marcellinus watched as the fallen aviators were carried away reverently to the peak of one particular conical mound. A pilot's body was not separated from his vehicle; rather, the two were taken and burned together on the pyre as if they were one thing, the ashes of man and wing rising together into the air. The pilots' eagle masks were not even removed. It seemed that the *Cahokiani* honored their fallen heroes just as reverently as any Roman comrade, mother, or vestal virgin.

Two Thunder-Birds had landed, one in a cornfield far distant, another at the northern edge of the *Urbs Cahokiani*. The nearer Bird was being carried back into the palisade by its squad of pilots; from Marcellinus's vantage point it looked like an enormous crawling insect. In the distant sky two other aerial bombers had turned in formation and were flying back towards the mound, their giant wings flexing in the invisible air currents. And, in the air far above him, barbarians wearing the individual wings still danced like dragonflies, wheeling and swooping in victory.

One of the small wings separated itself from the throng and spiraled down towards him. It shot over his head at speed and looped around. Its pilot pushed up his craft's nose to spill air, and landed running along the plateau towards Marcellinus. Ribbons fluttered behind the wing.

Time to sell his life, so soon? Reluctantly Marcellinus reached for his gladius.

The pilot shrugged out of his wing harness and laid the wing carefully against the slope of the mound. He appeared unarmed.

She. Once the pilot began walking and her hips twitched left and right, there was no doubt.

Sisika wore a light leather tunic, haphazardly cut, and a breechcloth. Her eagle mask now hung around her neck. In her hair she wore a band studded with eagle feathers. Her face was painted with the same swirling marks as the rest of her tribe. Back east she had not worn such marks, perhaps adapting to local customs. That, too, had been bravery, he now realized: to come all that way just to see the Romans for herself.

"Chieftain, daughter of chieftain," Fuscus had called her. Once again, understanding had eluded Marcellinus. Here on her home territory, Sisika's poise and authority were clear.

If ten warriors had landed around Marcellinus he might have snatched up his blades and gone down fighting. And if he was not dispatched, he should steer the gladius into his own stomach and fall upon it. A staunch Roman should choose death over defeat.

But he wasn't going to. He had already given his life for the Imperium. No need to die for it, as well.

He'd been ordered here on a fool's errand by an Imperator he disdained. He'd barely managed to keep control of his own army, and then lost it trying to conquer a city for gold they obviously didn't have. He had no reason for pride, and thus no need to die pridefully. The hell with it. He unbuckled his armor and tossed it down the slope and sat there in his simple tunic, a simple man. Let them make of him whatever they would; Marcellinus was done.

For all he knew they might torture him, drawing out his death over a week of agonized mutilation. But Marcellinus thought not. From the warriors who had let his legionaries flee in defeat, and the guardians who had allowed him through the gates to the mound, he guessed that this was not a nation of true savagery. Fearsome enough in battle, but less vicious than his own race, who called themselves the civilizing light of the world, yet could not master such a simple, glorious thing as flight.

At last the reaction hit him. Deep pain plunged through his heart and stomach at the loss of his Legion. He deserved to live with the guilt of having failed them. Avoiding the pain that was rightfully his by ending his life: that would be true cowardice. And if, after all, these civilized savages chose to burn him or tear off his limbs, that would be his just desserts. Marcellinus had rarely shown mercy. Let him be shown none in return.

Sisika squatted on her heels six feet away, staring into his face. He tried to imagine how rough and uncanny he must seem to her. How did she know he wouldn't attack her? Perhaps the mound was a place of peace, and in clambering up here Marcellinus had unwittingly claimed sanctuary. Or perhaps, having spared her once, she assumed he wouldn't hurt her this time.

In hindsight it seemed odd that they had declared war on a people they understood so poorly.

"Sisika," he said, and pointed at himself. "Gaius."

She put her head on one side, bird-like, but seeing the harsh disdain in her eyes, Marcellinus did not smile.

Above them, humans still soared. He tried to imagine Sisika being shot into the air like a ballista bolt and unfurling her wings, the mounds and longhouses far beneath her.

Marcellinus was battle-torn and filthy. He had cuts on his head, burns on his arm from splashes of Greek fire. His leg was gouged bloody and he had lost a chunk of skin from his shoulder, wounds he did not remember getting. What kind of idiot luck had kept him safe? Perhaps he'd just fought well. Yet all the while the ribbon-sparrows like Sisika had flown above him, noting his position. Perhaps they'd allowed him a path.

Marcellinus did not believe in luck. He must have survived for a reason. The fates had something more in store for him.

Soon he would be the only Roman left alive within the City. He was the farthest west any Roman had achieved, surrounded by a whole new world, completely independent of the Imperium. There was wonder in that.

Down on the battlefield they had begun to clear the plaza of bodies. No one appeared to be in charge. They all just seemed to know it was the proper next thing to do. Maybe they'd let him help. And later... well, Marcellinus was not such an old dog that he couldn't learn new tricks. He had overcome greater odds and swayed in stronger gales over the years. He was nothing if not adaptable.

"I fly," he said to Sisika. He held his hands palm upward, sliding one behind the other till his thumbs locked, then flapping his fingers, as if using lamplight to throw the shadow of a bird onto a wall. "I help you. Teach you how to fight your enemies even better. Show you things you need. In return, I fly."

She shrugged, not understanding a word.

"Whatever I have to do," he said. "However long it takes."

Below, three braves walked in through the palisade gates carrying the

Legion's golden Aquila. It looked unharmed, down to the two plaques mounted on the pole beneath the eagle, the "S.P.Q.R." of the Imperium, and "XXXIII Hesperia" under that. Chattering excitedly, the braves began the long walk up the mound with their trophy.

Well, they'd won it fair and square; nobody could deny that.

Marcellinus stood as the trio reached the plateau. They noticed him for the first time and jumped back in alarm.

He could slay them if he chose. They were young and unarmed, and Marcellinus still had two blades at his feet. But Sisika was watching, and the battle was lost an hour since.

And if the eagle of Roma was to be planted at the peak of this immense mound to look out over Nova Hesperia, that was something. It wasn't how the day should have ended. But maybe it was enough. Let there be gold in the Great City, after all.

"Here," said Marcellinus, and held out his arms to them. "Let me carry that for you."

To Love the Difficult
Amy Sterling Casil

"He who does not at some time, with definite determination consent to the terrible-ness of life, or even exalt in it, never takes possession of the inexpressible fullness of the power of our existence."

-*Rainer Maria Rilke*

That morning, MacKenzie was in his usual spot behind the counter at the Pik-A-Mart.

His John Deere cap had melted onto his face, and below the green brim, Mac's remarkably long nose had grown like Pinocchio's, with the tip nearly joining with his chin.

It was so ridiculous that Terry Herle laughed to see it, figuring that the Pik-A-Mart window was plastic and maybe it was warped, and he'd just never noticed before.

"Hey, Mac!" he said, rapping on the frame and trying the door. It was locked.

"Mac—what's hangin'?" Terry said, rapping again and rattling the doorknob. He really needed some java. "Gotta get my Starbucks."

Mac kept a junior Starbucks cart in the back of the store, and you might think that this was no remarkable thing, but Portland was a genuinely small Midwestern town. Terry remembered Mac bragging that he had to pay plenty just for the privilege of putting up that green-and-white sign, getting their beans, using their cups, and even paying extra for the essential little round brown cardboard things that kept a guy from burning his fingers.

Mac's nose wavered back and forth for a bit, but then the John Deere cap straightened itself out, and so did Mac. He looked toward the door, grinning his familiar grin and giving Terry a thumbs-up.

As Terry tried the knob again, the door practically flew open, and he grunted in surprise.

"Hey man, what's up?" he asked as he stumbled over the black rubber welcome mat.

"Hi there," said Mac as Terry righted himself.

This was almost as weird as the vision through the window. Terry felt like Mac didn't *know* him.

"I'll have the usual," Terry said as he walked to the counter. He put his elbow on the counter, then rested his chin on the heel of his palm in a "pensive" pose.

"Yeah?" Mac said. "And..."

"Mac!" Terry said, laughing uncomfortably, because he really didn't like this type of joke. "You've known me for ten years. Terry Herle—John Jay County's most famous resident."

Mac's eyes narrowed. "Ah, the most famous," he said slowly.

Terry started to feel like he was catching on. "Quit pulling my leg," he said. "Like you could forget the world's most successful blogger?" he added.

Mac nodded and turned toward the mini-Starbuck's barista cart. He started to grind beans and fill a little stainless steel cup with dark brown powder.

"The author of the 'Wellcome' Poem?" Terry said, as Mac squirted steam into a big stainless steel cup filled with milk.

"Never, man," Mac said, squirting some yellow gunk into the tall paper cup, dumping some brackish coffee into it, then sloshing in the hot, foamy milk.

"There you go," he said, pushing the cup at Terry. "Half-caf latte with skim milk and a shot of sugar-free hazelnut."

This was indeed "the usual."

"Thanks," said Terry, grinning to himself as he got one of the little brown cardboard rounds out of the stainless steel rack and slipped it over the bottom of the cup. Then, he popped on the plastic top, humming softly to himself.

"Sure," said Mac. "How could anybody forget the 'Wellcome' Poem?"

Terry rocked back and forth on his heels, grinning as Mac recited his masterpiece.

If you would have asked Terry Herle in tenth grade if all grown up, he would have become a more famous poet than Edgar Allan Poe or Henry Wadsworth Longfellow, he would have shaken his head and said, "Nope—not me."

Mac crossed his arms and brayed,

> *Wellcome*
> *Wellcome*
> > *Smell some*
> *Well come*
> > *Smell some*
> > > *Wellcome now!*

It repeated like that for a while.

"What did you think, pulling my leg like that?" Terry asked, inwardly relieved that the natural order of things had been restored.

"Pulling your—really had ya there, didn't I?" Mac said.

Terry nodded, forcing a grin. He still felt uneasy, because Mac really had him going for a while.

"Girls still won't leave ya alone, will they?" asked Mac. "How's that one you were telling me about from Terre Haute?"

Terry shrugged. "Tina? Aw, Tina comes by the blog every day. Sends me smokin' hot pictures, too."

"Heh-heh," said Mac. "I'd like to see *those*—"

"No can do," said Terry. "I'll just have to leave her up to your imagination." After all, Tina hadn't sent those pictures to *everyone*. They were special—for the world's most famous poet and blogger.

Terry Herle.

It was a pretty funny trick, Terry thought on the way home, Mac's little joke. For being a little hole in the wall, Portland, Indiana was pretty fortunate. It wasn't every little town along every highway through waving fields of grain that had famous residents like Terry.

Terry guessed that Mac probably thought it was a good idea to let some of the wind out of his sails. Maybe Mac had a point, he thought, sipping his steaming latte. It was never a good idea to get a big head, even if you were the world's most famous blogger.

Not far from his house, Terry stopped beside the waist-high white picket horse fence and looked over at his neighbor's property. Big red barn next to a little white farmhouse. It was a pretty scene, unless you were used to scenes like that. They were pretty much the only scenes around Portland, and if Terry was honest with himself, he was sick of them.

He could have gone for some graffiti, or maybe a bus stop with a bum begging for change getting beaten up by half a dozen raging crackhead gang members. As he struggled to imagine what gang members looked like, he suddenly got a cartoon image of a big, blobby black kid, a short, skinny kid with a purple knit cap pulled down over his face, and sharp-looking character with a messenger cap and a toothpick sticking out of the corner of his mouth.

Hey, hey, hey, he thought.

Um. Well, somebody probably already took that idea.

He looked back at the classic farm scene next door and decided to take a picture and run with it anyway. Maybe there was a poem in it. Everyday things. Found poem. He slipped his cell out of his pocket and took a couple of candid shots, then emailed them to himself. This was tomorrow's blog post—easy.

> *Horses... grass*
> *Too pretty to last - well*
> > *Kiss my ass...*

It could use a little work.

Not to worry, though—Terry had all afternoon. Plenty of time for a nap, then he could photoshop those pictures of the house and barn, polish up the poem, and take some more good long looks at the bodacious Tina from Terra Haute.

Five dollars—a half-caf latte. Custom-made Edward Green loafers—three thousand dollars. Living the life of the world's most famous blogger and poet? Priceless.

Imagine Terry's surprise when he woke up from his nap, the internet was completely out, and his laptop wouldn't turn on.

After kicking his desk a few times and storming around the house causing his ex-wife's mug collection to fall crashing to the floor, Terry threw open the back door and stomped out onto the porch, hollering, "Nooooo!!!!!"

This display roused his old yellow dog, who had been sleeping happily under the back porch.

"Howwwwa-roooo," yowled Pinky. That was the name Terry's gladly-departed spouse had given the dog. She wasn't the kind of woman worth remembering, so most of the time, Terry didn't. Terry had always called the spavined creature "dog" and as far as Pinky was concerned, that seemed to work just fine.

"What the hell have they done down at the..." Terry struggled to remember just *where* Portland's power came from. "Steam plant," he said, kicking a pot of geraniums off the porch.

The old red clay shattered and a half-dead collection of sticks and turdlike clods of mud exploded at his feet—he imagined for a moment that the weedy geranium was looking back up at him and wailing, but no—that was ridiculous. This type of thought was what you got for being creative. Geraniums didn't cry, whether they were green, dead, on his porch, or in some old lady's window garden.

He looked across his back yard toward the horse farm next door. He thought for several moments, but had no memory of the name of the woman who lived there.

When he'd tried to talk her up by the mailbox last year, the peppery gal had the unmitigated gall to tell him she wouldn't know about his poems, because she never used the internet.

Unbelievable. Who said that, these days? Even the Unabomber Ted Kaczynski would have used a satellite hookup to his death cabin if it had been available. What kind of nut didn't use the internet? If she hadn't been a female, Terry would have been *really* suspicious.

Shaking his head, he went back inside and gave the laptop another try. Still no go. It was getting pretty dark inside the house. He must have taken a longer nap than he thought. Glancing over at the microwave clock, it wasn't flashing "12:00". It was dark and sort of greasy-looking. Same for the DVR in the living room, except it wasn't greasy, it was dusty.

He got his travel alarm clock out of his sock drawer, and even it had stopped. It read 1:17—and the little "day/night" picture was stuck half-way between blue and yellow. What was that supposed to mean? He opened the back with his thumbnail and two crusty, whitish batteries fell out onto his pillow.

Terry jumped back as if they were a pair of night crawlers. What was it that his heinously ungrateful heifer of a former wife Kim had said about toxic batteries? They needed to go with the toxic waste to the toxic waste dump. He knew it seemed weird, but Kim had always been the one to fix things around the house. She paid the bills, too, and cooked the meals.

It was the most amazing providence, he thought, that his blogging had taken off right after that bitch shook her skinny fist in his face, moved to Muncie, and took up with the car salesman.

Nobody was driving cars too much any more, so Terry wondered how her lazy ass liked it riding a solar-powered bus and living in what-ever welfare dump she'd ended up in with that fat, unemployed, former Nissan-hawking good-for-nothing...

For some reason, Terry thought maybe he'd just blown a fuse, and he wandered back into the kitchen, idly trying to recall where the fuse box was. In the cellar? Hadn't been down there for—

Instead, he considered the refrigerator door a moment, then pulled the latch. A beer would go down—

He gagged, staggering back. He couldn't even *tell* what was in the fruit drawer, and he'd never seen a milk carton exactly *that* color.

Something wet touched his left wrist and he screamed like a little girl.

It was Pinky's long, raspy tongue. The hound had pushed the porch door open with his nose. Now he was in the kitchen sniffing curiously at the horror inside Terry's refrigerator.

"Get your damn nose out of there, dog," Terry snapped.

Pinky rewarded this masterly guidance with a deep sniff. With a filthy look, he turned around and walked crookedly back out onto the porch. Muttering quiet oaths, Terry followed him. He put his hand to his forehead shielding his eyes, scanning the horizon.

Now, if the power had been out long enough to do what it had to the refrigerator—

Terry had a horrible vision of the old Dutch guy who fell asleep under a tree. The image was hazy, but he could google it in a minute.

He shook his head. Nobody was doing any googling at the Herle house. The thought of all the blog comments he was missing swirled and tore at his mind. How much ad-click revenue?... the adulatory messages piling up from his posse, and new pictures of Tina—

Trip L'Twinkle, he thought. Wee Willie Winkie. No—Rip! Rip van Winkle.

With a cold shudder, the thought crossed his mind—What if he'd been asleep for a hundred years? He was waking—finally—

and the world had changed irrevocably?

Pinky howled again and looked toward the horse farm, his ears erect and quivering, and his tail rigid as an old stick with a little bit of yellow fur glued on it.

Now, the dog's existence spoke against that, he told himself. He might have been asleep for a century, but his dog sure as heck hadn't survived a century of somnolence.

Terry reached in his pocket and pulled out his cell phone. When he flipped it open, it was as dark as the inside of the refrigerator. Somehow, this didn't surprise him.

Pinky kept looking toward the farm next door, making little cries in the back of his old hound throat.

Squinting, Terry made out a thin stream of smoke rising from the white farmhouse next to the big red barn. Somebody was there, somebody was home, and they had a fire in the fireplace.

He bit his lip. He wasn't sure what the woman next door would say if he showed up at her door with his crazy story. No internet, not friendly—face like a smashed green cabbage. Then, he remembered—the Pik-A-Mart—Mac. Mac would know what had happened and what to do.

Terry ran down the hall and burst through the living room, barely noticing the condition of the curtains. They had advanced beyond needing a wash to greasy, then partially plastered to the windows, and were now approaching threadbare horror movie condition. Not good, Terry, he thought. Very not good.

He stumbled off the front porch and into his front yard.

It wasn't anything like it had been that morning. He could barely see the red bricks that marked the way to the curb. Brambles and briars bowed aggressively over shoulder-high weedy grass.

Pushing his way through the scratchy, reeking foliage, with Pinky shuffling behind and whining, Terry made it out onto the road, which also didn't look so great. The asphalt was cracked, with huge potholes that had most certainly not been there on his morning walk to the Pik-A-Mart. Trash was piled everywhere, and a little green battery-powered car was crumpled against an elm tree looking like a turtle on its back, only instead of legs it had old, cracked gray tires. Judging from the weeds poking through its empty windows, and the cobwebs connecting the tires to the wheel wells, it had been there a while. Terry saw something round and whitish in the passenger side window.

His throat filled with acid.

"Come on, dog," he said to Pinky, who had begun to growl back in his throat.

After just a few steps, Terry's legs started to hurt and he found himself wheezing. He stopped, coughing and hacking and clutching his chest.

With a sudden start, he wondered—what if there had been an attack? Some kind of biological weapon?

His feet were killing him. What could get worse?

His shoes had disappeared. His $3,000 Edward Green loafers, virtually fitted just for him! All Terry could think was that while he napped whatever godforsaken comalike nap he'd taken, someone had crept into the house and stolen them right off his feet.

His naked, thorny toes peeked from a pair of shredded gray-white gym socks.

Grimacing, he hobbled toward the Pik-A-Mart. It was a long, cold and fearsome trip, nothing like the pleasant jaunt he'd taken that morning. Once he got into town, there wasn't a house that looked occupied. Most were boarded up, and his chest felt even tighter as he passed the Lutheran Church and saw its double green doors ajar, creaking softly back and forth.

His spirits raised a little as he saw the Pik-A-Mart's windows were intact. Getting to the door, he tried the knob hesitantly. The door swung open easily and he went inside. The lights were out here too, and even from the door, Terry could see that the refrigerated cases were empty. Their glass doors had been smashed and jagged shards littered the store's center aisle.

Terry went around the side.

"Mac?" he called.

He wasn't surprised when he got no answer.

Somehow, in the space of—how long?—the Pik-A-Mart hadn't just been picked-over. It had been decimated. A few cans were scattered here and there—crushed and bent, and nothing anybody would have wanted in the first place. Beets. Sauerkraut. The only untouched display was, bizarrely, the "personal" products shelf, where four pregnancy tests huddled next to boxes of Trojans and sealed black packages containing "male and female" enhancement lotion.

That stuff was expensive, Terry thought. If looters came in, why wouldn't they go for that in addition to beer, pork rinds and cigarettes?

"Mac?" he said again in a softer voice, approaching the overturned Starbucks cart. He'd had a cup of joe from that very cart just that—

Terry stopped himself. It couldn't have been *that* morning. Even the worst looting incident couldn't have done what he'd seen in his house, the town, and the store, in a single day.

A brown workboot peeked from behind the Starbucks cart.

"Mac?" he said again, kneeling and peering around the cart as Pinky growled.

There was no leg attached to the boot. It was just a shoe, a steel-toed workboot with the laces undone. Terry started to laugh as Pinky's low growl raised in pitch and something huge and furry leapt out of the interior of the cart with a metallic crash and flew straight at Terry's face.

Terry shrieked as he fell back on the filthy floor, his assailant hissing and scratching at his cheeks. It was going for his eyes!

Grabbing hold of something fat, flabby and furry, Terry tugged with desperate strength. With thin, prehensile hands, the beast had attached itself to his collar.

Pinky yowled and he leapt onto the beast, sinking his teeth into what Terry figured must have been its hind quarters. The creature scrambled desperately, clawing Terry's neck and cheeks. With a mighty groan, he dislodged the creature, hurling it four or five feet away where it hit the floor with an audible "splat," forming a striped gray-brown circle with four squat legs splayed from under the flat fur patch.

The creature's abnormally-small hissing head turned and Terry saw two dark rings around its beady eyes.

It was a raccoon. The biggest, fattest, meanest one Terry had ever seen.

Righting itself, the raccoon reared up on its hind legs and staggered toward Terry like Terry was a bouncer, and the raccoon an angry drunk he'd just evicted from his barstool for the night. The hair on Pinky's back was standing straight up. He was snarling and growling at the raccoon, who was spitting and hissing back in an alarmingly psychotic, rage-filled tone.

Looking to his left, Terry saw that the inside of the upended Starbucks cart was filled with shreds of bright cellophane and plastic. Cheetos, regular and flaming hot, Doritos, Ruffles, Lays, Fritos, Tostitos, Funyuns, and of course—Terry saw the red outline of a cartoon pig that signified spicy hot pork rinds.

Terry had inadvertently trespassed upon Rocky the Mad Raccoon's junk food stash.

The raccoon continued to advance. Terry kicked at him with his sock-feet, afraid that the thing would grab hold and start chewing on his big toe. He knelt, snatching the work boot and slung it by its undone laces at the beast. It hit the coon in the belly with a satisfying thud of hard rubber against soft, fatty fur. The raccoon flew back into one of the empty steel shelves, and with a last hissing screech of fury, scuttled out the front door of the Pik-A-Mart like a furry, striped, pissed-off crab.

"We got him on the run for now, Pinky," Terry said, pulling the old yellow dog close. "But I've got a feeling he'll be back."

Suddenly, a buzzing hiss rose up and Terry snapped his head around to see a flickering form behind the Pik-A-Mart counter. It was more like a weird, projected shadow than anything else.

Heart leaping, Terry wondered if it was the dead spirit of Mac, still haunting his store. He could see the outline of a green cap shadowing a totally blank gray face.

"Howzit," the shadow said.

Terry's eyes narrowed and he backed slowly away, getting cautiously to his feet.

"Howwww-zzzzziiit," said the shadow. It buckled, then wavered back and forth in a greenish-yellow cloud of light.

Pale streams of twilight shot through the store and straight through the shadow, illuminating the empty, broken shelf behind the counter where Mac had formerly kept lighters, plastic flasks of lighter fluid, shotgun shells and small cigars.

Terry backed out of the store with Pinky. "Be seeing you, Mac," he said, keeping his eyes on the weird Mac-shadow. It didn't look dangerous, but he didn't plan to stick around to find out if it could solidify, or do something worse than buzz and sputter "Howzit."

Terry looked toward the center of town, which was littered with bricks, burnt-out car hulks and overturned trash bins.

Then, he looked back down the way he had come. Pinky stayed at his side, back arched, hackles raised, sniffing the air suspiciously.

Terry's body ached. He poked gingerly at his chest where the raccoon had clawed him. "Better find something for this," he muttered, looking down at his blood-streaked fingers.

Visions of some horrible infection, like cholera or botulism, went through his head. No—if you got bit, it was tetanus. Or rabies.

He felt slow—strange, but he emphatically did not want to die foaming at the mouth while trying to swallow tough red strands of yellow dog sushi or whatever horror the disease would force him to before the end.

With renewed purpose, Terry staggered back toward his house. A slight rush of hope warmed his face as he saw the intact, silver mailbox of his neighbor the horse farmer, with the red mail flag raised. Well, if the *mail* was still coming, he thought, as he squared his shoulders, then started trudging down her ridiculously long, rutted mud driveway. At least somebody had cleared the weeds around this place, he thought. And the house didn't look that bad—at least not compared to his place or back in town.

It wasn't until he got to the porch, examined the wicker rocking chair, clean flowered cushions, and the corn cob pipe resting on a wicker side table alongside an old four-cornered green glass ashtray that he realized—

He still could not remember his neighbor's name.

Karen? Corinne? Kayla?

He knocked. Pinky sat quietly and unceremoniously beside his right ankle and cocked his head attentively, like he knew what he was doing, and had been there before.

"Uh, Karen?" he called. "Are you home?"

He heard soft footsteps.

The lace curtain moved aside a couple of inches. He saw a single eye peering out at him, above a thin pale nose and a pair of narrow lips.

"It's Terry, your neighbor," he said.

"I know who you are," came a low, not particularly-friendly female voice.

"Uh, I got into some trouble just now. I was wondering if you had some..." he struggled to think of the right word. "Bactine," he said finally. "Or, uh," he was really struggling now. He could picture the small brown bottle in his mind, and see the nasty bright salmon color. "Merthiolate."

No answer.

"Something to put on the cuts," he said. "It was a raccoon."

"I've got whisky," said the soft female voice.

"Um," said Terry, "Would you mind letting me in?"

The curtain fell back. Terry stood on the porch with blood dripping down his waist into the top of his trousers for what seemed like fifteen minutes.

Finally, the door opened and a slender, graying woman with narrow, piercing blue eyes appeared. Terry could see around her shoulder to a combined kitchen and dining area stacked high with crates and boxes of all shapes and sizes, leaving barely enough room for a small round table, two chairs, and a flickering Coleman lantern.

"My name's not Karen," she said.

It was only then that Terry noticed the ominous black revolver in her hand.

"Whisky's in the cupboard," she said. "Rags are on the counter."

Terry stepped around her into the hall, acutely aware that he now had a long-barreled Smith & Wesson at his back. His dad had made somewhat of a hobby of collecting and cataloging guns. This one wasn't a newer model, but considering the type of rounds that it could hold in its chambers, at such close range it would blow a hole somewhere between the size of a tennis ball and a softball in his back or side. He wondered what that would feel like. Dad used to say getting popped by a big caliber gun like that was something like a deer getting shot by a 30-ought. The deer didn't feel a thing, dad said. As this was something dad had just read in a book, or picked up while drinking Burgie with his pals, Terry didn't really see the point of comparing his flank to that of a wandering buck in the forest going about its business until it was cut down by a drunk, whiskered guy in a Pendleton shirt hunkered down in a hunting blind.

"I'm sorry," Terry said, shuffling by the boxes in the kitchen until he reached the cupboard. She instructed him where to look solely with her eyes, not speaking a word.

He opened one cupboard, and the way her mouth turned down at the corners let him know that wasn't it. He opened the next cupboard, and saw a dark, fat bottle of Maker's Mark.

"I really thought your name was Karen," he said.

Considering that she had a gun on him, Terry really didn't feel like speculating any more about what her name may have been. He remembered that day by the mailbox, where she'd given him that flat, fishlike stare and said frigidly, "I don't use the internet."

He took down the bottle of Maker's Mark and set it on the counter. He hoped she didn't see his hands shaking as he uncorked the bottle and took the least-filthy of a pile of gray rags by the dry-looking tap and poured whisky on it, then started to daub at his torn cheeks and neck.

It stung like a *motherfucker* and his face felt so *weird*, but he started hoping that Maker's Mark would kill tetanus—or maybe even rabies, although fat chance. Even Terry knew that rabies was a virus and those probably drank whisky and multiplied.

He heard her sit in one of the kitchen chairs, but didn't dare turn.

"I didn't think you'd wake up," she said softly.

"What?" he said, turning quickly, which tore a round of searing pain from the whisky and the raccoon scratches.

"You look like shit," she said. "You should see yourself."

Terry wasn't entirely sure he wanted to. He had felt something while wiping his face, and it was just too weird to countenance. Something springy and bushy and rough and—

"Go ahead," she said. "Look at yourself in the glass." One of the cupboards had a paned-glass front and it was easy to see his reflection in it. Terry moved slowly forward and peered at the glass. He saw twin versions of a hollow-cheeked, blood-stained, bearded stranger staring back at himself. The reflection wore a tattered plaid pajama top and looked like something out of one of those old nostalgic movies, like a

World War II escape-from-the-concentration-camp adventure. The type of movie that always had a sad ending.

The longer he looked, the bigger the bloodshot pop-eyes staring back at him got.

"Holy—holy shit!" he said, staggering back.

"I've seen worse," she said in her soft, even voice. "Best pour yourself a couple shots of that whisky," she added. "Shot glass in the cupboard. It isn't too dirty."

Terry's head reverberated. The gun was resting in her hand on the table, sort of pointing at him, and sort of not. He was certain that in an instant, she'd lift it and squeeze the trigger if he did the least thing to spook her. So, he found the shot glass and gingerly poured Maker's Mark into it, but not carefully enough, because oily dark gold whisky poured out of the sides and onto the counter.

"Better wipe that up," she said.

Nodding, he did as he was told. Then he downed the shot, and after it burned its way down his esophagus, he actually felt a tiny bit, just an iota, better.

"What—what the hell is—" he said in a whisky-hoarse croak.

"Have a seat," she said, not unkindly. She moved the gun around into what could be thought of as a neutral position, and indicated the second chair at the table with a brief gesture of one of her thin, fluttery white hands.

"What happened?" he said. "I was down at the Pik-A-Mart this morning. Mac was there—I had a whole blog post to do. I was going to—I took a picture of your farm. Do some Photoshop, put it up and—"

She was nodding, and a small smile played around the corners of her narrow mouth. "I have no doubt," she said. "Seems to me there's still a few folks left asleep. I think the Johnsons are still taken care of over on the other side of town. Got Reverend Baker and his cat, too—their house was fine just a week ago. Constable's still in his office, hasn't moved for a year, but he's still breathing."

"What?" said Terry.

Still holding the gun, Terry's nameless neighbor stood and went to the counter, pouring him another shot of Maker's Mark deftly with her left hand, and setting it down on the kitchen table in front of him before reseating herself.

"Undo your pajamas," she said. "No—wait—" she said quickly. "Drink another shot, then have a look."

Terry looked at the empty shot glass, then around the room. "Where's Pinky?" he asked.

"Under the table," she said. Pinky's head poked out, and his jaws gripped a long beige rawhide bone, which he was masticating with gusto. At some point during Terry's long nap—or whatever it was, Pinky had lost a few teeth.

"Where'd he get that?" asked Terry. He hadn't seen her give it to Pinky. Heck, he didn't remember seeing Pinky since he stepped inside the house.

"I guess you could say that's still your dog, Mr. Herle," she said. "But I've been feeding him these past five years. Can't bear to see an animal suffer."

"Five—years?" Terry said.

She nodded. "It's twenty-twenty-six," she said. "Seems like Nostradamus and the Mayans were about nine years off."

"Nostra-Mayans?" said Terry, feeling like an idiot. He remembered something vaguely about the end of the world being December 21, 2012. BFD. A bunch of gullible dumbshits went and camped out on hilltops all around the world, it was on the newslinks, and nothing happened.

"The believers thought that on that day, the sun would enter the mouth of the great worm Ouroboros—in their idea, the Milky Way," she said, as if that would mean something to him. "But of course the Milky Way is only what we see from our vantage here on Earth. There is no great worm in the sky."

He shook his head, then looked toward the counter.

"It was merely a coincidence that the great worm turned on December 20, 2021 instead."

"You can get the next shot yourself," she added.

Terry had no memory whatsoever of that date. Five years ago! After a bit, he got some dim memory of placing a bet for the playoffs, just a day before.

Online gambling.

So if it was just a couple of days before, it had been hard winter in Portland, and it wasn't likely he'd be walking down to the Pik-A-Mart in his socks.

He stood up and got another shot, downing it quickly. That way it didn't burn so much, and it really was making him feel better, even if he was trapped with a crazy woman with a gun.

"I was checking my ad revenue this morning," he said. "It doubled in the last month."

"I just bet it did," she said, nodding.

"I had five hundred emails overnight," he said. "Two dozen comments and a new set of pictures from Tina—in Terra—"

"Terra Haute?" she asked.

He turned, nodding.

"Terra Haute's glassed-over," she said. "Indianapolis, Muncie, Chicago—all gone."

"What?" he said. Kim was in Muncie. With the car salesman, living in a welfare shack.

"You had people there—Indianapolis?" she said.

"Muncie," he said dully. "Glassed-over—"

"Nukes," she said. "Big ones. Old ones. Working ones."

"But why—why are we okay?" he asked. "How could—I mean we're not that isolated here. We—"

"Had a wedge here," she said.

"A what?"

"A wedge," she repeated. "A piece of the GMID. A large, global computer. Most people didn't realize, but it did a lot, before everything—happened."

"I—I never heard of it," said Terry.

"It wouldn't matter," she said. "It 'protected' us when everything went nuclear. Stuff blows in from time to time, of course, but it's not set in the soil like it is everywhere else. Then came the biochemicals, and after that just to make sure everybody was dead, they sent the big dogs through places like Muncie, Springfield and Peoria. And Chicago, L.A. and New York."

"GMID? Big dogs? Wedges?" Terry's head felt light. She was babbling some kind of crazy survivo-babble.

"Global Mainlink Information Dispersion… GMID," she said. "Some people think it started the wars, but I think it just tried to—mop up. Protect people. Do the best it could."

"Wars?" Terry asked, his tongue feeling thick and heavy.

"You don't think just one war could do all this?" she said. "They fought until there wasn't anything left. Just a few bits and pieces of the GMID here and there. Wedges, like here in Portland. The least little corner of Indiana."

"But why here? Why not—"

"I guess you could blame me for a little bit of that," she said. "I'm not originally from here. I was—manager—of this wedge. They, uh—well, the people in charge decided to spread the wedges around to out-of-the way places. They sent people to maintain them. You know," she said. "In case of war—have them out of the way of big military targets."

She took a deep breath and grabbed the shot glass and fat brown bottle of Maker's Mark. She poured a shot, downed it, and then she said, "It was just my luck the day the nukes went off that it was my three-day downtime. I'd just bought this farm and was taking measurements for an armoire upstairs. An *armoire*," she said, her voice mixed with equal parts of wonder and disgust.

"I thought as long as I was going to work here, that this would be a peaceful place to settle down," she continued. "Looked like I wasn't going to get married." She gazed out the kitchen window.

Terry wished for the shot glass back, but now it was resting loosely in the fingers of her left hand, while her right hand was casually covering the grip of the Smith & Wesson.

"Why not try horses?" she said. "This was some beautiful country back when, Mr. Herle. Very beautiful country."

She had an odd accent. She wasn't from Indiana, of that, Terry was certain.

"Where the fuck have I been for the past—" he blurted, losing track of the years and passage of time, and wars and nukes—she had rushed through.

"Five years?" she reminded him. "You've been next door in your house lying on your couch. Now, do as I said," she said in a steely voice, her narrow, glittering eyes meeting his. "It's time. Undo that pajama top and look down."

Terry looked down, and he didn't really need to undo the buttons to see down down his skinny pale chest to something that looked really bad. Weird. Like big red welts with sucker-like holes in them.

"You can see," she said. "Where the wedge fed you."

"Fed me!" he cried.

"Pop pop," she said. "The wedge didn't think about niceties like tube-feeding down your throat. It just shot nutrients straight into your stomach. Then it sucked the waste out of your colon when it was done."

"Like a—!"

"Yeah," she said. "Sort of like a colostomy. The wedge had this idea," she added. "That it would save as many people as it could, and wake you when the bad times were over. I believe it keeps people content while they are asleep. Or so I have heard."

Terry lifted the ragged pajama top away from his chest and squinted, horrified, thinking that the whisky was probably spilling out of the hole in his gut all down his side.

"Self-sealing," she said. "When you woke up and—well, what most people do is rip the tubes out, first thing. They were set up to self-seal. It's not a good idea to do a lot of strenuous activity at first. But I see you already got into that." She pointed at the raccoon's dirty work marring his neck and chest.

"I don't remember waking up," he said—about coming to and ripping any tubes out. Then, after a moment, he said, "It was a raccoon."

She nodded. "A lot of animals out now, around these parts."

"Why would I—wake up?" Terry asked.

"The wedge is running out of power, Mr. Herle. Not enough food, either. So it's shutting people off, one by one. Based upon—I guess who it thinks can make it. Or maybe who it thinks isn't worth—" She cut herself short and her narrow lips pursed.

Terry let his pajama top drop back onto his caved-in chest. "It shut me off," he said. "I guess I should have—"

"Died?" she said. "Well, some do."

"I didn't die," he said.

"No," she said. "Obviously not."

Terry folded his hands on the table and looked down at his long, cracked fingernails. How could he lie there—five years?—not knowing where he was, or what was happening? How could he not know there had been a war—heck, wars? That Kim, rest her evil soul, was fried to a crisp and glassed-over with the bastard car salesman in Muncie. Those two, and everybody—anybody.

"I'm—" he said thickly. "I'm not a—a famous poet," he said.

She shook her head. "I don't think so."

"It was the wedge, you say," he said.

He felt a hot burst of shame realizing what his unconscious mind had come up with.

"I thought I wrote this poem," he said. "The Wellcome Poem."

She nodded. "It tried to make things easier on people. A little nicer. What was the poem like?"

Terry began to wonder if he had really seen her by the mailbox, or if that had been a figment of the—wedge—as well.

"I—I don't know," he said.

"It's all right," she said.

"Well come, well come, smell some," he mumbled.

He could not imagine sounding any more like an idiot.

"Oh, my God," said Not-Karen. "That's—"

"What a fucking bastard," he snarled.

She nodded again, smiling that sad smile. "You've got that right, Mr. Herle. The wedge is a real fuck-ing bastard." She separated the curse word with a strange pause in the middle.

"I wish I was dead," he said.

"It'll be okay," she said, without a trace of smile on her face. "Everybody says that."

"Everybody?" he said.

"Well, you're not the first one to wake up," she said. "Two families and the veterinarian woke up last year—they formed a search party and left the wedge bubble, headed toward Terra Haute."

"Terra Haute! But you said that was—"

"Yeah, glassed-over. They didn't believe me. Had family there, all of them."

"Did they—"

"Make it?" she said. "Don't know. But it's not good out there, Mr. Herle. Outside of the bubble."

"Not—"

"It's only been five years," she said. "That's not enough time for any of the hot stuff to die down. There's still biologicals out there, and enough radiation to give a frog two heads."

"That's—that's disgusting," said Terry.

"I pride myself," she said, suddenly grinning and showing a full set of clean, strong white teeth. "Maybe you should have a bite to eat. There's plenty of food. Not to worry about that."

Terry's stomach growled. He looked anxiously down at the raw, sucker-like hole right below his ribcage and saw with relief that it remained, as she had said, sealed shut.

"What—what do you have?" he asked, feeling a little strange that he was giving short-order cooking instructions to his neighbor whose name he still did not know. Not-Karen. "I meant, what should I eat after—"

"What do I *not* have?" she asked.

Terry thought of the empty shelves down at the Pik-A-Mart. "There's no real person down at the Pik-A-Mart," he said.

"Oh—you must have liked that store," she said. "The wedge remembered for you." She got up and opened another kitchen cabinet to reveal neat rows of cans. She was, however, still holding the gun.

"Let's see," she said. "Spaghetti-O's, Chef Boy-Ar-Dee ravioli, Durkee beef tamales, Dinty Moore, corned beef, chipped beef, and potted meat product."

"Dinty Moore," Terry said. He might be realistically starving after five years of force-fed Soylent Green, but he still hadn't come to the level of thought that found "potted meat product" palatable.

"An excellent choice. Would you like Tabasco?" she asked.

He looked down at his chest.

"You're right," she said. "I bet that flesh down there is probably still pretty raw." She pulled the tab on the top of the can of stew and dumped it into a white Chinet bowl, added a plastic spoon and set it in front of him.

He looked around and realized that while he'd seen smoke rising from the chimney before, the room was now cold and whatever the smoke had come from, the fire was out.

"Hope you don't mind it cold," she said. "Don't have enough wood right now to bother with cooking things if they're already cooked."

Dinty Moore stew was always fully-cooked, even if congealed when cold.

Terry put the spoon in the brown, chunky liquid and lifted a hunk of meat only slightly better-looking than fancy dog food and a square of waxy potato to his lips.

It tasted—amazing.

Terry shoveled more stew into his mouth and chewed, although his mouth felt weird, almost raw.

"Take it easy," she said. "First solid food—"

"For five years," he said, mumbling through bites of stew.

She nodded. "You're waking up," she said. "Catching on. That's really good."

For the first time, her voice contained some thin hint of excitement or happiness. Looking up, he noticed that her eyes had lost some of the cold glare they'd had before, and there were smile-lines around her mouth, even if her thin lips were not smiling, and looked as though they may never have smiled.

"After you finish," she said, "We can turn the radio on. See what's going on down in Way-Way-tango."

"Way—Way?" he mumbled.

"Way-Way-Tay-Nahn-Go," she said. "Spelled H-U-E, H-U-E, T-E-N-A-N-G-O. It's a city in Guatemala. They had another wedge."

After he finished his stew, Terry stumbled up the stairs after her, wondering how he'd ever find the right way to ask her name, and wondering just where in the hell Guatemala was. Somewhere, he recalled, in South America.

"What's that?" Terry asked, as Not-Karen sat at a small desk upon which rested an old stereo receiver, put a pair of headphones on her head, and twisted a knob on a nearby open metal box filled with plastic toy-like contraptions and weird little coiled copper wires.

"It's a radio," she said, not turning.

"But if everybody's dead, what's the point of calling—"

"Huehuetenango," she said. "We still have some satellites, and they're not dead there. Other places too," she said. "Some folks up in Fairbanks, got another station in Alberta, though I haven't talked to them for a while."

"Canada," he said.

Not-Karen didn't bother to reply as she twisted the knob, little lights on the inside of the box began to glow, and crackling noises came from the stereo receiver-thing.

Terry sat on the small, narrow bed. It was covered with an old, patched quilt that smelled of cedar. The bed creaked. "You've got power," he said approvingly.

She removed the headphones for a moment and swiveled around in the chair, fixing him with a steely gaze.

"I have a generator for the radio," she said. "Not much else."

"Oh," he said, folding his hands on his lap. Pinky came sauntering in and jumped up on the bed, pushing fretfully against Terry with his hind legs. There was no surer proof that what she'd said was true—Not-Karen had been looking after his dog for the past five years.

Man's best friend, he thought sourly. Scratching under the pillow, the dog extracted and began to mouth an old plastic squeaky toy shaped like a hot dog, and he sure as heck had never gotten Pinky anything like that. Child-like dog toys ruined a hound's better nature.

Not-Karen picked up an old-fashioned microphone on a coiled black wire, continued to fiddle with the dial and started saying something in Spanish.

"Well, I guess Tina in Terre Haute was as real as a three-dollar bill," he said softly, reaching over to scratch Pinky behind the ears. Pinky, interpreting this as an attempt to snatch his toy, growled. Terry gave him a dirty look, but considering his host's temperament, he just shook his head at the dog, and didn't cuff him back of the head as he would have before—the wedge.

Not-Karen didn't seem to have heard him, but he saw her back stiffen slightly.

Then, her voice said brightly, "Hola! Como 'stas?"

Through a storm of clicks and hums came a rough-sounding voice. "Hola, Carina. Bien, y tu?"

"All right," she said in English. "Somebody else woke up today."

"Muy bueno!" came the rough voice. "A—man?" The radio clacked and popped. Terry didn't like the tone the guy was using.

"Yes," said Not-Karen—or Carina? Was that her name?

"Is your name Carina?" blurted Terry.

She looked over her shoulder for a moment, her eyebrows meeting in a harsh line. She raised her finger to her mouth.

Terry fell silent, nodding. Carina—Karen—not so different. He felt a little bit better. And he hadn't even had to ask her name!

"Ah, I can *hear* heeem," said the voice with its *Yo Quiero Taco Bell* inflection.

"He's still kind of out of it," Carina said.

Carina. Kind of a pretty name, thought Terry. How could he have forgotten that? How could he have not realized he had some important government employee living right next door? *Before* the world blew up.

"Tell heeem my seven daughters would love to meet him," said the voice.

Seven daughters? Terry leaned closer. Imagine that—

"Cut it out, Nacho," she said tartly. "You know nobody's going to make it three thousand miles."

After a pause, Terry heard the voice say, "Xochilt had her baby yesterday." The tone was completely different, far softer.

"B-boy or girl?" she asked.

"Girl," said the voice. "Muy bonita. Very—"

"Healthy, Nacho?" she asked, voice trembling.

"Si," said "Nacho."

Why she'd give the guy a nickname after some kind of chips and cheese was beyond Terry. Even he knew that wasn't an authentic Latin dish.

"Praise the Lord, In-ah-see-yo," she said in a heartfelt tone.

Now she was calling him something else. Who were these people? But a baby, Terry thought—that sounded really good. Really hopeful.

"We have lit all the candles," he said.

"I'll say a prayer too. Tell Xochilt I'm praying for her too. And—"

"Ramon," said "Nacho" or "Nasseee-yo" or whatever his name was.

"Yes, Ramon," she said.

"You know we are worried," said the rough voice.

"I haven't found anything yet," she said. "I can't see any evidence of what could have killed Ramon."

"Thank you for looking, Carina."

"I won't stop," she said. "If it's out there, I'll find it. Then we can figure out what to do."

"I pray every night," said Nacho.

"As do I," said Carina. "Look to the baby now—our time is up."

"Hasta la—" said Nacho, but he was cut off in mid sentence. She threw a switch and the metal box went dark and a whining noise came from the stereo-like receiver.

"It—it sounds great that they've had a baby—Carina," said Terry, sitting back on the bed.

She removed the headphones slowly, then set them down on the bedside desk with a crack. Turning suddenly, she snapped, "What?"

"I said it seemed good, Car... Carina," he said.

"That is *not* my fucking name," she growled. "Now get your ass out of my bedroom. There's a door down the hall and a cot and an army blanket."

Terry felt his mouth fall open. She stood stiffly, thrusting her hand in the hip pocket of her oversized plaid shirt. The grip of the big gun was clearly visible, the barrel almost poking through the fabric.

"I'm—sorry I don't remember your name," he said.

Her lips formed a tight line and her eyes blazed. "Out!" she snarled. And this time the gun came out of the pocket.

Terry stumbled down the hall, and something hot and wet came down his cheeks into the deep, raw raccoon scratches. It stung worse than ever. Probably—probably rabies, he thought as he threw himself on the cot and drew the scratchy blanket up around his shoulders. Pinky stuck his head in the door for a moment, then sniffed around Terry's face. After a brief chuff! as if to say, "You loser," the dog left, padding down the hall toward her room.

"Those," she said coldly, pointing at some gnarled, feathery green foliage pushing skyward out of the ground at the back of her house, "Are parsnips. You can pull shit out of the ground, put it in a basket and wash it in the stream, can't you?" she said.

Not-Karen threw a big wicker laundry basket, the kind with two handles, on the ground next to the patch of parsnips.

Terry nodded, swallowing hard. The raccoon scratches had crusted over and scabbed up overnight. It hurt to talk.

"Where—where's the stream?" he asked.

She looked down at the parsnip patch, and the corners of her mouth turned downward.

"You sat in that house of yours all day, every day, even before the wedge put you out and fed you like a coma patient," she snapped. "Of *course* you don't know where the stream is." She put two fingers to her mouth and whistled loudly.

Pinky came trotting out of the house and sat by her side, gazing up at her with big, black, adoring dog eyes. Terry thought the dog was smiling, and if he could have spoken, he would have said, "I love you soooo much."

She raised one thin, stringy white arm and gestured across the horse pasture. Terry blinked. He remembered horses being there, but there certainly weren't any now. He supposed they were in the big red barn.

With an excited grunt, Pinky took off across the field much faster than Terry would have thought the old hound was capable, bounding toward a stand of trees about half a mile distant.

"He's going toward the stream," he said slowly.

"That's right," she said. "So pull up a dozen parsnips and get to it. Watch out for any sudden movements you see when you get down there. There's more and more—critters," and she had an odd tone when she said that word, "every day."

Terry felt his brow wrinkling. After his run-in with the raccoon, he wasn't eager for any more Wild Kingdom action. In fact, he felt a little feverish, and wondered if it wasn't the rabies coming on. Did rabies come on overnight? Or did it stay in his bloodstream... move into his brain right away? What was the word?... incubating.

"Maybe you could give me the—" he said, unwilling to utter the word "gun."

Not-Karen immediately understood his meaning. "In a pig's eye," she said, squatting back on her heels and looking skeptically at him. "I hope that even in your fogged mind, you won't make the mistake of thinking I'm stupid."

"N—no," Terry said, stepping back.

"Parsnips," she said. "A dozen. Wash them and bring them back."

"But there's water here," he said, pointing to the cistern by the back porch where she drew water for tea, soup and plain old drinking.

She shook her head, pointing toward the stream, where Pinky had already disappeared in the grass. Scowling, she turned sharply on her heels and stomped back into the house.

Terry thought about just washing the parsnips in the cistern and not telling her. Deciding against that, he surveyed the parsnip patch for a moment, then knelt to grab one of the feathery green parsnip tops, telling himself to think "caveman" and "woman's hair." He tugged.

It was a lot harder to pull parsnips than one might think. And half a mile is quite a piece, for a guy who hasn't walked for five years and just ripped some feeding tube out of his gut and tore out a colostomy tube, too. And survived an attack by a mutant, possibly rabid 'coon drunk on stale cheetos and Junior Mints.

After two weeks, Terry had come to the conclusion that the coon couldn't have been rabid, since he hadn't begun frothing at the mouth, and no matter how much he might have fantasized about it, had not yet tried to tear out Not-Karen's throat. After the scratches had sealed over to dull, crusty rust-colored scabs, Terry had used some of Not-Karen's cheap disposable razors to shave. And in the bathroom mirror, seen something almost resembling his old, doughy face—though he'd never, he thought, ever be doughy again, no matter how many cases of Dinty Moore Not-Karen had stowed in her survivalist larder.

He, of course, still didn't know her true name and would rather have washed parsnips all day long and eaten them raw than ask her. He'd found some old junk mail in a drawer in the kitchen addressed to "Mrs. Phoebe Long," but he had a distinct sense that Not-Karen was no Phoebe. Nor had she ever been, he was certain, a "Mrs."

He had gotten an answer to the mysterious death of Ramon, the Guatemalan baby's father. Apparently some "rogue" biochemical agents were loose in the area of Huehuetenango, which had been a much bigger town than Portland, Indiana. Huehuetenango was located in Guatemala, which was not in South America, as his faulty memory had told him. Guatemala was a country south of Mexico, but north of the Panama Canal. Terry had apprised himself of these geographical facts while sneaking looks in Not-Karen's North and Central American road atlas.

Not-Karen was looking for some indication of what the "rogue" germs might be.

Her desire to help the Guatemalans was not entirely altruistic. Their wedge was dying, she told Terry over breakfast the other morning.

"When it's gone," she said, "The bubble's going to give way and we won't just be alone. Everything that's out there is going to come rushing in. It's already happening in Huehuetenango. That's where the stuff came from that killed Ramon."

"But they're having babies," he said. "Maybe the poisonous stuff isn't so bad."

Not-Karen had shrugged, looking down at her fingernails. After a long pause, she'd said, "I wouldn't count on it."

Terry had discovered what had happened to the horses. There was a row of half a dozen long graves, from a fresh, soft one to old, sunken ones, back of the big red barn.

At first, Terry had thought these were the graves of people, and spun a horrified imagined scenario where Not-Karen was a crazed, cannibalistic serial killer. But kicking at the dirt on the old sunken grave, there was no mistaking the big teeth and elongated skull of a horse, with some of its mane still attached and half a fine-furred, conical ear that most certainly never belonged to any person.

When he asked her over a plate of cold corned beef hash and parsnips, she'd rubbed at the corners of her eyes and told him that she'd shot them one by one. And taken as much flesh as she could, and preserved as much as possible, and then eaten as much as she could. With those that had awakened before—she had shared.

"It's not bad," she said. "You'd never mistake it for steak."

"I—I bet that was tough," Terry said, realizing with a start that she might take that *really* the wrong way.

"No harder than any of the rest of this," she said, looking steadily in his eyes, and he realized that for once, she'd taken what he'd said charitably—even kindly. "Every living soul I ever cared about is gone. There's not too much harder than that."

But I'm here, Terry thought, and immediately told himself he was still an idiot. He had always been an idiot. There was no chance he would ever not be an idiot. He didn't even know her real name, was too scared to ask, and he could tell she cared five thousand times more about those distant voices from Guatemala than she cared about him.

Or his dog, he thought. Pinky. Slavishly, everlastingly, he was *her* dog now.

Most of him didn't blame the old hound. If somebody had taken him in and fed him when there was nothing else to be had, he supposed he'd get attached to that person, too.

Most of all, he thought, he felt a dull sense of rage and loathing toward the "wedge." He didn't precisely know why. After all, the thing had done pretty much the same thing for him as Not-Karen had done for Pinky when the bad stuff started to happen. Tried to take care of him. Fed him. Tried to keep him safe.

Maybe, he thought, regarding his hands, which had begun to grow stronger and calloused from work—now, Terry Herle with calloused hands - that was really something. Maybe Not-Karen did care about him a little. He could tell she'd never let anything happen to Pinky. And he got the gist of what she'd said about the horses. They were going to die anyway, so she'd done it quickly, and made the best of it.

Not a bad thing to do, he thought. But then it was time to pull and wash more parsnips. Without realizing, there was a little spring in his step when he headed down to the stream. He spent quite a while down by the water poking around with a stick. He had it in his mind that there might be fish in it, as he'd seen glints of silver, and small, fast-moving streamlined bodies in the water.

And that seemed like a very good thing.

Terry sat on the bed, listening to the radio crackle. Ignacio had bad news. Huehuetenango's first baby wasn't eating well, and cried all the time. She was losing, not gaining weight.

"Did they—did they try soy milk?" Terry suggested. He remembered that his brother's daughter hadn't taken to regular baby formula, and was losing weight too. She hadn't thrived until they did soy milk. Don and... they were in Denver. Terry knew Denver was gone, too, just like Muncie. Just like everywhere else.

Not-Karen glared at him, and her eyes flashed. She licked her lips, and seemed to decide something. She turned back to the microphone and asked Nacho, "Do you have any soy milk?"

"Que?" asked Nacho.

"Soy formula. I know your daughter can't breastfeed enough. Have you tried supplementing with..."

"Oh, I see," said Nacho. "Leche soya," he barked. Terry could tell that it wasn't meant for Not-Karen, but for the other people who were listening to the ham radio beside him.

A muttering and rustling came through the receiver.

"Yes, we have some cans of dry milk," he said. "We'll try that. But Carina, maybe it is the water?"

Not-Karen cleared her throat. "No," she said quickly. "Don't think that. The wedge would protect the water to the end, Nacho. I can promise you that."

"It's dark in the building where the wedge is, Carina. There's no power left at all," he said.

"There's a... residual barrier," she said. "You wouldn't see it from the outside. It should stay up for... two, maybe three years."

"Oh!" said Nacho. "*Dios mio*, that's good."

"So don't worry," she said. "Try the soy milk," she said. Her fingers were quick, but trembling, as she turned the dial and powered down the radio.

Terry stayed on the bed, not moving, his hands at his side.

"You weren't telling the truth," he said softly.

She turned.

Her mouth was turned down at the corners. She wouldn't meet Terry's eyes. Finally, she lowered her head and shook it.

"No," she said. "When the power's gone, that's it. There is no barrier."

"So, the water could be poisoned," he said.

She shook her head. "Possibly," she said. "Probably. But what's the point in telling them? They've got to have some kind of hope. Nobody could go on, if they knew the next day their gut would shred up inside their bodies from radiation, or their hair would fall out, or they'd come down with some horrible mutant smallpox and die like dogs, covered with pus and sores."

"Rabies," said Terry.

Not-Karen looked at him, her eyes widening. "I thought you were getting better," she said.

Terry tried to smile. "No," he said. "That's not what I meant. For the first two weeks after I—woke up—I was sure I had rabies from the raccoon. When a couple of weeks went by and I didn't get sick, I figured that he wasn't rabid. I wasn't going to get it. I started to feel like—well—"

"Like you had some hope?" she said.

He nodded.

"That's the way I feel like every time one of you wakes up," she said. "I feel hope, right up until the day you leave."

Suddenly her anger meant something different. Terry felt like he ought to say something, but before he could form the words, she'd already left the upstairs bedroom and gone downstairs with Pinky.

"Midnight snack," she called back up the stairs in a voice so small that he barely heard her. "You can have some if you want."

It turned out that she had saved a bag of marshmallows, which they stuck in twos and threes on seafood forks, and roasted over a precious can of Sterno. Marshmallows, Terry realized, were one of those miracle foods like Dinty Moore and Spam that, if sealed properly, never seemed to go stale.

Well—that was an overstatement. They were pretty hard to jam onto the forks, but the big white puffs roasted up well, turned soft, and once done, were toasty, gooey, sweet and very edible. Terry delighted in watching the pale Sterno flame ignite the outside of the marshmallow, and then blowing it out before stuffing the crusty, sticky mess into his mouth.

Terry told Not-Karen about scout camp. Then, his cheeks flushed with some sort of foolhardy, marshmallow-fueled happiness, he told her a ghost story, about the "Boo Hag," a witch who fooled men into thinking she was a beautiful woman, until one day, nothing but flesh and sinew, she attacked and ate her unwary husbands.

Not-Karen laughed at that.

Then, thinking of the fish in the stream, he told her about the times he'd been fishing with his uncle, and about catching the four-pound bass that had fought like a demon and how its sharp teeth had closed on his finger when he was taking out the hook. He told her how good that fish had tasted, cooked in a heavy cast-iron pan over a fire he'd made himself.

He told her about riding his skateboard in the summertime, playing World of Warcraft with his best friend, and spying on his big sister and her boyfriend when they made out on the living room couch.

He told her how he got started in blogging, but she waved her hand and said, "Enough. Fishing and boy scouts and skateboarding and making out is real. The internet—no."

"I—I guess you're right," he said after a long while.

He hadn't understood what she had meant for days after he'd awakened. Now, he thought that he did. Long before the wedge put him to sleep, food had lost its taste. Soft skin had lost its feel under his fingers. The scent of a woman's clean hair was as dull as dead straw, the feel of her lips remote, as if he was being kissed through parchment.

Now, though he didn't want to think about it, he remembered why Kim had left him for the car salesman. He knew why she and that man were both dead now, while he was here, alive, in a strange woman's farm house telling her more about his life than he was even sure that he remembered.

"You've got books," he said slowly, looking toward the old-fashioned sitting room with its Persian rug and deep mahogany bookcases—a room that she never used.

"That's right," she said. "I brought back some boxes from the library. Maybe a month after it happened. That was when the car still ran." Not-Karen's Volvo was covered under a tarp in the barn, and Terry had already checked out its four flat tires and utterly dead battery unit. Not that there was enough power to charge it anyway. Portland's charging stations were all but one, outside the bubble, Not-Karen had informed him, and the one that was inside had been drained not long after the last wave of nukes had hit.

"Do you—" he said, rising from the kitchen table, "Do you think there's any poetry?"

Yes, there was poetry. Not-Karen even gave him a candle to read by, and found a shawl for his knees.

Terry spent the rest of the night in the living room. Reading poems.

A few nights later, after dinner but before the ham radio call to Huehuetenango, Terry sat at the kitchen table waiting for cold soup, and feeling a stab of shame as he remembered what he had thought he was, how he believed things to be, during those lost five years.

What—even then, why had he thought that? What did it matter, even if he had been famous to a faceless internet audience that never-was? How many people had been taken in by soft-porn pictures of girls who never were? He wondered if there had ever been a Tina from Terra Haute, or if she was some years-dead incinerated corpse of a 55-year old man, his internet scam caught short by the brief blast of a thermonuclear explosion.

Terry's comfort, which wasn't much, was that he knew he hadn't been bragging like a fool to the real Mac at the Pik-A-Mart, but just a digital simulation, replaying the same tired phrases over and over. A dumb, fake 'Mac,' who would have said whatever Terry wanted to hear.

His face burned with shame upon recalling these things. It reminded him of one of those junior high dreams where he walked to school buck naked, and even the newspaper he held in front of his privates somehow kept slipping aside. One time, he'd gone through an entire school day like that—in his dreams. Some guys might have dreamed that the cheerleading squad was excited by his giant schlong.

Not Terry. At Terry, they had laughed and pointed while his dick shrank to the size of a button mushroom.

It wasn't that he wanted to think that way. It was more along the lines of, he couldn't help it.

Biting his lower lip, he sat at the kitchen table thumbing through a slim, yellow paperback book of German poetry. Rilke was the poet's name. The poems were written in German on the left side, and English on the right. By looking at the two together, Terry thought he could almost discern the deeper poetry in the strange German words.

"Hey," he said to Not-Karen, who was carefully opening a can of Campbell's tomato soup at the counter. He swallowed hard. He wanted to say her name, but still did not know it.

"Listen to this," he said, and he started to read the poem on the English side of the page.

From under the table, Pinky raised his head, dropped his plastic hot dog, and made a questioning "whuff" in the back of his throat.

"Suddenly from the green all around you," he read softly, licking his thumb and holding the page open so he could see better in the flickering light of the Coleman lantern,

> ...something-you don't know what-has disappeared;
> you feel it creeping closer to the window,
> in total silence. From the nearby wood
> you hear the urgent whistling of a plover,
>
> reminding you of someone's Saint Jerome:
> so much solitude and passion come
> from that one voice, whose fierce request the downpour
>
> will grant. The walls, with their ancient portraits, glide
> away from us, cautiously, as though
> they weren't supposed to hear what we are saying.

And reflected on the faded tapestries now;
the chill, uncertain sunlight of those long
childhood hours when you were so afraid.

"Rain-er Mah-ree-ah, Rill-key," he said, closing the book.

Not-Karen had scraped the last of the red soup from the can. She turned, facing him, a gentle, strange expression on her face, her eyes shielded and dark in the lamplight.

"It's Mah-rye-ah," she said.

"Mariah," repeated Terry. "Rain-er Mar-eye-ah..."

"Rill-kuh," said Not-Karen. Then, suddenly, her eyes seemed to shine and glint through her lashes and she said, "That's my name. Maria."

"Marr-Eye-Ah," Terry said, feeling the sound of it on his tongue as his heart seemed to stop.

"My name is Mariah Rye-Nuh," she said. Then with a liquid lilt, she said, "Maria Rainer. I was born in Moon-ken—you say Munich. I am a doctor of computer languages—I was the head of COMSON. It was the project that created the science behind the wedges, the living computers—nanocomputing—for the GMID."

Terry listened, not really comprehending. After a moment, he said, "That's why you never got married." He immediately felt more stupid than he had for days, and started to apologize.

But she laughed, a sudden, sharp bark. "Ja," she said. "Yes. That is why I did not marry. I was married to my numbers and the beautiful little half-live creatures. It is a whole world that is gone. An internet on a level that you cannot imagine, Mr. Herle." And she pronounced his name "Hurr-luh," as he knew was the correct German way to say it, not "Hurley" as everybody and their brother had always called him and his dad.

Not that they were actually German or anything like that. He supposed he had a great-great-great Grandfather who'd fought for the Kaiser. Or maybe Hitler, but it couldn't have been that. And he knew how to say "Ich hab eine hammer" and "Kai-zu-slaw-den" for the town by the air base where his grandfather the Air Force Sergeant had been stationed. Back when there were big-ass jets and internal combustion engines.

"Now you eat by lantern light, wake when the sun comes up, and shoot horses," Terry said.

"And eat them," said Maria, smiling bitterly. She fumbled in the cupboard for something. He watched her take down the Maker's Mark and for the first time, he noticed another clear bottle behind it, which she stood on her toes to reach and slipped it from the shelf.

"What's that?" he asked as she put the bottle on the counter.

"What else?" she asked, smiling merrily. "I suppose now that you have discerned my name through Rilke, we should have a toast."

The bottle of clear glass had German writing on it, and Terry could smell it from across the table when she poured.

"Schnapps," he said. "We used to have it every Christmas."

"The true schnapps," she said. "Apfelwasser."

"Ours was supposedly pine-flavored."

"Oh, ja," she said. "You can have that too." And she said "haf" like German people did.

So, it takes about two hours for two people, somewhat malnourished, to drain a bottle of apfelwasser, which is an acquired taste, but which goes down smooth and light after about two shots.

Schwarzwalders said, that such was the water of life, and with life, came love. Or so the Schwarzwalders said. No trees grew now in that forest.

"I will do the parsnips today," said Maria as they went out onto the back porch.

"There aren't that many left," said Terry.

"Ja," she said, smiling. "No matter. We will plant more."

She was, Terry thought, a remarkably beautiful woman.

He watched her straight, lightly muscled back and the lean, longer muscles bunching in her thighs and calves as she strode across the field with the parsnip basket, Pinky running at her side, stopping playfully every few steps, and leaping at her for attention.

Terry stood for a while with his hands on the railing, then sat in one of the cane-backed chairs on the porch, took out a corncob pipe, and stuffed it with some of the pipe tobacco that Maria had stashed in a small wooden box in the library, a room where he now spent many hours. It was there he had found the poetry.

Rill-kuh, he thought. Now, that was poetry.

He wished that he could truly read and understand the German. And after a moment, it came to him. He had time. To read, to learn German. To—to even write poetry. There was paper in the library, and plenty of pens and pencils.

He had just lit the pipe and had begun to form a few words in his mind, taking a deep, satisfying draw on the pipe, when he heard Maria scream.

Terry was not a young man, it must be understood, when he jumped the porch railing and ran across the field. He tripped, once, and went down on his knee with a bitter crash and cold, teeth-jarring scrape of both knees. He was up, quickly. It didn't cross his mind that Maria's gun was still in the cutlery drawer until he had reached the stand of trees.

She screamed once more, and he heard a deeper, throatier cry.

"Maria!" he yelled, pushing through the small saplings near the stream as their young branches slapped him in the face and shoulders.

He was breathing heavily when he reached the clearing where he usually washed the parsnips.

The basket lay half-in the stream. The parsnips were scattered in the water, most of them floating away. He couldn't see Maria, but he saw footprints in the sandy mud, and broken branches scattered about.

"Maria!" he called again.

He heard rustling to his left and turned to see a thicket of branches moving.

Her head appeared through the leaves. He ran to her, kneeling quickly. "Are you hurt?" he asked.

She put her finger to her lips, shaking her head. Her eyes were enormous, with the whites showing. She grabbed his wrist with surprising, steely strength.

He started to say something else, but her eyes widened even more, and something huge crashed into his back. He fell forward into the branches as Maria tumbled away.

Terry saw a flash of yellow fur as Pinky, snarling and growling in a way he'd never heard, leapt over his head. He tried to rise, but whatever it was, still lay on his back. He smelled the odor of death and rotten meat, and heard deeper snarling than Pinky could ever make. Something tried to bite his shoulder, horribly close to his neck.

"Get away from it!" Maria screamed.

Whatever "it" was, was four or five times the size of the raccoon. Most of Terry's breath had been knocked out of him, and he grunted as he struggled to throw the beast off and get to his feet. More from instinct than anything else, he threw his right arm back, elbow bent, and felt the hard bone connect with a meaty, furry body.

There was no mistaking the canine yelp that followed. Terry rolled over to find himself face to face with—he supposed he had been expecting a big, wild dog—maybe a Doberman or a German Shepherd.

It had ice-blue, utterly undoglike eyes and was snarling with the biggest, longest yellowish teeth he'd ever seen.

"Wulf!" cried Maria

Yeah—a wolf. It leapt again, and Terry twisted at the waist, raising his forearm to fend it off. Its jaws snapped right by his cheek. Pinky clung to the wolf's shoulders with a desperate death-grip, his skinny yellow body flung this way and that.

"What the—fuck—" Terry cried as he wrestled with the wolf. "Get off him, Pinky!" he yelled. "He'll kill ya, ya dumb dog!"

The wolf's jaws grazed Terry's chin. This time, the hard side of his wrist caught it in a soft spot between its jaw and ear.

Dumb luck. The wolf yelped, then made a gargling growl and scrabbled against Terry with its hind legs. Terry bashed its nose with the hard part of his forearm, and it yelped again.

"Goddamn son of a—" Terry screamed.

He looked into its weird, blue-white eyes for a frozen moment, then he threw his knee up as hard as he could. The wolf finally let go, and Terry got up, grabbing any branch, anything he could.

The wolf's body was twisting, and it was ready to leap again, when he planted his steel-toed boot in its ribs. These had turned out to be a decent fit, after he had retrieved then from the Pik-A-Mart. He had never been so pleased with any footwear in his life. His foot felt not a thing as he stepped back, kicking the wolf again. It let out another agonized yelp and skidded away, Pinky still attached.

The wolf backed away, snarling, while Terry reached backward, looking for anything he could use. His fingers found a rough, dry branch, and he grabbed it and tugged. The branch came away and he raised it. Good-sized, if dry, the branch was about as thick as three of Terry's fingers. He swung it toward the wolf, which backed away as the wood whistled in the air.

Now he saw that the wolf was underweight, maybe weighing about eighty pounds, and that it had open sores on its flank. It circled warily, long yellow teeth bared, red gums flashing. Pinky clung to its back with his teeth sunk into the loose fur and skin looking like a weird parody of a dog on a pony ride.

"You son-of-a-bitch!" Terry yelled, swinging the branch and hoping he wouldn't whack Pinky. He caught the wolf on the left side of its head and it yelped and stumbled, forelegs suddenly giving way.

"Get off him!" Terry cried.

The wolf was scared now, and he'd hurt it. Terry grabbed Pinky behind his shoulders as the wolf tried to scramble away. Terry whacked it with the branch and heard a distinct crack, not of wood, but bone. Pinky's jaw seemed to be locked into the wolf's skin, and his dark eyes rolled wildly.

"Pinky!" Terry tugged at the stubborn, terrified dog.

Finally, Pinky's jaw popped open with a spray of foamy pink wolf blood mixed with dog spittle. It happened so suddenly that Terry staggered back, with Pinky's legs kicking and flailing about.

With a low growl, the wolf acceded the field. It lowered its head, gave Terry a long, blood-chilling look, and loped crookedly away down the stream, leaving a ragged muddy track in its wake.

Pinky whimpered in Terry's arms. Looking down, Terry saw that the dog's right paw hung at a terrible angle.

Maria came out of the bush, brambles in her hair, and immediately reached for the dog. "Oh, my poor hund," she said, taking Pinky from Terry's arms.

She looked quickly up into Terry's eyes as she did so. "You saved me," she said. "You were very brave."

Even as he felt a chorus of stabbing, shooting pains along his side, shoulders and back, Terry felt himself smiling.

"Aw," he said. "It was just a—"

"Just a wolf?" she said. "He has been eating human flesh. Did you see how bold he was? This is what they become, when they do such things."

Terry looked down the stream in the direction the wolf had fled. He shivered. The wolf had seemed to know exactly what he had been doing—a practiced ambush from behind. He had only been deterred by Terry's arrival, his steel-toed boots, the lucky branch, and a loyal old yellow dog.

"His leg," Terry said, touching Pinky's paw. The dog cried out. "Maria, we should—" He thought of the Smith & Wesson in the cutlery drawer, and the horses.

She looked up, eyes blazing. "No," she said, cradling Pinky. "No, we shall *not*. I don't care what it takes. We will save him."

Terry followed her as, carrying Pinky in her arms and cradling him to her chest, she walked slowly across the field to the house, weeping silently.

Pinky's nose was hot the next day, and his forehead fiery. It was hard to tell if a dog actually had a fever or not. Terry recalled the vet telling him that, from the days before he had stopped going out of the house, before Kim left, and before the wedge shoved him down on the couch and started feeding him comatose man pap.

Maria smashed some aspirin with a spoon and fed it to Pinky mixed in dollops of meat-flavored baby food. In all the food she had accumulated, she had somehow brought in cases of Gerber—for emergencies, she said. Pinky wouldn't take much of it, but he could be coaxed to swallow a few bites of veal or chicken goo with a picture of a cooing baby on the small glass jar. After Maria was finished with the dog, Terry sniffed the open jar. It didn't smell half-bad. He tried a bite—didn't taste bad, either.

Pinky's lower right leg was broken, but at least the bone hadn't gone through the skin. It was therefore Terry's job to carry the hound out back so he could take care of his business, which, feeling poorly as he obviously did, Pinky executed on three legs, trembling, while giving Terry the most mournful gaze of humiliation and resentment ever seen on man or beast.

When later that night, Terry came to Maria's bedroom, she stopped him with a steely glare. Without a word, he tightened the belt of his robe, nodded at her, and turned and left. It was going to be the end of her bed for Pinky, and the cot for Terry. Women, he thought. Women were like that, and for some reason that thought was a comfort to him.

As Terry lay on the rock-hard, lumpy cot and pulled the rough army blanket up to his neck, a dark green torture device which seemed to be woven from sisal and twined razor-wire if it was made out of anything, he found himself staring at the dimly-lit ceiling in the moonlight, thinking about Rilke, and... smiling.

The next day, Pinky was a bit better, ate a whole jar of baby food, and hopped a few times when Terry put him out beside the garden for his morning duty. The humiliated stare was a little less intense. And his nose was cooler, and wetter.

That night, it was still the cot for Terry, and the bed and quilt for Pinky.

The night after that, Maria reached Huehuetenango. Ignacio, voice barely audible, told her that during the day, the baby had died.

"I'm sorry," she said to the distant receiver. "We will light a candle."

"Hold on," said Terry. He had the book of Rilke in the pocket of his robe.

That afternoon he had been reading some more, both the German and English, and thinking about it.

"For the baby," he said. "I have something to read."

"All right," said Maria. "My friend has—something here," she said. "A poem." She made it sound like he had written it.

Terry looked over at her, surprised, but her eyes were veiled. He took the microphone and cleared his throat, beginning to read.

>We lack all knowledge of this parting. Death
>does not deal with us. We have no reason
>to show death admiration, love or hate;
>his mask of feigned tragic lament gives us
>
>a false impression. The world's stage is still
>filled with roles which we play. While we worry
>that our performances may not please,
>death also performs, although to no applause
>
>But as you left us, there broke upon this stage
>a glimpse of reality, shown through the slight
>opening through which you disappeared: green,

evergreen, bathed in sunlight, in truest woods.

"Oh," said Ignacio when Terry was finished. "That was beautiful. You are a great poet, Mister Terry."

"But I—" Terry said.

Maria reached out quickly and took the microphone. "He is a wonderful poet," she said. "He is too modest. I shall pray tonight for the baby's soul. My thoughts and prayers with you and your daughters."

"You have found no information on disease?" asked Ignacio.

"No," Maria said. "Not yet," she said. "I will keep looking."

She turned the radio off with a snap.

"Maria," Terry said. "Why did you—"

"Lie?" she said. "Sometimes lies are more true than the truth. This is something we Germans understand."

"Rilke wasn't German," said Terry as she took his hand and led him toward the bed. He noticed that a flat silk pillow had been placed on the floor. For Pinky.

"Exactly," she said. "Rilke was from Prague. A Bohemian."

"Isn't Bohemia a beer from Mexico?" asked Terry as she put her fingers across his lips and drew his hips toward hers.

Six weeks later, Maria sat at the radio, turning the knobs and trying every frequency, but there came no answer from Huehuetenango.

With a grief-stricken sigh, she turned the radio off.

Thinking about what to say, Terry found he could say nothing. Instead, he said, "I've come to the end of the book." He took the thin yellow volume of Rilke from his pocket and sat on the bed.

Then, as she faced him with tears streaming down her face, he read,

> You, whom I do not tell that all night long
> I lie weeping,
> whose very being makes me feel wanting
> like a cradle.
>
> You, who do not tell me, that you lie awake
> thinking of me:—
> what, if we carried all these longings within us
> without ever being overwhelmed by them,

letting them pass?

Look at these lovers, tormented by love,
when first they begin confessing,
how soon they lie!

You make me feel alone. I try imagining:
one moment it is you, then it's the soaring wind;
a fragrance comes and goes but never lasts.
Oh, within my arms I lost all whom I loved!
Only you remain, always reborn again.
For since I never held you, I hold you fast.

"Es eine lieder," Terry said slowly. He had both come to the end of the book, and learned a few words in German. "It some song," was what he had said.

"Ich weiss," said Maria. "Ein lied," she said. "Not 'some song.'"

"Oh," Terry said.

Tears tracked down her cheeks.

"I was a lonely woman," she said. "Wisst du was ist Einsamkeit? Do you know what is—loneliness?"

"Ja," Terry said. "Ich... weiss."

She put her slim, trembling hand to his cheek.

"The baby died," she said. "In Guatemala."

Then, she slowly lowered her hand and took his.

"But this baby," she said, putting his hand to her flat belly.

"This baby," he said wondering, feeling tears of his own squeezing from the corners of his eyes. "Maria," he said, his voice thick with emotion.

"Yes," she said. "Ja, Terry. A baby. And it is yours."

"Meine Gott," he said. And no one needs some translation to know what that means. "My baby. Ours."

"Ja," she said. And while he held her in his arms and stroked her hair, he felt the soft skin of her cheek beneath his trembling fingers. Each of her ribs. The muscles of her back. The still-strong flesh of her haunches, firm and powerful. He smelled the life of her, and something different, beneath her smell. Heard, distinctly, the barest beating of the tiniest of hearts. And he drew her to him and held her close and they stayed like that on the bed—oh, for such a long time, until light fingered across her bed and Pinky thudded to the floor and padded over to his water bowl.

Maria raised herself up on her elbow and said, "You must take him out, Terry, I won't have him going in the house."

Terry got up in the frigid morning, threw on his robe, and carried the old dog down the stairs. It was not precisely necessary, as Pinky's broken leg was nearly healed. Terry watched the sun rise with streams of pink fingering over the stand of trees by the stream as the dog looked up at him with veiled dark, shame-filled, yet somehow wise eyes.

Then Terry went back in the house along with the dog, and he held Maria's hand as they ate cold corned beef hash at the kitchen table in the pink and golden dawn.

That night, there was nothing from Huehuetenango, again, but there came another sound.

Crackles and pops, followed by the faintest voice, broken, barely audible.

"Hello! Hello! We are from Edo. We are a small community—twenty five men, women and children. Can you hear?"

Maria's face registered surprise. "Yes," she said in a trembling voice. "We are from America. Indiana. There are only two here," she said. Looking quickly over at Terry, she added, "Well, perhaps—three."

Terry knelt beside her, leaning toward the radio.

"I am—a scientist," she said. "I know about the wedges. Und meine mann, he ist hier."

Terry looked toward her, the strangest light feeling in his heart, as if something had just sprung to life in the room, and he didn't even know what to call it.

"He is a poet," she continued. "And we are—we are expecting a baby. Sometime in the spring."

"A baby," the voice said. "We will turn the prayer wheel for you."

Terry grasped Maria's hand. Questioning, he looked at her, and she shook her head, lowering her face and smiling. Her hand brushed his cheek.

He thought she was going to say something about prayer wheels be-ing pointless, but instead, she whispered, "Terry—no wedge survived—in

Japan. None—at all."

"Does that mean—" he asked.

"Yes," she said. "It means people can live outside the wedges. It means—we could someday be—"

"Free," he said, "But I think, already we are. And alive, and it does not matter."

The poet kissed her deeply and the radio went dark.

Snow Comes To Hawk's Folly

J. Kathleen Cheney

One

"No, let go." Imogen wrestled the feed bills out of Patrick's chubby hand and fixed him with her sternest look. "These are Mama's papers. Not toys."

He reached for her cream-colored braid instead, and it began to unravel under his touch. Only a moment before, he'd been contentedly stacking wooden blocks in the corner of her office. Now they lay strewn across the rug. Imogen set the bills on the far side of her desk, picked Patrick up, and carried him in the direction of the kitchen. "Let's go see Miss Mary, all right?"

As she walked along the farmhouse's white-painted hallway, Patrick tugged at the sleeve of her cambric blouse. "Where Papa?"

"Papa's out with the horses," Imogen said, trying to untangle his chestnut hair with her free hand. "If you're good for Miss Mary, I'll take you out there after your nap."

Patrick wrinkled his nose, much as she'd expected him to. "Papa, now!"

"Later," she said firmly, "after your nap." Her husband Guaire served as the trainer for the farm's racing stables, something for which he was eminently suited—as he'd been a racehorse for nearly a decade before arriving at Hawk's Folly Farm. A puca, one of the Lesser Folk, he had the ability to take on horse form. A family out of Ireland had kept him *bound* in horse form, racing on iron-shod feet. It was a painful thing for anyone with fairy blood to contemplate. Iron burned.

But Fate had, Guaire maintained, brought him to the perfect place in the end. Hawk's Folly had a history of collecting unusual people.

Imogen swung open the door to the kitchen, a cheery room that always smelled of bread, cakes, and soap. She found Mary there, reviewing a menu with the cook. "Mary, I hate to ask, but can you keep track of him for a bit, just until I can get the checks written out?"

Mary Sanders came around the table with a broad smile. The fresh-faced girl actually enjoyed wrangling a difficult two-year-old, partially a preparation for dealing with her own child, due in a month or so. She tucked a dark strand of hair behind one ear, then lifted the toddler from Imogen's arms and carried him off down the hallway.

"I'm sorry, Mrs. Dougherty," Imogen said while she braided her hair once more. "I'm simply not getting any work done. I need to find another nursemaid, and soon."

The cook laughed. "One that will stay more than a week? Good luck, missus. That boy is a terror."

And they all knew it. Patrick had a gift of unbinding—not a surprise when both of his parents did as well. It was part of his puca heritage. Things came apart under his touch, and unfortunately he hadn't yet learned to be judicious about the things he unbound. He broke things, undid them, split them, and unraveled them. Fortunately, his gift didn't affect living things, so Imogen had no worry that he would hurt Mary or the baby.

Imogen sighed and headed back toward her office, stopping to gently press her heel on a squeaking floorboard. She tugged back her full skirts to gaze down at the offending spot. Patrick couldn't work nails out of the wood. He couldn't affect anything made of steel or iron. But he *could* loosen the boards around them. She would have to get one of the stable hands to put a nail in that board after the next race. The Victorian farmhouse—built back in the late 1880s by her first husband—wasn't even twenty-five years old yet, and she certainly didn't want it falling apart before Patrick reached adulthood.

She'd nearly made it to her office when a brisk knock sounded on the front door. Imogen paused in the hallway and heard the downstairs maid's feet pattering in that direction. She leaned to one side so she could see, but couldn't make out who their visitor was.

After a moment, the young maid darted back along the hall to find her, her apron twisted in restless hands. "There's a gentleman calling to see you, missus."

Imogen wondered what gentleman would call on *her*, not her husband. "Did he give you a name, Beryl?"

"Mr. Finnegan," the girl said, her cornflower eyes wide. "He sounds Irish, too, like Mr. O'Donnell."

Imogen didn't recognize the name. She walked down to the foyer, young Beryl at her side. A tall gentleman waited in her front sitting room, his back to her as he surveyed the collection of photographs on her mantel. He was well-dressed, wearing a finely-made tweed suit and holding a bowler in his hand. His hair looked almost white, not gray—as creamy as Imogen's own coarse locks. He turned toward them then with a smile on his handsome face.

His features seemed too perfect for Imogen's taste, an unearthly beauty. Under her suspicious gaze that appearance wavered, briefly showing her the face underneath. Dark eyes gazed back at her, but she couldn't keep the rest of the illusion at bay.

"Beryl," she said softly, "go find Mr. O'Donnell and tell him I need him."

The girl gazed at Mr. Finnegan raptly, her mouth hanging open.

Imogen pinched the girl's elbow. The maid squeaked in surprise and looked up at her, so she repeated her request. After one more sidelong glance at their visitor, Beryl dashed down the hallway toward the back door—the fastest way to get out to the practice track.

Imogen turned back to her guest. "Mr. Finnegan," she began, "may I ask why you're here?"

Her visitor smiled though the layers of illusion. Imogen blinked, trying to get a clearer view of him. She couldn't make a good guess of his age. He looked no older than her, perhaps thirty or so, but she suspected that wasn't an accurate estimate. For his glamour to baffle her so, he surely must be one of the Fair Folk, and could be quite old.

"I'm new to Saratoga Springs," he said with a lilting Irish accent. "I've purchased one of the neighboring farms and wanted to make myself known to my neighbors."

Imogen didn't cross the threshold into the sitting room. "How kind of you. It's wise to be on good terms with one's neighbors."

"Tell me, Mrs. Hawkes," he said with a languid gesture toward the mantel, "are any of these photographs of your mother?"

Imogen pressed her lips together, trying to decide how to answer that. He'd called her Mrs. Hawkes—which indicated he believed her to be married to Henry Hawkes still. But Henry had passed away in the spring of 1901, seven years past. That lapse also indicated that her visitor didn't know about her new husband. Now Imogen wished she hadn't sent Beryl off to find him.

"Mrs. Hawkes?" her guest prompted.

"No," she answered. "My mother preferred not to have a likeness made." The fourth daughter of an English earl, Eugenia Villiers 'Smith' had held strong opinions about everything, including the frivolity of portraits.

Mr. Finnegan remained standing next to the green-striped sofa, apparently aware that it would be impolite to sit down until she did so. "She was English, I hear, although your accent is quite American. Have you lived here your entire life?"

"Yes, I've lived on this farm my entire life." Where was this interrogation going? Safest to answer, though, since she didn't want to offend one of the Fair Folk. She didn't need that sort of bad luck attaching itself to her.

The very fact that he stood there in her sitting room worried her. For one of *them* to have crossed the ocean to come to America would have been extremely difficult. That fact had always, supposedly, kept them in Ireland and the nearby lands. Evidently, the creature in front of her had circumvented the obstacle the ocean presented.

"And you married the owner of this property?" he asked then.

He wanted to understand who *owned* this land. Who *controlled* it. That she could grasp, as the Fair Folk were affected by territorial boundaries. "Yes, the land passed into my hands when he died."

The dark brows rose. "You husband is dead? I hadn't heard that."

Imogen decided she'd better spit out the truth. "I remarried a few years ago. My current husband is alive. Perhaps whoever discussed my affairs with you confused the two men."

"And may I ask how I should address you, then?" He folded his hands and waited.

"Mrs. O'Donnell. My husband should be here in a few minutes."

"He's old enough to be your father," Finnegan said in a vexed tone.

And that revealed he knew more about Guaire than he should. Guaire *had* been twenty by the time she'd been born—old enough, although one would never know it to look at him. Whoever this man was, he'd clearly been prying into her affairs. Imogen felt her temper rising. "That needn't concern you, Mr. Finn…"

And then she realized *exactly* who he was.

Finn *was* his name—or at least the name by which her mother had known him. His hair wasn't pale with age, not any more than hers. The man standing before her had sired her.

Her hands had clenched into fists at her sides. She had numerous reasons to be angry with him, but Beryl had invited him in, so she was hesitant to give him the discourtesy he deserved. "Why don't you drop the glamour? It does nothing more than confuse my eyes."

The illusions wrapped around him faded away like mist, leaving a man who looked near her own age, had her warm brown eyes, cream-colored hair and dark brows—a striking combination. He was still handsome, but his perfection had faded, leaving more rugged features. "How did you know?"

"I can see through glamours, for the most part." Her half-puca blood had some advantages, although she couldn't actually take horse form. But his glamour shouldn't have been able to fool her at all. That was why she'd assumed him to be one of the Fair Folk—a *true* fairy. Being of the Lesser Folk, though, her father shouldn't have the ability to baffle her. That served as a warning to her that Finn had more power than she expected, or perhaps greater skill. She would have to be wary. She leaned back and peered down the hallway, hoping to intercept Guaire before he came in. Her father might recognize him. "What do you want, here, sir?"

"I came for my daughter." Finn smiled. "You are my child, aren't you?"

As if he had some right to her. Imogen raised her chin and gave him a hard look. "I am my mother's child."

"You cannot deny that I'm your father," he said, opening his arms wide.

"You sired me, no more. Paddy O'Donnell is more of a father to me than you ever were."

His nostrils flared. "So you married him?"

Imogen bit back the urge to laugh in his face. She understood his earlier questions now. He'd assumed she had married *Patrick* O'Donnell, a retainer of her mother's family who'd escorted the 'widow' and her infant child to America. Paddy had decided to stay in Saratoga Springs and had been hired on at the farm as a trainer by Henry's mother. Throughout Imogen's lonely childhood, Paddy had been there, a surrogate father.

"I married Paddy's nephew," she explained.

That actually seemed to take him by surprise, as if his own interpretation of the facts couldn't possibly be wrong. "I wasn't aware O'Donnell had family here."

In truth, he didn't. When Guaire first came to Hawk's Folly, his Irish accent had made it simplest to explain him away as a 'nephew' visiting Paddy from the old country, even though no such relationship existed. Imogen just hoped that Beryl hadn't found that supposed nephew. She glanced back down the hallway and was gratified not to see him there.

And then the front door of the house opened. Guaire stepped into the foyer, his customary wide grin lighting his face. Like her father, his rugged features didn't show his age. He had the same warm brown eyes, combined with the unruly chestnut locks his son had inherited. He wore work clothes suitable for the stables, a collarless shirt with a tweed vest, and trousers that had seen more than their share of wear. He dropped his cap on the table in the entryway. "Ginny, I hear we have a guest."

Imogen froze, waiting for an explosion.

"I'm amazed you're even alive, boy," her father said.

Guaire slowly turned toward the sitting room. His eyes settled on the man therein and a rare anger burned in them. Imogen laid one hand on his arm, eager to forestall chaos. "Don't let him provoke you. Beryl invited him in."

"Then invite him out," Guaire said in a cool voice.

She understood his fury. Long ago, Guaire had come to her mother's aid, helping Eugenia Villiers flee from Finn and return to her family. He had paid for that interference. Finn had come after him seeking revenge, and Guaire had spent nearly two decades in hiding. When Finn found him, he'd bound Guaire in horse form and sold him to a racing stable—an imprisonment which would last another decade.

"How did you find my child?" Finn asked Guaire in an amused tone. "And get her to marry you? I am quite impressed, boy."

Imogen set a hand on Guaire's stiff arm. They both had reasons to despise the creature who stood before them, but they needed to handle him carefully. "Mr. Finnegan, I think you've been here long enough. You should go now."

Finn's jaw clenched, but he clearly recognized the power of her ownership of the land. He couldn't stay if she didn't want him. He settled the bowler on his head and took a step toward the door. Unfortunately, just then a banshee-like yowl filled the air, followed by the patter of bare feet.

"Papa!" A naked two-year-old came barreling down the hallway and slammed into Guaire's legs. He clung like a monkey, bouncing in excitement.

"Where are your clothes this time?" Guaire asked in an exasperated tone.

"Miss Mary," the boy said, and held up his hands.

Imogen eyed her father, who watched the child with something resembling avarice. She cast Guaire a pleading look. With one last distrustful glance in her father's direction, he picked up the boy and marched toward the back of the house, out of her father's sight.

She blew out a pent breath, relieved that the two hadn't lost their tempers. On the rare occasions when Guaire did get angry, he had the potential to make the house fall apart—and he was only three-fourths puca. Her father came from purer stock and could likely do far worse if roused.

"You have a child," her father observed. "I didn't know."

Imogen crossed her arms over her chest. "Your informant was clearly behind the times. What do you want here?"

His eyes narrowed. "A question for a question? How did Guaire find you?"

He was offering a bargain, and her fairy blood would hold her to it. But answering his question would force him to tell the truth in turn, which was all she wanted.

"He didn't find me. I purchased him. From a dispersal sale, sight unseen, at auction." There was no harm in admitting that. Her father could tell the whole countryside that she'd bought her husband in horse form. No one would believe him. "What do you want?"

"I'd lost track of him after Boston," her father said. "I did have some concern that he ended up in the slaughterhouse."

The most damning of her father's crimes, in Imogen's mind. Unlike a full-blooded puca, Guaire didn't have the ability to speak while in horse form. Trapped so, Guaire might easily have been slaughtered, unable to explain that he wasn't a horse, no matter how he might appear. "What do you want?" Imogen repeated stiffly. "A question for a question."

Finn removed his hat again and ran fingers through that cream-colored hair. "Your mother cheated me of the chance of ever knowing you. That's all I came for."

Imogen considered his statement, and then asked, "How did you find me?"

"A question for a question?" When she nodded, he said, "I met one of the Villiers' old servants who was pensioned off and lived in Ireland. He told me that your mother hadn't actually married some Mr. Smith as her family put about, but that he'd been fabricated to explain her pregnancy. So I hired an investigator in New York, who tracked down your mother's address and also found your marriage lines."

Her mother hadn't lived secretly, but she'd always believed that the fictitious Mr. Smith would protect their names from scandal. Unfortunately, old servants did gossip at times. Imogen suspected that her mother's two-month long disappearance in Ireland—and subsequent return and pregnancy—had been the most interesting thing to happen in that family in decades. The servants must have found the gossip irresistible.

"What is my grandson's name?" Finn asked.

Imogen weighed the question, wondering how complete her answer had to be. She didn't want to give him the boy's true name, as it would give her father power over her son.

"I only ask his given name," Finn said. "Not his true name."

"Patrick." Imogen wrapped her arms more tightly about herself, and added, "I'm not comfortable with you here."

He inclined his head. "I think I understand, but I will swear by my own blood that I mean no harm to you, your son, or any in your household."

It was a vast promise, Imogen knew. "And Guaire?"

"He is a part of your household, is he not? I mean no harm to him. I never intended for what I did to him to carry on so long, but once I'd given him over to the Boyle family, I found I couldn't easily get him back."

"I have trouble believing that," Imogen said. She had never nursed anger toward her father for his questionable treatment of her mother or for his absence from her own life. He'd always been a distant and almost mythical figure in her mind. But what he'd done to Guaire—that filled her with fury.

"I could have tried harder," Finn admitted with an elegant shrug, "but he proved to be a valuable racer, and they didn't want to lose him. I hadn't realized he was fast."

Guaire had passed from one racing stable to another, all within the Boyle family. Each would race him for a few years under forged papers, and then pass him to a cousin. Only when Guaire passed to an heir uninterested in keeping a stable had he gone up for sale—and Imogen bought him, thinking a retired racehorse of his caliber might be a good match for her brood mares. That had turned out to be the best purchase of her life.

She gave her father a hard look. "Swear it, then."

He pulled off a glove and bit his thumb. He held it out for her to see, blood and all. "I swear by my own blood that I mean no harm to you, your household, your child... or your husband."

Imogen didn't know what to make of that. He would be bound by that oath, as his kind always were, just as she and Guaire would be bound by any oath either of them made.

He wrapped his glove about his thumb and squeezed it. "I have no other children. I only wish a chance to know the one I do have."

Imogen couldn't imagine what it would be like to be separated from Patrick, and that thought tempered her anger. "I will consider permitting you to visit with me, but I will need to discuss the terms of it with my husband first. I will put his preferences above yours at all times. If

Guaire says no, then there is no bargain."

Finn nodded. "And he has cause to refuse me, I know."

"I'll send word around to your place tomorrow," she said, "to let you know what he and I have agreed upon."

"I had hoped you might be pleased to meet me, but I didn't factor him into my reckoning." Finn shook his head and handed her the bloodied glove. "Tell him of my promise, at least."

Imogen gingerly took the glove. Might some charm be woven into its fibers? She could rarely sense such things, but Guaire always did. "I'll tell him."

Her father made an urbane bow and left her there in the hallway, feeling stunned.

Two

Guaire peered down from their bedroom on the second floor, staring out the window that looked over the stable yard and the green roof of the stable. Finn had ridden away on a chestnut gelding, heading the long way around to his adjacent property rather than cutting through the west pasture. Guaire had no idea what Finn was doing here—in the New World, in New York, or in the front sitting room downstairs.

For the most part, Guaire hadn't given Finn a thought for years, not even married to his daughter as he was. Now Finn had walked into their lives with the ease of an old friend, and Guaire didn't know if he could forgive him, much less trust him.

But Imogen was Finn's daughter. Seeing them together, one couldn't have any doubt of that. Her mother had raised her in denial of the puca side of her heritage, to be serious and cool, to restrain the wildness that ran under her skin. But it had always been there.

He was still staring out the window when Imogen came looking for him. "Patrick is down for a nap," he whispered before she could speak.

She came and put her arms around him, and pressed her face against his neck. He set his lips against her hair. "This scares me, Ginny."

"I know," she said. "Me, too. I couldn't see through his glamour at first."

Guaire pulled back and his eyes met hers. "He's always been… unusual. He's old and powerful, and much stronger than I am. If he tries to take you from me, I may not be able to stop him."

Imogen pulled a stained glove out of her pocket. "He swore. On his own blood, he swore that he meant no harm to anyone in this household."

Guaire caught the scent of blood on the thing—a binding. Even so, for their kind the exact words of an oath were the ones they must obey. They could bend and evade the oath any other way. "Ginny, what exact words did he use?"

She repeated her father's words, which were a broad oath indeed.

Guaire still didn't trust it. He sat down in the wide chair before the window and pulled her to sit in his lap. When she'd settled comfortably, he asked, "What did he say about Patrick?"

So Imogen repeated every bit of that conversation as well, answering when he had questions. And once she'd relayed everything to his satisfaction, she asked, "Is it true that he has no children other than me?"

"I don't recall his having any children," Guaire admitted. "I don't even know how old he is, darling. Old, more than a hundred years, for sure. But no, I'd never heard of anyone saying they were his get."

"Except me," she said.

"I just don't know, Ginny." He sighed heavily. The Fair Folk had convoluted ways of thinking, putting multiple layers of meaning into what they did and said. Pucas were of the Lesser Folk; they had simpler ways. But as he recalled, Finn had always been an exception to that. "He's one of the hard ones, and I can't think like that."

"Motives within motives, my mother said," she whispered.

Which matched with what he recalled of Finn. "I'm going to send Billy to Sheepshead with the horses," Guaire told her.

August was almost gone. The Saratoga meet had ended, and the next races for them would be those at Sheepshead Bay, out on Coney Island. It meant hours on trains, and it was a trial for Guaire to be surrounded by steel for so long anyway. It was time for Billy Sanders to take on more responsibility anyway, he reckoned.

"I would be more comfortable with you here," Imogen said. "Until I understand why he's come, at least."

"Ah, then, I won't be traveling for the next decade or so." Guaire's arms tightened about her. He hadn't known his own father. He would have liked to, he'd always thought. And he knew that Imogen felt the same, despite all the ill her mother had claimed about Finn. "If you're wanting to talk to him, Ginny, I'll not argue, but watch your words. And I'm thinking, I would want to know why he left Ireland. Crossing the ocean's a terrible thing. You were a babe when you did so, but I remember it, and I'll not be doing that ever again. I have to ask myself why he did."

"You don't think it was to find me?" she asked with a furrowed brow.

He pressed a kiss to her forehead. "As much as I'd like to believe he did so, I can't, Ginny."

"He bought the Hammersly place," she said. "Whatever reason he has for coming here, he landed very close."

Guaire had noted that as well. Imogen liked to believe in coincidence. She liked to believe it had been a coincidence that he'd ended up in her stables rather than some other owner's. But he'd never had much faith in randomness. "You know I said 'twas Fate made you buy me? We'll have to hope that Fate knows what she was doing when she led him here as well."

Imogen decided to go herself, a way to talk to Finn that wouldn't bring him anywhere near her family. So one of the stable boys saddled up Captain for her, and she rode the old bay gelding through the west meadow toward the Hammersly house.

She'd never before set foot on the farm her father had purchased. It had belonged to William Hammersly, who had wanted to acquire Hawk's Folly so fervently that he'd shot one of her prime horses, tried to steal Guaire in horse form, and nearly kidnapped Imogen herself. She wasn't certain she liked her father as her neighbor any better. Even so, when she reached the farmhouse, she steeled her nerves and slid down from Captain's back.

The house was older than hers, dating from the Civil War, with a wide porch and small windows. Since no groom appeared to take Captain's reins, Imogen tied them to the porch post and walked up the steps. The house seemed strangely quiet, no servants bustling about, no hands working near the tired stables. Only a handful of horses grazed in a distant paddock, the caretaker's private property, she recalled.

Dark curtains hung over the windows, and Imogen couldn't see any light within. She lifted her hand to rap on the door, but stopped, asking herself again if she really wanted to pursue this. But a night's sleep had convinced her that the opportunity to learn about herself outweighed her fear of her father, so she knocked on the door loudly.

It only took a moment for the door to open, Finn himself standing at the threshold. "Have you made up your mind?"

She'd expected a more traditional greeting before he pursued his answer. "Yes. We've decided that we'll try to work out some terms. A chance to get to know each other."

He looked pleased. Perhaps relieved, she decided, although his expression hardly changed at all.

"Won't you come in, then?" He stepped back and, after a brief hesitation, she followed.

The inside of the house smelled dusty, and the furniture was still covered. A line of steamer trunks ran along the main hallway, as if he'd carried them inside but never bothered to unpack them. "How long have you been living here?" she asked.

"A week," he said.

The air in the house was stale. "Don't you have anyone working here?"

"No, I saw no reason to hire people on if you didn't want me to stay." He went into the front sitting room and pulled the Holland covers off two chairs. At the first sight of each—one a tall leather wingback chair, and the other, a smaller feminine version in a burgundy floral brocade— his expression hinted that he'd never bothered to look under the covers before.

"Did you buy this place sight unseen?" she asked.

"I asked my agent here to find something as close to your land as possible," he said and gestured for her to sit in the more feminine chair. "I didn't care what the house looked like, although the land itself is pleasant."

Imogen sat, asking, "Do you know who lived here before you?"

He sat across from her. "One William Hammersly, now deceased, from what my man said."

"Hammersly wanted my land," she told him, "and was willing to go to extreme lengths to get it. Lengths that caused his death, in a way."

Her father regarded her with one raised brow. "You killed him?"

Imogen tried to return that sardonic expression, but suspected she failed miserably. "No."

He sat back and crossed his legs. "Then how did you deal with him?"

She explained how Hammersly's greed finally led him to the use of magic on track-owned lands, something the Saratoga Racing Association didn't permit. The next day he'd collapsed in an apoplectic fit. Whether there were supernatural forces involved in that, or if the man's excesses had merely caught up with him, Imogen had no idea—nor did she want to know.

Her father seemed to appreciate the tale, though, and they discussed her relationship with the previous landowner for a time. Neither of them broached the subject of her mother or of Guaire, which kept them in neutral territory, a surprisingly amicable discussion. But since she'd told Guaire she'd be gone no more than an hour, Imogen told her father she would have to go.

"And will you allow me to visit your house again?" he asked when she rose. "I would like to get to know my grandson."

Imogen frowned. "I am still considering that. Perhaps you can come next Wednesday for tea."

He inclined his head, and then surprised her by asking, "Do you know where I can hire reliable servants?"

He would have to go into town. And sooner or later, people would begin to talk about how much he looked like her. Or how much she looked like him. And while her mother had claimed to be a widow when she arrived, Imogen had let slip once that her father was still alive in Ireland. How long would it be before people started assuming familial connections between them? "Do you intend to tell them you're related to me?"

"What do you suggest? I know what your mother told people. What would happen if they discovered that I am your father?"

He didn't look old enough to be her father, so it was unlikely people would believe that. She said so, and then added, "Perhaps, if people ask, you could say we are cousins."

"If asked, I am willing to say that," he conceded.

So she gave him a quick listing of where he could seek out household help and, citing the time, sped out the door.

Guaire was waiting anxiously at the stables when she rode in. He helped her down from Captain's back. "You're late. Are you all right?"

Imogen nodded. "For now, I think I trust him."

"For now," Guaire repeated. "One day at a time?"

"The best I can do, I think."

It wasn't until after sunset that they had time to go over her discussion with her father. Guaire heard it in her voice: for all that Finn's presence worried her, she wanted him to stay. She wanted him to be her father, whether he'd earned that privilege or not. And Guaire would support her in that, whether he liked Finn or not. But he intended to be cautious.

After a great deal of discussion the next day, Billy Sanders agreed to take the three-year-olds to the races at Sheepshead Bay in Guaire's place, Billy's first outing as their official trainer. The young man fretted over being gone so close to Mary's time, but Mary just reminded him that their child wasn't due for a month or so, and sent him on his way. The rise in his pay helped soften his worry, Guaire thought.

And Guaire talked to people in town that week, running down shopkeepers and trainers and grooms. In the three years since he'd arrived, he'd made plenty of friends. If anything were happening in Saratoga, he heard of it.

"He's setting up stables," Guaire told Imogen over Sunday dinner. Finn had hired a full staff for the house and a handful of grooms. "Breeding is my best guess."

She regarded him with a troubled expression he wished he could wipe away. "Where is the money coming from?"

"Fairy gold?" Guaire suggested, only half serious. He'd never been concerned with wealth or fine things. Most pucas weren't. They spent their lives in search of the next bit of mischief instead. Even though Guaire hadn't had a single cent to his name—or a shred of clothing—when he'd first come to Hawk's Folly, apparently Finn chose not to live the same way.

Imogen shook her head at his jest. "He bought the Hammersly place, and now he's buying horses? He has to have money somewhere."

"Is that a lot?" Guaire asked. Imogen had a head for business; he didn't. The question of funding honestly hadn't occurred to him.

"I hadn't thought about it until now," she said, "but yes. He's laid out a great deal of money. I would be flattered if I truly believed it was so he could see me."

Guaire watched her finish her dinner, the narrow line between her dark brows never easing. In this sort of situation, he wasn't the most help. He didn't think the way Finn did, with the deviousness more commonly associated with the Fair Folk. What Imogen needed was someone who could think like her father, someone who had a brain as convoluted as old Finn's.

And Guaire knew exactly on whom to call.

When Wednesday afternoon came, Finn sat down with Imogen in the front sitting room, a civilized thing, revealing that her 'wild' father understood the rules of polite society. He looked quite at home on her green-striped couch, his teacup and saucer balanced on his knee. They spoke of the weather in that part of the country, what he could expect when winter came, and the yearling sale that would come in the spring.

So far Guaire hadn't heard anything odd being said about her father in town, which meant Finn must be comporting himself much like any other new landholder in the Saratoga area. And he wasn't seducing every girl in town yet, either. Imogen considered that a good sign.

They drank the last of their tea, and she rose, indicating it was time for him to leave. He stood as well, a hopeful expression on his handsome face. "May I see my grandson today?"

After a moment of weighing the consequences, Imogen sent Mary to bring Patrick. "For a few minutes," she told her father. "He'll need to take his nap, soon."

Guaire came in through the front door then, brushing his shoulders. He cast a wary glance at her father, but turned back to her. "Are you all right?"

He had white flecks in his dark hair, melting down to droplets of water. Imogen reached up a hand, bemused. "Snow?"

"A cold wind came in fast," he said, with a worried shake of his head. "I think it's going to snow the night through."

"It's September!" Imogen protested. "We shouldn't be seeing snow this early."

Mary came waddling down the hallway then, her face flushed. "Mrs. O'Donnell!"

Imogen turned away from Guaire to the girl. "What is it, Mary?"

"The nursemaid," Mary said, leaning against the doorframe. "I went to find her, but she's gone."

Guaire set a hand under Mary's elbow to support her. "Where's Patrick?"

The girl looked as if she might faint. "I don't know, sir. They're both just gone."

Guaire ran down the hallway, leaving Mary in Imogen's hands. Imogen turned to her suspiciously silent father. Finn still waited in the parlor. "What have you done?"

Trapped by the two of them blocking the doorway, Finn regarded her with raised brows. "Whatever do you mean?"

Mary had gone from flushed to a pasty white. The girl gasped, and then grabbed frantically at Imogen's arm. "Oh, Lordy, missus!"

Water started to pool on the floor at Mary's feet; Imogen knew exactly what that meant. She lifted her skirts with her free hand and tucked them up, casting an angry look at her father.

"I am not responsible for that," her father said, pointing at Mary's belly.

Imogen wanted to scream at him, but contained it, worried for the girl. She stepped closer, sliding her arm about the girl's bulky waist. "Mary, have you been having pains?"

"For a while, missus, but..." Mary stared down at her belly wide-eyed, as if surprised that the child inside intended to come out. "It wasn't supposed to be for another couple of weeks," she protested. "I thought it was just in my head."

And now it was snowing. Imogen wasn't sure she could get the girl into town, not in the buggy. She certainly didn't want to deliver a child, but it was beginning to look like there wasn't much choice unless they could get a doctor out to the farm.

Guaire came jogging back up the hallway then, his features set. He touched Imogen's arm in passing and said, "No sign of them. I'm gonna head out to the stable and see if anyone's seen them."

"Ask if any of the hands has delivered a child before," Imogen called after him as he whisked out the front door. When she turned back, she was relieved to see the cook bustling down the hallway toward them.

Mrs. Dougherty's eyes went wide at the sight in the hallway. She replaced Imogen's arm with her own, taking Mary's weight. "Uh, I'll take Mary back to the kitchen, missus, and get one of the girls to clean this up."

"Take her to the guest bedroom instead, Mrs. Dougherty," Imogen decided, "I suspect the doctor may not make it out here. Have you ever helped with a birth?"

The cook looked scandalized, as if such things didn't mix well with kitchen duties. "Of course not, Mrs. O'Donnell."

Imogen wanted to stamp her foot, but she had to stay in control. Someone else was going to have to handle Mary so she could start looking for Patrick. "We'll think of something, Mary." She managed to keep her voice even, at least. "Mrs. Dougherty, could you get her settled and then call Dr. Williams and see if he can come out?"

The cook nodded jerkily and drew Mary away toward the guest bedroom. They paused when the girl gasped, then moved on.

Imogen turned back to her father, her ire barely under wraps. "What have you done to Patrick?"

"I've sworn to you, child," he said in a placating tone, "that I mean no harm to your family."

"Yes, but you didn't swear not to steal my son! I know exactly how oaths work." She couldn't keep the bitter anger out of her voice. The betrayal stung worse for the fact that she'd actually granted him some leeway. She'd wanted to believe him, wanted to believe in a father who might actually care about her. Now her palm itched with the desire to slap him.

He stepped forward, easily within reach of her hand. "Imogen, I promise you that I didn't take your son. I didn't have him taken by someone else, and I don't know who did this. I will do what I can to get the boy back to you."

"Swear it," she said between clenched teeth. He did so, solemnly, as if he wanted her to believe him. And he was bound by his words, just as she would have been. "I had better not learn that you've deceived me somehow," she added. "Because if you've done anything to my son, I swear I'll take your hide."

Three

Imogen shivered as the cold seeping in from the foyer touched her heated cheeks. Her father still waited in the sitting room under her baleful gaze. He'd sworn that he hadn't taken her son, but how far she could trust him?

Guaire had gone to the stables to see if perhaps Patrick had disappeared into some horse's stall. That would have been one of the safer possibilities. The horses all knew Patrick was a puca. They would never harm him, knowing him to be part horse himself. But people were a different matter.

"Where did the nursemaid come from?" her father asked coolly. "That girl said the nursemaid was gone, too, so I would suspect her first."

Imogen shook herself out of the fog that clouded her mind. She needed to *do* something. "Moira? I hired her from the Women's College. She had letters of recommendation."

"And how long has she worked here?"

"Just a couple of days," Imogen admitted. He was right; there must be some tie between the new nursemaid and Patrick's disappearance. She held up a hand, thinking hard. Surely it had to have been planned if the nursemaid was somehow involved. She should go into town and discover as much about the girl as she could.

She needed to search the house; she knew the nooks and crannies of it far better than Guaire did. She needed to find someone to take care of Mary. And she needed to think of who might profit from taking her son. She couldn't do all three.

The front door opened and she looked for Guaire to step inside, but instead an elderly woman in a wine-colored walking suit strode regally through the portal, her elegant nose in the air. The mother of Imogen's first husband, Victoria Hawkes-O'Donnell had a touch of fairy blood herself, along with a great deal of training and a far better grasp of the evil that people might get up to—the very person Imogen needed at the moment. Paddy O'Donnell followed her inside, dusting snow from his sloped shoulders much as Guaire had done.

Imogen ran to the door and threw her arms around the old man, so relieved to see him that she shed a few tears before controlling herself. She stepped back and, after taking Mother Hawkes' hand, told them about her son's disappearance.

Mother Hawkes regarded Imogen with narrowed eyes. "How long?"

"I don't know. Mary's gone into labor, so I didn't want to ask her a bunch of questions."

"Oh, pish-tush, girl," Mother Hawkes snapped. "She can answer between contractions. We need to know how much of a lead the kidnapper has, and she has a better chance of knowing than anyone else."

"I don't think a doctor will be able to get out here," Imogen said then. "Not in time."

"Just because you spit out that boy of yours like a watermelon seed," her mother-in-law said dismissively, "it doesn't mean little Mary Sanders will do the same. We probably have a good day or two. I'll go question her."

"What if the doctor can't come?" Imogen asked.

Mother Hawkes turned to Paddy, who'd kept a solicitous hand under Imogen's elbow the whole time. "Patrick, how many foals have we delivered between us?"

"It's not the same thing, Victoria, and you know it." Paddy rolled his eyes at Imogen. "We'll take care of young Mrs. Sanders. Now, what else needs doing?"

"I need to search the house. Guaire is out searching the stables and outbuildings." Imogen cast a glance back at the parlor then, figuring she'd best introduce her father.

But Finn was gone.

Self-control had been Eugenia Villiers Smith's mantra. She'd stressed that Imogen must always control herself or risk having her tendency to unbind things wreaking havoc. Imogen had lived by that instruction all her life, always muting her emotions, always smothering her temper. People had always believed her cold and unfeeling. She'd heard it in the whispers behind her back and in the gossip of other girls at school. It was only when Guaire came into her life that she'd learned to loosen her control and allow her feelings to show.

But now she had too much to lose. She had to keep herself under control. So Imogen searched every crevice of the house, the activity keeping her from focusing on her fear. She was all right so long as she could keep *doing*.

The occasional cries from the guest bedroom didn't seem too close together, hinting that Mary indeed had a long labor ahead of her. At least Mrs. Dougherty had reached the hospital on the telephone. Dr. Williams promised he would drive out first thing in the morning, relieving Imogen's worry on that score. Evidently the town wasn't getting nearly as much snow.

Her mother-in-law strode into the parlor where Imogen had been pacing, and rubbed her hands together briskly. "It's freezing in here. Have one of the maids lay a fire in here, for heaven's sake, Imogen."

She hadn't even considered that, and with Mrs. Dougherty short-handed no one had gotten around to it. Imogen rang the bell by the door. "What did Mary say?"

"She last saw them about two o'clock," Mother Hawkes said.

"About the time my father showed up for tea," Imogen said, resuming her pacing. Snow fell on her shoulder, and she hissed in anger, wanting to strangle her father. "He swore to me he didn't have anything to do with this."

"Girl, rein in that temper of yours, or this house is going to fall apart!" Her mother-in-law pointed at the ceiling.

Imogen glanced upward and saw fine lines crossing the plaster on the ceiling—lines that hadn't been there before. The snow on her shoulder was plaster dust. She took a calming breath, wishing suddenly for Guaire to return. He needed to hunt for Patrick as much as she did, but she still wanted him with her. They always faced things better together. She sniffled, then opened her eyes.

Beryl stood in the entryway to the parlor, regarding the failing plaster with a concerned expression. "You rang, missus?"

"I know you're all busy, Beryl, but could you find time to bring in some wood for the front parlor? And also the guest bedroom. We'll need a fire there, too, tonight. That one first, actually."

The girl nodded and swept off back in the direction of the kitchen.

"Why would he do this?" Imogen asked.

"I don't rightly know," Mother Hawkes said. "I can't imagine your husband stealing away a child, but given how your mother talked about your father, he seems to be cut of a different cloth. More like one of the Fair Folk than a puca, almost."

Guaire had said that of him as well. A tear slipped down Imogen's cheek, and she wiped it away with the back of one hand. "I thought he wanted to get to know us. I thought…"

"Now," Mother Hawkes said, "you need to keep calm, girl. There are some possibilities other than blaming your wayward father. It occurs to me that we should check whether our old friend Sebastian Wells has resurfaced in town—that driver of Hammersly's. He probably feels he has a score to settle with you. That's one possibility."

While William Hammersly had been her chief persecutor, his bag of magical tricks had been supplied by a young man out of Albany, eager to sell his wares to a gullible-but-wealthy client. The exposure of Hammersly's perfidy had led to that of Sebastian Wells also, resulting in his punishment by that branch of the Racing Association in Saratoga Springs who regulated the use of magic on their turf. Imogen had never asked what, specifically, was done to the young man, but the fact that he'd also been trampled by Guaire in horse form wouldn't leave him with any liking for either of them.

"I hadn't thought of him," Imogen admitted, feeling calmer now. "There's also the nursemaid. We don't know who she worked for."

Mother Hawkes nodded, brushing plaster dust from her silver hair. "So we need to investigate this nursemaid and find out what happened to Mr. Wells. I can head into town and do that."

"I'll get one of the hands to hitch up the buggy," Imogen said, heading toward the door.

"You'll do no such thing. Haven't you noticed, girl? We've had a few inches of snow, it's past sunset already, and there's no moon up yet. We can't go till morning."

Imogen realized that the light in the room came from lamps. The sun had set while she searched. "I can't just stand here and do nothing!"

Mother Hawkes directed Imogen out of the parlor. "I'll ring up a couple of friends in town. You go find your husband and bring him back to get some food in him. You're neither one of you any good if you can't stand."

"If it's Wells, what would he want? Wouldn't he try to contact us?"

"Let me worry about that," Mother Hawkes said, almost gently. "Now, go find that husband of yours."

And Imogen went, at the moment wanting to see Guaire more than anything else.

Guaire had searched the stable, the feed storage areas, and all the paddocks near the house. He could take horse form and cover the paddocks more quickly with eyes better suited to the dark, but without Billy to organize them, the hands were coming to him for instructions. They wanted to find Patrick, too, but the horses had to be fed, no matter what.

It took all of Guaire's patience to answer in civil tones, but he bit his tongue and set a couple of them to work while Jack and Tommy headed down to check the dower cottage and paddocks on the far end of the property.

The snow had stopped, at least, leaving a white blanket of a couple of inches that masked the earth under his feet. Guaire stopped in his office, frustrated and shaking with worry.

Imogen found him there. She came inside and slipped her hand into his, her fine eyes downcast. "Mother Hawkes says you need to get something to eat," she said in no more than a whisper.

He could hear the anguish in her voice, the self-control she held tightly about herself loosening for him. Guaire tugged her into his arms, and she sobbed against his shoulder. "We'll find him, darling," he whispered against her hair. "We'll find him."

She drew back and rubbed the heel of her hand against her cheek. "We don't know who took him, Guaire. And the snow would have long since covered any tracks. I don't even know where to start."

He felt better for having her close. She was the stronger of the two of them, the linchpin of sense and order that held the farm together. "Let's go in and eat, or the old lady will come out here and twist our ears. She's done that to me before and, saints preserve us, it hurts."

His wife let out a wet chuckle, and for a second he felt like a hero. Guaire wrapped an arm around her waist and led her back toward the house, waving the younger stable hands back to their work. When they reached the kitchen, Mrs. Dougherty had a meal of greens and fish laid out for them.

Imogen told him of Mothers Hawkes' ideas. As if to reinforce her words, he could hear that woman talking loudly into the telephone she'd had installed in the hallway. Guaire had never used the contraption himself—too much iron in the thing to make it bearable for him to touch—but he knew it could save them time. An occasional muffled cry from the front hall told him that Paddy was still occupied as well, playing midwife.

As Guaire finished the last of his greens, Mother Hawkes came into the kitchen, her narrow nose held in the air. "There you are," she said. "Thank heavens you sent for us, boy."

"*You* sent for them?" Imogen asked him, sounding surprised that he'd come up with the idea on his own.

Guaire shrugged. "I'm not smart enough to follow what Finn's up to, Ginny, and I know it. I sent a telegram, asking if they could return."

Mother Hawkes nodded sharply. "Good thing you did, too. Now, what have you found so far? Any tracks?"

Guaire tucked the last of his bread into a pocket, thinking he might find an appetite for it later. "No, and with this snow, we're not like to see anything when the sun rises, either."

The elderly woman pulled out a chair and sat, smoothing her skirt. "Well, then. I've been on the telephone, and I've good news, or bad. The girl you hired, Imogen, that Moira Kennedy? She never left her boarding house this morning. Apparently she slept the whole day away, and her landlady had trouble rousing her when she went to check on her when I called. The girl's a mite confused, but unharmed."

Imogen stared. "Was she drugged? Or perhaps… something else?"

Mother Hawkes gave her a dry look. "I suspect something else. A potion, or a spell, maybe."

Imogen caught her lower lip between her teeth.

Guaire took her hand. "Can you find out what happened to her?"

"I'm going to go up to town in the morning," Mother Hawkes said. "If there's something to be found, I'll find it. I may need to go down to Albany as well. I talked to some friends at the Racing Association, and they say that young Mr. Wells is still in Albany, but he could have hired someone."

"How could someone with ill intent have slipped past the wards you've set here?" Imogen finally asked.

Guaire had noticed the wards the first time he stepped hoof on the farm, simple charms meant to protect the house and stables. Not powerful enough to keep out one of the Fair Folk, they could still deflect harmful actions from humans. But they weren't infallible.

"Power, skill, lots of patience," Mother Hawkes answered, "any or all of them. Or perhaps there's a hole in the wards that I didn't see before Patrick and I left for Canada. However it happened, it looks like whoever passed herself off as your new nursemaid managed to fool everyone. Did you speak to her yourself today, girl?"

"Only briefly," Imogen said. "Moira came in after lunch to watch Patrick while my father and I had tea."

White brows quirked upward. "And what are you thinking, girl, letting *him* in here?"

"He's my father," Imogen said softly, sounding as if she were close to tears. "He swore to me that he didn't take Patrick, or have anyone else do it for him. He said he'll help find him."

"Hmmph." Mother Hawkes crossed her arms over her chest. "Some help he is, disappearing like he did."

Imogen nodded slowly, as if acknowledging that had taken the wind out of her. She didn't want her father to be at the bottom of this, Guaire suspected, no matter how culpable Finn appeared at the moment. "I've no reason to take his part," he said, "but I don't see any reason for Finn to take Patrick, or to lie about helping. Pucas don't steal children."

"You've always said he's more like one of the Fair Folk," Imogen said, "and they do steal children, don't they?"

"They need human followers," Mother Hawkes inserted. "So they might steal a human child, but not one like Patrick."

Guaire shifted on the hard chair. "He's Finn's descendant, though, and his presence gives Finn a stronger hold here. A tie to the human world."

Imogen's shoulders slumped. She was sick with worry, and tired.

"You need to get some sleep, Ginny," he said, "it will seem clearer in the morning."

She shook her head. "I can't sleep."

Guaire leaned closer and whispered in her ear. "Imogen Amelia Villiers Hawkes O'Donnell, go to sleep. Sleep until dawn."

After shooting him one disbelieving glance, she crumpled slowly toward him. Guaire lifted her out of her chair and into his arms as he rose. And for once, Mother Hawkes kept her sharp tongue in her mouth. She just nodded approvingly.

Imogen woke at dawn with her mind clear. She was in her own bed, warmly bundled in blankets. Guaire sat in the chair by the window, looking toward the east as if waiting for the sun's permission to rise. "Did you sleep at all?" she asked him.

"No," he said softly. He never needed as much sleep as she did.

"Have we heard anything?" she asked. "Has anyone contacted us?"

"No." He rose and came to sit on the edge of the bed. "Jack did tell me someone was out at the cottage and took one of the quilts. I'm about to head down there and start looking."

She sat up. "Did he find any tracks?"

"No." Guaire stroked the back of his hand along her cheek. "Too dark last night. Mother Hawkes wants to head into town as soon as you're ready, to find out what happened to that nursemaid."

Imogen nodded again, grateful that Mother Hawkes hadn't left without her. She needed to be out doing something.

"You're not angry with me?" Guaire asked cautiously.

She sighed. She *should* be angry with him. He'd used her true name to force her to sleep. Even half-blooded as she was, it still had power over her, and since her mother hadn't thought to give her a secret name, her legal name was her true name. Fortunately, almost no one knew of her Villiers ties, as most paperwork used the name of her supposed father, 'Smith.' "I understand," she said. "I wouldn't have been able to sleep, and I would have been far worse off this morning. I should be grateful."

"But you're not," Guaire said.

"Well, no." She pushed back the quilt to get out of bed. Guaire had, for the last three years, been the sunshine in her life—mischievous, happy, and unfailingly lacking in seriousness. He had taught her to laugh and to smile, to let slip the self-control that her mother had so thoroughly ingrained in her. She went to him and put her arms around him, and pressed her face against his neck. His arms came around her.

"I understand your reasoning," she said after a moment.

"So you'll not cast me off your land?" he asked in a solemn voice.

Imogen shook her head, amazed that he still asked that every time they disagreed. But she owned the land and he could only stay with her consent. "Never," she whispered.

"I'll go on, now, then." He kissed her and headed for the door, but turned back, a smile quirking one corner of his mouth. "And Mary didn't wait for the town doc. Paddy delivered a nice little filly a few hours past midnight. Mary screamed the house down, but she's fine now."

Imogen flushed as Guaire closed the door behind him. She'd completely forgotten about Mary Sanders. She was relieved that crisis had resolved itself, at least, but felt guilty she'd managed to sleep through it. After saying a quick prayer for Patrick's safety and a heartfelt thanks for Mary's safe delivery, she shook herself and went into the dressing room to get ready. Half an hour later she was dressed in a dark suit and bundled into a warm coat for the buggy ride into town. She pinned on one of her felt hats, and wrapped a shawl over that for warmth.

Mother Hawkes looked as if she'd had a long night, shadows darkening the fragile skin under her bright eyes, but Imogen knew the woman was far tougher than she appeared. "Now, girl," Mother Hawkes said, "We'll go to the boarding house first, and then decide what we should do from there."

Imogen flicked the reins and got the horse started down the drive toward Lake Avenue. "Should we stop and see the police? Would they be able to help?"

Mother Hawkes tucked her jacket firmly around herself on the buggy's seat. "I doubt it, Imogen. Let's keep that option open, though, should we decided something mundane is going on here."

They'd left Paddy behind at the house to wait to see if any information showed up there, so Imogen hoped they had all their bases covered. She hoped there wasn't a magical explanation at the bottom of Patrick's disappearance, but 'mundane' seemed the least likely possibility at the moment.

Four

Guaire stood behind the old cottage at the far end of the farm, wondering what he was looking at. All about the back door he saw footprints in the remaining snow. He knelt on the edge of the wooden porch to get a better view. They had to have something to do with his son's disappearance. "You've never seen prints like these before?"

Jack, a grizzled hand who'd been at the farm as long as old Paddy had, shook his head. "Nope. Not this close to the house."

Guaire glanced up at him. "Dogs?"

"No, foxes," Jack said. "Middle toes are sorta separate, see? Can't imagine why a whole pack of them would come up here. They usually stay out in the fields or by the stream."

The suspected foxes had milled about the back porch, it appeared, sometime after the snow had stopped. Careful not to disturb the tracks, Guaire stepped farther away from the porch and tried to get a better perspective. Jack pointed in the direction of the stream that ran across the edge of the property, and Guaire crunched that way, finally spotting what Jack already had.

In the early light, the fresh snow clearly showed the fox prints running in two straight lines as if the creatures had decided to proceed in file. And over all those tracks, two thick slashes cut. Guaire gazed at the odd arrangement for a while, trying to figure it out. The prints and cuts looked like something he'd seen before, he simply couldn't place what. "Could you come and look at this?"

Jack stepped carefully through the snow to join him. "I keep looking at it, Mr. Guaire. I know what I'm seeing, I just can't put a name to it."

Guaire felt relieved that he hadn't imagined that odd sense of familiarity. "So our fake nursemaid brings Patrick here to wait out the snowfall, and then does what?"

"Well, there are some very faint footprints in the snow, a few feet away," Jack pointed out. "So faint that I'm not even certain. But if I'm not imagining them, then they're too big for Patrick. Smaller than a man, though. And if they're *hers*, she was barefoot."

Barefoot? Guaire knelt in the snow next to the spot Jack pointed out. Running parallel with the odd track of the foxes he saw a faint indentation that seemed far too light to be a real footprint. It did indeed look to be a bare foot, and likely a woman's from the shape of it. It was as if the walker had stepped lightly atop the snow.

Guaire laid a hand on one of the footprints, trying to sense if any charm or spell had been used to mask the woman's prints. Nothing came to him, adding to the puzzle. If she had used a spell to look like their nursemaid, she'd dropped it at the cottage. He stood again, and saw Jack still contemplating the odd trail left by the foxes.

Jack rubbed a hand across his unshaven chin. "You know," he said in a musing voice, "I heard that up in the Yukon, they use dogs to pull sleds."

Guaire crunched back over that direction, and stared down at the tracks slack-jawed. The ruts left by a sleigh—*that* was what the wide imprints resembled. He measured the distance between the two tracks with his hands, only about a foot across. "Is a dog sled this narrow?"

Standing over him, Jack shrugged. "Don't know about that, Mr. Guaire. Just what it looks like to me."

Guaire rose. "I'm going to follow these tracks, see how far I can get. Can I leave my clothes here?"

The older hands all knew the family's secrets, so the request didn't appear to surprise Jack at all. "Want me to take them back up to the house?"

"Yes. And could you let Paddy know what you found? Tell him where I've gone?"

When Jack nodded and headed back inside, Guaire tugged off his jacket. Never as sensitive to cold as humans, he didn't really need the thing. He quickly stripped off his clothes, folding them haphazardly, until he stood naked in the snow behind the cottage. Then he gathered his will about himself, feeling the weight of a horse gathering into him, the heat and the strength of the animal.

His breath steamed in the sudden chill about him, as if he'd sucked every bit of heat from the surrounding air. He stamped a hoof to test the thin layer of ice atop the snow, and crunched through easily. In this form he caught a lingering scent, a faint odor of animal above the clean tang of the snow. And moss and earthy bodies, smells that didn't remind him of foxes at all.

Guaire trotted to the place where the tracks of the sleigh could be seen and followed them down toward the stream. In horse form he could go all day without tiring, but his eyes didn't see the same, forcing him to tilt his head this way and that to get a good view of the tracks past his muzzle.

He couldn't make out the faint impression of a female foot, either—too shallow to be obvious—so he followed the ruts left by the sleigh, down along the bank of the stream and toward the edge of their property.

At the boarding house on Caroline Street, Imogen and Mother Hawkes went upstairs to inspect the nursemaid's room. Hunting for clues, Mother Hawkes called it.

"I'm so sorry, Mrs. O'Donnell," Moira Kennedy said in a tearful voice. "I've never missed a day of work before anywhere, I promise! I must have come down sick of a sudden to sleep like that."

"Pish-tush, girl," Mother Hawkes snapped, evidently her new favorite phrase. "We're not angry with you. Just let me look about here. I need to get a sense of whether anyone tried to poison you."

Moira's eyes went wide at the mention of poison. She grabbed up a beaded rosary off her nightstand and then flattened herself against the wall to get out of Mother Hawkes' way.

Imogen waited at the doorway. The girl's small room was tidy and clean, and she didn't get any sense of anything wrong there, but Mother Hawkes was a far better judge of that sort of thing.

Mother Hawkes ran her hands along the sides of the narrow bed, searched under the pillows, drew back the blanket, and looked under the bed. Scowling, she went to the desk in the corner which apparently served as the girl's vanity table as well and inspected the personal articles there, pausing as she handled the girl's boar-bristle hair brush. She lifted the thing to her narrow nose and sniffed. After another inspection, she put it down and turned back to Moira. "Now, girl, did you dream?"

The nursemaid turned a helpless look on Imogen, who simply gestured toward Mother Hawkes. "It's all right, Moira, just answer her."

"I did, ma'am. I dreamed of running in the snow, barefoot. It was the oddest thing, 'cause I used to do that when I was a little girl. I would pretend to be Our Lady of the Snows. Made my mother fume, I did."

"Was it a bad dream?" Mother Hawkes asked. "Did you feel scared?"

The girl shook her head vehemently. "Oh, no, ma'am. It was like I was warm and safe the whole time, even if it was snowing."

The arching white brows drew together. "And do you remember anything else from your dream? Did you see anyone or anything?"

Moira appeared to think that over. "There were little dogs. Little white dogs. But that's all I remember."

"Little white dogs," Mother Hawkes repeated slowly. "Never heard of a dream like that before. Hmmph."

The girl turned back to Imogen. "I'll never miss another day, missus. I promise I wouldn't."

Imogen had been so lost to her own worry that she'd forgotten the girl must be worried for herself. Jobs weren't easy to find. "Don't fret, Moira. We know it wasn't your fault. And thank you for answering our questions."

The girl seemed relieved to be forgiven her lapse, unaware of what had happened back at the farm. "Should I come in later this afternoon, then, Mrs. O'Donnell?"

Imogen froze, uncertain what to tell her. No one in town knew yet, save certain friends of Mother Hawkes.

"Just in case you're catching, girl," Mother Hawkes interposed smoothly, "better take another day off—with pay. Just remember to keep what we discussed here to yourself, will you?"

The girl nodded, and Mother Hawkes swept Imogen from the room before she could say anything else. They headed down the steps of the boarding house and were out in the chilly air before Imogen got a chance to ask anything.

"So what did you find?" Imogen demanded as she untied the buggy's reins. She felt guilty for keeping the horse out waiting in the cold. At least the temperature had risen once the clouds faded away. The snow was melting off, although it appeared that it hadn't carpeted the town as heavily as the farm anyway.

"Nothing," Mother Hawkes said as she climbed up into the buggy. When Imogen settled next to her, she added, "And that's rather interesting."

"What do you mean?" Imogen snapped the reins to start the horse walking.

"I mean that there wasn't any obvious sign of magic in the room, or about the girl's person. None of her hair had been taken from her brush—she really needs to clean that thing more often—so I don't think anyone used that to take on her appearance. And she didn't have bad dreams, all of which suggests that whatever was done to her wasn't dark magic."

"But you think it was magic of some sort?" Imogen asked, thankful that out on Caroline Street, no one would be likely to overhear their discussion.

"No one dreams about snow and little white dogs. Not for an entire day. That's just not natural."

Imogen wasn't sure if she was joking or not. She cast a sidelong look at her mother-in-law, and decided that Mother Hawkes was simply thinking aloud. She sighed. "So what do we do now?"

"I have an idea," Mother Hawkes said, "but I will need to go on to Albany. I can check on Wells, and find out if he's behind this."

Imogen half-hoped that Hammersly's former driver *was* their culprit. The racing association had vanquished him easily. "And if it's not him?"

"Then I've a couple of friends in Albany with whom I can confer, experts on folk like your father. They can give us some guidance if it's one of them."

"But I need to stay close to home, in case Patrick shows up."

"Oh, I didn't mean you, Imogen. The buggy would take too long." Mother Hawkes set one leather-gloved knuckle under her chin. "What I need is a motor car."

"Do you even know how to drive one?" Imogen didn't, nor did Guaire, and there was no likelihood of them ever possessing such a vehicle. Too much metal.

"Do you know where I could get one?" Mother Hawkes countered.

Imogen only knew of one automobile, but she knew exactly where to find it. After William Hammersly died, his Pierce Arrow Touring Car had been stored at his estate in one of the stables. Her father unknowingly purchased the contraption along with the rest of the property. He'd complained to Imogen at tea the day before about storing the motor car. He couldn't use it either. And he wasn't certain he could sell it, because the thing was apparently heavily laden with charms or spells; since Hammersly had originally hired Sebastian Wells as his driver, it hadn't particularly surprised Imogen to learn that vehicle was charmed as well.

"My father has a motor car," she told her mother-in-law, "stored under a bunch of tarpaulins in his stables somewhere."

"Excellent," Mother Hawkes said, wrapping her scarf over her hat. "That's where we should go next."

"Well, he did promise he would help," Imogen said grimly, expecting to have to wrangle it out of him. During the drive from town, her urge to strangle him had begun to resurface.

Once they'd arrived at her father's house, Imogen waited on the porch until a young girl answered the door—apparently a kitchen maid by her dress. "Is Mr. Finnegan here?"

"No, missus," the girl said. "Mr. Finnegan left early this mornin'. Don' know when he'll be back."

Imogen heaved out a frustrated sigh. "I need to get into the stables," she told the girl. "Who's in charge down there?"

"Mr. Reid, missus." The girl wiped her hands on her apron. "Is there anythin' else you're needin'?"

Imogen shook her head and headed for the stables where Mother Hawkes already stood talking with a couple of the stable boys. The older woman knew everyone in the area—at least anyone associated with the horse trade. "He's gone," Imogen snapped.

Mother Hawkes rolled her eyes. "How like your cousin to leave when he promised we could borrow it."

Imogen kept a straight face. She'd momentarily forgotten she was passing her father off as a cousin. "Annoying of him. If Finn complains I'll remind him of his promise."

"I suppose we'll have to find that tiresome Angus Reid, then," Mother Hawkes said. "Knows his horses, but a duller young man I can't recall."

Imogen pressed her lips together. Angus Reid was probably ten years older than herself. Only Mother Hawkes would have the nerve to call him a young man, or tiresome. Privilege of age, she reckoned.

One of the stable boys, a strapping youngster with fair hair and what looked to be a twice-broken nose, shook his head. "I can show you where it is, ma'am. It's out in the old stable."

They followed the young man around the aging stable. Once they'd reached the back side of the stable where horse vans might have pulled up in the past, he opened the wide doors to show them a canvas-covered hulk. With a grin, the young man dragged off the heavy tarpaulins, revealing a shining contraption of wood and steel and rubber. Imogen stayed well back from it. The simple fact that it had belonged to Hammersly made her inclined to dislike the thing. And while the seats might be leather, too much of the rest of it was steel for her to feel comfortable around it.

Mother Hawkes had no such reservations, though. As diluted as her fairy blood was, she'd never had trouble handling iron. She walked around the motor car, running a gloved hand along the metal and wood body. She reached up to touch the seat and the wheel that steered the thing. "This is amazing. As many protective spells and charms as young Mr. Wells laid on this beauty, I expect it'll run just fine."

The stable boy's blond eyebrows rose, but he didn't dispute that claim.

"Can you drive that thing?" Imogen asked again.

Mother Hawkes hitched up her skirt and climbed—still managing to look regal as she did so—into the front seat. She surveyed the machine's levers and pedals for a second. "Of course, I can. Thankfully this one has a steering wheel instead of a tiller. I hate those things. Can you give it a crank, Winston?"

The stable boy went to the front of the vehicle, tugged on something with his right hand and began turning the crank with the left. After a moment, the car's motor chugged to life. Mother Hawkes fiddled with something near the steering wheel, and the motor roared. Imogen took a few more steps back.

"Wells might have been a greedy liar," Mother Hawkes yelled over the din, "but he loved this vehicle."

"Are you safe going alone?" It wasn't far to Albany, but Imogen had heard stories of motor cars breaking down. "Paddy won't like it."

Mother Hawkes scowled, and then gestured for the stable hand to come closer. "I'll need an escort, then. Winston, how would you like to make twenty dollars in one day? Without resorting to pugilism."

That explained the nose, then. Not too surprisingly, the young man agreed to accompany her mother-in-law; Mother Hawkes almost always got her way. Winston threw open the stable doors and Mother Hawkes directed the vehicle out at a slow, majestic roll, without even a hiccough from the roaring motor. The red wooden spokes of the wheels gleamed in the sunlight as though not a speck of dust had settled on them in the last three years. The young man closed the stable doors and climbed up in the front seat next to the elderly woman, a wide grin on his face.

"I'll let you know what I find out in Albany," Mother Hawkes yelled down at Imogen. "You get home and tell that husband of mine where I've gone. And tell him not to worry." She waved and turned the wheel, and the motor car began cruising through the stable yard, wavering at first, but then steadying and gaining speed.

Shaking her head, Imogen headed back to where her buggy waited. She only hoped Guaire would have news for her when she reached home.

Guaire followed the trail left behind in the snow, picking along the stream and down toward the tracks of the Saratoga Lake Railway. His hooves squelched in damp ground. The layer of snow had begun to melt off. The trail he followed would be gone in a few hours, he knew.

In the last hour he'd begun to find bits of fabric scattered along the way. Not torn, he decided. Only after finding more than a dozen did he understand what they were—squares and diamonds of old fabric, not ripped, but un-sewn. They were bits of the quilt the false nursemaid had stolen, the thread in them unraveled by his son's gift. Patrick was likely only doing it for amusement, but he was also leaving a clear trail for his father to follow.

As Guaire approached the railroad tracks, he caught a scent in the air that smelled odd to him—not right for foxes. He cast an eye on the rails, only a stone's throw away, and wondered if foxes pulling a sleigh could get it over them. But the question didn't matter, because the trail abruptly disappeared a few lengths short of the steel rails.

Guaire twisted his head about to peer down at the trail. Even in the slushy snow that was left, he couldn't make out what had happened. He turned about to look at it with his other eye, but didn't get any better picture. Frustrated, he cantered a short distance away and let go of horse form.

The change let loose a hot wind in all directions. The snow at his feet melted away. He would be quite warm for a while, so he padded back over on bare human feet to look at the trail with human eyes.

The tracks ended abruptly, almost as if the sleigh and the creatures that drew it had flown up into the air or sunk under the earth. Or as if they had walked through a portal into the fairy realm, gone between one stride and the next. Guaire knelt in the snow on one bare knee and snatched up a diamond of sodden pink cotton that had been abandoned next to the tracks.

Only a true fairy could open a portal into Faery; one of the Lesser Folk shouldn't have had the power to do so. Guaire puzzled at that realization. None of the Fair Folk had any cause to act against him or Imogen, so Finn must be the at the heart of this after all, the theft of his grandson intended as punishment… or blackmail. And even as Guaire thought that, he heard a whicker behind him.

Guaire rose to face Finn, his sudden anger making him want to pull things apart, only he hadn't a stitch of clothing or a single piece of tack on him.

Neither did his nemesis. In horse form, Finn was a magnificent crea-ture, a liver chestnut with ivory-pale mane and tail. And while Guaire made a smallish horse, barely fifteen hands, Finn was much larger, well over seventeen.

"This is your fault," Guaire yelled at Imogen's father. "Who have you called down on us?"

Finn stamped one hoof on the slushy ground. "Go home," he rumbled in a deep voice.

Guaire stepped closer to the stallion. "Who took my son?"

Finn tossed his pale mane and stepped delicately closer. "Go home."

Guaire wouldn't back down. Finn could hurt him badly in this form, but he wasn't going to simply walk away. "Who took my son?"

Finn just shook his mane again.

Guaire heard an odd sound then, halfway between the chirping of a bird and the bark of a dog. Huddled amidst some stones half-covered by snow, he spotted a bundle of white fur with narrow black eyes and a dark spot of a nose. The creature stood and shook itself, revealing that it was, indeed, a fox, only all in white. It regarded him with its tiny ears pricked forward, as if waiting.

For a second, none of them moved.

Then the white fox chirped at them once more and began trotting toward the spot where the tracks disappeared. Finn spun back on his hindquarters as if preparing to give chase, and Guaire heard him say, "Trot home to your wife. Guaire Michael O'Donnell, trot home."

The change came over him suddenly, Finn's command forcing him into horse form in order to *trot*. And even as he tried to fight it, circling this way and that on hooves in the ruined snow, Guaire saw the other stallion follow the fox into a white hole in the fabric of the air and earth. And then they both were gone.

Five

Imogen sat in her office, trying to keep herself calm. She wasn't certain how long it would take Mother Hawkes to drive the motor car to Albany, much less to find whoever she was hunting. She wanted her son back, *now*.

Jack had come up to the farmhouse to tell them about Guaire's plan to follow some odd tracks. His report that the fake nursemaid had waited out the snow at the cottage while they'd all been frantically searching the house stung. And the news that the woman had apparently walked away from the cottage barefooted in the snow worried Imogen. There weren't too many explanations for behavior like that, other than insanity. Jack's story of foxes pulling a sleigh made Imogen wonder if madness was catching.

She chewed on her lower lip. Paddy came and sat with her after a time, looking tired from his night's work. She had him to thank for the safe delivery of Mary's daughter, yet another thing in the long list of things that he'd done for her.

He patted her knee and said, "Everything that can be done is being done. We'll find your son."

"I shouldn't have let Finn come here," she said. "Mother Hawkes didn't say so, but she doesn't think that human magic was involved. That leaves my father. If I hadn't let him come into my house, Patrick would still be here."

Paddy sat back in his chair. "Why did you let him in?"

"Well, he was already in the house before I found out who he was," Imogen waffled.

"I mean the second time. Why let him into your home? Into your life?"

"I know that I'm fortunate," she admitted. "You and Mother Hawkes are better parents to me than my own ever were, and all the people who live on the farm—the Sanders, and Mrs. Dougherty and Jack and Tommy—we're like a bigger family. We take care of each other. But somewhere in the back of my mind, no matter how many bad things my mother said of him, I always wanted my father to care about me."

Paddy nodded. "Are you thinking, then, that he's responsible?"

"He has to be. He swore to me that he didn't do it, but he must have been able to twist his words around to escape the oath." Paddy understood that concept—he'd been around her entire life and had seen her struggle with oaths and promises before.

"Exactly what did he swear?" Paddy asked.

Imogen closed her eyes and thought back on her father's oath. "He said he didn't do it, that he didn't have someone do it for him, and that he didn't know who did it."

"Sounds like he didn't do it, then," Paddy said with a shrug.

Imogen shook her head. "No, there's some way he got out of a proper oath. He left as soon as my back was turned so I couldn't ask him anything else."

After a moment of cogitation, Paddy said, "Of course, he might not *know* who did it, but I wonder now if he had a good idea, and didn't say that."

Imogen regarded the polished surface of the table. Her father could consider the word 'know' an absolute, and therefore have escaped giving her the truth. She closed her eyes and wished that she had answers.

The telephone rang in the hallway, and Imogen followed Paddy out there. He plucked the earpiece off its hook, and after a moment of wrangling with the exchange operator, he finally seemed to be talking to his wife. Shaking his head, he yelled into the receiver. "We don't need one."

Imogen threw a quizzical look at him.

He covered the mouthpiece with his hand and said, "She wants to buy that motor car from your father."

Imogen rolled her eyes. "What did she find out?"

"What did you find out?" he shouted into the mouthpiece. His head nodded as he listened. "Let me tell her." He turned back to Imogen and said, "She's pretty sure Wells isn't involved, because he's still peddling the same type of wares he was three years ago. She doesn't think he could manage anything as clean as what was used on that girl."

Imogen sighed and brushed a loose strand of pale hair back from her eyes. "I suppose I'm not surprised."

Paddy turned back to the telephone with a whistle, and then listened for a while longer. "No, we haven't found out anything else here. Now come on home, or Angus Reid is going to fire that boy you connived into going with you."

Imogen drifted back to her office. She sat on the arm of the sofa and chewed on a nail for a moment, trying to decide what she should do now. She'd only been there a moment when Beryl appeared at the doorway, nervously twisting her apron. "Um, missus?"

Imogen glanced up. "Yes, Beryl?"

"There's a horse tryin' to get into the kitchen, like. Honest, missus."

Imogen dashed toward the back of the house. Through the small pane of glass in the kitchen door she glimpsed a horse trotting in a tight circle outside—a chestnut stallion with compact lines and a dark mane.

It was Guaire, for some reason unable to get out of horse form. "Beryl, go get me a blanket," she called back as she opened the door and jogged down the stairs.

Guaire's sides were lathered, something he rarely did to himself. When she reached the bottom of the steps, he came to her and laid his muzzle against his chest. "What happened to you?" she asked.

He shuddered, but didn't change back into his normal form. Imogen glanced back and saw that Beryl stood at the top of the stairs, a quilt clutched in her arms and her eyes worried. At Imogen's gesture, she handed over the quilt and went back inside.

Guaire backed up a few steps as Imogen unfolded the quilt. Then he changed, the customary wave of hot air flowing out all around him, a strange side effect that Imogen never had understood. His body steamed in the chilly air.

She wrapped the quilt about him, more to protect their employee's modesty than his—Guaire didn't have any. "Did you find anything?"

He nodded, looking grim. "Let's go inside."

Once Guaire had gotten himself dressed, Paddy joined him and Imogen in the office so that Guaire wouldn't have to repeat his story.

"White foxes?" Imogen repeated when Guaire told her of the creature her father had followed. "Foxes aren't white."

"Up in the far north parts of Canada," Paddy inserted, "there are white ones in the winter."

"This isn't the far north," Imogen said irritably. "And it isn't winter. It's September."

Guaire shook his head. "They weren't foxes in the first place, Ginny, so if they wanted to be pink or green, they could."

Her lips pressed together. "What were they, then?"

"Hobs, I think. They smelled more like hobgoblins."

Her shoulders slumped, and she laid one hand over her mouth. Paddy scowled and settled back in his chair.

"One of them was waiting for Finn," Guaire added. "It led him through to the other side. That's when he sent me packing."

"Sent you packing?" Imogen rose, her dark eyes alight with anger. "He used your true name on you? After all these years I can't believe he remembers it!"

It had been thirteen years since her father had used Guaire's true name to force his compliance while a human farrier put iron shoes on his hooves. Finn hadn't resorted to *that* name this time.

"He must have gotten a hold of our marriage lines," Guaire said with a shrug. "The name on that piece of paper has the same effect."

"But you have a true name, Guaire," she protested. "He has to use *that* one."

"No, he doesn't." He took one of her hands. "And I don't think he's forgotten my true name. He was testing me, don't you see? If the name on our marriage lines isn't as valid as my true name, then our wedding vows don't mean anything. So he used that to see if it bound me the same."

She laid her forehead against his, and for a moment simply let him hold her. He suspected she was trying to calm herself to keep from tearing things apart. Her father was in for a rough greeting the next time she laid eyes on him. "I wish I understood why he's doing this to us," she whispered.

Guaire held her away far enough that he could look into her eyes. "I don't think he's doing it to us. I think he's trying to help."

Paddy snorted.

Imogen shook her head. "Who, then?"

"I don't know. But I had a lot of time to think about it while I was trotting back here. Whoever she was, she wanted to be followed. She waited until after the snow had stopped so she would leave tracks. Patrick was unraveling the quilt along the way and left bits in the snow; she didn't stop that. And she left one of her creatures behind to make certain."

Imogen's eyes narrowed and her lips pressed together. Guaire could almost see the wheels of her clever mind turning. "And my father went through to the other side instead of you?"

"I think your father was meant to do the following," he said. "I don't know that I could go through. I've never been on the other side."

Some creatures of fairy blood lived their whole lives in the human world, happy to be away from the pretenses and faded glories of the fairy courts. Being part human, Guaire had never considered visiting. He would be seen as inferior there. Nor did he know of any way to open a portal, or even access one created by another.

Imogen frowned. "So Patrick is merely bait to draw out my father?"

"That did occur to me."

"Will Patrick be safe then, if my father went?"

Guaire wanted to tell her that Patrick would be fine. He wanted her not to worry any longer, to hear her laugh. But he always told her the truth. "If your father is being baited by a fairy, then there's no knowing what that creature might do."

"Bread." Paddy's voice startled him. The old man rose and headed for the door. "After talking to her friends in Albany, that's the only suggestion Victoria had," he said. "I'll ask Mrs. Dougherty to start baking some."

Imogen paced the office floor. She'd visited with Mary in the guest bedroom, and taken a turn holding tiny Elizabeth Sanders. She'd read the race results out of Sheepshead Bay again. She'd tidied all her paperwork and straightened the clothes in her dressing room. Mother Hawkes hadn't returned yet, and Paddy had gone to set the stable boys to work while Guaire returned to that spot near the tracks to see if he could figure out anything more.

They had all left her alone to fret and, fearing for the structure of the house, she couldn't even do that properly. There was nothing she could do but wait. She had to wait and hope that her father would somehow retrieve her son—a father she'd never really known or had any reason to trust.

Other than his promise; he'd said he would help.

Trust was not one of her virtues. All her life, her mother had trained her to trust no one. It had been hard for her to trust Guaire at first. She wasn't certain she could extend that to include her father. So she paced the office, counting the steps to keep herself calm.

"Ginny!" Guaire's voice split the quiet in the house, and she ran for the front parlor, hoping he'd found Patrick.

Instead, he supported Finn in his arms. A livid burn crossed her father's face at an angle, the width of her hand. The skin had blistered and reddened, and one eye had swollen shut. On that side his eyebrow had burned away. She ran to his side and helped Guaire settle him on the couch. The hunched way her father sat suggested that he had other injuries, more painful ones.

"What happened?" she asked.

"I found him on the railroad tracks," Guaire said softly. "On the rail. I had to drag him off by one foot."

Imogen looked down at her father in horror. That wide, reddened stripe across his face was a burn left behind by contact with the steel rail. In dragging him off of it, Guaire would have exposed the rest of her father's body to the steel, which meant burns everywhere.

"It'll heal," her father said through clenched teeth.

"What about Patrick?" she asked. "Where is he?"

"On the other side," Finn managed.

She set her hands on her hips. "And how do I get him back?"

He looked up at her with his one good eye. "You can't go there."

"I will," she said. "We'll find a way."

"She won't negotiate with you," Finn said. "I'll go back. I just need to rest a bit."

Guaire folded his arms over his chest. "How did you get through to the other side in the first place?"

"Who is she?" Imogen demanded.

Her father sagged back against the sofa, as if too weary to stay awake. "Snow," he said in a worn voice, and closed his good eye. "Snow."

"Yes, I know there's snow," Imogen snapped. "Who has my son?"

She felt Guaire's hand wrap around her elbow. He drew her out into the hallway, and said softly, "I think he answered you, Ginny."

"What do you mean?"

"One of *them*—the Lady of the Snow. He must mean her."

She stepped back. "Do you know her?"

He shook his head. "No, of course not. One of them wouldn't have anything to do with the likes of me. She must have found a way to make a foothold on this side of the ocean, something named for her or someone setting up a shrine for her."

"Something named for her?" Imogen tried to imagine why anyone would name something for a fairy, and then decided that it didn't matter. "So will she give me Patrick back?"

"Ginny, we have no way to get to her. She traveled through Faery. I can't even begin to guess where she might actually be, other than on this side of the ocean."

Imogen turned back to consider her father's slumped form. He looked unconscious. The burn across his face seemed less red, though, which made her wonder how quickly he would heal. "I'll bet *he* can."

She headed into the parlor to shake him back to wakefulness, but Guaire stopped her with a gentle hand. "Not yet, Ginny," he said, "We need his cooperation. Go back to your office and wait for me. I have an idea."

"You want me to do what?" Paddy asked.

Guaire puffed out his cheeks. He'd known the idea would be unpalatable to the old man. "And you have to mean it," he added. "It's the only thing that will work. Otherwise it'll be hours or even days before he's ready to travel again, weak as he is."

Imogen's father might be looking better, but his continued somnolence suggested that the exposure to iron had eaten away his strength. Even if he could walk to the spot out in the snow where Guaire had found him, Finn surely didn't have the strength to access a fairy portal now.

Paddy crossed his arms over his chest, scowled down at his boots for a moment, and then marched off toward the kitchens. Guaire let loose the breath he'd been holding. He could offer sustenance to Finn himself, but he doubted it would do any good. It had to come from *human* hands—like Paddy's.

Paddy returned with a torn-off hunk of bread in his hand. The warm scent rising from it reminded Guaire that his own stomach was empty, and he hoped Mrs. Dougherty had made more than one loaf. They were going to need them.

"Let's get this over with," Paddy said in a gruff voice. "Is there something magic I'm supposed to say?"

Guaire shook his head. "No. Just offer it to him."

Paddy shook his head again, but marched into the front parlor, where Imogen's father had roused somewhat. Finn sat with his head back against the sofa and his eyes closed. Not too gently, Paddy tapped his foot against Finn's to get his attention. Finn's dark eye opened—the other still appeared to be swollen closed—and fixed immediately on the bread in Paddy's hand.

"An offering," Paddy said simply, and handed over the piece of bread.

Finn took the bread and tore off a piece. Before eating it, he glanced up at Paddy's face. "Thank you."

"Help find my grandson. That'll be thanks enough," Paddy said, and stalked out of the room. He stopped in the hallway where Guaire waited. "How long?"

"Give him a bit." Guaire cast a careful look inside the parlor, up at the lines of cracks in the plaster. Imogen had done that, he'd heard, a rare lack of control from her. He turned his eyes back on her father, chewing a second piece of the bread now. "You're not a puca at all, are you?"

"Come now, boy," Finn said. "You should know better."

The swelling around his eye had receded, Guaire noted. "Our kind doesn't respond to offerings of food, other than in kindness."

Finn opened that second eye and wiped at the crusted corner with the back of one hand. He tore off another piece of the bread and chewed thoughtfully.

After a moment of silence, Guaire left him alone in the parlor, reckoning Finn's strength still faded enough to keep him from leaving. He headed back to the office where he found Imogen pacing, cradling one of Patrick's wooden blocks in her palms.

She came to him and grabbed his hand. "What happened?"

"Your father accepted an offering of bread from Paddy," he said. "His strength is coming back."

Imogen licked her lips, clearly picking up what he'd not said. "Only real fairies do that."

"He has to be part 'real' fairy then, Ginny, else he wouldn't gain strength from it. Which means you are, too... and Patrick." It would explain a great deal about Finn, especially why his behavior seemed more like that of one of the Fair Folk than a puca. "Blood forges ties between this world and theirs. Children with human blood are like anchors, giving a fairy a hold here once they're acknowledged. Whatever she wants of him, she knew that you and Patrick would be leverage against him."

"So what does she want? Could he have stolen from her? Cheated her?"

"I don't know," he admitted. "And I don't think he's going to tell me."

Her lips pressed together. "It doesn't matter. As soon as he's able, I want to go after Patrick."

"He won't take you with him, Ginny. I'll go."

Her eyes blazed. "Oh, he'll take me."

Mother Hawkes would be proud of her daughter-in-law at that moment, Guaire reckoned, for such a demonstration of willfulness. "Then he'll take us both."

"No," her father said. "There's no point in your falling into her hands as well."

Imogen felt surprisingly calm and collected at the moment. She crossed her arms over her chest. "I'm going with you. He's my son, and if I have to cut out some fairy's heart to get him back, I will."

Her father's single brow rose. The one that had burned away hadn't grown back yet, despite the fact that the burns across his face had faded, little more than a sunburn now. "You would do that?"

"For my son, yes." In truth, Imogen doubted she could do anything of the kind. With fairies, though, posturing was almost as good as action. Guaire held his tongue throughout, letting her take the lead.

Finn nodded approvingly. "You do have a backbone after all, child. Perhaps you *can* face her down."

"What do you owe her?" she asked. "Why does she want you to come to her?"

"I owe her no more than you owe me," her father said. "As for why she wants me to come to her, I cannot know the motivations of another."

He'd answered, when he strictly didn't have to—a gift to her, of sorts. But his answer didn't make sense. Imogen took a deep breath to calm herself. "I want to go now."

Guaire had remained silent until then. "Can we get back through that portal?"

Her father's eyes flicked toward Guaire. "You, as well?"

"He comes along, too," Imogen said. Whatever had to be done, she and Guaire would handle it best together. "No argument, Father."

"You've never called me that before," Finn said, fixing her with an odd expression.

Imogen didn't know how to respond, uncertain what her slip of the tongue revealed. She only hoped it wasn't too much. "May we go now?"

His head inclined. "After you."

Imogen lifted the bag that Mrs. Dougherty had loaned her, which held two more towel-wrapped loaves of bread. There had been enough left from the first for Guaire to get something to eat, but her nerves had been too jangled for her to stomach it.

Guaire stepped behind her and leaned close to whisper in her ear, "Well done."

Imogen waited atop Guaire's back near the railroad tracks. She'd hastily crammed his clothing into the bag along with the bread. Last bits of snow lingered about the rocks. The sun had started its downward trek, casting long shadows. The rails stood out in relief against the old wooden ties.

It was the first time she'd seen her father's horse form, his pale hair translating into a creamy mane, striking against his chestnut coat. She watched him with a troubled eye, not entirely certain he would do as he'd implied. He hadn't actually made a bargain with her, which left her dependent on his goodwill.

A sharp yip caught her ears, and she saw a fox jump up onto one of the stones near the tracks. It was white, exactly as Guaire described—the white dog of Moira's dreams. It let out a long string of yips which sounded oddly accusing to Imogen's ears.

"I will follow." Her father's voice, deep and sonorous in this form, startled her. It didn't come from his muzzle—not possible in horse form at all—but from somewhere within.

The fox turned about on the rock and leapt off. It darted toward an open area in front of the tracks and then disappeared. Guaire raced after it, faster than her father. Imogen dug her fingers into his mane, and the world changed between one step and the next.

Six

Guaire's breath steamed as he picked his way though rows of snow-capped tombstones. An early snow had hit this place as well, more heavily than at the farm.

They hadn't asked enough questions, Imogen thought, or not the right ones. She shivered and tugged her field jacket tighter about her neck, grateful it wasn't full dark yet. Guaire stopped and she slid from his back. "Where are we, do you think? And where is my father?"

He tossed his mane, which she took to mean that he didn't know. She laid one hand on his withers and looked around, trying to figure out where they had ended up. A wooded mount rose behind them, with graves laid out in tight lines in its shadow. Red oaks and maples grew on the mountainside, not the sort of trees they would find around Saratoga Springs. She inspected the expensive stones about them, crosses and obelisks each with a cap of snow. "LeClaire, Monette," she read aloud. "Papineau. They're French names. Could we be in France?"

Guaire snorted.

This seemed like a place in their world, not any fairy realm. A black squirrel climbed up on a dark stone nearby, its bushy tail fluffed out. Imogen regarded it cautiously, thinking that it might be another of their adversary's minions, but when she moved toward it the creature dashed away up a tree. Likely a real squirrel after all.

"Are we really in this place or not?" she asked.

Guaire walked a distance away from her and changed, a hot wind heralding his return to human form. The snow on the ground about him melted for several feet in all directions. Imogen dusted off a tombstone with one gloved hand and set her bag atop it to draw out his clothes. Guaire wouldn't feel the cold for some time, but she would feel better if he weren't naked in this strange place.

"Look over there." He pointed toward a spot near the crest of the mountain's slope.

Imogen turned to survey it while he drew on his trousers. A small cluster of buildings had been constructed near the high point of the mountain. Overlooking the countryside, a cross marked the apex of a chapel. No bell-tower, though; fairies hated the sound of church bells, if she recalled correctly. "If this is a graveyard, then this must be consecrated ground. Fairies can't live on consecrated ground, can they?"

Still shirtless, Guaire ran a hand through his dark hair. "Well, it must be named for her. That would make it her territory."

"You mean the graveyard is named for her?" She looked about, but didn't see anything that would tell her the cemetery's name.

"I'll bet this is one of those Catholic graveyards," he said with a shrug. "There are old churches and such named for her—the Lady of the Snow. She can claim those."

Imogen tried to recall why that sounded familiar. "You mean *Our Lady of the Snows?* That's another name for the Virgin Mary, Guaire, not some fairy."

"She's old, Ginny," he said as he buttoned his shirt. "She had that name long before your Virgin Mary did. Think about it. Do you think the Virgin Mary ever even saw snow, living in Palestine as she did?"

Imogen couldn't argue with his logic. "So even though the church named the place after the Virgin Mary, the fairy can still claim it because… she had the name first?"

"Names are important." He drew on his jacket. "Every time someone uses that name, the Lady can draw on it—sort of the way an auction house gets a percent of the money from a yearling sale."

She shot him a guarded look, not sure if he'd slipped into blasphemy there. "So they're inadvertently… feeding her?"

He nodded. "She can draw strength from their prayers, I suppose, and use it to gain footholds in the human world."

"Like *this* place," Imogen said, looking about the chilly landscape. She hoped her son was warmer than she was.

"Until they build a bell tower," Guaire added, with a nod toward the chapel on the hill. "Then it won't be so welcoming for her. She'll have to find another foothold."

If her father could use Patrick as an anchor to the human world, Imogen wondered what the fairy could claim once evicted from this cemetery by the sound of church bells. She brushed snow off another French-inscribed headstone. "Do you think this might be Quebec? They speak French there, don't they?"

Guaire cast a blank look at her, which told her he was the wrong person to answer that question. They didn't race their horses in Canada, so he had no reason to take an interest in that country.

"Do you have any idea where my father is?" she asked then.

He took her hand. "I suspect our guide took him through, and dumped us in the human equivalent of their location. So now we need to beg for help."

She could feel the warmth of his fingers, even through her glove. "What do you have in mind?"

"Bread?" He shrugged. "Could be just more squirrels out here, though."

"Well, they need to eat, too." She dug in the sack and pulled out one of the loaves. "Where should we put it?"

Guaire regarded the torn chunks of bread Imogen had piled on one of the tombstones. The light was almost gone. Soon they wouldn't be able to see much of anything, and the wind carried the scent of more snow on the way.

"What if they aren't here?" Imogen asked, worry leaking into her voice. "What if we're alone? How do we get home?"

He shook his head. Usually she was the strong one, but this all had to be far outside her experience, and doubly frightening. "They're here, Ginny. I smell them. Hobs, I think. They're watching us."

"Are they dangerous? Would they hurt Patrick?"

He shot a glance at her under his brow. "I think not. He's bait, so there's no profit in hurting him."

She wrapped her arms about herself and pressed her lips together. A black squirrel climbed up onto the stone where the bread lay and picked up a chunk in its paws. It chittered at them, sounding not too different from the fox they'd seen earlier.

Guaire took a careful sniff and caught that earthy scent that spoke of hobgoblin. "We need to speak with her. We need to go to the other side."

The squirrel tossed the chunk of bread at them, a supremely un-squirrel-like action.

"Please," Imogen begged. "Please, I must find my son."

A wave of cold swept over them as the sun set, sharp enough that even Guaire could feel it. He moved to draw Imogen into his arms, but paused when he heard familiar childish laughter. Imogen turned and ran toward the sound, her feet sure in the snow. Guaire followed. Even if it was a trap, they had little choice.

He saw the Lady then, a tall slender creature standing at the place where two of the snow-garbed paths crossed. On her hip she carried a child. Wrapped in a tattered quilt, Patrick seemed unaware of any danger, but laughed and waved at them, his dark hair as wild as ever, despite the fairy's gentle attempt to straighten it with long, delicate fingers.

Her hair was white and wild—not the smooth cream of Imogen's hair, but the icy white of frost. Her skin had a similar pallor, only enough color in it to show that some blood flowed within. She stood barefooted in the snow, her garments like a fall of silken rags in shades of mossy green, but laced close about her waist. She was beautiful in a way that spoke of cold and remote places.

One of the old ones and still powerful, she had no real use for them, Guaire knew. The Lady of the Snow needed no fairy court to adore her; she held enough borrowed power not to require anyone's supplication, but seeing Imogen and the Lady together, he suspected he knew now what the Lady wanted from her. They were startlingly alike.

Imogen had stopped in her tracks as if a wall prevented her from going closer, only a couple of feet from Patrick's outstretched hands.

"Mama," Patrick cried merrily.

"Hush," the fairy said, her voice like the fall of dry snow.

Patrick fell silent. Guaire bit his tongue and stopped a few feet farther back.

"My son," Imogen said, reaching toward Patrick. "What do you want in return for my son?"

"Imogen!" Finn's voice thundered through the twilight. "Don't bargain with her."

Imogen glanced back. Guaire heard hooves nearby, careful steps plodding through the snow. He could smell Finn approaching from behind, still in horse form, but he didn't take his eyes off the Lady, certain she was more dangerous.

"This is unfair," Finn said.

"Hot-tempered father of an impetuous child," the Lady said. "She has already offered. There is nothing now to do save make a deal." Her fingers stroked through Patrick's hair again, a gesture Guaire had seen Imogen make a thousand times.

"I gave you my word." Finn followed that with angry stamp, a thump on the snow covered pathway. "You have what you want. Don't trifle with my daughter."

"She wanted to talk with me," the fairy said. "I heard her say so."

Guaire stepped to her side, drew her back and inserted himself between them. "Lady, deal with me in her stead."

He felt Imogen's fingers knotting into the back of his jacket. "No," she hissed.

But he had the Lady's attention now. She surveyed him with dark eyes, startling in so pale a visage. "You are the rarest creature," she said. "A puca with a constant heart."

Not knowing how to react to that statement, Guaire gazed down at his son instead. Patrick scowled mightily, a mulish expression, irritation at being restrained rather than true anger. A square of fabric floated to the snow, a pale bit of blue floral cotton, and then another.

"Yes, he would escape me eventually," the Lady said, stroking Patrick's hair. "One can't hold a puca against his will, I learned long ago. Not without their true name." She glanced up at Guaire. "I've watched over you for years, young one."

She definitely meant *him*, Guaire decided. "What do you mean?"

"A question for a question?"

Foolishness all his own, blurting out a question like that. It implied he was willing to bargain. He took a deep breath. "Yes."

"Then tell me." She pointed behind him with her chin—at Finn. "Why did you help Imogen's mother leave him?"

That query surprised him. It must be the one thing the Lady couldn't know—his reason for helping Eugenia Villiers escape Finn's grasp so long ago. "He took up with another woman, and she felt betrayed. She begged for my help to return to her family. She'd lost her love for him, she said."

The fairy's pale head tilted. "Do humans lose love? Misplaced like a necklace left behind, tangled among rumpled bedclothes?"

A rhetorical question, that one, and not part of their bargain. More squares of cotton dropped from the quilt to the snow. Guaire felt Imogen's shuddering breaths against the back of his neck. She was right to be afraid, for this creature was far more powerful than anything she'd met before, and colder.

The Lady shifted Patrick on her hip. "You were punished for your compassion. It is, I suspect, a trait from your human side. The puca are not known for that, either." Her dark eyes flicked up to meet his, startling in the suddenness of the movement. "I wonder what you would give to get your wife and son back home."

She hadn't asked a direct question, once again not part of the bargain. Guaire pressed his lips together. He should not have provoked her. He wasn't clever enough to outsmart her kind.

"You dealt with me," Finn said. "Let them go."

The corner of her pale lips lifted. "Do not think to order me, child."

Guaire wondered how many people had dared to call Finn 'child' in the past. But then, the Lady had the right—he was certain of it now. "You said, Lady, that you've watched over me. What did you mean?"

Her head tilted. "I do not hold you to blame for separating them. Finn was the one who betrayed her, and she would have found a way to leave him, whether you helped her or not. Death would have been an unjust reward for your actions, I think. So once he trapped you in horse form, I watched over you. If your life had been threatened, I would have intervened."

Imogen stepped from behind him before he could stop her. "You knew what my father did to Guaire? And you allowed him to be tortured like that?"

The Lady turned her eyes on Imogen, her expression curious rather than offended.

Imogen made up for the Lady's coldness with fury. "He spent ten years with iron shoes nailed to his feet. He was crippled with pain and he still had to run. Why did you do nothing then? They shipped him across the ocean in the metal hold of an ocean liner, the bars of his stall iron, the floor under his hooves steel. He could barely stand when I first laid eyes on him. And you could have done something?"

Guaire took Imogen's hand. "Why should she have?"

Imogen fixed him with a frustrated look.

The Lady stroked Patrick's hair. "True, the journey across the ocean must have been unpleasant. But tell me, young one," she asked, glancing up at Guaire again, "what did you gain of all your trials?"

Guaire didn't owe her an answer, but if she'd truly watched over him all those years, he thought he should try to be civil. "If I hadn't come across the ocean, if I hadn't been trapped so, I wouldn't have my wife and my son. I thought Fate brought me to that farm. Now I wonder if it was you."

The fairy inclined her head, as if acknowledging that. "Finn is too much like his father—too hot-tempered, a trait I see my granddaughter has inherited also." Imogen gasped, apparently just then grasping that the Lady of the Snow was Finn's mother. The fairy reached out one white hand to touch her cheek. "Would you really have cut out my heart, Imogen?"

Guaire leaned closer to whisper, "You don't owe her an answer, Ginny."

The Lady turned her dark gaze on Guaire. "I have answered your question, and you mine. The rest of this is not your concern."

She flicked her slender hand in his direction, and Guaire felt himself falling. He landed on loamy, damp earth, only a hand's span from the railroad ties. He could feel the steel through the air and, alarmed, rolled away from it without getting up. Then he took several deep breaths to calm jangled nerves. No moon had risen yet, plunging the countryside into blackness, but somewhere nearby he heard the chittering of the hobgoblins. It was no doubt their joke to set the portal so near the railroad tracks.

She'd finished with him, the Lady of the Snow, and sent him on his way like a truant child. As she would likely do with Imogen in a few minutes—or twenty years.

Imogen felt cold with Guaire's absence. The Lady's casual gesture—her *grandmother's* casual gesture, she amended in her mind—demonstrated far more power than she'd ever seen before. "Where did you send him?"

"A question for a question?" the fairy asked. The snowy ground about her bare feet was littered with dozens of pieces unraveled from the quilt.

Imogen suspected she already owed a dozen answers, and wished she'd remained calm enough to keep track of what she'd said. "Yes."

"Tell me, Imogen of the shaking hands, what do you think of this father of yours now that you've met him?"

The bargain bound her into telling the truth. Imogen licked her chilly lips. "I'm not certain I can trust him, but he's not as bad as my mother led me to believe." She heard a hoof thud down in the snow behind her. "Yes, he betrayed her, but he'd never made her any vows. She should have known better than to expect more."

Patrick wriggled one arm out of the quilt and stretched it out toward her. Imogen reached a hand toward his, but couldn't seem to touch his fingers.

"I sent your husband back to the place where you entered the portal," the Lady said. "That was not an enthusiastic endorsement. Your father may want to stay in your world, but it's time for him to come home."

Imogen closed her eyes and mentally pictured the quilt that captured Patrick's arms loosening enough that she could reach his hand. Then felt his warm fingers touching hers.

The fairy sighed, shifted Patrick in her arms, and kissed his forehead. She held him out to Imogen. "I lack the enthusiasm to fight both of you at once."

Imogen grabbed Patrick and held him close. It was a step in the right direction, but not the same as having him safe home. He threw his arms about her neck. "Mama, puppies!"

She shook her head. "No puppies."

"Puppies," Patrick insisted.

"Hush, child," the Lady said again, and Patrick fell silent. "We've been having that same fascinating conversation for an entire day. He has to be the most stubborn creature ever born."

Imogen dared to look up at her, surprised by the almost-maternal affection in those words. "He is, I think."

"He will take a human wife one day," the fairy said. "As will his children, until no one remembers the likes of me. Even this little one, his world will be circumscribed. Too many things he cannot do and too many places he cannot go. Too much iron. Your world has no place for us any longer."

Imogen carefully chose her words so they weren't a question. "I wonder if that's why you want my father to leave it."

"Imogen," she heard him say, a warning tone.

"It is time for him to take a wife," the fairy said. "I gave him twice a hundred years to live in the human world. In all that time you were his only child, and he managed to alienate your mother and thereby lose you. So Finn will stay here where I can oversee him, take a proper mate, and honor his vows."

"That's…" Imogen stopped herself, and reframed her reply. "If he does so, I will never see him again."

"True," the fairy said. "But I wonder why you care. You believed he'd conspired to take your son. You hold anger against him for what he did to your husband. I would expect you to be pleased to be quit of this side of your family."

The Lady had included herself in that, Imogen noted, and recalled Guaire's claim that blood gave the Fair Folk ties into the human world, once acknowledged. For a moment silence reigned, broken only by an occasional grunt from a frustrated Patrick. "I've barely begun to know my father. Yes, I feel anger for what he did to Guaire, but I'm trying to understand. I never will if you force him to leave me."

"You cannot live here, child," the Lady said. "You are too human. For you to know him better, he would have to live in your world."

Imogen could hear her father snort, and suspected he resented their bargaining with his fate. She had no real power over the Lady, though, so it was little more than a charade. It would, however, shape the remainder of his life. "I would prefer that he stay near me."

"What would you offer me to allow him such a choice?" the Lady asked, a real question this time.

Imogen pressed her lips together. This was what it had come to—making a bargain that would allow her father to stay in the human world. And she had nothing to bargain with, save herself, which might have been the fairy's design all along. "I am only half human," she said, "but if you will accept it, I will offer you bread as long as I live."

The Lady regarded her with raised brows. "That would give me a doorway into your world."

Patrick wriggled, evidently working his way loose from the Lady's spell again.

"I understand," Imogen said. "It's all I can offer."

The Lady nodded. "Then I accept. Now, I think you should take that child away before he unravels the world." She laid a hand on Patrick's tousled hair. "May you have your heart's desire, little puca, when you are old enough to understand what you wish for."

Imogen opened her mouth, but the world changed around her, and she stood in the darkness near the edge of her own farm.

Imogen appeared between one breath and the next, holding Patrick on her hip. Guaire ran to them and threw his arms about them. Imogen shivered, and he held her tighter, grateful that the Lady had consented to give his family back.

"Papa, puppies!"

Patrick grabbed his shirt to get his attention, so Guaire drew back and lifted the boy into his arms. "Are you all right, Ginny?"

Nodding absently, Imogen looked about them in the falling dark. "Where's my father?"

He didn't really care at the moment. "What happened?"

Imogen stamped one foot. "She was supposed to turn him loose."

"Puppies," Patrick insisted.

"No puppies," Imogen said, evidently having heard the request before.

"No puppies," Guaire repeated, so Patrick would know his parents agreed on the topic.

"Oh, wait." Imogen slung the bag from her shoulder and withdrew the last loaf of bread, and began tearing pieces off of the loaf. She scattered them on the rocks where the fox had waited. "Until I can set up some proper arrangement," she said under her breath, "this will have to do."

As if that opened a door, her father came trotting through that space between one realm and another. And Imogen looked relieved, like she wanted Finn back, so Guaire held his tongue.

Imogen's father stood in her front parlor, clutching his hat in his hand much as he had the first time she'd seen him. "So I have a year," he said, "to take a wife. That was my bargain with her, that I do so in exchange for Patrick's return."

Imogen hadn't spoken to him that night, too exhausted to do much more than collapse in bed once they'd explained to Paddy and Mother Hawkes. "I'm grateful you were willing to do that for him. For me and Guaire as well."

"I would rather have gotten him back by stealth," Finn said in a tired voice, "but I learned long ago that she usually gets her way. I should have known better than to try."

He sounded suspiciously like a child who'd been caught trying to steal a cookie from the plate behind his mother's back. If it hadn't been her son in jeopardy, Imogen might have found his penitent tone amusing. "Why not tell me in the first place?"

"I didn't *know* it was her, Imogen, I only suspected. I should have questioned how the information about your existence fell so easily into my lap in the first place. She manipulated me every step of the way."

They were an odd family, she reflected wryly, bound by fairy blood to bargaining and oaths rather than the human example of talking out problems over dinner. That was a skill she was going to have to cultivate. "I hope you don't resent my interference, father."

"I was surprised," he said. "I expected you would prefer me gone. But

I am grateful. That world is no place for one of my kind."

"You're half fairy," she pointed out.

"Half," he said firmly. "I've always frustrated her because I take after my father."

Imogen pressed her lips together. Her own mother had felt exactly the same way. "I..."

"Mama, mama, mama!" an excited voice gasped in the hallway.

Imogen had given Moira a few more days off before bringing her back to watch Patrick, neither she nor Guaire willing to let their son out of their sight quite yet. She went out into the hallway and spotted Patrick waddling in her direction, his movement impeded by the bundle of fur he awkwardly carried.

"Mama, puppy!" Patrick crowed. He had his arms wrapped around the chest of a piebald puppy almost as long as he was, and surely far more patient.

Imogen glanced up at Guaire and Paddy, who had followed him in. Guaire held a battered fruit crate in his arms and wore a resigned expression on his face. The crate had been stuffed with an equally battered blanket, and its contents squeaked.

"Someone abandoned a litter of puppies at the entrance of the drive," Paddy said with a suspicious glance in her father's direction. "They're lucky Victoria didn't run them over with that motor car."

"They're real dogs," Guaire said before Imogen asked. "Not hobs in disguise."

Imogen sighed. "I thought we said no puppies."

"Well, now we have puppies." Guaire retrieved the long-suffering black-and-white mongrel from Patrick's arms. "And don't think to send away a fairy gift. It would be unwise."

She cast a glance at her father, but he just smirked. "You agreed to let her into your life, Imogen. I suggest you simply expect odd things to happen."

"It could be a coincidence," she said faintly.

Her father settled his hat on his head, nodded to Guaire and headed for the door. "Yes, child, it could be a coincidence. But I promise you, in our family, nothing is."

The Curious Adventure of
the Jersey Devil
Michael D. Winkle

A stout, rosy cheeked man with a mustache like whale's flukes sat at a desk and chewed the end of a pencil. He laboriously printed words on wrappers dug from trash bins and posters torn from fences. He winced in the flickering lamplight and picked up what had once been an ad for Carter's Little Liver Pills. He crumpled it.

He opened his battered old diary and scribbled.

> *Have two dollars left. Watson's has cheated me out of $155. Dreiser has sent back two stories he told me he would buy, one even advertised to appear in his next number. There will be no money from the house next month. I owe $15 since July on the mortgage. Everything is pawned. W. led me to believe he would buy the house and now backs out. I am unable to write. I can do nothing else for a living. My mind is filled with pictures of myself cutting my throat or leaping out the window, head first.*

Charles Hoy Fort looked over his entry and sighed. That was the most interesting thing to emerge from his pencil all week.

"Oh, Charles," murmured Anna.

His wife had entered the room unseen. If she was not as quiet as a ghost, she was certainly as pale as one after her long bouts of illness. Fort fancied himself as tall and strong as any man he'd ever met, but he felt helpless in his fight to keep a roof over her head.

Anna smiled thinly. She was four years her husband's senior; in recent times she seemed to age faster than he, as if leaping forth from her head start.

"We'll get by, Charles. We always have."

"Really," said Fort. "We owe, we owe, our debts great sucking leeches, draining our silver and currency and leaving our dried husks behind. Dreiser has forgotten us, the newspapers need no reporters, and Matt! Dear Uncle Matt! Remember how he wrote he was dead broke, yet he included a check for twenty dollars?"

Anna bent over her husband and kissed his brow. "You mustn't brood, Charles. People are good, in the main. You must have faith they'll pay what they owe."

"Faith," moaned Fort. The small lenses of his spectacles misted over. "Oh, Mama. You know I've no faith. I don't believe the priests in their pulpits or the doctors in their laboratories. People are no blasted good, and institutions are worse."

"Hush, now, Charles," said Anna. "You do get into such *states*. Come to bed. Things will get better."

She lifted the glass chimney of the lamp and snuffed the flame. "At least we've still got the house."

— New York City, January 10, 1909

As he and Anna crowded up to the counter, Charles Fort stepped in something wet. The fact he could tell it was wet with his shoes on did not bode well for walking in slush.

The women of the soup kitchen shoveled an approximation of food onto metallic plates. Charles stared at the herring heads on his platter. They stared back.

The angel of the fish heads shrugged. "Sorry, sir. The middles is gone by the time they gets to here."

Charles made no comment. Anna groaned at the sight of the ogling heads and bristling tails. The noise was the twist of a knife in his heart.

He picked up a wooden bowl and elbowed his way along the smelly conveyor belt of people to the huge soup pot. Purple gizzards and J-shaped chicken necks danced in the boiling water. A severe woman, her fat-spattered apron hard as corrugated tin, plunged a dipper into the grease-encrusted cauldron.

The woman poured a gray-brown liquid into Charles' bowl. Shreds of green flesh swam in the liquid like microbes in a drop of water. The sight of the broth made him ill, but he did not spill any.

Charles led the way to a table. The penniless people of New York turned a wall of soiled coats to the Forts. Charles edged around the table and spotted the bung-shaped heel of a loaf of rye on the communal platter. A thin cougar of a woman snatched up a ladle.

"You dare take anything from here, and I'll smash you in the puss!"

They sat in a far corner. Only a few rats crowded them. Anna sighed, her eyes lost in the dark bags of her lower lids. "Too bad about the house," she said.

— Bristol, Pennsylvania, January 17, 1909

The baby cried. John McOwen hoped he was dreaming.

The baby still cried. John wriggled onto his side.

"Marsh... Claire's cryin'..."

Claire bawled all the louder. Marsha McOwen lay as if drugged. John almost fell back to sleep, inured to the noise.

He opened an eye at a *crunch* and *creak* from above. *That* was unusual, like roofers at work. He sat up and spat the tip of his mustache out of his mouth. Claire burbled in the next room and cried again.

John rose and rubbed his eyes. The cold floor against his bare feet helped him wake.

He heard a long, crackling scratch, like a needle dragged across a phonograph record.

"What on earth?"

He stepped through the gloom into Claire's bedroom. The baby waved her arms and legs in her bassinet. Cold light from the streetlamps threw everything into relief.

A screech like a factory whistle made him jump. He dashed to the window. Something followed the tow-path along the Delaware Division Canal. It padded like a dog for a moment, then it rose on its hind legs.

John gasped; the thing was plainly visible against the snow, but he still couldn't tell what it was. Huge wings swelled partially open over its shoulders like umbrellas. John made out the head of an eagle, but something like horns stuck out the back of its skull.

The thing hopped like a bird, glancing up at the sky as if searching for Halley's Comet. It had to be a bird, though it stood taller than a man. However, it dropped to all fours again and trotted off, following the tow-path out of sight.

"What was that?" asked John. "Sweet Lord in Heaven!"

Claire bawled.

Patrolman James Sackville turned the corner of Buckley Street, blinking as the wind cut into his face.

He pulled the flaps of his overcoat close. He set his bull's-eye lantern on the boardwalk. Its thin trickle of smoke whipped away as he re-wrapped his scarf.

Marching through the snow at two o'clock in the morning, he thought. *Ah, what a life. Well, Boyo, we all pull the graveyard shift eventually.*

A dog barked. Sackville ignored it and crunched down toward the canal. A little mutt somewhere howled squeakily, and dogs of a deeper pitch joined in.

Damned odd, thought Sackville as he stepped onto the tow-path. *It's not me disturbing them.*

He heard and saw nothing, yet he suddenly turned. At first he discerned only a large mass in the dim light of the oil lamp. It rose taller than he, and walls of dark feathers sprang from its sides. It shrieked.

The constable stumbled back. The creature turned itself around with a sweep of one yards-long wing. The wash sent a great ball of snowflakes whirling between the policeman and the thing, like a scene in a shakable Christmas globe. The beast retreated in jumps, stretched out kangaroo-long by its flapping pinions.

Sackville pulled his service revolver and gave chase, firing as he ran. The beast's wings spread wide as an aeroplane's. It pushed itself into a glide with pawed hind feet. It hissed like a locomotive. The patrolman fired again.

Nothing that big could get off the ground, he told himself.

The creature's wings drew in, sprouted skyward, and swept down.

Snow burst up in sideways tornadoes. Its paws left the earth. Sackville glimpsed a rope of a tail. The beast rose six feet over the narrow footpath.

Swearing, Sackville fired once more. The creature sailed over the water and vanished into the night.

The patrolman edged along the canal trying to keep it in sight. He stepped on something that crunched like a fallen pecan.

He moved his boot and glanced down at a tiny frog, sparkling with ice crystals, spread-eagled on the path.

— Broadway and Sixth Avenue, New York City, January 20

Charles Fort stared up at the imposing marble palace that housed the *New York Herald*. It might have been the Parthenon of Athens: A likeness of Athena stood high over the entrance, flanked by two bronze bell ringers for the building's huge clock.

Several bronze owls lined the roof. Others stood poised, wings outstretched, on cornices. James Gordon Bennett, Jr., the owner of the *Herald*, had a "thing" for owls. His life's ambition was to build a two-hundred-foot owl-shaped mausoleum in Washington Heights that would stare down on Manhattan.

Fort stared down owlishly, himself. He had pared away the loose threads, and he took small steps so no one would notice the holes in his shoes. Did he dare approach the *Herald*, one of the most prestigious newspapers in the world?

"Well, why not climb the highest mountain?" he said aloud. "At least Mr. Standish gave me some names to inquire after."

Charles adjusted a brown accordion folder under his arm as he entered the lobby. A circle of marble counters, with windows like Grand Central ticket booths, lined the walls. He passed between a pair of busts that stared at each other so intently he hunched down, as if they were duelists with pistols. One bust possessed a kindly, clean-shaven face with a high brow, prominent chin, and long curly hair. This was, Charles believed, James Bennett Senior, although he had been in life a notoriously ugly man, once chased out of a brothel because the whores couldn't stand the look of him. The other bust was narrow of cheekbone and small of chin, with short hair parted in the middle and a bushy mustache that did not quite hide an angry scowl. Charles could only speculate as to the model's identity, though there was enough family resemblance to suggest a sort of Cain to the first figure's Abel.

Charles crossed the tiled floor, whistling in amazement. The noise and activity were also like Grand Central, with men lined up at windows or bent over tables or milling about discussing something in this or that section of the newspaper.

Fort scanned the signs over the windows. ADVERTISEMENTS, read one. SUBSCRIPTIONS. PERSONALS.

He grinned at the last. Every journalist in New England knew the *Herald* personal columns were composed of barely-disguised solicitations from prostitutes.

Arrows pointed down a short hall to the editorial department. A rail-thin woman at a pine desk guarded the entrance to this kingdom of jangling phones, smoking cigars and yelling sub-editors.

The female sentry's fingers danced over the keys of a shiny black Underwood. The woman's neck was long and smooth in the best Gibson Girl tradition. Her jacket and skirts were navy blue, with white lace at the wrists and hem. The puffs at the shoulders put one in mind of a wing chair. Charles stood, cap in hand, hoping his presence would eventually attract her attention as the gravity of Saturn disturbed Uranus.

Finally—perhaps because he blocked her light—the woman looked up, her smile a tiny curve like an eyelash in her face.

"May I help you, sir?"

"I have a letter of introduction to Mr. Reick, the city editor," explained Fort, pulling a worn gray envelope from his breast pocket. "I was hoping perhaps someone might deliver it to him?"

The woman's eyelash-smile turned upside-down. "Mr. Reick is no longer with the *Herald*. He's over at the *Times*."

"Oh." Fort slipped the gray envelope back into his pocket. He drew out a brown one. "It happens I also have a letter of introduction to Mr. Charles Lincoln, the managing editor. I was hoping—"

The woman yanked her paper from the typewriter. "Mr. Lincoln is no longer with us. He, too, is over at the *Times*."

Charles replaced the brown envelope. "I fear I have no more rabbits in my hat. May I speak to whoever *is* city editor?"

The typist rose. "Please have a seat, Mr.—?"

"Fort. Charles Hoy—"

"Mr. Fort. It may take a while to find an editor. They come and go like flies on a horse. Mr. Bennett always seems to find something offensive about them."

Charles adjusted his spectacles. "I was given to believe Mr. Bennett lived in France."

"He does," said the woman. "I doubt he's ever seen any of the men who work for him."

"Then how does he determine whom to hire and whom to fire?"

The typist smiled her barely-visible smile again.

"That process has yet to be explained by science."

Charles tapped his fingers on his knees. He checked his shoes; in an attempt to save an unpalatable chunk of bacon fat from a waste bin, he had knocked a plate of grease onto them. His attempts to wipe them clean with an equally greasy rag at least gave a couple of toothless reprobates a good laugh.

Fort rose as a burly middle-aged fellow filled the office doorway. The man plucked a cigar out of his mouth. Round eyes in a round face narrowed to slits.

"I'm Murphy. City Editor. Who in hell are you?"

Charles worked his flannel cap as if knitting. "Uh—the name is Fort, Mr. Murphy. I have worked as a reporter at a number of dailies over the years, and..."

Murphy stared him down and up. Fort imagined seeing with his eyes via some odd visual sympathy. He could not miss the frayed seams, the knee patch, the soiled shoes.

"And I take it you're in need of work?" asked the editor.

"Not to put too fine a point on the matter—yes."

Murphy savaged his cigar again. "You sure you didn't just get kicked off the Buffalo Southern?"

Charles frowned. "I have clippings of my previous work, Mr. Murphy. And letters of introduction from Mr. Standish of the *Albany Democrat*."

He pulled his clippings from his accordion folder. The round-faced editor snorted. "Forget it. The *Herald*'s hit bad road. We can't afford to hire a half-literate typesetter, let alone more reporters."

"But Mr. Murphy—I've worked at papers here in Manhattan—"

Leather soles clapped marble tile. Men in brown suits rushed through the hall as if escaping a flood.

"He's come! He's here!" cried one.

"The Commodore! He's here!" cried another.

Mr. Murphy's jaw dropped, his cheroot clinging to his lip in defiance of gravity.

"The Commodore?" asked Fort.

"Bennett!" snapped Murphy. "It can't be! He never comes to the States any more! He ain't been here for years!"

The running men piled through the door of the editorial department. The noises from the lobby faded as if the crowd had been struck dead. Now a yip-yapping chorus rose, and a ground fog of black and white lap dogs flowed around the corner. They moiled and barked at the ends of black leashes, resembling bundles of yarn granted life.

The owner of the dogs swept into view next, the nexus of the leashes held in his gnarled fist. He was the very image of the scowling bust in the lobby, but wrinkled and soured with age.

Mr. Murphy snatched the cigar from his lips and flipped it somewhere behind the typist's desk. He gave a smile that would frighten an alligator.

"Mr. Bennett, sir!" he called. The dogs lifted their pug noses and yapped, sounding more chipmunk than canine. "What a surprise! What brings you to the States?"

The elderly man's mustache drooped into an inverted "V". "News, sir, news! A story that I wouldn't trust to my own departed mother without my careful supervision. By the way—who the hell are you?"

Charles wished he could fade into the wall. James Gordon Bennett, Junior, was like an ogre of legend, his life a mythic saga of the newspaper industry. His favorite sport as a youth had been to rocket across the countryside atop a coach and four—stark naked, rumor had it, even in winter. Not even engaged until the age of thirty-five, he escaped matrimony at a party held by his fiancée's family by urinating into the fireplace. True, he built the *Herald* into one of the greatest newspapers on earth, but he could fritter away millions on a whim, and he had personally insulted everyone from Admiral Peary to the Kaiser.

"Er—Jack Murphy, sir," his round-faced employee stammered at last. "City Editor for the past six months."

"I must have been drunk," said Bennett. "You're soft and fat and you smell like a two-cent cigar."

He snapped his head toward Charles. Fort's spectacles fogged. "And who in holy blue blazes is this?"

"No one, sir," answered Murphy, his overwhelming presence of a minute before gone like the crew of the *Mary Celeste*. "A bum—a walk-in—says he's a reporter. Can you imagine?"

Fort detected sniffings near his toes. The black-white carpet of dogs smelled the grease on his shoes. One tugged at his laces as if at spaghetti.

"I *can* imagine," snapped James Gordon Bennett, Junior. "The man looks ready to work. Looks like he *has* worked, at real jobs. He looks *hungry.*"

The old man's ceramic face softened as he regarded his miniature sled team. "And my dogs know a real reporter when they smell one. You! What's your name?"

Charles managed not to jump out of his suddenly popular trashers. "Fort, sir. Charles Fort."

"Charles Fort? Visited Charles Fort in Ireland once. They say the place is haunted. What do you think?"

"Well, Mr. Bennett, there are more things in Heaven and Earth—"

The old man spat unerringly into a nearby spittoon. "Don't know anything about Heaven. Don't expect I'd qualify. Sounds boring anyway, sitting on clouds and playing harps."

The pug-nosed animals reared up at Charles, stubby tails wagging. Bennett hauled back as if reeling in a marlin.

"I do know how to run newspapers, though, Fort. So happens I have a special project I was going to toss to the sharks in yonder, but I think we need a little new blood at the *Herald*. How's about it?"

Fort's heart did not so much skip a beat as try to stick several *thump-lumps* in the same instant. "I'll give it my all, Mr. Bennett."

"That's what I'll be wanting, Ford," said James Bennett. "Now follow me."

The newspaper tycoon pulled as if tacking into the wind. The tide of lap dogs receded. Charles followed as obediently as any of the yarn-haired Pekinese.

"Do a good job, and you'll rise fast, Ford," said Bennett. "I hear there's a City Editor position opening."

Fort glanced back at Mr. Murphy and winked. The round-faced man slapped papers off the typist's desk.

Mr. Bennett's office was predictably palatial, with marble inlays, chandeliers, enormous landscapes and portraits, countless statuettes, and teakwood doors leading Lord knew where. Fort could have fit the house he no longer owned into it, halfway to the attic.

A cheery fire crackled on the hearth. Cigars lay, already cut, on a great black desk nearly as long as the Wright Brothers' first flight. This morning's edition of the *Herald* and the *Daily Telegram* lay on the desk. Fort wondered how all that had been arranged, if Bennett's arrival was sudden and shocking. The rumors, apparently, were true: Bennett's office was eternally kept as if the tycoon were about to step in off the street.

The *Herald*'s owner drew a folded newspaper from his vest and slapped it down on the polished desktop. It was a Jersey City daily. JERSEY DEVIL FLIES OVER PENNSYLVANIA, JERSEY, read the headline.

"You mean to tell me you haven't heard a word about this?" demanded James Bennett as he led his entourage of lion-faced dogs to a corner.

Fort thought about the nights spent fighting drunks and prostitutes for rat-gnawed mattresses in the communal rooms.

"I fear I haven't been keeping up with the papers," he explained. "I have been otherwise occupied."

Bennett grunted and left his pooches. He drew forth another paper, the *Philadelphia Public Ledger*. Under the heading JABBERWOCK IN MORTAL COMBAT, they showcased the famous drawing of Tenniel's monster from *Through the Looking Glass*.

"Well, since you've been under a rock, let me enlighten you," the old man said as he hung up his hat and overcoat. "The country's between wars. The economy has gone to the outhouse. Taft is nothing but Roosevelt's marionette; can't do a damned thing on his own. Men are out of work—but you know that part. There was a time I wouldn't let the *Herald*—or even that yellow rag, the *Telegram*—touch manure like this. We made the news, we didn't squeal up to the trough halfway through a nine-day wonder."

Bennett paused to light a gilt-covered Havana cigar.

"But times change, Fred."

"F-Fred?"

"We have to tighten our belts, put our nose to the grindstone, and roll the dice."

All that would be difficult to do simultaneously, thought Fort. Aloud he said, "Is this, eh, phantasm really that newsworthy, Mr. Bennett?"

The millionaire puffed dragon smoke. "It's goddamn newsworthy if I say it's newsworthy! Besides—" The old man raised a hand suddenly. "You were going to give me that spiel about there being more things, et cetera, than are in my philosophy. How about your philosophy, Ford? Do you believe things exist beyond the scope of modern science?"

"Well, Mr. Bennett," said Charles, "there have been reports of unusual phenomena throughout history. Not fairy-tales, or miracles, or spiritualists' floating hands, but events recorded in publications like the *American Journal of Science* and the *Comptes Rendus.* Lights and objects in the sky, unheard-of creatures seen after a volcanic eruption, people and ships mysteriously vanishing—"

"All right, all right. You're not reading for Oxford." Mr. Bennett stared past Fort for a moment. "What I tell you now does not go past that door. I know this Jersey Devil will be the biggest story in the *Herald's* long career. I know, because I've seen the damned thing myself."

He motioned Fort to a leather chair in front of his dreadnaught of a desk and slid into the one behind. Fort found the chair incredibly comfortable, sensuous in a way. Besmirching it with the worn seat of his pants seemed blasphemous.

"It was November, 1865," began the tycoon. "The war was over. DeLancey Kane, Leonard Jerome, and other sons of the rich and famous formed the Coaching Club. I joined to bring a tad of excitement to their sluggish blue blood. Stuff their races, toss the silk toppers and goddamn flowers on the horses. We charged off across New York, Jersey, and Pennsylvania for a fortnight at a time, buying what we needed along the way.

"It was Thanksgiving. Some misshapen innkeeper tried to force turkey on me instead of muttonchops. He found a lamb quick enough when I pulled out my wallet. Anyway, I drove my coach south from New Brunswick to Hopewell. The fillies lathered up and collapsed in Hopewell; I bought four fresh stallions and a new coach while I was at it.

"There was moon enough, and snow enough; I could see the farm-houses and fields. The road looked level and hard, so I decided to see what my new team could do.

"They charged along without quaver or whinny for a good half-hour. I cracked the whip anyway; horses never could go fast enough for me.

"We'd almost reached Ewing. All four stallions suddenly just scraped to a halt. I stood up on the box as they snorted and reared. There was something in the road hunched over a dead deer. It rose, big ogling eyes on me, as shocked as I was. Must've been used to dirt farmers on broken-backed nags; didn't expect James Gordon Bennett to come tearing up so fast.

"But here it was, and so was I. It spread out a set of wings that filled the road. It had those goggling eyes, and these horns or ears on its head—thought it was a screech owl first, with those tufts they have. Biggest damn owl in Creation. But it had arms and legs, like.

"And a voice, by Lucifer! Never heard anything shriek so loud in my life, like a zooful of monkeys. My horses danced back, and I just dropped onto the box.

"The thing jumped, or flew, or half of each, right over me. It thumped on the roof of the coach behind me." The old man held his hands up and swung back and forth in his chair to illustrate his story.

"I spin. The Jersey Devil crouches, backside to me. Only thing handy's my whip, so I give it a snap under the tail. It squawks like a chicken and drops over the back of the coach. Hah!

"Well, the horses plunge forward, and I near about flop down on my face, but I figure I've seen the last of the Devil.

"Then a taloned paw reaches up from the end of the coach and sinks claws like railroad spikes into the roof. The Devil drags itself into view, puffin' like a foundry and screechin' like a tomcat, as we rattle along. I don't let that intimidate me, of course. I give it a right thrashing about the head and shoulders.

"Well, the Devil claws its way up anyhow, its nails scraping the roof loud and echo-y, like when you scratch an empty steamer trunk. I steadies myself as the coach hits a bumpy stretch, then I give it what-for. But don't let me catch you using 'what-for' in a newspaper column, Ford."

"No, Mr. Bennett," said Fort.

Bennett paused a moment, slowly straightening in his huge armchair.

"I figured the damned thing'd let go," he continued, "but I forgot those blessed wings. It spread 'em and rose like a kite, what with the wind spilling over the coach, but it still held on like its claws were nailed in. I snapped the lash again, and dip me in turpentine if it didn't grab the leather with one foreclaw or paw or whatever.

"I hooked one arm over the seat. I would not relinquish the whip. It let go of the coach and flapped. Near pulled my arm off, but I kept the lash, and it *was* a goddamn kite, sailing behind my runaway coach. You should have seen it, Ford! I laughed my lungs up."

"Yes, Mr. Bennett. It must have been, uh, hilarious," said Fort.

Bennett frowned. He dug out another cigar and snapped a match alight.

"I mean," he continued as he puffed, "it was *so James Bennett* of me. A scene no dime novelist would ever conceive of. Conceive of. That's ending a sentence with a preposition. Don't do that, either. But there I was, James Gordon Bennett, horses galloping crazily, hauling the Devil himself on a leash. But then the thing let go and flapped its way up into the night."

Fort nodded sagely. "And that's why you want to—"

"I ain't finished," snapped Bennett. "And don't use 'ain't.'... But I thought it was over myself, truth to tell. I stood up on the coach roof and shook both fists at the black sky, a-yelling and a-whooping like an Apache. Amazing a branch didn't take my fool head off. Anyway, I shut up quick when I saw the damned thing dropping down feet first, like one of those parachutists you see at county fairs. I fell back over the box and nearly onto the horses. The Devil went right through the roof, *crunch!* Damned cheap construction... paid good money for it, too.

"Anyway, I dragged myself back up. There was just a big hole in the roof. My whip lay there, the lash end hanging into darkness. It was my only weapon, so I grabbed the stock. Thunderation if *it* didn't grab the tip and yank! I pitched headfirst right into the coach with the Jersey Devil!"

Bennett tapped ashes into a crystal bowl. Fort hunkered at the edge of the big leather chair.

Bennett puffed again. "And what do you think it did?" asked the old man.

"It slaughtered you like a pig?" Charles suggested.

"No, it didn't slaughter me," said the newspaper owner sarcastically. "Would have been less embarrassing, though."

Again a moment of silence, except for footsteps and muffled voices from outside Bennett's sanctum.

"You've probably heard certain vicious rumors," the old man continued slowly.

"I'm sure, if the young woman were really your daughter, you would have done right by her, Mr. Bennett."

"Not those rumors, you moron! I mean about how I rode my coach stark naked in the dead of winter. Well, it's true as far as it goes. I wasn't naked by choice. That thing, that Jersey Devil, started ripping with beak and claw. I yelled like a little girl, but finally I realized it was just tearing my clothes, yanking off a clawful at a time as you'd pluck dandelion fluff.

"The horses ran off the road into a field. They got mired. The Jersey Devil peeled off my coat, jacket, braces, shirt, pants, boots, unmentionables—everything. Then it kicked open the door and flipped me out in the snow.

"I ran like a plucked chicken. Hell, I *was* a plucked chicken. Last I saw of the Jersey Devil, it was biting my whip into licorice bits. Eventually—when my pale blue buttocks froze together—I limped back. The Devil was gone. Somehow I worked the team out of the mud and rode into the nearest town, screaming like a banshee."

"Most understandable, Mr. Bennett," said Fort.

"Humph—well. I hove in at Atlantic City yesterday on my way to inspect the *Herald*, and I heard right on the dock that *it* was back. I don't know why it's flapping all over New England this winter, but it gave me an idea."

Bennett drew powerfully on his cigar, which crackled like a string of fireworks.

"You know anything about the *Herald* expeditions, Ford?"

"Indeed, Mr. Bennett," said Fort. "The *Herald* financed David Stanley's search for Dr. Livingstone, and McCreary's trek across Africa, and Admiral Peary's search for the Pole."

The old man snatched the cigar butt out of his mouth and waved it around. Fort winced as hot ash flew.

"And they all got too big for their britches! Goddammit, who'd ever have heard of Stanley, if I didn't kick him toward Zanzibar and tell him to find Livingstone? He was a deserter from the Union Army—*and* the Confederate Army! Who paid his bills? Who outfitted him?"

"Uh—you, Mr. Bennett?"

"Of course me, don't be an ass!"

Despite his outburst, Bennett smiled. "My problem was, I was too far from the action. Darkest Africa sells papers, but I couldn't control operations from here or in France. But this—"

He slapped ring-laden fingers on the Jabberwock woodcut.

"A little expedition, right in the *Herald's* back yard, with a payoff greater than finding a hundred Livingstones: A living monster in our midst! What do you say, Ford?"

Fort straightened. "I'm all for it, Mr. Bennett! Only—just for the sake of vouchers and the like—the name is Fort."

Bennett stabbed his cigar out on a newspaper illustration that resembled a winged jackass. "Ford, Fort, Rumpelstiltskin! You'll be able to afford a new name when we're done, and a peerage to go with it! Now, come on!"

Bennett called in mewling acolytes to take care of his Pekinese troupe. He led Fort down through the fairy-castle building, and the pair exited through a cramped bay below street level. Blocks away they found the millionaire's rented motorcar. He truly did try to "sneak up" on the *Herald*, thought Fort.

The rows of seats made the limousine resemble an omnibus. Bennett sat behind the driver and Fort sat behind the tycoon.

"Now I understand your obsession with owls," Fort commented.

Bennett twisted in his seat. "What?"

Fort pointed out the bronze figures on the roof of the *Herald* building. "Your owls, Mr. Bennett. You said you thought the Jersey Devil was a giant owl at first."

Bennett pursed his thin lips, then he guffawed. "I never thought of that. Must've been—unconscious, like. Hell, that damned Devil *is* an obsession."

They left Publisher's Row and frightened horses and pedestrians down to the Battery. The long Ford touring car rolled past the docks until it reached a Studebaker surrounded by men in blue sailor's uniforms. The second automobile resembled a delivery van, with a boxlike structure replacing the back seat. The men gathered and saluted as the touring car pulled up. Scrolled lettering on their caps spelled out *Lysistrata.*

Fort stepped out in the tycoon's wake, smelling fish, garbage, oil and gasoline on the cold salt breeze. Gulls collected in a lazy cyclone behind a sagging restaurant. Out in the harbor, the Statue of Liberty held her torch up to the gray Atlantic as if searching for an heirloom in the world's largest and dampest basement.

The old man signaled. One sailor drew aside a tarp curtaining the back of the Studebaker; another lowered a plywood tailgate.

"Here," called Bennett, his breath puffing like his cigar had earlier. "Boots, caps, worsted union suits. Browning cameras and an Edison film camera. Can you operate a camera, Mr. *Fort?*"

"Yes, Mr. Bennett."

"Smith & Wesson .44 revolver. Winchester bolt-action 30-30. Hundred rounds for each. You've handled firearms, haven't you, Fort?"

"Certainly, Mr. Bennett. But you mean for me to shoot this creature?"

Bennett's face wrinkled like a monkey's. "After what it did to me? Yes, dammit, I want you to shoot it! Man, beast, angel, devil—no one does that to James Gordon Bennett!"

The old man reached in and dragged a green canvas package into the sunlight. "I want pictures, of course, but any yellow rag can give you pictures. I want the beast itself!"

"But Mr. Bennett," protested Fort. "Such a valuable specimen, like a living dinosaur, or a Martian dropping to Earth—I'm not sure I could bring myself to squeeze the trigger."

"You see what I saw, Fort, you'll shoot first and ask questions next Thursday. Anyway, this here's an officer's tent, army surplus. Back there, twenty gallons of gasoline. That's why I had the Studebaker altered instead of getting a truck—only trucks available were electric! This Devil's been spotted at Bristol, Woodbury, Camden, Gloucester, Burlington, and points between. No batteries on those goddamn goat-trails. Don't trust that electricity stuff anyway. A man can see and smell and feel gasoline. Oh, and before I forget—"

He pulled out what looked like a black leather shaving kit. He unclasped the top, and a green bouquet blossomed.

"Two thousand dollars for expenses, fines, bribes, talcum, hospital bills, whatever. More if you need it; wire the *Herald*. Do we have a deal?"

Fort blinked at the cabbage head of bills. His mouth might have become the receiver for a wireless message: "Absolutely, Mr. Bennett!"

James Gordon Bennett, Junior, swelled like one of the owls he so admired. He seized Fort's hand.

"What did I say? I know 'em when I see 'em. I'd go with you if it weren't for my back—and the outstanding warrants. Fort! Bring me the head of the Jersey Devil!"

— New Jersey Pine Barrens, January 21

The Studebaker putted along at an amazing clip. Charles marveled at the automobile's smooth motion; even the engine hummed sweetly, without the rattle and bang of most gasoline-powered runabouts. The cratelike structure replacing the back seats actually seemed like a good idea for picking up small loads or pieces of furniture. A picking-up truck, one might call it.

"Scientists might miss eclipses and report planets that aren't there, but they sometimes give us new contraptions that change everything," remarked Fort.

Anna touched her fingers to her pillbox hat. The canvas flaps that served as doors for the vehicle did not keep out the January wind.

"I'm not at all sure I like so much change," she said. "Heavens! Rattling along a road so fast! People never used to rush about like this!"

"We reporters must put the *new* in newspaper," quipped her husband.

"All that money," said Anna, "and all that equipment. Mr. Bennett trusts it to someone he's never met before?"

"Mr. Bennett knows an honest soul when his dogs smell one. Besides, he could lose lock, truck, and barrel and scarcely notice it. Once in Paris he bought a restaurant and gave it to the waiter who served him."

"Gracious," was Anna's only comment.

Fort squinted at a wooden sign ahead. RAINESPORT— MERCHANTVILLE—CAMDEN, read faded paint on cracked boards. An arrow pointed west. "Hold on to your garters," he said.

He turned sharply, passing through a forest of pine, oak, and cedar. The stunted trees looked like stage props. Cleared shoulders of the road revealed sandy loam scarcely different in color from the patchy snow.

They rolled over a wooden bridge. The stream below shone a dull orange from the local iron deposits.

"An odd sort of country," Fort remarked. "Just the place for an odd sort of creature. A habitat calls out for things to habit it, I think. A hole or a quarry fills with water. Eventually fish appear in it. Do you really think birds carry fish eggs stuck to their claws and drop them there, like the nature books say?"

Anna worked her hands into her muff. "I never gave it much thought, Charles."

Fort pulled back the canvas door and studied an abandoned shack as they rolled by. Trees and vines had converged on it like wreckers. Branch hands and creeper ropes seemed to pull away planks.

"I think a new-filled pond or lake sends out a signal, a yearning; or perhaps magnetic fields or Roentgen rays if *yearning* is too anthropomorphic. And something else somewhere, in charge of migrations and rains, sends minnows and perch to fill it. And a unique land like these Pine Barrens? It seeks something unique to live in its squat woods and leeched-out soil."

Anna lay back sleepily.

"Such an imagination you have, Charles."

The new sign read HOG WALLOW, with an arrow pointing north, and SOOY PLACE, with an arrow pointing south.

Charles stepped from the car with the map Mr. Bennett had provided. He stared at the road sign as if it might reveal more information up close.

"No Hog Wallow on this map," muttered Fort, "and I'd be worried if I actually found Sooy Place."

He scraped his new boots on the running board before climbing in. "Nothing for it but go back the way we've come."

Anna glanced toward the horizon. "It will be dark soon, Charles," she murmured. "I don't relish trying to find our way out of here at night."

"Never you worry, Mama," said Fort as he backed into one fork of the road. "Camden can't be far from here. And if not Camden, then another town just as good."

— Underline: West Collingswood, New Jersey

"'Snot so bad out this evening," remarked Chuck Klos, the bookkeeper.

George Boggs, the banker, huddled in his overcoat.

"Not so good, either. I don't know why you insist on dragging me along on these winter walks."

"It brings color to the cheeks and poetry to the soul," said Klos.

Boggs grumbled. The bookkeeper smiled up at the two-story house owned by neighboring Camden's fire chief. He squinched his blond eyebrows together.

"When did Chief Embry put up a gargoyle?" he asked.

The bank manager peered out from under his furred cap. Something sat on the gable roof of the wood-frame structure. Curved wings hung to either side, outlined against a purple-pink cloud, and a beaked head rose above a wide, eagle-like breast. The object appeared to be a bird, but, judged against the attic windows, it stood taller than a man. At first the creature studied the late afternoon sky as if watching for something, then its large, brassy eyes shifted to the banker and bookkeeper.

"It's not a gargoyle," said Klos. "It's a bird."

"No bird's that big, except maybe an ostrich," said Boggs.

"What would an ostrich be doing on the fire chief's house?" asked the bookkeeper.

The bank manager spotted a red-painted box on the side of a telegraph pole.

"I don't know," said Boggs, "but seeing as it's on the chief's house, I think I'll alert the fire department."

A crowd gathered in twos and threes. Eventually the jangling bells of a great red water wagon echoed along Grant Avenue. The bird on the roof perked its ears and looked north.

"Its *ears?*" mused Klos.

Boggs stepped to the curb as the horse-drawn vehicle rattled up. The driver pulled the reins, and Chief Embry stepped down.

The muscular fire chief's eyes grew wide beneath the rim of his gilded helmet. "Great day in the morning," he sputtered. "What's that on my roof?"

"I don't know, Chief," said Boggs, "but I figured you might not want it there."

Firemen hopped from the wagon and gathered around. The Chief glanced back at them.

"Get the hose," he ordered.

The creature divided its attention between the earth and the sky as slickered men unrolled the thick beige hose. The fire fighters connected the brass couplings to the water tank. Two of them aimed the nozzle as others engaged the gasoline-powered Waterous pump.

More people emerged from houses across the street. Chief Embry frowned.

"Keep back," he called. "There's no telling what that ostrich or vulture or whatever it is will do."

Klos and Boggs edged away. "I don't know about you, George, but I think we could have waited for it to leave on its own," whispered Klos.

The jet of water shot up, drenching the strange bird. The slickered men fanned the spray back and forth. For a moment the creature did nothing but fold its odd pointed ears. Finally it leapt.

The crowd, now upwards of three dozen men, women, and children, gave a collective gasp. The strange bird landed in the cobbled street several yards from the fire wagon. The horses whinnied and reared.

"Turn it on him!" yelled Chief Embry.

The firemen shifted around. Klos hopped in place, trying to see over Embry's neighbors. The bird spun, but with its wings folded it was no longer a bird but a four-footed beast like a wolf or lion.

The jet of water crashed into it, concealing it beneath white spray. The beast zigzagged over the street, shaking its head and lashing its tail.

"Hoo! What *is* that thing?" called someone.

Some raggedly-dressed boys scooped up loose cobblestones and lobbed them at the prancing beast. The creature rose on its hind legs and opened its wings in a maple brown curtain. Its screech echoed down Grant Avenue. It fell forward into the full strength of the hose and galloped toward the crowd.

People screamed and ran. Chuck Klos held his ground.

What is it? he asked himself over and over. *What?*

The firemen trained the stream right on the creature's beak, which merely divided the water like a ship's prow, then finally dropped the hose and ran with everyone else.

The beast seized the hose in its huge talons, ripping canvas and rubber with its curved orange beak. Water spurted anew into its face.

Klos's retreat became a slow rotation, taking a few steps then turning to watch the monster. The horses dragged the fire wagon in a wide circle, their whinnies almost like human screams. The gargoyle-beast fixed its brass eyes on the bookkeeper. It jumped.

Klos raised his arms to fend it off. Cold wind buffeted him as the thing flew overhead. Animal legs and a long, curved tail hung from the beast. It banked to the left and vanished around a corner, its palm-leaf-sized primaries whisking the cobbles.

Klos reached the corner just in time to see it sail north along Mount Ephraim Avenue, straight for Camden.

"That's some ostrich," he concluded.

He stepped on something and slipped. He reached down and picked up a prune-pit-shaped body with straw-thin legs. It was a tiny gray frog, crushed by his weight.

"A frog? Out in this weather?" The bookkeeper shook his head. "Nothing makes sense today."

— <u>Camden, New Jersey</u>

Mary Sorbinski dropped flour-dusted dough into an iron pie pan. She crimped the edges with thumb and forefinger and sliced away the overhanging crust-to-be with a paring knife.

Land sakes, could those grandchildren go through pies! Ned's and Theo's broods had stormed through her home every Thanksgiving, Christmas, and New Year's, leaving her each time with barely enough left over to feed little Scott. And now Ned was moving out west, he and Melissa and their five brawny boys.

One more visit then I shan't see them for years, Mary thought. *Maybe all the hungry mouths weren't so bad.*

Scott barked at something in the yard. Mary hoped it wasn't that ragged fellow who dug through the trash bins. She never liked the look of him.

She heard a crunch, as if a branch had fallen. The terrier's barking rose in pitch and tempo. Scott *never* carried on like that. Mary brushed her hands on her apron and snatched up her broom on the way to the back porch. The terrier squealed like a pig as Mary opened the door.

A nightmare of curved talons, burning eyes, and bristling feathers stood in the yard. It held the terrier like an apple in one handlike claw.

Mary screamed and swung her broom, slapping the creature on the side of the head. The thing scissored its wings and glared at her over a massive aquiline beak.

Mary raised the broom and brought it down like a sledgehammer. The creature's neck accordioned with the blow. The horror let out a hyena's laugh. It dropped the terrier and flapped back several feet.

"Get away! *Get away!*" cried the woman.

She scythed the broom before her. The monster beat its wings wildly and rose from the frost-rimed grass.

Mary tumbled back on the porch, her broom up like a pike. A strong yank left her with splinters in her palms.

The air popped with the creature's powerful flaps. It rose above the porch, rattling the shingles. The broom, discarded as quickly as it had been stolen, clattered on the walk.

"Scott!"

Mary rose with a grunt and staggered into the yard. She scooped up her dog as the monster vanished over the roof.

The terrier gurgled. A wet gash, like a crimson grin, split his stomach from side to side. Mary screamed again.

The Studebaker rattled along the streets of Camden. Fort relaxed within his overcoat. He didn't want to admit that he, too, had been worried. Not of devils, Jersey-born or otherwise, but of the cold night.

Anna can do without another bout of pneumonia, he thought. *Such irony! That day in the hospital when I woke up to find her taking care of me. Little Anna Filing, a long way from England, nursing the great world traveler. I'm glad I've had the chance to take care of her in turn.*

I simply wish I could take a bit better care .

"What on earth is going on up ahead?" asked Anna.

Fort blinked away his idle thoughts. Streetlamps, bull's-eyes and electric torches lit the paved avenue ahead like a Chinese New Year parade. A crowd milled around a quaint wooden cottage, spilling so far into the road the Studebaker could not creep by. Fort stopped.

"I'm experiencing journalistic atavism, Mama. My reporter's instincts tell me there's a story yonder." He pulled back the canvas and stepped down. "Stay here, Anna, and keep the motor running. One never knows about crowds. A laughing audience one moment, a lynch mob the next."

Anna nodded. Fort approached the crowd and shrugged; one cap-covered back of a head looked much like another. He tapped a shoulder at random.

"What's all the commotion?"

A man with a black comb of a mustache glanced back. "They say it's the Jersey Devil! Frightened an old lady to death!"

A bonnet turned, revealing a woman's face like the seed-disk within a sunflower. "Swallowed her dog whole, I hear," she said solemnly.

"I heard it knocked a trolley car off the tracks," came a disembodied comment from deep in the crowd.

"—burned down a church with its fiery breath," added an even more distant ghost.

The jackpot! thought Fort.

He shouldered his way toward the house. Two constables stood on the front porch, shooing the crowd as if it were a flock of geese. Fort dug into his pocket and pulled out a notebook and pencil. He climbed boldly onto the porch.

"Officer! I'm with the *New York Herald!* Might I ask what happened?"

The first policeman, a muttonchopped fellow in heavy blue serge, eyed Fort skeptically. "You might, but there's no guarantee you'll get an answer," he said. "*New York Herald?* You got here blasted quick."

Fort allowed himself a smile. "My good fortune, Officer. We've only just motored into town."

The constable turned to the crowd again. "Go on, then, go about your business! What happened has happened. There's nothing to see."

"What did happen, Officer—?"

"Cunningham," said the muttonchopped man. "I'm damned if I know. Don't quote that. Apparently old Mrs. Sorbinski's dog was attacked by a wild animal."

Fort nodded solemnly and scribbled on his tiny pad. "You have a lot of wild animals around here, Officer Cunningham?"

The policeman shrugged. "Raccoons... even a bear, once in a while."

Fort scanned the dispersing crowd. A hundred or more people still lingered in front of the house. "All this for a raccoon?"

Cunningham shrugged. The second officer watched something fall from the eaves. He hopped to the ground and picked it up.

"Hey, Tom," he said, "have a look at this!"

Cunningham and Fort stepped over. A small frog squirmed in the second officer's hand.

"It fell off'n the roof!" exclaimed the officer. "Look—there's another!"

A tiny amphibian dropped from the roof to the sere winter grass.

"Don't frogs sleep all winter, like snakes?" asked the second constable.

Cunningham shrugged again. "Heat from the house must have awakened them. The woman's kitchen was hot as a furnace when I got here."

"But what were they doing on the roof?" asked Fort.

A shrill cry echoed through the night before Officer Cunningham could answer. The people in the street set up their own palaver. Arms pointed north.

The crowd shifted away from the Sorbinski house. The policemen clumped down from the porch. Fort followed.

The dome of a hill rose three blocks off. Several teenaged lads trotted toward it, pointing at a water tower on the summit. Something clung to the tower like a cicada, black against the purple clouds.

The policemen marched steadily toward the hill. The crowd followed like sheep. Fort edged along to one side, trying to watch everything.

The blot on the water tank dropped away with the snap of flags in a stiff wind. The first line of people stopped; others bumped into them. Fort thought of water roiling as it hits a dam.

He could not blame them for their reluctance. What *was* this, gliding down from the park? It screeched again, and people stampeded back screaming along the brick lane. The policemen drew their revolvers. The blasts of the handguns made Fort wince.

The creature dipped low, almost brushing the street, then it angled up over the officers. Fort trotted after the flying thing. The panicked mob reached the Studebaker and split like a flood around a boulder. Anna's face bobbed up at the windscreen.

Abruptly she drew back. A dark comet dropped out of the night and landed with a *bang* on the roof.

"*Anna!*"

Fort ran. He saw only the hindquarters of the beast and the vast, curved wings hanging to either side. A few paces ahead Officer Cunningham raised his pistol, aiming on the run.

"Hey!"

Fort rammed Cunningham like a rhinoceros. The officer stumbled and regained his stride. He glared at Charles.

"My wife is in that motorcar!"

The creature lifted its wings vertically, like the sails of twin sloops, and flapped with an audible *voop*. The Studebaker shook like a cracker box as the monster lifted into the air. The policemen clopped past the car, firing a few times more.

Fort reached the vehicle and yanked aside the canvas. Anna!"

His wife lay huddled on the seat, pale as the frosty ground. Fort jumped in.

"Mama, dear, are you all right?"

Anna straightened and nodded weakly. "I'm all right, Charles. But perhaps I should have stayed in the city."

Fort promised Anna he would return to their hotel room momentarily, but he interviewed the desk clerk, then a businessman from Trenton, then a roustabout on the street.

Police motortrucks rolled by, and Fort followed like the scraps of newspaper in their wake. He heard that something had clambered about the roof of a house on Vanhook Street. By the time he reached Vanhook, someone told him that a "Jabberwock" was drinking from a horse trough on Third.

He returned to the hotel very early in the morning. He undressed in the dark and slipped into bed like a man home from a drinking binge.

"Charles, you said you'd be right back."

Fort sighed. "I'm sorry, Mama. So many fellows were rushing down the streets, herd instinct took over. But I filled my notebook. Mr. Bennett will have the greatest story ever come the Sunday edition."

Anna's thin fingers brushed his cheek. "But he expects you to *shoot* it, doesn't he?"

"Does that worry you?"

Somehow he knew she smiled.

"I'm not worried about you, Charles. But I don't think the beast intended to harm me. It was confused. Frightened by the crowd and the guns."

Fort rubbed his mustache idly.

"I've been rather against shooting it, if there was something actually to shoot, all along. Maybe I can convince Mr. Bennett that the creature would be more valuable alive. A mascot for the paper, perhaps."

"What about the incident in his youth?" asked Anna.

Fort frowned. "I'll have to be convincing."

— The Pine Barrens, January 22

The trees crowded the road aggressively, scraping the windscreen with their branches.

Is this the same road we arrived on? Fort wondered.

The Studebaker, dents marring its roof and bonnet, rattled along at twenty miles an hour. Charles Fort patted the hard lump in the pocket of his greatcoat. He carried the Smith & Wesson despite his talk against gunplay.

"Do you know where we are, Charles?"

"We're headed north, Mama. That's all we need to know."

They passed a gray-brown sign. Their choices of destination were CEDAR CREEK and MARY ANN FURNACE.

"Well," said Fort, "let's try Mary Ann Furnace. Perhaps they, or she, can direct us to Trenton."

The trail ended at a dirt clearing, a skillet with the road for a handle. Half-fallen shanties lined the clearing. A cracked, empty foundry furnace did, indeed, sit near the trees, near a grassless expanse of slag and clinkers.

"Dear!" said Fort. "This must be a Piney town."

He climbed out of the Studebaker, musing. *The first "boom" of the*

Industrial Age exploded right in this wilderness during the Revolution, when iron smelters churned out weapons for the American cause. Leftover Indians, farmers whose crops failed in the poor soil and other human outcasts provided cheap labor for fifty years. Then better grades of ore found in the Midwest turned the boom to a bust. The poorly paid laborers became poorer still, and they shunned and were shunned by the rest of the population, who dubbed them Pineys. Generations later, "proper" folk still gossiped about mental retardation, deformities, polygamy, and inbreeding among these self-exiled Pineys.

"Charles, I think we should turn back," said Anna. "I've never heard good about these people."

"Now, Mama," said Fort. "They are probably just the victims of bad press or wishful thinking. Jersey-ites must find *someone* to look down upon, after all. I'll make some simple inquiries and we'll be on our way."

Fort left the motorcar and headed for the nearest shanty. A barrel, a wagon wheel, and two rickety chairs flanked the door—there was no porch—and old burlap served as curtains for the rough-cut windows. The door hung open on leather hinges.

He knocked on the frame. "Hallo?"

The shanty consisted of a single room with a cot in one corner, a pot-bellied stove in another, and a kitchen area in a third. Fort ventured in and studied a rude kitchen table. A willow-backed chair lay overturned. On the table proper sat a chunk of rye bread with a single bite taken from it, next to a pewter bowl half-full of porridge.

"As if he just up and left," muttered Fort.

He rubbed his chin. Why would a man, hardened to life in this infertile forest, jump from his chair and his lunch and flee his home and few miserable possessions?

"Only if the Devil himself were after him," he said aloud. "Best not to mention this."

Something rattled on the pine shingles above. Sleet? The rattle passed on like a swiftly-moving spring shower. Fort stepped outside and shaded his eyes against the sun.

"Only a few cirrus clouds this morning," he observed.

A dull patter came from the dusty earth. Dots of sleet or rain fell between the shanties and the car. A few dark specks hit the windscreen. Anna bounced as if startled from a nap. She leaned forward and squinted through the glass.

Now squat conifers at the edge of the forest shook as if from heavy precipitation.

"Curiouser and curiouser," muttered Fort. "A localized shower? From a near-cloudless sky?"

He headed for the trees. Tiny objects bounced on his cap and shoulders. He brushed his head and stared up.

"What the—?"

Something slimy dropped into his mouth. He spat it into his hand. It was a frog, smaller than a nickel but fully formed. Its throat pulsed in and out as fast as the eye could follow. It jumped and vanished into a hopping, bouncing, chirruping sea of its brethren.

"Frogs, like on the old woman's roof," murmured Fort in amazement. "But where did these or those come from?"

He scanned the winter sky more carefully and gasped. Tubes, or hoses, or pipes crisscrossed the sky. He could just see their silver-white etchings, like glass in water. Some of the tubes ran parallel to four or five companions, like electric cables in a basement. Others hung alone in the sky. Some were wispy fishing lines as high as the winter cirrus; a few hung low to the ground, like aqueducts.

One of the near-invisible tubes curved slowly into an "S". The top of the "S" straightened after a moment, curled the other way, and made a backward "C".

He barely noticed his wife pushing open the curtain-door of their vehicle.

"Charles! What in Heaven's name are those things?"

"I—I—" He swallowed. "I am the very definition of 'flabbergasted'," he finished.

Some of the aerial tubes met at nexus points like train tracks at a roundhouse. Others simply ran from horizon to horizon, like the arches of Heaven. None of them seemed to have actual ends.

The moving tube had a ragged terminal point, however, and it spewed some manner of fluid.

"That one's like a loose firehose, the way it's whipping around," he called. "Good heavens!"

The ragged end of the sky-artery, wide as a train tunnel, swept by only a few yards up. Dark particles streamed out in its wake. Fort threw himself to the cold ground. He climbed to his knees as the tube drifted skyward again. More frogs plopped down like rain.

"Cosmic arteries with frogs for blood cells," he murmured. "How can it be? What does it mean?"

Fort heard the patter of batrachian precipitation out among the scrub oaks. He rose and ran after the tube, which now resembled a waterspout.

"Charles!" called Anna from the Studebaker. "Where are you going?"

"Not to worry, Mama! I'm just having a closer look at that frog depositor."

The tube swung well over the trees. Just as Fort reached the brush, however, it swung ponderously back.

Fort retreated a few steps. He sucked uncertainly on his mustache as the edges of the artery dropped lower than his shoulders.

The walls of the tube were of a deeper blue than the sky. They seemed membranous. The writer's hair stood up, popping his cap from his head. The prickling sensation flowed out of the ground and through his body.

That's how you feel when you're about to be struck by lightning!

The rubber look of the walls gave him a desperate idea. He worked the .44 out of his pocket, took steady aim, and fired, thinking to rupture the artery. He felt a concussion, as if he stood in an elevator car that suddenly hit bottom. And now a curious light-headedness—so light, in fact, he could paddle both feet without touching the earth.

"I'm floating up! The frogs drifted down! It works both ways!"

He dropped the revolver. It fell like the steel from which it was made.

A selective force of gravity?

He made frantic swimming motions as if diving to the bottom of a pool. He saw the blue walls, and the tires of the Studebaker below the rim of the tube-end, and now the lower half of his wife as she ran across the clearing. She shouted his name, then he felt a giddy acceleration...

He woke, although he was certain he had not slept. His feet crushed dry grass as he settled to earth.

The first thing Fort noticed was the cold. He stood in the middle of an empty lot, its weeds and thistles crusted with frost. He faced a boardwalk and a puddle-dotted street. Everything was slightly blurry; he had lost his spectacles.

A fence lined the near side of the street, ending on his left in a scattering of unpainted slats. A woman bundled up for winter marched determinedly into view past the end of the fence. She stopped abruptly, boots skidding on the icy walk, and stared at Fort. Then she screamed and vanished behind the fence again, the clop of her boots marking her passage.

"Unaccountable," said Fort.

He glanced down at his pale, naked form. "Great Scott!" he cried. "No wonder she ran! No wonder I'm cold! Where on earth am I?"

He looked around frantically. On his right, perhaps a quarter-mile away, stood a gray brick building. A huge sign proclaimed GRIFFIN BREWERY—BRENTFORD, LONDON, W.

"London!" cried Fort. "But what of the Pine Barrens? The Piney town? Anna? My clothes?"

"Charles..."

Fort shifted his cold feet. "Anna?" he asked of the air. His breath smoked. The situation was intolerable on so many levels.

"Charles, where are you?"

His wife's voice sounded near but weak. Fort squinted in its apparent direction. A patch of grass shone brown there. The frost had melted in a ten-foot circle.

"Anna?" He crunched toward the brown patch, wincing as grass stalks stabbed his feet. He entered the rough circle and stepped on a yielding surface. He waved his arms frantically. The wintry ground folded downward, like a painted canvas puckering out of its frame. He fell, skidding on the cold grassy earth of Brentford, London West.

Giddiness enveloped him again. He passed into the blue tunnel, then gravity returned. The orange dirt of the Piney clearing slapped him in the face.

He pushed himself up with Anna's help.

"Oh, my God, Charles, you disappeared into that thing!" she babbled, her voice cracking like ice in hot tea. "How did it happen? Where did you go?"

She looked him over.

"Where are your *clothes?*"

The components of a dark pantsuit fluttered down from on high. A glint of light on a dual hailstone, and Charles' spectacles hit the froggy dust.

"My wardrobe is scattering to the winds. Help me harvest it, my dear, before I catch my death!"

The couple carried the lost vestments to the truck. Fort outlined his brief misadventure as he dressed.

"I can sympathize with Mr. Bennett in one aspect at least," he concluded as he buttoned his shirt. "It is most disconcerting to find oneself naked, in the out-of-doors, in the dead of winter."

He raised his chin, studying the sky-arteries as he buttoned his collar. "Whatever the tube is, it can shift frogs—and men—but not clothing, or guns, or spectacles."

He rubbed his glasses with a handkerchief, thankful they had not shattered.

"How is such selectivity possible?" asked Anna.

"I've no idea. Yet the experience reminds me of several newspaper accounts from somewhere in America, roundabouts 1888, and England, 1904. Men appearing, stark naked, out in the street or the countryside, with no memory of how they got there. Perhaps it's some kind of quite literal animal magnetism—a pull on living things but not on clothes and shoes. But I wonder how they got *off* me, without me unhooking them?"

Anna Fort closed her eyes. "It's all beyond me, Charles. I just want to—to—" She paused. Fort slipped on his coat.

"Go home, you were about to say."

Anna stared at the orange dust at her feet. "I didn't mean that."

Fort touched a finger to her chin. A minuscule pressure tilted her face up. He found her eyes, kindly nanny's eyes surrounded by wrinkles of worry and pain.

"Yes, you did," he said. "If you didn't, you should have."

He stepped to the back of the Studebaker and unlatched the wooden tailgate.

"Charles, what are you doing?"

"By all accounts, Mr. Bennett is a difficult man to please," explained

Fort. "He won't settle for merely a story. He wants the Jersey Devil itself."

He found a box of Pointer Smokeless Powder shells. He slipped the 30-30 cartridges into the Winchester's magazine.

"Charles," said Anna, "what makes you think you're going to find this creature? Half the state's gone hunting for it without success."

Fort nodded at the transparent tubes over the clearing.

"I think it will come to us, my dear. I believe in an underlying Oneness to wonders."

Anna shook her head. "Charles, I don't follow you at all."

Fort set the rifle aside.

"An unaccountable creature has appeared in and vanished from the Pine Barrens in an unaccountable fashion for two hundred years. And here, in those very Barrens—an unaccountable means of transportation: frogs appear, men disappear. Of the many things in which I do not believe, coincidence ranks high. I think ol' Jersey travels through those tubes, passing from here to England, or Outer Mongolia, or Mars. And I think he will return."

The couple concealed themselves in the nearest shack. Anna started a fire in a rusty stove. Charles sat with the rifle across his lap, the warped front door open far enough to give him a view of the clearing.

He tugged at his collar, the circle that had remained unbroken during his brief excursion *au naturel* in Brentford.

"I've been thinking, Mama," he began. "I know that is often cause for alarm, but I'm wondering if I might have an hypothesis concerning yon tubes."

Crude as the shanty was, it possessed a counter, sink, and well pump. Anna placed a battered little pail beneath the spout and lifted the rusty cantilever arm.

Fort rose and set the rifle across his rickety chair. "Oh, Anna, let me do that." Fort grunted the lever down and groaned it up again. Water trickled into the dented bucket. He wondered whether the slight redwood stain of it came from the pipe or the Barrens.

"After *Monsieur* Verne took us under the sea and around the moon (huff), and before H. G. Wells arrived on the scene with a *whoosh*, a fellow (grunt) named Professor Hinton wrote of scientific marvels to put either of them to shame. Only he was no scribbler of mere fiction."

Anna found a pewter coffee pot as timeworn as the bucket. Fort hauled up the latter and poured half its contents into the former.

"Hinton wanted to illuminate for the benighted populace the geometries outside mere length, width, and height," Fort continued.

"I fear he would find little wick in my lamp, Charles," said his wife. She set the old coffee pot on the stove. "Geometry for me stops at dress patterns and crazy quilts."

Fort indicated the knothole-dotted table. "Sit, my dear, and I shall attempt to be less obscurant."

The couple sat facing each other. The rough boards of the table formed the slightest suggestion of a plane, and they were dingy enough that a finger could draw upon them as well as chalk on a blackboard.

He drew, or rather wiped, a line on the table, a pale streak in the grime, with his index finger. "What we call Length is a dimension, a physical property we're all familiar with." He etched a second line perpendicular to the first. "Width lies at right angles to Length, giving us Area, like the floor of a house."

Fort fished his pencil from his pants pocket and set it, point up, on the table. "Height stands at right angles to the previous two, creating Volume. Professor Hinton suggested a direction at right angles to the other three: the polyphemic Fourth Dimension, which we mere mortals cannot see, except with the mind's eye."

Fort scratched a square in the waxy patina of the wood.

"We can draw a square with four lines and fashion a cube with six squares. In four dimensions we could use eight cubes to form what Hinton named a tesseract. Similarly, a point passing around a radius forms a circle, and a circle, spun like a watch at the end of a chain, describes a sphere. Turned through our Fourth Dimension, a sphere would create a hypersphere."

The light slowly faded from Anna's eyes.

I would never make a successful lecturer, thought Fort, *except perhaps on the subject of curing insomnia.*

Then, however, his wife's eyes sparkled, and a girlish smirk forced back her worry lines.

"Oh, Charles! How you complicate things!" Her smirk became a Cheshire-cat grin. "One does not need a Tolstoi to explain Billy Whiskers. I've read all that you are trying to say in a children's book. The one with the talking squares and rectangles."

Fort adjusted his spectacles. "*Flatland?*"

"Yes, that's the name," said Anna. "The square is visited by a sphere, who—forgive me, dear—explains dimensions far more clearly than you do. It was easier to follow things from the square's point of view, as he struggled merely to understand our world."

"Easier indeed!" said Fort enthusiastically.

He scratched a smaller square within the first he drew.

"Imagine Mr. A. Square, Esquire, secure in his quarters, doors sealed against any polygonal invader of Flatland. Imagine him, even, warm in his little Flatland sweater."

He sketched a line three-fourths of the way around the inner square, as if it lay tucked in a pocket. "All the peoples, all the history, all the natural phenomena he knows about exist only on his tabletop world. He knows nothing of us, the space below and above the table, or all the rest of the earth. So far as he is concerned, no one and nothing can get at him. Yet I could reach down, pick him up like a playing card, and set him down outside his fortress—pluck him right out of his tiny smoking jacket, while I'm at it."

Fort touched the square-within-a-square, wishing he had a playing card handy to better illustrate his analogy.

"We need only replace A. Square with me, and my arm with that glassy tube, to re-create my curious trip."

"I suppose it's possible, Charles," Anna said slowly, "but where did those strange tubes come from?"

Fort waved toward the raw pine rafters above. "Perhaps they have always been there. My arm still exists after I've withdrawn from the table; so does yours, and everybody else's. As our four-cornered little friend can only see them when we touch the table, so can we only perceive these tubes when they intersect our land of Three Dimensions."

Fort paused, eyeing a crooked stud in the roof as if it were the work of Michelangelo.

"These hyper-cyclones might always waver and whirl just outside our view. I fear I mutilate Milton, but he wrote something like, 'Millions of spiritual creatures walk the earth unseen, when we wake, and when we sleep.' Only think of yonder vortices rather than spirits."

Anna drew her already-narrow shoulders closer together. "Goodness, Charles. The thought gives me a most uncomfortable shiver."

"Then pay my ramblings no mind, Mama. My hypotheses rise and fall faster than Parisian fashions."

Fort took up his position at the door again. Anna poured coffee, found among the motorcar's supplies, into tin cups, found in the shack. "I feel like a burglar, Charles."

"These people have little to burgle, Mama."

"Where do you suppose they went?"

"Perhaps there was a trade," suggested Charles. "A shanty town of Pineys for a blizzard of frogs. Perhaps they mingle even now with the Roanoke colonists or the ancient Mayans. Perhaps other men have been traded for amphibians. A royal personage gone, and a squat amphibian deposited in his place—*voila!* The Frog Prince!"

Fort shifted slightly to see the Studebaker among the trees. It was certainly visible from the air, but the Jersey Devil did not seem to fear vehicles. "Or they most mundanely saw our Devil drop out of the sky and fled. There's not much, as I say, in the way of material possessions to root them here."

Anna sighed. "At least they had roofs over their heads, Charles."

Fort winced. "That will change, Anna, darling," he promised.

Anna set a cup on an old crate by her husband. "It's not your fault, Charles. We've been two of the thousands of destitute in New York. Perhaps it's the city. Out in the country—living simply—it may be different."

Now Fort sighed. "Ah, Mama. All my life I swore I would travel to the big city, be a reporter, a Great Writer, a Literary Giant, hoisting pomposity on halberds of witticisms. Well, the pen is mightier than the sword, but high rent beats 'em both." He leaned back slightly. "The simple life, eh? I'd say we should take Mr. Bennett's motorcar and his money and set ourselves up in a farmhouse at Fly Creek or Lake Seneca—but I would feel I had done poorly by him. Bothered by conscience! Perhaps that's why I never excelled at journalism."

Anna smiled. "Posh, Charles. You're an honorable man. That's nothing to be ashamed of. Now set that gun aside and have some coffee."

Fort lay the Winchester carefully on a rough bench and took up the steaming cup. He regarded the weapon for a long moment. After draining his coffee, he rose.

"Well, there is conscience and there is conscience. I'll write stories for the *Herald*, because it's a newspaper, and it would look queer with no filler to hold apart the advertisements, but I shan't kill for it. I'm going to fetch the camera from the truck, Anna. Mr. Bennett will have to settle for pictures."

He drew the heavy revolver from his coat pocket and placed it on the table. He felt lighter, morally as well as physically, when he left the shack.

Most of the sky-frogs had hopped off into the bushes, but a few lay underfoot, torpid or dead.

Not from falling, he thought. *Just from the cold. The anti-gravitational force in the tubes softened their landings as well as my own. How does it work?*

He scanned the zenith again. The tracing of arteries was barely visible, like fingers just brushing Flatland, perhaps.

"One does not need a Tolstoi to explain Billy Whiskers," he said to himself. "I'll have to remember that."

He wondered why the tubes seemed static, now, over the clearing. A tangle, as of fishing lines? But the loose one, coiling about like an anaconda with indigestion: Fort believed something had gone wrong with it.

Quite arrogant, diagnosing illness in a phenomenon never before seen by Man. I stand firmer in thinking it has something to do with our flying devil. The frogs it dropped here, and the frogs on the old woman's house, if nothing else.

Fort paused by the rear fender of the Studebaker. He still gazed skyward, but he no longer watched the tubes.

He saw no feathered forms, not even of the more mundane variety.

"We may be in for a bit of a wait," he said aloud. "The beast would be a winged jackass indeed to emerge in daylight."

He stepped round to the plywood tailgate. Where was the camera?

Fort hauled himself half up onto the incongruous superstructure of the vehicle. A splinter or two caught at his pants.

The black Kodak lay beyond the officer's tent and the gasoline cans, nearly touching the backs of the seats.

"There you are, my pretty," he said. "Of course you sit as far from convenience as possible. Oh, well, another necessity first, then I shall step around front for you."

He unhooked a beltlike strap that held one of the five gallon cans to the wall of the box and dragged it out with a bang and rattle.

No more than one gallon left in this one. When we do happen upon a town, we must purchase more petrol.

He hopped down and found the spout for the vehicle's fuel tank. He unscrewed the lid and upended the can, slipping the latter's metal funnel into the spout.

The gasoline made a *plump-plump-plump* as it disappeared into the Studebaker's guts. He tried to decide whether it sounded more like a heartbeat or a huge baby suckling on a bottle.

He idly scanned the haze of branch and bush and vine as he waited for the last of the refined oil to trickle away.

Fort knew, of course, that human beings depended on their eyes more than any other sense organs. Now he realized that something in the human makeup also *recognized* eyes before any other feature of a living thing. He knew, because from the jackstraw tangle of underbrush he picked out two glaring bronze orbs.

With the eyes like the foci of an ellipse, he next sketched out a pantherlike shape, chest hissing over crumbly fallen leaves, hindquarters slowly rising, foreleg drawing back for a spring.

Fort thought of the volatile power of gasoline. He hurled the steel canister at the threatening form, its liquid contents spraying all around.

The underbrush shook wildly. Fort patted his pockets.

That would have worked more effectively had there been more petrol... and had I not given my matches to Anna for the fire.

He jumped for the driver's door of the Studebaker, crowded between steering wheel and seat, and slapped the canvas door down. *A poor shield,* he thought as he scooted across the passenger's side.

He expected the canvas to be shredded like tissue. Instead a sirocco of orange soil clouded over the bonnet and the windscreen. Wings snapped sharply, and a shadow, darker than the iron-stained dust cloud, dropped down before the car. Fort heard a now familiar screech.

The dust settled. Fort stared out the glass at the Jersey Devil.

No longer was it a goblin-shape in the night; the sun glinted on aeroplane-sized wings and a barrel-wide mahogany chest. The creature's body was leonine, its hindquarters a brindled yellow, its tail ending in a teardrop of walnut-brown hair. It sat upright on its haunches. Even with hind legs folded, it would tower over any man.

Mahogany-brown feathers covered its hefty upper forelegs. Its forearms were the same burnt umber of the Pine Barrens' soil, and they ended in wicked bird-claws. Its brass-gold eyes stared back at him over a curved, raptorial beak. A foot beyond its heavy eye-ridges, two ears, like those of a horse, perked up.

It was not the creature's unearthliness, but its familiarity, that shocked Fort the most. He recognized the Jersey Devil.

"A gryphon," he murmured. "A gryphon, right off a heraldic shield."

The bird-animal bristled into a tan-brown pinecone and dropped onto all fours. Its great wings snapped shut against its sides.

And now it's more feline than fowl. That's how it travels in the daytime. I would never have expected it to prowl about like a leopard.

"Prowl—and spring!"

The creature leapt over the bonnet, its eyes and beak like archer and arrow in one. It hit the glass, head and neck folding up momentarily, black talons scraping audibly aside.

Fort dragged himself over the seats into the cratelike rear.

A huge pine box, he thought. *How appropriate!*

He scuttled over the folded tent as the Jersey Devil batted the windscreen with its meat-hook claws. The glass held. The monster ascended in a flurry of wings, then a heavy mass thumped onto the thin wooden roof of the limousine-turned-truck.

By heaven, its claws sink right through!

Black nail tips appeared, vanished, appeared, vanished, as the bird-animal crawled across the ceiling. It would reach the tailgate before he did.

Fort slapped himself around one hundred-eighty degrees like a seal on ice. The angry beaked head poked down into view, upside-down at the rear of the Studebaker. The beast's screech made his head ring.

Fort rolled into the front seat and flowed out the passenger's side like some viscous fluid. The Jersey Devil entered the back as he left; at least, the vehicle rocked so hard he half expected it to overturn.

Fort lurched to his feet and ran, a stitch developing in his side. It always happened when he was forced into exceptional activity.

And how does that promote survival of the fittest, Dr. Darwin? That, and fainting?

The door to the shack burst open, and out popped Anna, the Winchester in her arms.

"Anna! No!"

She ran with a stamina undreamt of by Fort. Husband and wife skidded to a halt before one another, scattering gravel and dead frogs.

He accepted the rifle. "Get back to the house!" he barked.

Anna had no time to obey. With a deep *pop*, the Jersey Devil's talons penetrated the canvas over the Studebaker's door. In seconds the stiff material turned to vermicelli.

"It must know what Man's weapons can do," said Fort. "A warning shot should discourage it."

"And if it doesn't?" asked Anna.

"There are more bullets."

The gryphon's axe of a beak poked into the daylight. Its eyes, as hypnotic in their intensity as a serpent's, found the couple.

Fort lifted the barrel high and fired. The blast seemed muffled, somehow. His hair—bodily as well as head—stood on end.

"Charles!" warned Anna.

He looked up into the opal blue tunnel, which had again drifted over the clearing.

"Damn and blast! Not now!"

Too late; already his boots lost their purchase on the rusty earth. He caught his wife's flailing hand in his own. She rose as well.

Better than leaving her with that ravening beast, he decided.

The gryphon, however, no longer raged. It froze, half out of the Studebaker, beak agape in what could only be described as a mask of astonishment. Then the translucent wall of the artery eclipsed the sight.

Fort came to consciousness pre-irritated, scowling, arms crossed. Once more he hung naked in a bluish Limbo, and he felt again the pricking of winter grass against his feet as he touched to earth.

He forgot himself upon hearing a sharp gasp.

"Mama!"

His wife, looking even more frail naked, collapsed—toward him, fortunately. He crooked his knees as he intercepted her. He hugged her close and straightened again.

"Mama, dear, you should have waited in the shack."

Her thin fingers closed weakly on his bare shoulder. "And remain alone with that creature? No, Charles."

She steadied herself, but Charles held her loosely still, a goose-pimpled scaffolding.

"Together, for better or for worse," commented Fort. "And hitherto I thought we had plumbed the depths of 'worse'. Where could we be?"

He squinted, his spectacles gone with his apparel. He made out a vast plain and the jagged outlines of distant mountains.

It's cold again. Well—suppose we had dropped in the open Pacific?

Something grunted low and loud. It sounded like a bomb bursting underwater. The Forts, clinging to each other, shuffled around like Chang and Eng, the Siamese Twins.

A huge creature grazed on the frost-rimed stalks twenty or thirty yards away. A virtual freight car with legs, it flicked a horselike ear as it crunched up a wicker chair's worth of yellow grain. Two curved horns on its snout, one behind the other, weighed down the heavy skull all the more. The foremost horn stood as tall as Charles.

"Mama," he said, "your eyes are better than mine. Tell me what you see."

"I fear I see a rhinoceros, Charles," answered the shivering woman. "Only it's covered with long, stringy hair like one of those Himalayan yaks."

Fort muttered a word that made Anna frown. "Sorry, Mama, but... it's woolly, like its more famous cousin, the mighty Mammoth. And, like the Mammoth, dead many thousands of years." He cupped his hands and blew into them. "Wells argued for Time as the fourth dimension. So did that Einstein fellow who's been in all the science journals."

He shook his head free of associations and metaphors. "And time is the one thing we lack. Our way back may vanish soon, if it even exists. Look for a discoloration in the grass, Mama, or any visual distortion!"

The Forts broke their hug and scanned the rhino-cropped steppes.

"It must be here as before—it must!" said Fort.

Anna pointed a pale finger. "Charles, look. A shimmer over the grass—like summer heat over a tar road."

Fort hugged his wife again. "And here there is emphatically no summer heat! Come, Mama."

The couple minced toward the dancing air. Fort smiled grimly as the frosty earth opened beneath him.

He braced himself this time. They could not lie about if the Jersey Devil still raged.

Light grew beneath them. It was the sunlight reflected by the Jersey soil, shining up the tube, Fort decided.

Anna jerked her hand suddenly from his. He collided an instant later with a grizzly-bear-wide and granite-hard form. He wrapped his arms around it reflexively. Neither bears nor boulders were shingled with feathers.

The figure let out a startled caw and reciprocated by crushing him close with iron-strong forelegs. Wings beat so near, so powerfully, the floating man's ears popped.

After a moment of terror, Fort felt the pull of gravity. So, apparently, did the Jersey Devil. The lion-bird released the two-hundred-thirty-pound extra load, and once more Fort hit the ground with a thunderous "Oof!"

Fort pushed himself to a kneeling position. The glint of spinning glass caught his eye. He reached out and snatched up his spectacles before they hit the ground.

"Hah!"

"Charles..."

The name came out as a moan. Fort froze on left hand and both knees, right arm still extended, like some chubby pink Labrador at point.

The Jersey Devil sat cat-fashion perhaps twelve feet away. For the moment it moved no more than they, except that eyelids or nictitating membranes snapped shut and opened again.

Fort found himself at a loss for words—even at a loss for thoughts. The creature was awesome in action, and unmoving it was a sculpture of terrible beauty, bronze and ebony, oak and copper.

The bird-beast drew one foreclaw closer, slipped the other out farther, and bowed like a circus horse. Its wings flowed out and down, putting Fort in mind of some Dumasian cavalier doffing his hat.

Why? wondered Fort. *Not that I question our good fortune.*

The renegade sky-tube wavered over the nearby trees.

Because we used the tube? It was more a case of the tube using us, but "Jersey" doesn't know that.

Fort slowly climbed to his feet.

"Uh—yes, good Jersey Devil. We are the mighty Nature Spirits, descending to this mortal sphere to see to the apportionment of, er, frogs."

The huge aquiline head rose again and turned, its wicked beak now in profile. The sky-artery swept toward the abandoned furnace at the north edge of the clearing.

The gryphon padded, then trotted, toward the furnace.

"Charles?"

Anna had made it only to her knees. Her husband lifted her to her feet.

"What was it doing?" she continued. "It looked like it was humbling itself before a king."

"I believe we're in the club, Mama," said Fort. "We rode the tube and returned. Perhaps he regards us as fellow travelers."

The gryphon galloped up beneath the sky-artery and sprang many yards high.

Only to flutter back down like a plump hen.

"Oh—wait a minute," said Fort.

The tube sailed languidly on. The Jersey Devil followed and leapt again. A high, magnificent jump, but again it fluttered to earth.

"It *tries* to use the tube," Fort observed. "Tries but fails."

Anna studied the ground. "Charles—Our clothing!"

Fort lowered his gaze to a scattering of haberdasher's flotsam. "Ever pragmatic, my Anna. Quickly, then—grab what you can before the tube or its pursuer returns."

The couple watched through the doorway as the winged creature sprang once more at the tube. It rose straight up the central axis, yet again it dropped in a fluster of paws and feathers.

Fort sat on a rough bench holding the single gray sock he had rescued. He wondered which foot was colder.

"You were right about the beast and the tubes being related, Charles," Anna remarked.

Fort finally worked the sock over his right foot. "I assumed the creature came and went by the tubes," he said. "Yet the artery rejects him, while it seems inordinately fond of me."

He slipped on his boots, both recovered, next. "Unfortunately, I have no idea how I induced the frog-flinging phenomenon to conduct me elsewhere. I had no wish to fly off, leaving every stitch of clothing behind."

He rose again and joined Anna at the door. The gryphon landed one final time. It simply squatted, head low and ears drooped forward, like a scolded puppy.

"Look, Charles. There's the rifle. He's practically sitting on it."

Fort shook his head slowly. "We no longer need it, I'm sure, Mama. If the Jersey Devil wished to slay us, he would have done so while we played subarctic Adam and Eve."

Fort drew thumb and forefinger along his chin, feeling two days' worth of stubble.

"Wait a moment, Anna... All I did the first time, in my panic, was fire the revolver into the air." His eyes widened. "And I fired a warning shot with the Winchester the second time. By God, or Whoever's up there pretending to be God, that may be it!"

The couple drew back into the shanty. Anna drew her mouth into a pucker.

"The gunshots?" she asked.

"Not the bullets. The reports. I've read of such falls, like those frogs, and even of reversed precipitations—like what happened to us—in those endless days of newspaper reading in the library. I came across 'snatchings', accompanied by loud detonations, but no signs of explosives, or wind-storms, or volcanic activity found afterwards. Sheets on clotheslines sucked into the sky, stones shooting up from fields, tiles drawn magnetically from a roof..."

He indicated the Jersey Devil, which sat like a statue now in the clearing.

"In those cases I believe the flows induced the noises—but possibly the noises can induce the flows. The pistol's crack changed our tube's direction, temporarily, from downward to upward. Why, if individuals as extraordinary as our Jersey Devil use sky-arteries to travel, that may be the answer to the gargoyles and monsters of the Middle Ages. In olden times church bells rang to drive away demons. In China they bang gongs to scare off dragons, in Nepal they crash cymbals to rid themselves of mountain devils."

"But Charles—why wasn't anyone drawn up when the policemen fired their weapons last night?"

Fort waggled his mustache. "Perhaps the tube, like a storm, had already passed on. The arteries themselves must vanish *here* and reappear *there* on occasion, or even blinkered modern folk couldn't help but notice them. I suppose the Jersey Devil's been flying about New England seeking them—always a bit late, like a commuter missing his train—until today."

A loud wail, part steam whistle, part bittern, and part alley cat in heat startled the Forts. The gryphon howled into the winter air, its stance more lupine than avian.

"I thought perhaps there was something wrong with that particular tube," said Fort softly. "Now I'm sure of it. The mere fact the beast's had to chase it across the map tells us something's amiss. His gooney-bird leapings speak of desperation. Now this..."

The Jersey Devil wailed again, not stridently like a parrot or a baby, but almost musically, like a grim Gregorian choir. Fort spotted the dark lump of the bolt-action rifle near its taloned forefeet.

"Charles, you're not going out there!" Anna cried suddenly.

What was this wild talent she possessed, that she could read his thoughts before they even formed? Fort took his wife's hands in his.

"Anna, dearest. This is no mere animal. If he knows the workings of the tubes, he may be quite above us in braininess. And you were the one to say he was only frightened and confused by the crowd."

He pushed the warped pine door open. "Look at him. That's no monster. By thunder, he looks ready to cry. Besides, I hold a distinct advantage—I succeeded where he failed. That's why he bowed to us.

"And before you say selflessly that we should both go," Fort continued quickly, "I believe only one ambassador of our little Third Dimension should approach him. He cannot possibly fear a single thin-skinned human being. Also—I have an idea of how to speak to him."

Anna Fort finally nodded. "You are certainly eloquent enough, Charles. Very well. But I'll stand ready by the door, just in case."

Fort stepped out. He walked slowly toward the bird-beast. For its part, the Jersey Devil shut its beak with a wet clack and bristled.

"Whoa, there, J.D.," said Fort, spreading his empty hands. "They say these signals are universal. See? I have no weapons. I mean you no harm."

The gryphon's feathers settled. It folded its wings in a precise feline manner (though the usual run of felines did not have wings to fold). The human pointed at it.

"You," he began.

He shaded his eyes and scanned the wide, wide sky. The renegade tube undulated high above. He swung his index finger toward the tornadic column.

"Want to travel in that." He held both hands palm up and lifted an imaginary load. "Fly through it and return—wherever it is you came from. Well, that conveyance may be as common as subway trains where you come from, but trains can derail, or collide, or run out of steam. Something happened, and you're stuck here."

The winged creature looked toward the tube as Fort pointed. Dogs commonly watched one's moving digit. More evidence of intelligence beyond the animal, thought Charles.

Fort located the rifle on the rusty earth.

Here's the hard part.

Fort pointed to the earth between the bird-beast and himself.

"The tube was here," he explained.

He indicated the rifle. The gryphon's only reaction, fortunately, was to emit a sort of "Clorp".

"Then I lifted the magical Thunderstick!"

He pantomimed raising a weapon high.

"I fired, and the Thunderstick made a mighty *bang!* Then—"

Fort knelt and grabbed a couple of torpid frogs.

"And whoosh! Up I went!"

He tossed the amphibians into the air.

"Savvy? Capisce? Okee-dokee?"

The Jersey Devil apparently understood. It narrowed its eyes and smiled.

Smile? An illusion of barely-opened beak, surely.

It sat up, curled a foreclaw into a fist, and thumped itself on its feathery chest. It pointed to the sky-tube.

"Indeed. You in the tube, up this time. The thing is, though..."

He stepped carefully over to the Winchester and pointed down.

"We will need this. Do you understand? I am going to pick it up now."

Fort knelt and picked up the rifle by the stock. The Jersey Devil watched but made no sound. Fort rose and cradled the weapon in his arms, careful to point it away from the creature.

"Good... Good." He nodded up at the aerial artery. "Now if our errant tube would just cooperate." The bird-beast abruptly spread its pinions and leapt. Fort stumbled back in surprise. It sailed over the forest; dry leaves hissed like a tough vaudeville audience. The creature mounted higher and arced gracefully around.

"And here I thought we were getting somewhere," said Fort.

He walked back to the shanty, the Winchester in the crook of his arm. He stumbled over branches and slipped on frogs, his attention on the spectacle in the sky. Anna stepped out to meet him.

"Charles, what is it doing?"

"I'm not sure, Mama," admitted Fort.

The gryphon wheeled in pursuit of the twisting artery. It hooked the lip of the sky-tube with its foreclaws. It gave a hawkish cry and tugged. The tube shifted.

"It's fighting the tube," observed Charles. "Like a man trying to straighten a large tarpaulin."

The Jersey Devil hauled the artery over the clearing.

"Best go back in, Mama. I'll try not to take another unexpected trip, but if I do—perhaps you can call me back again."

Anna stepped away reluctantly. The gryphon landed nearby. It let out an excited cackle and trotted toward Fort, unmindful of the rifle.

The artery loomed like a hot-air balloon. Fort aimed up. "Here goes," he called.

He fired and felt the electric tingle. He lay the Winchester aside and dropped flat.

The gryphon nudged him with its monstrous raptor's head, as a cat bumps in greeting. It padded out beneath the tube and sprang. It rose up the cosmic esophagus without a flap of wing.

Fort rolled on his back. The sky tube drifted away like a cloud, diaphanous and unhurried. Even as he watched, it and the network of arteries faded, leaving only the feathery cirrus to decorate the sky.

"Intriguing," he remarked. "Sending J.D. through must have corrected or balanced something. The sky's back to normal—or what normally passes for normal."

"Charles?"

Anna's pinched face hove into view. Her husband smiled.

"Well, Anna, I believe New Jersey has seen the last of its Devil—at least until he can get that errant sky-tube repaired."

Anna helped him up. "But Charles—you didn't even get a photograph."

"True—but it's been my observation that photos don't mean any more than signed affidavits or hands on Bibles. People would believe it if they'd the inclination, or call it a Barnum exhibit if they did not. It's just as well. Old Jersey's been in and out of the Pine Barrens for two hundred years. Draw more attention to him, in this day of machine guns and howitzers? I shan't do that to the poor beast. Let him be a nine days' wonder and be forgotten."

"I'll have a story for the *Herald*, if not J.D.'s head, and if Mr. Bennett won't accept it, another paper will."

— New York City, January 23

Charles Fort entered the lobby of the *Herald* and nodded to the busts of Bennett Junior and Senior. He patted his accordion-file of notes as if it were a satisfactorily full purse. He approached the woman with the eyelash-smile.

"Good day to you, Miss," began the writer. "My name is Fort. You may remember me from the other morning. I telephoned ahead about my assignment for Mr. Bennett?"

The woman's smile grew microscopically wider. She rose.

"Of course, Mr. Fort. We've been expecting you. Please follow me."

The woman led the way to Bennett's extravagant office. She opened the door and announced, "Mr. Fort is here."

Fort stepped in, doffing his cap. The woman closed the door behind him. For a moment Fort saw only the back of Bennett's chair, like the shoulders of a headless giant.

"Mr. Bennett?"

The chair turned. In it sat a large man with unkempt, graying hair, small, ice blue eyes, and a long bar of a nose that bisected his oval face.

"Good morning, Mr. Fort."

Fort gasped. Every New Yorker—most everyone in the country, for that matter—knew this man—millionaire—Congressman—nearly President.

The man rose and extended a plank of a hand. "Hearst. William Randolph Hearst."

The writer shook the proffered hand. William Randolph Hearst's grip was weak and clammy despite his size. His strength massed in other areas: in his penetrating stare, in his palpable willpower, in his pocketbook...

"Mr. Hearst. Of course. It's very—*democratic* of Mr. Bennett to let you use his office."

"Isn't it, though?" asked Hearst. He indicated the sensuous leather chair Fort occupied three days ago. "Do sit down."

Fort obeyed, shifting his brown folder to his lap.

"I'm not sure I understand, Mr. Hearst. Where is Mr. Bennett?"

Hearst sat again and leaned dangerously far back. "The Commodore? He's probably Commodore-ing his way to France by now. See, there are reasons he doesn't visit the States—a backlog of warrants and subpoenas stacked to the ceiling of the Criminal Court. Most buried in the legal tomb by now, but that editor, Murphy? Unpleasant fellow, but he informed me that the Commodore had pulled into port. And I never could resist a joke. The right words in the right ears, and the legal necromancers freed a few skeletons from Bennett's closet."

An ivory-shelled telephone on the huge desk rang. William Randolph Hearst lurched forward.

"As a matter of fact, if the old buzzard got my telegram—" He snatched up the receiver. "Hello. William Randolph Hearst speaking."

Fort heard an angry splutter, like a duck landing in a puddle. "What the hell are you doing answering my phone?" screamed James Gordon Bennett over the wires.

Hearst shrugged. "Somebody has to."

Fort winced at the stream of invective spilling from the receiver. The gryphon could not have screeched so loud. Mr. Hearst merely smiled.

"Always have a flowery turn of phrase handy, don't you, Jimbo? By the way, my offer for the *Herald* still stands."

The receiver shook in Hearst's grip.

"Easy, Jim," said the millionaire. "Remember your blood pressure. By the by, the Harbor Patrol ought to be steaming your way any minute. I'd hop aboard the *Lysistrata* and sail on if I were you."

The *clack* from the other end made Fort jump. Hearst set the receiver in its cradle and gave a bark of laughter. "Grand, just grand!"

Fort wiped his brow. "Yes. Quite the knee-slapper," he said weakly.

Hearst leaned forward, eyes hard as gimlets.

"Oh, that was just a joke, Mr. Fort. When you consider that the doings of the so-called Commodore are the main reason I lost the Presidency, it's like ringing his bell and running. Nothing will come of it."

Fort stared down at his frayed accordion folder. "Nothing indeed." He sighed. "Well, thank you for letting me hear the punchline, Mr. Hearst. I'll take no more of your time."

Fort rose, feeling old, tired, and sad. He had seen godlike forces at play in the Pine Barrens; the Olympians contested one another just as much in Manhattan.

"Wait," said William Randolph Hearst. The word was not shouted, but it came with more authority than any of James Bennett's bellowing.

"Yes, Mr. Hearst?"

"When I bribed my way in here, I heard a lot of rumors about some secret assignment Bennett had. What were you covering for the old geezer?"

"Mr. Bennett sent me in search of the Jersey Devil."

Hearst's tiny eyes widened. He reared back in the Commodore's chair and guffawed.

"My God, is our billy-goat-gruff *that* desperate? We've already re-placed the Devil with the Man-Eating Tree of Madagascar—and that only in the Sunday supplements."

Fort felt himself flush. "Mr. Bennett had reason to believe there was something to the Devil reports," he said.

"Mr. Bennett hasn't come up with a good story since the Central Park Zoo Massacre of 1874—and he made that up. Look, Fort, I take everything—even practical joking—seriously. I did my research on the

Commodore—and on you."

Fort's spectacles steamed over. "Me, sir?"

Hearst smiled grimly. "I knew this would ruin your hope to work here. I've already reimbursed the *Herald* for the truck, the supplies, and the pocket change Jimbo gave you. Keep 'em, if you can use 'em."

Fort rubbed his glasses. "That's very generous of you, sir."

"There's one more thing," said Hearst. "I could get you a position at the *Morning Journal*, but if I read people right, I have an idea you might like even better."

Fort frowned. "I don't follow you, Mr. Hearst. We don't want handouts, Anna and I."

Hearst waved that away. "I contacted a certain Theodore Dreiser, and he told me about a certain uncooperative publishing firm. He also said you were something of a novelist."

Fort sat back down.

— New York City, April 1909

The money from the car and the weapons stayed in the bank. Bennett's "pocket change" paid for a lease on a narrow, dirty boarding house. Compared to the communal rooms downtown, it was heaven.

Fort carried in a well-wrapped package as Anna cleared the kitchen table. The writer tore the brown paper like a boy on Christmas morn. He opened the box and pulled out several large volumes. Orange letters on blue cloth spelled THE OUTCAST MANUFACTURERS.

"Oh, Charles," said Anna. "Your first book!"

Fort set his arm over his wife's shoulders.

"Yes, Mama. Things will be different from now on. No more fish-head stew, if I have anything to say about it."

Anna shuddered. Fort gave her a squeeze and stepped over to his writing desk. "And there's no time to rest on my laurels. I'm thinking of another book."

"Another book? Already?" asked Anna, pulling the last of the novels from the cardboard box.

"Yes. A book of frogs, and monsters, and visions in the sky. A book with volcanoes of dialogs and hurricanes of soliloquies."

He pulled up a proper sheet of ruled paper.

"There's more in heaven and earth than is dreamt of in our philosophies, wrote Shakespeare, or virtually wrote he; we've had a glimpse of it, Anna. The Jersey Devil showed us. Now, like Galileo with his Jovian satellites, I must yank the blinders of convention off the world."

He touched pencil to paper, smiling at the familiar scrape.

Dangerous Creatures
J. Michael Shell

Book One
Glamorous Creatures

I

The Clans of Glamour

Though he'd heard many reasons why he shouldn't have been, Jasper was walking through the Old Woods. Some said there were snakes in there, fat as table legs, with venom laced fangs as long as toothpicks. Others said there was briar and bramble that would catch you up like barbed wire, and leave your ensnared corpse to be picked at by crows. There was a madman in there—a wolf, a bear, and a lizard as long as a horse, with fire red eyes and a taste for flesh. He'd even heard that a cannibal, escaped from an act in a traveling circus, had set up housekeeping with a giant cauldron for making stew. But Jasper had put a bit of rum into him, and with that courage decided to take a shortcut back to his dormitory. "Besides," he thought, "they probably tell those stories just to scare us freshmen."

Jasper also knew that old man Peters, an alumnus and the college's wealthiest patron, was known to walk in those woods on occasion. In fact, Peters owned the property on which they stood, and had tacked up "No Trespassing" signs all around the woods' perimeter (which Jasper, of course, had ignored). Other than when entering his woods, Peters was rarely seen in public. Word had it he was an introvert of the highest order.

Jasper saw no snakes. No briars tugged at his clothes. In fact, the woods were fairly open, with a cushiony leaf-mulch floor. Sassafras and honeysuckle fermented in the air, and when he came to a stand of wisteria, the spicy sweet aroma nearly lifted him off his feet. It was then that his mind's voice whispered, in a tone that seemed to have gone soprano, "Why hurry? It's nice in here."

Jasper found a log and sat. Looking up, he noticed that no stars were visible. The canopy the trees had raised was dense and dark. Yet he seemed to be able to see, as if some very faint luminescence was washing over everything. "It's nice in here," he said out loud, and that high-pitched voice in his mind said, "Yes, so nice."

Jasper had had some rum, but his intoxication was turning narcotic. Warmth flushed through him, and he opened the first few buttons on his shirt. "So nice," the voice reminded.

When it was that the fireflies arrived he couldn't say, but he watched as they flew lazy patterns in front of his eyes. Before long, his eyes wanted to roll, and their lids occasionally fluttered. Even within this hypnosis, Jasper could hear the tiny voices, high like little bells, speaking around him. "What is your name, boy?" one of them asked, as the rest of them giggled.

"Jasper," he breathed.

After many more tinkling giggles, the same voice said, "Jasper is a cutie-pie name. It tastes like frosting on my tongue." Again, sweet laughter followed. Then the voiced shouted, "See us, Jasper!" and his eyes opened wide and cleared.

It was the fireflies speaking! They'd changed into beautiful girls perhaps the size of extra large dragonflies, and with similar wings (but pink and gossamer). One by one they flew very close to his nose. From that distance, they seemed full-grown and were all quite stunning. Some of them giggled into their hands as they hovered. Others did little dances, which often seemed risqué (especially since these firefly girls wore no firefly clothes). "You're very pretty bugs," Jasper managed to say, and the laughter and dancing ceased.

The winged girl who'd spoken first (whose name was Titanya) buzzed up to Jasper's nose and said, "Do we look like *bugs*, young man?"

Jasper wanted to say no. He wanted to say they looked like beautiful (though tiny) girls, but he was just too stupefied on rum and hypnosis to speak anymore. Turning to the other Faeries behind her, Titanya said, "I think he's sleepy, clanlings," and the laughter started again.

Jasper was somewhat aware, but he felt like he'd been breathing a little bit of ether. His body wasn't quite under his control. When his chin dropped to his chest, he noticed two of the tiny girls had lighted on him, and were tugging at the remaining closed buttons on his shirt. Just then, he heard another voice, slightly different from the voices of his present company. "Caught another one, have you?" it said in a delicate tone, just a touch less high than the others'.

"Mirabelle!" Titanya moaned. "Go home to your highborn and leave us to play. The Faerae clans have no quarrel with the Fiereste. Why must you Firesprites care what sport we pursue?"

Jasper managed to rock his head up and look at Mirabelle hovering before him. She was half an inch taller than Titanya, and lit as a lantern. "Hello," he said drunkenly.

"The Faerae have you, boy, do you know it?" Mirabelle shouted into his stupor.

"Pretty," he mumbled.

"They're pretty and Glamorous, human-child, but they find *you* pretty, too! They'll not let you leave till they're tired of the dalliance. Their tastes are strange, and they don't tire easily!"

"Why should you care how long we dally, Mirabelle?" Titanya asked. "I can see in your eyes, right now, a lust for him rising. Why fight it?"

Mirabelle fluttered lazily around Jasper's head. "I'm not averse," she said, swatting a lock of his hair. "But you Faeries have no compassion. You'll Glamour this child so long that his mind will go fey and shy. He'll have little to do with his own kind once you are through. And the only love he'll ever know is what he receives when he returns here."

"Which is why we keep them so long," Titanya said. "It's like feeding a puppy so it comes back for more." Then the other Faeries roared their little laughter and darted about like sparks.

"I'll show you some tricks, if you'll let him go sooner," Mirabelle tempted. "Techniques known only to the Fiereste."

"We've techniques of our own, Firesprite!" Titanya laughed. "Join us, if you will, but interfere and you risk the peace! As rare as our clans are become, another Glamour War could be the end of us all!"

Mirabelle seemed taken aback when Titanya spoke of war, and said, "I would *never* break the Treaty of Sighs! But talk breaks no vows. I only try to persuade you toward compassion."

"It's a *human*-child, Mirabelle," Titanya argued. "They call us bugs, but they breed like mice. There are plenty more whence this one came." Then she laughed in a lovely, dismissive way, and her clanlings laughed along with her.

"What if I agree to touch you each, once, with a Fiereste spell? Would you take one turn apiece with this pretty human, then set him free?"

"What spell could tempt us," Titanya asked, "from lingering pleasure? We can feed and water this pup for half a fortnight, till he is quite spent and we are quite sated. And we don't *take turns*! He's a large enough playground for all!"

"But can you do *this*?" Mirabelle cried, spinning like a fiery top and growing into a human-size girl.

The Faeries shrieked and buzzed their wings. Titanya shouted, "How dare the Fiereste keep such secrets!"

"'Twas ours to keep!" Mirabelle answered. "And I'll not teach it to you. But I'll touch you with it, each in your turn, if you'll settle for one dance apiece with our boy."

Jasper sat up and smiled. He knew he'd had a bit of rum last night, but how had he gotten out of his clothes? Things were brightening with dawn, and he realized he'd slept the night away in the old woods. And what *dreams* he'd had! Wonderful dreams that perhaps were best dreamt out of one's clothing. As he started dressing, he breathed the sweet morning air and smiled again, as thoughts of those dreams assailed him.

They'd seemed so real that they'd left him spent.

As he got his bearings and prepared to walk home, Jasper heard a fair voice behind him. "Don't you come back here, now," it said, "or I'll join them myself for a week or two."

Jasper turned and, for a moment, thought he saw a girl, but she disappeared. He laughed and said, "You must stay away from the rum, Jasper," to which he heard tiny giggles.

II
Dalliance Allies

In a little glade, on a ring of mushrooms, sat thirteen Faeries and six Firesprites. A couple of Pixies had stopped by the gathering, but after being practically ignored by the others they moved along. "Don't let the sky smack your ass as you leave," one of the Faeries said under her breath, which made the rest of them giggle loud enough to be heard.

The Pixies bent forward and patted their behinds at the Faeries. "Kiss it," one of them said as they left.

"Why must you always chide the Pixies?" A Firesprite asked the Faeries.

"Oh, Giselle, you know they're all lummoxes. Their Glamour is weak and they're *short*!" Said a Faery called Ophelia. "They aren't even of clans! They just wander about by themselves or in pairs. While *we* have the clans of Faerae, and you of Fiereste, they have Diddley-Squat and Poor-Little-Me." The Faeries all laughed in agreement, as they reached down between their legs to tear off pieces of mushroom to munch.

"Have you caught any man-children lately, Ophelia?" Giselle asked, changing the subject.

"None! None in so long that I've pulled out several handfuls of hair, and chewed my nails to nubs. But I thought you Firesprites don't approve of the way we diddle our captives."

"That's not it at all!" Giselle protested. "In fact, I could give you some pointers in that arena. The problem is that you dally too *long*! All that Glamour, not to mention what you do, leaves them fey-shy and dull. If you'd just show a little restraint, we could all enjoy ourselves and then let them go their way unharmed."

"Do I detect a note of horny in your voice?" Ophelia asked.

"I've pulled out a handful or two myself," Giselle admitted. "*Do* call me if you catch one."

"Will you stay for the duration of our dalliance if we do? Think of the ecstasies if Faerae and Fiereste partner for a game. Think of the orgasmic rays we could catch coming off of the captured!"

"Stop!" Giselle told her. "I can take but so much! Let's go *now*, and set a trap! I know of a path, where I've seen farm boys go. And sometimes they go with farm *girls*!"

"Oh, to catch a pair! Just like the old days!" Ophelia pined. "But it's hard enough to catch *one* anymore. It's why we keep them so long—it makes them come back for more."

When Ophelia said that, the other Faeries burst into laughter. "They always come back!" they squealed.

The Glamorous creatures hopped off their mushrooms and into the air—all but one. A Firesprite named Maribeth remained in her half-eaten seat. "Oh, come on, Maribeth," Ophelia said. "You *know* you want to."

But Maribeth dropped off her mushroom and stood on the ground. "I do, but I'll not," she said, turning and walking away (which is a Firesprite way of saying, "I'm ashamed of you").

"That's Mirabelle's sister," Giselle whispered. "Those two have the highest codes of conduct. Did you notice she *walked* away?"

"Yes, I feel so ashamed!" Ophelia said, mock contritely. Then she and the other Faeries laughed, and even the Firesprites giggled.

The moon was new, and the path was dark, which worried the Faeries that no one would use it. "Such a shame," Ophelia said to Giselle. "They don't see well, you know, and aren't likely to take this path through these dark woods. Not on a moonless night."

"You're too easily foiled, you Faeries," Giselle told her. "Watch this!" Tearing off down the path toward its entrance into the woods, Giselle looked like a little white rocket (only faster).

Not quite as quickly, but still very prettily, the Faeries followed behind her. "What are you going to do?" they asked her, when they all reached the path's point of entry.

For answer, Giselle flew circles around the two trees that guarded the path's location until both began glowing ever-so-slightly. "That might steer some our way!" she exclaimed when she'd finished.

"A lovely advertisement," Ophelia said. "But Titanya told me you Fiereste can spin yourselves large as a human. Why not do that, and attract us a boy? You're actually quite pretty, for a Firesprite."

Giselle ignored Ophelia's little jab, and said, "Titanya's a silly ether-brain. Where does she get such ideas?"

"She witnessed it done! By Mirabelle, in fact!" Ophelia said in an offended tone. "And Titanya's been nominated for Queen of All Faerae, which I think she'll win. Don't you speak so of our queen."

"She's not queen *yet*!" a Faery named Honeythorn insisted. "My sister, Thistle, is also nominated!"

"Nominated by Honeythorn," Ophelia whispered to Giselle. "Titanya has it sewed up like buttons."

"Well," Giselle said, "if she's to be your queen, I take back the 'ether-brain,' but I'll neither confirm nor deny her account. I'll have to ask Mirabelle about it."

"Good Pan," a Firesprite named Nell whispered to one called Prissi. "She's practically admitted it!"

"She should *do* it," Prissi whispered back. "I haven't slid down a belly or touched a boy-tongue in much too long. And what I really miss is..."

"Stop it!" Nell said, clapping her hands to her ears. "Do you think you're the only one with unindulged fetishes?"

"Sorry," Prissi said. "I just need it so badly I could *spin*!"

"Well *don't*! Not in front of these Faeries! Not till we've talked to Mirabelle!" Nell scolded in harsh whispers.

Prissi was somewhat sensitive to criticism, made worse by her long, unintentional stint of abstinence. A tear slid out of her eye, and when it hit the path, burst into a respectable flame.

"What in the nethers are you two doing?" Giselle shouted. "We'll find no game in burned up woods!"

"Don't yell!" Nell hollered back. "You'll just make her cry more!" Then she took Prissi into her arms and kissed her eyes. "Mmm," she said, teasing, "you taste like barbequed mouse."

Prissi smiled and stopped her arsonist tears.

Just then, Ophelia, who'd flown dangerously out into the open, called to Giselle. "Look!" she said. "A *pair* wanders near! They've spotted your glow in the trees. Let's all be a swarm of fireflies, and lure them to the path!"

The girls all donned a little bit of Glamour, till they looked just like well lit lightning bugs. They flew up into the glowing trees, and twinkled intensely. The human lovers came closer to see the show. "Look, Jackie," the girl-human said to her boy, "they're like ornaments on a Christmas tree!"

"I'd like to *catch* her cutting down a perfectly good tree for such a thing," Prissi said to Nell.

"Hush!" Nell told her. "And don't you dare cry!"

"What's down this path?" Jackie asked his girl, whose name was Jillian.

"It goes all the way through these woods to town," she told him.

"I don't want to go to town," Jackie said, taking her into his arms for a kiss.

"Me neither," she said, when their lips let go. "But there's a little clearing about a hundred yards in, full of lovely rye and wildflowers. I might be persuaded, by just the right boy, to spend an hour or two there tonight."

"*Bingo!*" Prissi cried out.

"Hush!" the other Faeries and Sprites scolded.

"What was that?" Jackie asked.

"It's me breathing heavily," Jillian told him.

"Let's go!" the boy-human said to his human girl.

For such a dark night, Jillian and Jackie had no trouble at all finding the clearing. Apparently, the fireflies had decided to join them, and the path, it seemed, was reflecting some memory of past moonlight. "It's beautiful, isn't it?" Jillian asked when they entered the clearing.

"Magical," Jackie answered, which made the fireflies stifle giggles.

After pushing the rye down in places to make a mat, Jackie and Jillian climbed into each other's arms and dropped to the ground. "This is going to be easy!" Prissi announced, which made the other Glamorous creatures roll their eyes.

"I think I heard a mosquito," Jackie said.

"Let her drink," Jillian answered, pulling his face back to hers.

While the lovers kissed and fondled, the Faery and Firesprite partners began to scheme. "Let's do a firefly dance for their eyes till they're all hypnotic," a Faery named Josslyn offered.

"Let's just do it fast," Prissi said, "with fire dust and breaths of ether."

"Let them get out of their clothing, first," Giselle wisely suggested. "Think of the time *that* will save."

To the Faeries' delight (and the Firesprites' elation at saving some time) the lovers deftly undressed one another in minutes. "Dust them!" Prissi shouted, once they were nude.

"Breathe sleep up their noses!" Nell cried.

"Let's watch for a bit," Ophelia insisted. "They might give us some ideas."

"If you get your ideas from human play," Giselle said, "you need my pointers more than you know."

"I *mean* we might get ideas about what *they* like. The more frenzied we make them, the more rays we'll catch!"

"I know what you meant," Giselle said, laughing. "I was pulling your wings."

The glamorous creatures ended up waiting till the lovers were well entangled. "They're not going to stop for a firefly dance," Ophelia told Giselle. "Go ahead and dust them. We'll help with some sleepy breath."

"You Faeries have used up your dust, haven't you?" Giselle asked. "It's no wonder you can't catch humans anymore."

"We're growing some new," Ophelia said in a tiny voice, seeming quite hurt by Giselle's observation. "And we still catch a few with our dances and ethers."

Ophelia looked like she was going to cry, and even though Faery tears don't burst into flame, Giselle felt sorry that she'd hurt her feelings. "It's okay, sweetie," she said. "And, look! Tonight we've caught a *pair*! Don't cry now, or you'll make me cry too—and that would be the end of the party."

"You'd probably roast our catch," Ophelia said, brightening a bit.

"Now watch," Giselle told her, "and see how *fire dust* confounds!" Then, to the other Sprites, she called, "Come, clanlings! To Glamorous endeavors!"

Tiny motes of light, like finely crushed spark or powdered fire, rained down on the lovers in the clearing. They'd tangled themselves in such a way that Jillian was on top of Jackie. She'd propped herself up on her arms, and was looking down at him when the dust began to fall. "I'm so hot, I think I've gone molten," she said, looking down into Jackie's eyes. Then her own eyes rolled, and, sleepy with Glamour, she laid her head on his chest.

Jackie folded his arms over her, and said with his last conscious breath, "Me too."

"They're ours!" Prissi screamed, darting around above the somnolent pair.

The other Glamorous partners joined her. They were all so excited that the clearing glowed. "No tears of joy, now!" Nell shouted, teasingly, as she buzzed past Prissi. Behind her, trails of leftover dust lit the air.

"Let's get them apart!" someone shouted.

"No, let's play with them tangled a while!"

"Yes! Slide between bellies while they're slippery and wet."

Then Giselle, still dusty, and the most luminous of all, hovered over the lovers and held up her hands. The others went silent. "Hear me!" she shouted. "See what our cooperation has wrought! A Pair! Thank Pan our unrequited desire has finally brought us together! Hurray for our alliance! Now on to the dalliance!"

"Hurray!" the Glamorous creatures cried.

Then Ophelia called out, in a joyously teasing voice, "Save your wind for our captured, Giselle! It's going to be a long fortnight!" And the Faeries and Sprites all trembled and sighed at the lovely thought of having the humans for so long.

The children of Glamour began their play with the lovers still in one another's arms. So relieved were they all to have two such marvelous playgrounds on which to frolic, that they didn't notice they were being observed. Up in a dogwood, resting in stout, white blooms, two Pixies and a Firesprite stared down on the scene. "Looks like fun," the Pixie named Dalla said to her walking-mate, Tealli.

"They'd probably let you join them," Maribeth said to the Pixies.

"Why don't *you?*" Tealli asked the Firesprite. "I can see it in your eyes, you're chomping on the bit!"

"You have no idea," Maribeth said softly. "But if I get caught up in it, I won't be able to stop it in time."

"I thought you Firesprites have self control?" Dalla said, smiling.

"We do, but it's been a long time, and longer since any have captured a pair. Do you know what delights our sisters are immersed in right now?"

"They're not *our* sisters," Dalla said.

"But they are," Maribeth told her. "We're all fallen from the same tree. Millennia ago, before the first great Glamour War, we were all of the clans Fiereste. The three factions that fought in that conflagration were changed forever by the maelstroms of Glamour they unleashed on each other."

"How do you know what occurred in millennia past?" Tealli asked her.

"I was there," Maribeth breathed, her eyes gone distant.

"She was there," Tealli whispered to Dalla, who giggled and rolled her eyes.

"Will you join them, or stay with me and help stop this?" Maribeth asked, with a touch of annoyance in her voice. Her hearing was good, and she'd heard the Pixies mocking her.

"We've really no taste for that sort of thing, Maribeth. We prefer to creep into the humans' dreams and play with them there. We don't need such a gaggle of girls to achieve it, either. We can do it ourselves."

"I know," Maribeth told them. "And that's just the kind of help I'll need. Have you ever slipped into Sprite and Faery dreams?"

Dalla and Tealli looked at each other and raised their eyebrows. "You've a wonderful mind, Maribeth," Tealli said. "But how could we do such a thing? Look how many of them are down there playing. And they're stronger of will than Pixies, as you know."

"But our *bodies* are stronger," Dalla said proudly. "We walk often, and let the Earth push against our feet. I'll bet I could wrestle even *you* into submission, Maribeth!"

"It sounds like fun, and we'll try it sometime," the Firesprite told her. "But now, do you want to crawl into Glamorous dreams or not?"

"I still don't know how we'd do it, but what will you give us if we try?" Dalla asked.

"The *ability* to do it, for a while, and an experience you'll never forget." Maribeth answered.

Again the Pixies looked at each other with widened eyes. "I'm not busy tonight," Dalla said to Tealli.

"Me neither," Tealli told her. Then to Maribeth, she said, "Why not?

We have no plans for the evening."

"Good, but we wait for morning, when the clanlings will rest. They dally in the night, then drowse on the captured all day—soaking up rays of afterglow."

"What if other humans come by while they sleep? Isn't it dangerous in that clearing in broad day?"

"Has your Glamour really gone so weak that you don't know?" Maribeth said with pity in her voice.

"We still know some tricks," Dalla said with downcast eyes. "And besides, we dally in dream. We've no worries of being discovered."

"Neither do they," Maribeth told her. "Such a large band of sisters will easily weave a web of dread over their site before they sleep. So thick will it be that even sunlight will dim, and no human will go near it. They're easily frightened, you know."

"So what shall we do till the dawn comes round?" Tealli asked.

"I want to watch," Dalla answered. "And Maribeth can give us the blow by blow."

"What's that?" Tealli wanted to know.

"Something I heard in a burly man's dream," Dalla told her. "It means she can tell us what's going on—in detail!"

"Mmm, how lovely! That should give us new ideas for our dreamscapes!"

Tealli and Dalla settled back in their blossoms to watch the game going on below. The Pixies had very good eyesight, and could see everything as if up close. Maribeth, of course, had such vision that she could watch amoeba dance. After a little silence, Tealli said, "So tell us, Maribeth, or we shan't help you! Give us the blow on blow!"

"*By*," Dalla told her. "It's blow *by* blow."

"Whatever, and we want to know secrets," Tealli continued. "Things about the clanlings that we might not know. We're very curious creatures, we Pixies. For instance, why are they all glistening so? They seem to be growing quite damp."

"You'd grow damp, too, if you were down there," Maribeth said. "You're more like them than you know. And we are all very much like *flowers*. A flower turns sunlight into sweet nectar. The girls are gathering rays of ecstasy as it shines from the humans. The nectar they make glistens on their skin. Soon they'll be covered as if in jam, thick and sweet. Their ebullience will rise to great heights as they slide around on those human torsos, and roll on their tongues—filling them with sweetness and ardor."

"Ooo, you tell it so *well*," Tealli cooed. "I'd like to go lick some off them."

"Mmm, they'd like that," Maribeth breathed, losing herself in thoughts of such play.

As the night wore on, Maribeth and the Pixies witnessed all manner of rapture and bliss. The clanlings below (who were stronger than you'd think) eventually separated the pair of lovers into two lovely fields of play. So enraptured were the humans that, even in their stupors, they moaned and sighed with mouths opened wide into silent cries. "Look," Dalla whispered to Tealli as the action heated up. "Maribeth is sweating jelly."

"I know," Tealli said. "I can feel the radiance myself coming off of the humans. And *you* are glistening a bit, too, honeybunch." Then she ran her finger down Dalla's arm and tasted it. "Mmm, like cherries," she said.

"Let me taste you," Dalla insisted, wrapping her arms around Tealli and touching her tongue to her cheek."

"Knock it off," Maribeth told them, "or you'll end up going down there with them."

The Pixies giggled, and Dalla said, "You're pretty well glazed yourself. We'll stop if you let us taste you."

Maribeth glared at them, and they stopped their teasing. But when they settled back into their blooms, they each had one of the other's fingers in their mouths.

When dawn began to crack her knuckles, Maribeth looked over to find the Pixies sleeping together in one big bloom. Dalla still had Tealli's finger on her lips. "Wake now, you two," Maribeth said. "Watch as the clanlings begin their repose. They'll rest in mental fields of bliss, lounging on the captured all day. They believe they've many days yet to go with their charges, and will sleep in peace beneath their protecting web."

"What's she going on about?" Dalla asked sleepily, untangling herself from Tealli.

"I don't know, but look, Helios rises. The Faeries and Sprites are snuggling down into human flesh for a nap."

"We could enter the man-children's minds and play in the dreams the clanlings have wrought," Tealli suggested.

"You'll not!" Maribeth told them. "I've much better minds, and more powerful dreams for you to behold."

"The clanlings'?" Dalla asked.

"Of course the clanlings," Maribeth told her. "Weren't you listening last night?"

"I still don't see how," Tealli said. "I doubt if we two could invade *one* Glamorous mind."

"What if you were *bigger?*" Maribeth said, with eyes shining and smile stretched wide.

Dalla and Tealli faced one another, and Dalla said, "I've heard tales, but could it be true?"

Then, as the clanlings slept, and the Pixies watched in wonder, Maribeth jumped up out of her bloom and began spinning wildly in the air. Larger and larger her spinning form loomed, till finally she stopped, holding out arms for balance, and stood, human sized, in the clearing.

The Pixies looked into each other's wide eyes, and said in unison, "That's so *cool!*"

"Care to join me?" Maribeth asked, staring up at the tiny girls in their tree.

"We can't do *that!*" the Pixies cried.

"Don't be so sure," Maribeth told them. "But it doesn't matter, I can touch you with it for perhaps an hour. Would you like to be big for a bit?"

"*Would* we!" the walking-mates squealed, hopping out of their blossom to hover near Maribeth's very big face.

"Here goes then. Hang on!" She told them, flicking them each into a spin with her finger.

In a moment the Pixies stood four feet tall in the clearing. "We're *huge!*" they cried.

"Hush!" Maribeth told them. "The clanlings sleep deeply, but you've very large voices now."

Giggling into their hands, the Pixies whispered, "We do. We really do."

The Pixies watched as Maribeth found a fallen tree and sliced out a section with a fiery hand. Then she used her fingers like red hot chisels to carve it into a big, wooden bowl. After dusting the clanlings sleeping on the humans, she said, "That will keep them somnolent, but not for long. Here, take this bowl. Pick all the Glamorous off of the humans and put them into it. Look everywhere, some might be hidden. When they're all in the bowl you must enter their dreams and play with them there. Keep them asleep while I rouse the humans. Do you think you can do it?"

"We'll find them all," Dalla said. "And as big as we are, we'll have no problem entering their dreams. We'll give them such ardor!"

"Make them quiver and pant!" Tealli added.

"Have fun," Maribeth told them. "Now go!"

The Pixies picked the Faeries and Sprites like strawberries. Maribeth brushed herself free of excess dust, then said a little spell into her hands. *"Naiad babies float through the sky—in my hands I'll hold them until they cry!"* Between her cupped palms, a cloud began to form. "Are you ready?" she called to the Pixies.

"We've got them all off and into the bowl," Dalla answered. "We'll go to their dreamscapes now. Don't talk to us while we're there, if you can help it, or you might draw us out."

"Go!" Maribeth told them. The Pixies closed their eyes and left.

With the sisters subdued, and the Pixies with them in their dreams, Maribeth could relax. The clanlings would have been quite annoyed with her if they'd awakened to what she was doing. They'd have fought ferociously to keep their captives, so strongly were their arousals arisen. But once she managed to get the humans on their way, there would be nothing left to fight over. And the clanlings would still have the night they'd spent playing to sizzle their dreams, and give them bawdy tales to tell. "If only they wouldn't insist on keeping them past their minds' limits," she said aloud, "I'd join them myself."

Maribeth walked over to the boy-human and squeezed her cloud over his face like a sponge. Little lightnings flew out between her fingers, as the cloud emptied cold rain onto his face. As his eyes began slowly to open, Maribeth dropped to her knees and gave him a kiss. "You owe me that, at least," she said, "and I'd take much more if I had the time!"

Jackie looked up at Maribeth bending over him. "You're naked," he said in a sleepy voice.

"So are you. But you are more naked than you know. The Faerae and Fiereste have seen your naked glow."

"Are those wings?" Jackie asked, his eyelids beginning to flutter again.

"Good idea," Maribeth said, turning her back on him and buzzing her wings.

The fierce wind blowing on Jackie brought him more awake. Maribeth stopped her buzzing, and turned to face him again. "Take your girl and go," she told him. "You might have to carry her. She's deeply Glamoured, and I can't keep those Pixies grown forever."

"What?" Jackie asked her—still sleepy, but beginning to move.

Then Maribeth heard the Pixies sigh, and noticed they'd shrunken a foot. "Oh no," she said. "I'm losing my grip on their Glamour! I didn't know they were so weak. Pick up your girl, this instant, and run—or a war may be fought over you."

"Where are our clothes?" Jackie asked.

"No time for dressing!" Maribeth told him. Then she reached up and tugged on a tendril of the dread the clanlings had hung over the clearing. She touched it to Jackie and his eyes opened wide with fear. Quickly he scooped up Jillian and ran, as best he could, with her in his arms. Maribeth watched them go, and said, "They're even cuter seen through larger eyes."

By the time the human lovers were gone, the Pixies were barely a foot tall. "They're gone," she told them. "You can come out now."

"Noooo," the Pixies moaned, with cries in their sleeping voices. "Help us staaayyy."

Maribeth spun back to Firesprite size, and with the Glamour she'd freed up, grew the Pixies a foot and a half. "It's the best I can do," she said, as they smiled—their eyes closed and their skins glistening with cherry dew.

"Be happy together in your dreams, sisters," Maribeth said as she started to flutter away. Then she changed her mind and flew back to lie in the bowl with the clanlings. "Come play in my dreams as well," she told the Pixies. "I could use a little bit."

The Pixies' smiles grew wider, as both big and little sighs drifted through the clearing.

III
Queens of a Feather

There are no boys among the Glamorous creatures. There once were, and may yet again be—but in the present time, over all the Earth, none can be found. It was half a millennium ago that the last of boy-Pixies melted away into the Pixie girls. Firesprite and Faery boys had been soaked up long before that. Apparently, the Pixies had not stressed their males quite so much as the clanlings had.

Though the Pixies were the last to go, in the end *all* the boys of Glamour vapored away and curled up in Glamour-girl minds. Why did the boys disappear? Because the girls made them love them so much that the boys could no longer abide being boys. So they slipped away into girl-minds to sleep. Do the girls know they have them? Oh yes! They know (though they can't *tell* they're there), and they've tried every way they can think of to get them back out. They want the boys out because the girls want to be adored again (and perhaps, though nobody's sure, that is why the boys stay where they are).

Mirabelle and Maribeth, Firesprite sisters, were very popular in the clans Fiereste. One day, when the old queen tired of the job, the clans nominated both the sisters for the chance to sit on the throne. The winner would be chosen by vote, which would be preceded by a lot of excitement.

The clans had actually nominated the sisters to see which one was more popular. It seemed that exactly half of the Firesprites liked Maribeth the most, and exactly the other half loved Mirabelle. With the vote they would all know, once and for all, who was really loved most, and their curiosity would choose a queen.

The sisters were very alike, but looked different because they did little things so they could tell themselves apart. Sometimes they were different colors, or simply had different colored hair. Sometimes one would tie a ribbon round a toe (which is considered risqué to all Glamorous creatures, who find *any* kind of clothing scandalous). They sometimes even made themselves different sizes, though they avoided doing that around Pixies or Faeries (who would want to know how it was done).

When the nominations had been heard, and only the sisters' names were called, the gathering of the clans broke into wild celebrations. Some of them had even brought stupefied (but lovely) boy-humans to play on for the night. It was quite a treat, as man-children were becoming harder and harder to catch. In the old days, the clans would have brought many, and also pairs (human girl & boy lovers).

It was a fine celebration, except that Maribeth was sullen all evening. Finally, Mirabelle took her aside and asked her what was wrong. "You've been soggy all night, sis, what's the matter?" Mirabelle said in a hiccuppy voice (she'd been drinking mead and sprinkling ether dust on the tip of her nose).

"I don't relish this vote, Miri," Maribeth said. "It makes us *rivals*! I love you too much to contend against you!"

Maribeth started to tear up, which worried Mirabelle more than a little. Firesprite tears, as you know, are highly explosive, and burst into flame quite readily. "Don't you *dare*!" Mirabelle told her, "or you'll make me cry, too, and the clans will be all night putting things out!"

Maribeth smiled and rubbed away her tears before they fell, as Mirabelle took her in her arms and said, "We'll never be rivals—*hiccup*—and you know it! Now tell me what's really—*hiccup, hiccup*—wrong!"

"You're nose is quite red from ether dust, Miri," Maribeth observed. "It's okay to be toasty around the clans, but you should keep your wits when you're with the Faeries."

"What are you coming to—*hiccup*—Maribeth?" Mirabelle said, squinting her eyes angrily.

"I heard you spun up some Faeries to human size, then let them each have a go with a boy-human."

"I did!" Mirabelle said, as if it were her business only.

"How could you let those Faeries see you spin, much less spin *them* up? If it gets around, there'll be no end of pestering till we tell them how."

"So, just don't tell them," Mirabelle said, finally getting her hiccups under control. "And I only spun them up to save the boy-human being diddled for a fortnight. They'd have mushed his mind if I hadn't helped. And didn't I hear you spun up two Pixies to save a human pair? *Pixies*, for Pan's sake!"

"Yes, but I didn't let them *dally* with the man-child while they were huge. Don't you know what could happen?" Maribeth asked.

"I *saw* what happened! They dallied and it was fun!" Miri answered.

"But what if *babes* were put in?"

When Maribeth said that, Miri burst into laughter. "You're kidding me, now I see! You had me going for sure. *Babes*! That's a hoot!"

"I'm serious, Miri! That's how it's done, you know!"

"Oh, come on, Maribeth. Even when the Fiereste boys were still around, babes were rare. We could barely have them with *Glamorous* males, much less humans! Babes won't take that were placed by human boys. Not in Faeries!"

"Probably not," Maribeth said. "But I'd hate leaving that to chance. Such a thing probably won't happen, but it could, and more likely in Firesprites than any other. Tell me you didn't do it that night with that human—not in a consummate way!"

"Oh, stop it, Maribeth! You're making me mad! I'll have no more to do with you tonight. You're ruining our party!"

With that, Mirabelle turned her back and walked away, which was a pretty rude thing to do. Maribeth wanted to, but didn't, cry, as Miri went back to the ether dust (and started hiccupping to beat all the nethers).

But it wasn't just anger that had flared in Miri, it was also concern. Maribeth had planted a seed of worry, which was why Miri hit the mead and ether dust even harder. In fact, she got so loopy that she tied ribbons on two of her toes.

Sad and unhappy, Maribeth decided to leave the party. She fluttered off to the clearing where she'd grown the Pixies. It was a lovely place, with pretty memories, and she sat in a dogwood bloom to snooze. Unfortunately, Mirabelle, in her drunken state, grew angrier with Maribeth as the night wore on. Eventually, she ended up following her sister's trail, deciding to give her a piece of her mind (ether-dusty though it was).

Immediately upon entering the clearing, Miri could see Maribeth up in the dogwood. She was just about to scream at her, when she realized her sister was asleep. Suddenly, a burst of drunken inspiration came over Miri, and she concocted a pretty dirty trick (which, in her defense, she'd have at least thought twice about if she hadn't been so in her cups). It was a complicated practical joke, to be sure, that would take quite a bit of high-powered Glamour. She'd have to keep her sister asleep, or stupefied into immobility, in order to pull it off.

But confounding a Firesprite into stupefaction, or keeping one asleep against her will, is very nearly impossible. Mirabelle could dust her sister, but that would only keep her asleep a very few minutes. Mirabelle needed much more time for her joke. In fact, she'd probably need hours.

Miri, however, was wickedly smart, and had a steamy imagination. "I can't stupefy a Firesprite," she thought with a naughty grin, "but if she were *human*-size, and already asleep, I could keep her that way for a very long time."

Then Miri saw the flaw in her plan, and the highly dangerous solution to that flaw. She could dust Maribeth long enough to grow her, then ether her up and dust her down again. But there was not enough Glamour in Miri to keep her sister grown for more than half an hour. She was sure she'd need more. The only way to borrow the extra Glamour she'd need was to attract the attention of a Demi-god (which is not attention you'd ordinarily want to attract). She thought about calling to Mab, who tended, occasionally, toward wickedness, and would probably like the prank.

But Mab was moody, and one could never tell how she'd react to having her attention tickled. *Pan*, however, could be counted on when mischief was involved. So Miri prepared herself, and chose her words carefully when she spoke at the Demi-god. "Pan, you scandalous rascal," she whispered, with eyes tightly closed, "hear my prayer. Grant me Glamour for a wonderfully dangerous prank. If you don't you're a horse's ass, but of course I'll still love you. How could I not?"

Mirabelle took a breath and felt her Glamour. Nothing! "Okay, then," she added to her prayer, "I'll grant you an hour with me if you're ever a satyr in these woods. And I'll wear a blue ribbon round my neck, and another about my waist."

Suddenly, Mirabelle felt it. "Ooey," she said. "That's nice!" She also knew that it was quite a gift, since Pan, if he chose to be a satyr in her woods, could take her anytime and for as long as he liked. But she didn't want to think about her promise to Pan, or dallying with a satyr (which *no* amount of glamour will stop from stinking). It was time to teach her goodie-wings sister not to judge, or scare her with thoughts of cross-bred babes.

Mirabelle spun herself up to seven feet tall (feeling the oats of her Pan-Glamour) and, after dusting her, picked Maribeth out of the dogwood. Then she laid her down in the clearing, and grew her to petite human size. "You're just lovely, all big," Miri said, as she tied one of her toe ribbons, which both were red, round Maribeth's pretty neck. Then she took the other and tied it around her own. "Now we look like mirrors," she said to the sleeping image of herself. "Oh, but I must shrink a little to make it exact."

Once she was perfectly the spit of her sister, Miri dusted Maribeth liberally, and glamoured her wings invisible. "Just a portrait of human," she said, vanishing her own wings as well. Then she walked drunkenly down the path to where it took her out of the woods. Looking the way she did, it was no time at all before she enticed a boy-human to chase her back in there.

Before she got to the clearing, Mirabelle stopped and turned on the boy who was following her. He also stopped, and faced her with cheeks blushed red and trousers blooming. "What do you have on your mind?" Mirabelle asked, touching his nose.

"Something that might please a pretty girl like you."

"I'm hard to please," Miri told him. "I'm a little drunk, however, and inclined to let you try. But here's what would please me most. There's a clearing up ahead..."

"Yes! I know it!" the boy-human said, overanxiously.

"Let me finish, silly," Miri told him. "I'm going to lie in the clearing, and pretend to be asleep. Do *everything* you can think of to wake me! Do you have some things in mind?"

"Many!" the boy told her, grinning to beat all the nethers.

"Okay. Count to three and then come," she said. Then she moved so quickly it startled the boy (but not so much that he didn't follow).

When the boy made it to the clearing, the girl he'd chased was lying asleep (or so it seemed) in a patch of wildflowers. "You're incredibly pretty," he said quietly. "Why don't more pretty girls wander about wearing nothing but ribbon collars?" Then he went to her, removing his clothing along the way.

Mirabelle had spun down to Firesprite size, and was watching from the dogwood where her sister had slept. Though the boy-human couldn't wake Maribeth, he tried very hard indeed. He loved her one way, then rolled her over. Then he tried again, and again and again. For a human he was quite insatiable. But when he was finally spent, Mirabelle Glamoured him up for one more bout. But this time, when he and Maribeth were face to face, Miri woke her in the middle of the game. "What are you doing?" she cried, once awake.

"So, I finally woke you!" the boy said, laughing.

Then Miri buzzed out of the tree, and spun herself up to Maribeth's size. "Good lord, there's two of you! You're identical!" the boy said in a delighted voice.

"Yes," Miri agreed, realizing she'd better pull the ribbon from her neck. If the Firesprites saw each other identical (while both were awake), they'd mistake themselves for one another, and never know who was who again. "Time for you to go," Miri told the boy, as she weaved up a little dread and put it on him. It frightened him so that he left his clothing, and ran naked from the woods.

"*What have you done?*" Maribeth cried, rubbing her tears back into her eyes lest she burn down the woods.

"That's what you get," Mirabelle told her, "for scaring me with tales of having babes, which you know won't happen! But if it happens to me, now it will happen to you." Then Mirabelle, finally sobering and having regrets, dropped to her knees and cried (wiping furiously at her tears before they made it to the ground).

"I'm sorry I scared you so," Maribeth told her. "I see now that I should have been a bit more delicate about confronting you. It's a million to one, I know, that such a thing could happen. But I have to admit, now that one of the chances is mine I'm a little scared, too." Then she went to Miri, and took her in her arms. "Did that boy-human have a nice time with me?" she said, kissing her sister's cheek.

"Quite a few times," Miri told her. "It was probably that red ribbon that inspired him so." Then she put her head on Maribeth's shoulder and said, "I'll never glamour you again, I promise."

"Where did you get all the Glamour to do that trick, anyway?"

"Oh my!" Miri said, rubbing her starting-to-ache little head. "I'm afraid I might have to lie with a satyr a while to pay for it."

"Serves you right. You'll stink for a fortnight!"

The vote came four months after the nominations. Mirabelle and Maribeth showed up for the results looking exactly the same, except Miri had a little blue ribbon in her hair. They stood together on a platform, and held hands as they waited for the results. A Firesprite named Prissi hollered the tally. "Exactly one half for one," she cried, "and exactly one half for the other! We have two queens!"

Miri and Maribeth smiled and kissed, happy to be queen together. But as their lips touched, both at once felt kicks in their tummies (which had recently become a tiny bit rounder than usual). "Oh no! I just felt something!" Mirabelle said.

"I felt it, too!" Maribeth whispered, wide eyed.

At that moment, a gusty breeze, with a slight smell of satyr on it, blew the blue ribbon out of Mirabelle's hair. "Which one are you?" she said to the Firesprite she'd been kissing, who was now her identical twin.

"I'm one of us," the other one said, "but I'm not sure which. Do you smell satyr?"

"That scandalous rascal has found a way to have us *both*! Now we can't tell which of us made that deal!"

"Oh my," the other said. "Do you think he had anything to do with what's in our bellies?"

"I wouldn't put it past him to have helped that along. I think we're to be queens during interesting times."

"And we'll never know which of us tricked the other."

But the trick was done, and, somewhere, a satyr was waiting to be paid.

IV
Meeting Marisa Rose

Though Pixies quite often walk alone, they are always looking for walking-mates. To them there is no stronger bond, and they seek it as intently as humans seek bed-partners (though Pixie pairs stay together longer and seldom quarrel).

One day, two Pixies met while walking, which is pretty rare for several reasons. First of all, Pixies themselves are rare (as are all the Glamorous creatures). Secondly, they're tiny beings, even shorter than

Faeries, who are slightly shorter than Firesprites. A Pixie can walk all day and barely cover half a mile. Of course, they can fly (and they do), but they like to walk and it makes their little bodies hale and hearty.

So, on this day a Pixie named Taia and another named Brini were walking around the same big puddle. When they spotted one another their eyes grew wide, as Pixies see meeting while walking as a sign of lives about to intertwine. "Aren't you Taia," Brini asked, hurrying to join the other pretty creature. "I think you know my sister, Tealli!"

"Yes!" Taia called out. "She walks with *my* sister Dalla!"

"There are no coincidences!" Brini said, quoting the sayings of Mab.

"There certainly aren't," Taia agreed, taking Brini in her arms for a greeting kiss.

Though no agreements were spoken (and, of course, no silly promises sworn), Taia and Brini held hands as they strolled, knowing they were walking-mates found.

As they talked about the weather, and how huge the puddle was, Taia broached the inevitable subject. "Have you found any good boy-humans to dream in? Or perhaps a pair of bed-mates?"

"Oh! You'll just love this!" Brini exclaimed, so happy that the subject was out in the air. "I've found one not far from here, who sleeps in a pretty blue room. He's at that human age where all he can think of are girl-human playmates. And here's the loveliest part—he's not had one yet!"

"Except in his dreamscapes, I'll bet," Taia giggled.

"Oh yes!" Brini beamed. "Especially when I show up in there. I've kept him sticky and sweaty in his sheets on several occasions. I think, tonight, he should find out what it's like with *two* playmates!"

"I just *knew* I'd love you when I saw you coming round that puddle," Taia said. Then those two sat down for a rest, held in each other's arms.

When night grew strong and settled itself deeply into the sky, Brini took Taia to the human house where the man-child slept. As they flew up to an open window, Brini said, "Careful, there's a metal web woven over this opening. Come down here, I've torn a corner of it away."

Though the room was dark, Pixies have very good eyes, and Taia said, "I thought you told me this room was blue. This is the pinkest blue I've ever seen."

"It's strange!" Brini said. "I'm certain this is the place. Might humans have Glamour that we don't know about? Could they have changed it?"

"Perhaps they crush berries or earth colors, they way they do to color those flat images they make."

"It would take a lot of juniper berries to cover all that blue," Brini said. "But, no matter, look there—under the covers he sleeps, though he must be curled tightly."

Marisa Rose was in her bed, but she wasn't sleeping. The smell of the freshly painted walls gave the room a feeling of new. Up until a few days ago, it had been her brother Jonathan's room—but he was off to college. He hadn't been out the door two minutes before Marisa couldn't stand it anymore and said to her mother, "*Can I?*"

Her mother laughed and said, "Yes, you can. But we'll paint it first. What color would you like?"

Now Marisa was in her pink room, lying still in her bed, trying to hear what sounded like faraway voices. And though they *seemed* far away, Marisa had the strangest feeling that they weren't. She felt like she wasn't alone.

"Come have a look!" Brini said. "He's a lovely face, and I've a tiny bit of ether I can breathe up his nose. Of course, I haven't any dust."

"Who does anymore?" Taia observed.

"Firesprites, but they keep it to themselves," Brini said with a pout.

"Theirs is too hot to handle, anyway," Taia told her. "Maybe Faeries could use it, but it would blister us, surely."

The Pixies lit on the pillow, which held Marisa Rose's pretty head. Immediately Taia knew something was wrong. "It *is* a lovely face," she said, "but isn't that a girl-child?"

"So it is!" Brini answered. "Now where did that boy get off to?"

"Have you ever been in girl-human dreams?" Taia asked.

"Of course! And I often play in pairs of bed-mates. But this one's too young. All you'll find in there are candies and ponies!"

"Let's go in and ride her ponies a while," Taia said. "As long as we're here, I mean."

Marisa Rose's eyes appeared to be closed, but they were actually squinted open a tiny bit. She could see the two bugs on her pillow, talking, though they were blurry, as she was seeing them through her lashes. She knew she could catch one, but she wanted them both and was waiting for them to move closer together. But her impatience ruled her, and the fear of catching neither made her spring like a cat. She brought her cupped palms down over Taia.

Pixies can move very quickly when frightened, and Brini was seriously startled. When that girl-child moved, she was out through the metal web in a flash. But she noticed that Taia wasn't with her. Where could she be? Then she heard the girl-child talking. "What *are* you," she was saying, and it scared the nethers out of Brini.

Marisa had a jar in her room, with holes punched into its lid. It was what she called her "Firefly Lantern," because she often filled it with the sparkling little things. But when she held the jar in front of her night-light to see what she'd put inside, it delighted her more than fireflies ever could. "You're a fairy!" she exclaimed.

"Hmph," Taia harrumphed. "Shows what you know. How would you like me to turn you into a snail, and then eat you right out of your shell?"

Taia was bluffing, of course. Even if she had that kind of Glamour, glass is the one thing that stifles it. She might work some through the metal ceiling over her, but the glass would direct it all up, and the girl-child would have to pretty much get in its way for it to work.

"If you could do such a thing, you'd have done it by now," Marisa wisely told her. Taia dropped onto her butt, and began sobbing into her hands. "Don't cry," Marisa said. "I always let my fireflies go after a while. I'll just keep you long enough for Show-n-Tell, though, of course, I'll have to find something for you to wear."

"Wear?" Taia said, ceasing her crying. "*Clothes*, do you mean? You have scandalous thoughts for such a young human. Let me into your dreams so I can see them."

"You're welcome in my dreams once I'm asleep," Marisa graciously offered.

"Well, I can't get in them through this glass, you know!"

"Don't try to trick me," Marisa said, laughing. "I'm not letting you go until *after* Show-n-Tell!"

What Brini saw from behind the metal web was terrifying. Taia was captive in a little glass house with a metal roof. The girl-human child was talking to her, and Brini didn't like what she was saying. "How dare she threaten to clothe my walking-mate!" she said out loud. "As soon as she falls asleep, I'll breathe every bit of ether I have up her nose! Then I'll punch her in the eye! I'll bite her lip till it bleeds and shove a dorsal-fly in her ear!" Brini went on about what she'd do for so long that she hyperventilated, and fell off the windowsill. By the time her head cleared and she'd buzzed back up there, the girl-child had a pile of little human clothes—which she was showing to Taia.

"You're not as big as Barbie," Marisa said, "but I think you could wear one of her miniskirts as a gown. Or maybe one of her blouses as a robe."

"You should be ashamed of yourself!" Taia told her.

"I'm not the one standing nude in a jar," Marisa giggled.

"Okay," Taia tried. "Let me out, and I'll put on clothes for you. A Pixie's word is as good as honey, so if you let me out you'll get to see me dressed as sure a worms eat dirt!"

Marisa eased the jar lid up a tiny bit, and slid Barbie's red plaid mini-skirt under it. When it fell over Taia, she swatted it away. "Forget it!" she said.

But Marisa picked up the jar, and told her, "If you don't put it on, I'll shake you!"

"You're cruel as well as scandalous," Taia said, quite amazed at the things she was learning about human girl-children.

"Put it on!" Marisa warned, threatening to shake.

"Okay, humiliate me if you must," Taia said, pulling up the skirt till it was under her arms.

"That's so cute!" Marisa squealed. "Wait till they see you at Show-n-Tell! And I promise not to shake you if you'll just be good till then."

Brini watched as the human-child did terrible things to Taia. "She's having too much fun tormenting my walking-mate—she'll *never* go to sleep. I won't be able to rescue Taia alone, not with that monster in there. I'll have to get help. I'll ask the Firesprite Queens!"

Brini, of course, meant Mirabelle and Maribeth, who'd recently been elected Queens of the Fiereste. Brini's sister, Tealli, had told her a wonderful tale about Maribeth Fiereste growing her as big as a goat. The Firesprite Queens were rapidly becoming living legends, and it was said that no one, not even they themselves, could tell which one of them was who. It was also rumored that Pan had planted babes in their tummies, but Brini would have to see those bellies before she'd believe *that* was true.

Firesprites are the fastest Glamorous creatures, but not by much. In two quick shakes of a lambkin's tail, our Pixie flew to the Fiereste meeting place hoping to find the queens. Unfortunately, as it was high night, there was no one around. They were probably all out playing. Still, Brini was desperate, and she started screaming, "Alarm! Alarm! A human beast has taken a Glamorous creature! Alarm!"

Just then, two beautiful Firesprites came out of a hollow tree. They both appeared sleepy, and were rubbing their eyes. As they walked, a little excess dust twinkled off of them. "Good Pan," Brini thought. "They've so much dust it falls from them like dander!"

"What's all this shouting?" the Firesprites said in unison, which made them look at each other and giggle.

It was then that Brini noticed that the two were identical. "You must be the Firesprite Queens!" she exclaimed. "Were you sleeping in there at this hour? Are you ill?"

The queens both rubbed their bellies, which Brini noticed were rounder than seemed normal, and one of them said, "What's in here makes us a little fey. We sometimes sleep all night and play all day."

"Yes," the other said. "And we often eat strawberries with vinegar."

"Are there really babes in there?" Brini asked, amazed.

"'Fraid so," the queens answered, in unison again, which made them smile at each other.

"Can I look in at them?" Brini asked.

"How could you do that?" one queen wondered.

"Pixies can see through anything, if we want to. I could tell you what kind they are, if you'd like. But I'm forgetting my errand! A terrible human has taken my walking-mate! It trapped her in glass and makes her wear clothes!"

"Aren't you Tealli's sister?" the queens asked. "Have you been drinking mead?"

Brini dropped to her knees and began to plead. "Please, great queens, help me save my walking-mate. Here, hold still and I'll look at your babes for you, and tell you their kind."

Mirabelle and Maribeth (though, of course, I can't say which was who) stood still while Brini peered into them. After a moment she said, "They're both boy babes, and yours," she said pointing to the queen on the right, "is several days older."

The queens looked at each other, and raised their eyebrows. "Quick!" one said to the other. "Find a ribbon!"

In a flash the queens were gone, and in another flash they returned with a pretty blue ribbon. "Now, which of us holds the older babe?" they asked.

"You do," Brini said, pointing.

With that, Mirabelle tied the blue ribbon around her waist. "I'm me!" she cried.

"Oh, I'm so glad you're you!" Maribeth exclaimed. "Though I wish we'd found out before that night with the satyr."

Both of the queens made a face as if something was stinking. Then they went to Brini and said, "You've solved the dilemma of which was who, and are welcome amongst the Fiereste any time. Someday we might even give you a gift. But now, let's go find your walking-mate. I'm certain she simply trapped herself in a cast off jug, or squeezed herself into a bottle. We'll have her out in no time."

"A human has her, I swear!" Brini cried.

"Come along then," Mirabelle said, putting her arm around the Pixie. "Let's go see."

Mirabelle and Maribeth were quite surprised when they peered through the metal web. "What's she wearing?" Maribeth asked.

"Clothes!" Brini whimpered. "That monster threatened to shake her to pieces if she didn't don them!"

"That's a young girl-child," Mirabelle said. "How did she catch a Pixie?"

"She set a trap with a boy for bait! When we came for his dreams, wham! The next thing I knew, she had Taia trapped in that little glass house!"

"That's a jar," Maribeth said.

"Yes—it jars me, too!" the Pixie told her, which made both the queens smile.

"Have you tried going in there and asking her to release your Taia?" Mirabelle asked.

"What?" said Brini.

"Go in there, right now, and tell her if she doesn't release that Pixie, the Queens of the Fiereste will take her to task," Mirabelle told her.

"Okay," Brini said, shaking like a leaf fluttering in a breeze. "I'll do it right now."

"Well? Are you going?" Mirabelle asked when Brini didn't move.

"I'm on my way," Brini answered. Then she slowly crawled through the tear in the screen.

"What do fairies eat?" Marisa asked Taia, who was mortified standing there in that dress.

"I'm not a Faery!" she said. "And right now I'd like to eat one of your fingers!"

"If you're not a fairy, what are you?"

"I'm a dangerous Firesprite, of the clans Fiereste! If you don't let me go, I'll dust all your ponies and spoil your candies!"

"I haven't any ponies," Marisa told her. "And I don't think you can do *anything*. So you'd better be good till Show-n-Tell, or I'll shake you up and sew buttons on your feet for shoes!"

The thought of having buttons for feet was about to make Taia cry again, when she saw Brini come buzzing into the room. "Save me, Brini," she screamed when she saw her, "or this human will take me to the land of Showindell, and we'll never be together again!"

With courage she didn't know she had, summoned up by the sight of her walking-mate captive and humiliated, Brini hovered in front of Marisa's face. "You let her out this instant," she cried, "or the queens..." but that was as far as she got. Marisa, who must have had sorceress blood, snatched her out of the air like a frog tongue-snatching a fly. Then she popped her into the jar with Taia. "Well, of all the nerve!" Brini said.

"Are there more of you about? Can you light up like fireflies?" Marisa asked.

"You're going to catch it now!" Brini said, shaking her fist at Marisa, who giggled. "The Firesprite Queens are outside, just beyond the metal web. Wait till they get their hands on you!"

Outside the window, Maribeth and Mirabelle had gotten into a discussion about names for their babes. Knowing they were going to be boys, they'd decided, was certainly going to save time. Now they wouldn't have to think about girl names anymore. "I like Jackie," Maribeth said. "Maybe I'll call mine Jackie."

"That's a *human* name!" Mirabelle said. "Don't you dare call my nephew a human name!"

"How 'bout Oberon?" Maribeth tried.

"It's better, but you've still got time to consider."

"And how about *you*, have you thought of any?"

"Peli!" Mirabelle told her.

"Peli is a girls name! Try Pelon of Pelonias."

"I can call him a girl's name if I want! He *might* be that *pretty*!"

"Hey, wait," Maribeth said. "What happened to that Pixie?"

"We sent her inside to get her walking-mate from the girl-child. Don't you remember?"

The Firesprites were sitting on the sill outside the window, with their backs against the screen. Maribeth turned her head to look into the room. "Good Pan," she said. "That child has *both* the Pixies in the jar now." Mirabelle looked and both the queens giggled. "We'd better get them out," Maribeth told her sister. "They're probably frightened to death."

"And what about the girl-human? Shall we punish her to keep her from stealing Pixies!" Again, they both laughed.

"We'll leave it up to her!"

In just under a flash, the Firesprite Queens flew through the tear in the screen, and hovered over little (big) Marisa, just out of her reach. "If you try, even once, to catch us," Maribeth told her, "we'll put you to sleep, and you'll wake with green teeth and a pimple on your nose the size of a raspberry. But if you listen to us, we might make you a deal."

"What *are* you?" Marisa asked. "You're bigger than my Firesprites, and you're all sparkly!"

"Yes, just some excess dust," Mirabelle told her, as she brushed it off. "And they aren't Firesprites, they're Pixies. *We* are Firesprites, and you'd not have trapped us in a jar!"

"Are you *pregnant?*" Marisa asked.

"Does it show that *much?*" Maribeth said, looking down at her navel.

"Now listen here, young girl-human," Mirabelle said. "You've a scandalous mind, and must be quite nimble to have caught two Pixies. We respect those qualities, but you must never trap Glamorous creatures again, or we'll punish you, and you really won't like it."

"What would you do?" Marisa asked, folding her arms defiantly.

"Would you like to have a tail?" Maribeth threatened.

"I might!" Marisa said, sticking out her chin.

"Spin her!" Mirabelle said, growing impatient. "Spin her down and we'll put her in her own jar!"

But Maribeth whispered to Mirabelle, "Do you know what happens if you spin down a human?"

"What?" Mirabelle whispered back.

"All of their Big spins down with them. That jar wouldn't hold her a second!"

"Oh enough!" Mirabelle said. "Let's just dust her and go!"

But Maribeth was presciently wise, even though pregnancy had made her a little fey, and she had a strange feeling about this child. "Listen to our deal, human girl," Maribeth said. "What is your name, by the way?"

"Marisa," Marisa told her.

"Okay, Marisa. If you let the Pixies out, of your own accord, we'll make you a FireFriend, and leave you the memory of this night. We'll also give you a way to call us in a time of dire need. You can only call once, but if you're good, we might come twice."

"How do I know you're telling the truth?" Marisa asked.

Though Mirabelle moved much too quickly for Marisa to see it, she definitely *felt* it when the Firesprite swatted her nose. "Ooww!" she said.

"If you question my sister's word again," Mirabelle told her, "I'll pull your nose *off!*"

"You're bery bery fast!" Marisa said, holding her stinging nose.

"Do we have a deal?" Maribeth asked.

"Okay, but how do I call you in a time of tired need?"

"*Dire!*" one of the Pixies yelled through the glass.

"Okay, then, *dire* need! How?" Marisa demanded.

"Just call us, silly. We're leaving you this memory, are we not?" Maribeth said.

"I don't get it," Marisa told her.

"Don't worry, you will when the time comes. But don't waste your call. You should wait till you're grown and know what dire means."

Marisa picked up her jar, and when she took off the lid the Pixies fluttered out. "Can I take that dress off you," Brini asked Taia, with a smile and blushy red cheeks.

"You're so *wicked!*" Taia blushed back.

"Do you think you might come see me again?" Marisa asked the Pixies, as Taia gave her back Barbie's skirt.

"If you swear not to trap us, we'll come and ride ponies in your dreams!" said Brini.

"And *Unicorns?*" Marisa asked.

The Pixies laughed furiously, and the Firesprites giggled. Then they all said at once, "You silly child! Unicorns aren't real!"

V
According to Mab

Time conducts itself quite differently with Glamorous creatures than it does with human-kind. Though we say Glamorous *creatures*, they are actually half-creature, half-luminous beings. Humans, of course, also have a foot in the Luminous Realm, but they don't know it, and even if they did, they seem to have no idea at all how to interact with the physics of luminosity.

Time, as it applies to the Glamorous, was a particular problem for the Firesprite Queens. While humans' perception of time is creature-linear, for the Queens time tended to move in fits and starts (and, occasionally, even slipped into reverse for a moment or two). The reason this was a problem for Mirabelle and Maribeth was that they were the only two Glamorous creatures in at least five hundred years to have buns in their ovens (so to speak). Perceiving and reacting to time as Glamorous creatures do, being pregnant was a trying proposition (which, perhaps, is why it rarely occurred even when the Glamorous boys were still around).

Mirabelle and Maribeth had been pregnant for seven years of linear time. Firesprites tend to become a little fey while engaged to motherhood, and this also played havoc with their interactions with time. It was a viciously cyclical problem, as pregnancy fiddled with time and time faddled with the pregnancy. But the queens never complained, and actually seemed to be enjoying the fey nature pregnancy had saddled them with—as if it were a kind of mild and pleasant high. It also made them seem more mysterious and wise to the other Firesprites. Their only real complaint was with their round little bellies. Occasionally time would slip, and they'd wake to find their tummies once again hard and flat. But it never lasted long, and as soon as time quit grinding its gears, their bellies would round again. Once, when their roundness returned after having been absent a day, Mirabelle said, through a pout, "I wish it would have stayed flat a little longer," and Maribeth answered, "I wish the boys would just go ahead and be born!"

But there was no hurrying that sort of thing, and for all the queens knew, their ovens might keep baking those buns for another hundred years.

While the queens had been pregnant for seven years, it had also been that long since they'd seen their FireFriend Marisa Rose. Marisa had a least one free call coming, but in seven years she hadn't used it, and the queens had never paid a visit of their own accord. Pixies, however, regularly showed up in Marisa's pink room, to ride with her on her dream ponies, and sample the sugarplums that danced through her head. Marisa even conversed, on occasion, with them while awake (once the Pixies began to trust her not to trap them again). But as Marisa grew older, and dreams of ponies and candies became dreams of a different nature, the Pixies stopped coming except when Marisa was asleep. They enjoyed giving her pleasure in dreams, but could not abide the waking questions she asked pertaining to details. "It is what it is," they'd told her the last time they showed up during waking hours. "You feel the ecstasy, don't you?"

"Oh yes, I feel it," Marisa had told them. "But I can't *imagine* most of those things happening outside of dreams!"

"Then they won't, and it's all your own fault," the Pixies had said, fed up with her questions. "Why don't you go to sleep now, so we can come in!"

Though she hadn't seen any Glamorous friends in over three years, Marisa knew they were still visiting her dreams. But, being seventeen in human years, her body was starting to insist that she receive some of her ecstasy while awake. In fact, it was starting to become *quite* insistent, which was made even worse by years of Pixie-diddled dreaming. "I need a boy, or maybe *two*!" she said to herself while packing her suitcase. It was spring break of Marisa's senior year, and she was going to see her brother. "Maybe," she thought, "Jon will have a friend who'll be just right, and I'll finally get my ashes hauled."

Actually, being Glamour-touched (not to mention a FireFriend) Marisa had grown into a fabulously beautiful young woman. She could have had her ashes carted away by any number of the boys at her school. But *being* Glamour-touched, ordinary boys just didn't do it for her. Though she'd noticed one or two of the prettier *girls* at her school, she was really more interested in beginning her waking sex life with the gender more suitably fitted to a complimenting dalliance.

"These babes of ours are never coming!" Mirabelle lamented, pouting terribly one day when her skin had turned a melancholy shade of blue.

"Don't fret, Miri," Maribeth told her. "They're waiting for something to happen, and I think whatever that is is on its way."

"Is your prescience aroused?" Mirabelle asked, hoping some inkling of the babes' arrival time might come through.

"Somewhat," Maribeth told her. "But all I'm getting is 'soon.'"

"Soon they'll be birthed?" Mirabelle asked, excitedly.

"I don't know, but I think it just means we'll learn something soon about this dilemma of the babes. Either way, it's encouraging, don't you think?" Maribeth said, smiling at her poor, blue sister.

"If you say so," Miri said, looking down at her big little tummy.

Marisa's brother had gone off to college just before she'd trapped her first Pixie. Now he was a teaching assistant at a college a hundred miles south of her room. It was spring break for him, as well, and he'd invited his little sister down to visit. When she arrived, on a big Gray Hound,

Josh was at the station to pick her up, accompanied by a friend.

If you've read the sayings of Mab, you know there are no coincidences. So don't be surprised that you've already encountered Jon's friend once before. His name was Jasper, and though he was no FireFriend, he'd once been touched by Glamour. He'd also, unbeknownst to him, placed a babe within a certain Firesprite Queen.

Jasper was an artist, and, believe it or not, an art critic had once called his paintings "glamorous." When Marisa stepped off the bus, she'd grabbed her bother into a painful hug. But over his shoulder, she'd spotted that glamorous artist. Their eyes locked, and they shared a thought (well, more of a notion).

The sparks that flew between Marisa and Jasper would not be damped by hurricanes, much less Jonathan or anyone else. I can't tell you how rare it is for two Glamour-touched humans to meet, or how that attraction *insists* (at least for a while).

By the time Marisa boarded the bus for home, her ashes were nowhere to be found, and the relief of it made her feel like a new girl. Though she and Jasper had seriously enjoyed their time together, no lingering attraction or bond grew between them. On the long bus ride home, she drowsed, thoroughly contented, but she was also thoroughly something else, which, when she found it out, would throw her into a panic. "I'm what?" she'd say, two months later, to the doctor at the clinic.

Marisa was grown, and now understood the meaning of the word dire. Though she hadn't seen the Firesprites in seven years, she remembered their meeting as though it were yesterday. One night, just after her surprise at the clinic, she called up that memory and looked into the eyes of Queen Maribeth. "I think this qualifies as dire need," she said to her memory of the queen. "I'd like to use my call now."

The image of Maribeth turned to her and said, "Right now?"

"If it wouldn't be too much trouble," Marisa answered.

Maribeth had seen the fear in Marisa's eyes, and went to find Miri. "Do you remember the human-child I BeFriended those years ago?" she asked, when she found her splashing vinegar on a strawberry.

"Yes. I heard her calling you just now."

"She seemed quite upset. I feel for her, and am going immediately. Do you want to come?"

"Yes, I do," Miri told her. "If I eat one more bite of strawberry, I'm going to burst."

Miri and Maribeth found the tear in the screen right where they'd left it. As they entered the room, they could hear Marisa sobbing, curled in her bed. "She weeps!" Miri said. "Maybe we should come back later."

"By her reckoning of time," Maribeth said, "she called us a day ago. *That* is why she weeps. She thinks we're not coming."

"She's impatient," Miri said. "Perhaps that's how she caught those Pixies!" Then they giggled into their hands.

The queens lit directly in Marisa's hair, blowing a tiny bit of ether at her to keep her from being startled. "It's all right, FireFriend, we are here. You can stop your weeping now," Miri said into her ear.

"I was so afraid you wouldn't come," Marisa whimpered, as the queens jumped down onto her pillow.

"But we did! Why are you still sobbing?" Miri wanted to know.

"She's distressed, sister, can't you see? Mellow your tone."

"Sorry," Miri said.

"I'm not distressed, I'm *pregnant*!" Marisa told the queens, sitting up in her bed. "And I certainly hope there's something you can do about it."

Mirabelle threw up her hands and rolled her eyes. "She's wasted her call!" she exclaimed.

"She's right, you know," Maribeth said. "That's a simple thing in humans. A matter of a few herbs swallowed to end the bout."

"Really?" Marisa asked. "Can you get them for me? Can you do it?"

"Certainly!" Miri said. "We can gather them tonight."

"How long have you been this way?" Maribeth asked, with a strange note in her voice.

"Two months," Marisa answered.

"Let me see," Maribeth insisted.

Marisa pulled up her nightshirt and showed Maribeth her belly, which still seemed pretty much unaffected. The Fiereste Queen crawled up onto it, and laid her head in Marisa's navel. "That tickles!" Marisa told her.

"Hush!" the queen told her back.

After a minute, impatient Marisa asked, "What is it?"

Maribeth stood on her belly and said, "The heartbeat of this babe calls out to something near, almost as if it is calling to the one *I* carry."

"Let me hear," Mirabelle said, joining her sister on Marisa's tummy. But as soon as she set foot onto it, both sisters could hear that heartbeat calling wildly. "It calls to *my* babe!" Mirabelle exclaimed, surprise showing in her eyes. "Did a human father this child?" she asked.

"Of course," Marisa said, laughing. "Jasper is quite human."

"Jasper!" Miri screamed. Then she fainted dead away.

Marisa picked Mirabelle off her belly, and laid her on a pillow. Maribeth flew over and woke her sister by fanning her with her wings. "Are you okay?" Marisa asked, as the Firesprite regained consciousness.

"Not really," she said, holding her head. "Do you know our babes are brothers?"

"*What?*" Marisa said.

"*What?*" Maribeth also said.

"It was Jasper that placed my babe seven years ago! And you know what Mab says about coincidences!"

"You've been pregnant all this time?" Marisa asked, incredulously.

"Thank Pan it hasn't all been *human* time," both sisters said at once, causing them to smile.

Maribeth and Mirabelle stayed with Marisa that night, mostly pacing around on her bed. Finally, Maribeth said, "This *is* a dilemma, but you are FireFriend, and have used your call. If you demand it, I'll gather a potent potion of flora, and relieve you of this burden. But I fear you carry an important child, kin to Glamorous creatures. He is half-brother to a Fiereste Prince, and cousin to another—stepson to my sister, and nephew to me."

"How do you know it's a boy?" Marisa asked.

"That's a good question, but I do."

"I *can't* have a baby!" Marisa wailed. "You have no idea what that means for a young girl. My life would be over! My *world* would be over!"

While Marisa and Maribeth had been discussing, Miri had been uncommonly silent and pensive. Finally, she said, "How would you like to *leave* your world. In *our* world you would be a princess, at least." Then to Maribeth, she said, "Wouldn't she?"

"I suppose. Her son would have claim to the throne."

"But the Pixies told me Firesprites *elect* their queens," Marisa said.

"Queens, yes, because there haven't been offspring in five hundred years. Our sons will be heirs to the throne, and so would any brothers, no matter who bore them."

"But how could I come to your world?"

"We'd have to spin you down to our size," Mirabelle told her.

"Which has drawbacks as well as advantages," Maribeth added. "For one thing, all your Big would become small with you. You'd be incredibly strong, but would have to get used to your strength. And you'd feel very heavy for a while."

"Tell her the worst part," Mirabelle whispered.

"Well," Maribeth said, almost as if embarrassed for Marisa, "you'd have no wings."

"I have no wings now," she told the queens.

"We know," they said, bowing their heads.

Marisa wasn't sure what to say. In fact, she wasn't really taking them seriously. "What if someone stepped on me?" she finally said, laughing.

"They'd hurt their foot!" Mirabelle said, quite seriously. "When we say you'd be very strong, we mean it. Imagine all the Big you are now, squeezed into someone our size. We're not even really sure *what* you might be able to do. We've never left a human little long enough to find out. Come with us and have your babe. Or make your decision now to end a prince—my son's only brother."

"And mine's cousin," Maribeth added.

"But what about my mother and my friends and—"

"Nobody said you can never return," Maribeth interrupted her. "You can come back tomorrow if you change your mind."

"Well, hell then, let's go!" Marisa told them.

"Why would we want to go to a hell?" Miri asked Maribeth.

"It's an expression, I think, like 'let's get the nethers out of here.'"

"Oh. That makes sense."

"So how do we do this?" Marisa asked.

Since Marisa would have no wings, and the sisters wouldn't be able to carry her with all her Big shrunk down, the queens decided to have Marisa walk, while still huge, nearer to the Fiereste gathering place. There, they could make a little home for their unwed mom, and keep an eye on her till she learned the ropes of being tiny. "How small will I get?" Marisa asked.

"We can adjust you as you like, but if you want to be accepted by the clans, you won't want to be much taller than we are."

"Hmmm," Marisa said. "Barbie's clothes would be a bit big for me then."

"*Clothes!*" the queens squealed. "You scandalous thing! You'd better get that notion out of your head *right now!*"

"I'm sure I'd get over the modesty part pretty quick," Marisa said. "But don't you ever get cold-? I know I would."

"You'll not!" Miri told her. "You'll have all your Big heat. In fact, you'll have to get used to that as well. But you'll learn to regulate it. I promise you, however, that you'll never be cold."

So convinced, Marisa set out into the aging night with a Firesprite on each shoulder. "Turn left here!" Mirabelle called.

"No, *right!*" Maribeth insisted.

"You two better fly, or you'll never get your bearings," Marisa told them.

"She's clever, for a human," the sisters agreed.

When the Firesprites and their human charge were very near the gathering place, Mirabelle spun Marisa down without a word of warning. "Why didn't you let her get undressed, first," Maribeth scolded. "Now she's buried in a mountain of clothes!"

But Marisa tore the clothes over her away as if they were made of wet tissues. "There she is now!" Miri cried. "See, no harm was done! How do you feel, tiny human?"

"Hot!" Marisa said, sweating to beat all the nethers. "But I also feel *great!* I feel like I could beat up a lion!"

"A *cat* you could!" Miri shouted, excited to have this human full of Firesprite-kin with them.

The three friends danced around, as some kind of joy infected them. Then Maribeth said, "Wait, stop! Mirabelle, do you feel it?"

"Feel what?" her sister asked.

"Time!"

The sisters were each holding one of Marisa's hands. When Mirabelle felt it, too, they both let go and took a few steps away from Marisa. "Yes!" Miri said, "I feel it diminishing!" Then she walked *toward* Marisa again, and said, "Now it *grows*!"

"What are you two talking about?" Marisa asked.

"Time!" Maribeth told her. "The nearer we are to you, the more rhythmic and linear it grows! If we stay close, our babes will come soon. They'll come as soon as yours comes!"

"And it will be a relief!" Miri told her. "If you stay with us till then, that is."

When Marisa didn't say anything, both the queens turned a sad shade of blue, which made Marisa feel sad as well. "Don't worry," she said. "When I called, you came—just like you said you would. What kind of FireFriend would I be to abandon you to eternal pregnancy."

The queens were so touched that they each shed a tear, which Marisa, with her great strength, managed to put out before the woods caught fire.

After doing a bit of "pacing off" while feeling time, the queens discovered that in order to remain in linear time, they needed to stay within a human foot of Marisa (which is fifteen hobnails to a Firesprite, twenty-seven slugs to a Faery, and six wiggle-worms to a Pixie). "I guess we're going to become pretty close!" Marisa joked.

"It'll be fun!" Miri laughed. "We'll make a big bed for three in our hollow tree! You'll be wonderful to snuggle, as warm as you are, and we can all lie abed and eat vinegar strawberries!"

"I guess you won't be doing much flying for a while," Marisa said, which turned the queens' smiles into frowns.

"She's right!" Maribeth said. "We'll be bound to within fifteen hobnails of earth till our babes are born!"

"Look out!" Marisa told Maribeth. "Miri's going to cry again!"

"Don't you *dare*!" Maribeth told her sister. "We've only a two foot circle round Marisa! If you run us out with your tears, we'll lose count on our months!"

Miri rubbed away her tears and plopped down onto her butt, wearing terribly pouty lips. "I miss flying already!" she whimpered.

"I know," Marisa said, comforting her. "Come to bed and I'll feed you a strawberry."

For over six months, Miri and Maribeth and Missi (which is what the Fiereste came to call Marisa) lived in close proximity. And believe it or not, there were only thirty-seven arguments, fifteen quarrels, and very little hair-pulling or nose-pinching or punching. Fortunately for all their sanity, Missi realized she could run incredibly fast with her Big shrunk, and the Firesprites loved to chase her through the woods—buzzing along below radar at a mere few inches from the ground. "You run almost as fast as we can fly!" Mirabelle told her one day after a lovely chase.

"I think I'm going to have to slow it down pretty soon," Marisa laughed. "Look at the size of my belly!"

"It won't be long now!" The queens shouted together, patting their own enormous tummies.

And their words turned out to be prophetic, because that night after her long run, Marisa, sleeping between the two queens, woke with a howl. "It hurts!" she cried out, overcome with labor pains.

"Try this," Miri said, breathing a tiny bit of ether up her nose. "Better?"

"A little bit," Marisa said, lying back. "Do you know how to deliver a baby?"

"It isn't even *born* yet, silly," Miri told her. "And to whom would I deliver our kin-child?"

"I *mean*, can you get it *out* of me?" Marisa screamed, as the pains bore down on her again.

But the queens only giggled, and Mirabelle said, "He knows how to get out, but it's a small door he has to squeeze through. I'll sprinkle one pinch of dust on your nose, and give you a tenth dram of mead, but that's all. You're going to have some pain to remember this night by."

"Great!" Marisa said, gritting her teeth.

Then Miri yowled, too, and threw herself down in the bed beside Marisa. "Mine comes, also!" she cried, and Marisa managed to laugh.

The half brothers were born side by side, with Maribeth tending to their mothers. Three days later, Miri and Missi dabbed ether dust on

Maribeth's nose as she bore their children's cousin.

The celebration that ensued amongst the Fiereste grew so wild that it attracted the Pixies and Faeries, until the largest collection of Glamorous creatures in at least five hundred years were gathered. And, of course, before long talk turned to the desire of many to have babes of their own. "Boy babes!" they all were saying. "There will be boys among the Glamorous again!"

Though our lovely mothers had their hands full with their babes, at least one of them (which was Maribeth) was growing concerned. "The Faeries are threatening war if we don't teach them to spin," she whispered to Miri one night.

"What good will it do them? Jasper diddled a *gang* of them that night, but only I took to a babe."

"They're consulting their old knowledge, and say they've come up with a spell to help babes take."

"Fiddle faddle," Miri said. "I think the only reason it took in us is because I attracted Pan's attention. He had a hand in this, I'll *wager*. Still, something must be done about the Faeries. We don't want war!"

"If they can catch a boy-human, I'll spin some of them up and let them try. But I'll never teach them the trick," Maribeth told her.

"Nor I," Miri said. "They'd get careless and give us away to the humans, of whom there are many too many. If they ever started hunting us..."

"Don't even *say* that," Maribeth told her. "And speaking of humans, our little one is homesick. Have you noticed?"

"Yes. She wants to see her mama, and show her the child."

"We should tell her, don't you think?" Maribeth said.

"Let's snuggle her deeply to sleep tonight, and we'll tell her tomorrow. Do you think she'll take it well?"

"Would you?" Maribeth asked.

"I'd cry!" Miri told her.

"Me too," her sister agreed. "I'd burn down the forest!"

Marisa named her baby Jasper, which made the queens moan and roll their eyes (though they secretly thought it was a cutie-pie name). The problem was that little Jasper was human, and had never been Big, which meant he could never be spun back up. If he ever were, he'd vapor away like a cloud. A second problem was that humans can only be spun down once. If Marisa ever went home to Big, she'd have to stay there. But the *worst* problem was that the queens hadn't told Marisa these things in the first place, and *that* caused all the nethers to break loose. But I'll tell no more in this book, except for this—Mirabelle named her very pretty baby Peli, and Maribeth called her son Oberon.

Book Two
Damnable Creatures

I
Megan's Story
The Most Potent Curse

She'd gone to Africa to quench her thirst. If there is such a thing as a vampire conscience, Dahlia had a little one—at least for a while. Of course, there are occasional newly-turneds who balk at drinking from humans, but it never lasts long. Nothing tastes (or refreshes) like a human.

Dahlia wasn't a newly—far from it. She'd been planting her pearlies in mortal necks (among other places) for a very long time. In fact, the snake that supposedly latched onto Cleopatra's breast was actually our girl in an amorous (and thirsty) mood. She might deny that (being vain about her age), but she told me the story in such detail that it *has to* be true.

As I've mentioned, Dahlia went to Africa in search of drink other than human. "Don't tell me vampires can develop consciences!" I said, a little startled (if not worried).

"You're all just so *pitiful*," she answered. "Perhaps if you were greater challenges."

"Not me," I reminded her. "You yanked me *out* of the human race, remember."

"Sorry, Meggie dear," she said, without a trace of apology in her voice. "You still look so human to me, though pallor *is* setting in nicely."

I was never sure how to take Dahlia's "compliments," though I'm still pretty grateful that she turned me instead of drinking me out of existence. Of course, if I ever pissed her off enough, she could *swat* me out of existence in a very thin minute. She *looks* lithe and lovely, and maybe even a bit frail, but don't be fooled. Dahlia is an Old World Drinker who's tapped elephants and tigers, as well as countless Homo Sapiens.

Anyway, this is what happened when she went on safari and didn't bring me along. "You're much too weak, still, sweetie," she told me before she left. "You'd slow me down. And if an elephant were to step on you it wouldn't kill you, but it might affect your looks. And I do so love your looks!"

"Are you really swearing off humans?" I asked her, finding it hard to believe.

"For a while, darling. I've kept count of my, shall we say, 'consumption total' over the years, and I'm about to hit a milestone that I'm just not ready to achieve."

"How many?" I asked her.

"Now Megan, darling, you're a bright girl and you'd probably be able to figure out my approximate age if I told you that. You know how sensitive I am on that subject."

"Half-a-million?" I pressed, more than a little intrigued.

But Dahlia only giggled when I mentioned that number, as if I'd complimented her looks. "Run along and play, darling," she told me. "I need to pack."

I remember when she left, all bandaged up like the invisible man (she insists on flying), wearing white linen gloves and those pitch black glasses of hers. "Cosmetic surgery, darling," she tells flight attendants and passengers alike. "I do so hope they did a nice job this time."

I offered to drive her to the airport, but she said she felt like walking (it was two a.m., and with the streets empty Dahlia could "walk" twenty miles in ten minutes). She did make me drive her luggage to the airport, and she said quite seriously, when I arrived, "What took you?"

"I *drove*, Dahlia! Remember?"

"Oh yes, that's right," giggle-giggle. "How else could you have carried all this luggage. Now listen to me, darling—check the mail everyday. I'll be posting letters to you quite often to keep you informed of goings on, and to remind you that you are mine. If you must dally, try to do it with human girls. I don't want any other Drinkers handling you, and I'd prefer not to have human males inserting themselves into my precious darling.

"Remember, Megan, to clean up your messes," she went on in a sterner tone. "The one thing I forbid, of course, is your turning anyone. I *should* insist that you not take human males into your bed—which, remember, is also *our* bed. But I'm a softy, and hate to restrict anyone's pleasure." Then she added, with another of her patented giggles, "Especially mine!"

I received a letter from Dahlia at least twice a week. I have to say I really did look forward to them. I started missing her almost immediately, or at least my body did. Dahlia knew tricks, perhaps *ancient* tricks, which she often used to keep me in a state of ecstasy for hours (and hours and hours). But when I started growing horns (about a day after she left) something she'd said came into my mind: "...human males inserting themselves into my precious darling."

Something I hadn't told Dahlia was this: I'd never *been* inserted into, at least not with one of *those*. I was, after all, only seventeen when Dahlia exited me out of the orphanage. Oh, I'd fooled around with girls, but as far as boys were concerned, I was an untapped resource. Had Dahlia known that? Could she tell it that night she showed up at the orphanage and picked me out like a pup from the pound?

There's really no telling *what* Dahlia knows, and I was sure she'd be able to tell exactly what sort of sexual escapades I dabbled in while she was gone. But the thought of actually being taken (impaled) by a boy was suddenly starting to cause my novelty glands to pump. Of course, I'd have to drink whatever human I chose for love-play (call it a show *then* dinner), but I was sure a male lover would be easier to do away with than a pretty girl. Call it a vampire conscience if you like, but at the time I truly believed that *whomever* I dallied with wouldn't survive the dalliance. Dahlia had only forbidden me to turn anyone, but there'd be hell to pay if she found out I let a human lover live. (Actually, there *was* hell to pay.)

Dahlia's letters were fascinating. Her descriptive prose was simply delicious. She intrigued me with tales of her exploits with elephants. I marveled at her stories of hypnotizing tigers, then lying naked in their fur while she drank them dry. Then she'd close the letter with something like this: "Be good now, Meggie darling, or don't, as you like. Do clean up your messes, though, or I'll take you over my knee when I return. Actually, I'll probably do that anyway."

I could hear her giggling at the ends of those letters, and by then I was more than ready to be taken over her knee, or placed under her thumb, or *something*! I had an itch that I was damned well going to have to scratch.

It was a parcel post delivery boy who caught my attention. Dahlia had sent me a beautiful carving of an elephant with a note that read, "They taste just like Asian humans with a twist of lime!" The boy who delivered it, dressed in cute little Khaki shorts, seemed just what the doctor ordered. "Come in," I told him, "please. The sun hurts my eyes."

"It must," he said. "You really keep those windows covered, don't you?"

"I'm pretty sun-sensitive," I assured him, knowing he had no idea what an understatement *that* was.

"Sign here," he said, holding out his electronic pad.

"Have you been doing this job long?" I asked him, hoping to entice rather than take.

"I'm a writer," he told me. "I just do this to make money."

"Can't you make enough money writing?" I asked him. The look on his face made me reconsider, and I said, "Oh! I'm sorry!"

"It's okay. Someday I will," he told me with a lovely vehemence.

"I'm new around here," I cooed. "I've come to live with my aunt." Then I decided to go for it, and said in an innocent little voice, "Would you take me out on a date?"

"Are you old enough to go on a date with me?" he asked.

"I'll bet I'm older than you," I said, and I'd have won that bet hands down.

"No way," he told me. "I'm twenty-three."

"Oh!" I said, feigning surprise. "You don't look that old. But I'm definitely old enough to go out with you. I'm almost twenty-one," I lied. The fact was, I'd been seventeen for thirty years.

"You wouldn't lie to me, would you?"

He was flattering me, though he didn't know it. Then the cat came out in me, and I started rolling him around under my paws. "You don't think I'm pretty, do you?" I said with a pout that I could see was clawing at his soul.

I knew I'd been a pretty human, but when Dahlia turned me I think she knew how much it would fair me up. She actually killed another Drinker once, an Old World male who had a mind to take me against my will (and Dahlia's). She pulled his heart out of his chest and tossed it through a window into the sun. I'll never forget the look on his face, or the one on hers. She smiled at me with her hand all bloody, and I *never* felt so precious in all my life!

"You're *too* pretty," the parcel boy told me. "But I'm no cradle robber. You're pretty enough to wait for, though," he said, which actually caused a little feeling of endearment to rise in me.

"I have a driver's license," I told him. "But I won't show it to you. I won't go out with a boy who thinks I'm a liar," I lied. "But I'll tell you this," I lied some more, "I was born in September of 1985. This September I'll turn twenty-one. So if you take me on a date before then, I won't be able to drink alcohol." Then I threw in the kicker. "But I can do mostly anything else."

"Okay," he said, which didn't surprise me. But what he said next did. "If you'd like to go to dinner with me tonight, I'd very much like to take you. And since you can't drink, I won't either. But I have to be honest—as hard as it will be, I won't so much as kiss you, or even hold your hand, unless you show me that driver's license. You don't look eighteen, and I have very strict principles."

"Me too," I said, trying not to laugh, because my principles included making him disappear when I was through with him. That's what I was thinking as I dug my license out of my purse. I showed it to him and it confirmed my lies. Then I caught his eyes with mine and drew him in for a kiss.

But he somehow shook off my hypnosis and said, "I've got to get back to work. I'll pick you up at eight, if that's okay."

"We're eating here," I told him. "I'm an incredible cook. How do you like your steak?"

"Bloody," he said, and I couldn't help but laugh.

"That's funny?" he asked.

"I took you for a well-done man," I told him, trying to recover.

"Why ruin a good piece of meat?" he said, as he headed out the door.

"Why indeed," I said to myself as he left.

His name was Albie, which, believe it or not, was short for Albion. Apparently his parents had been literature professors or some such, and had named their son Albion Blakely Jones. I had every intention, that night he showed up for dinner, to get my new experience from him and then drink him dry. But what happened instead did something to me that I couldn't explain. I'd never felt it before. Of course, I know what it was now—it's what Dahlia calls "The most potent of immortal curses." It was love.

That night, after we ate (and after I excused myself to throw up that food before it made me ill), Albie and I went into the den and got cozy on a couch. It didn't take long before his cute and my pretty touched tongues. It was starting to get heavy and, believe it or not, I was getting just a little bit scared. Remember, I'd never even *seen* one, much less had one inserted. But Albie seemed to sense my trepidation and stopped. "You're innocent, aren't you?" he said through a most amazing smile.

At first I wasn't sure what he meant, and said, "Hardly!" Then it dawned on me that he meant I was a virgin.

"You are, I can tell," he insisted. "So here's what we're going to do. You're going to give me a goodnight kiss, and then I'm going home. I'll call you tomorrow and see if you'd like to go out with me again, maybe to a movie. But I really want you to think about it first, because I won't be able to resist you again."

WELL! If I wasn't already, I'd have said, "I'll be damned!" But instead I did something I hadn't done since the night Dahlia turned me—I shed a tear.

After he left, I sat there dumbfounded. I even drank a bottle of wine, which affects me intensely if I don't feed first. I was thirsty, too, but I didn't drink that night. I just sat there and thought about Albie, and wondered what I was going to do with him.

I got a letter the next day from Dahlia, but I didn't open it. I knew, at some point, she'd exhort me, as she always did, to clean up my messes. But my mess just then was a boy named Albie, and the bigger mess was that I'd fallen in love with him. "Love, for immortals," Dahlia had told me during one of her many teaching lectures, "is the most potent curse. I cursed myself when I turned you, darling, because now I love you and can never let you go—which means I'm stuck with you forever. It's a most conflicted position to be in. Still, I managed to wait over four... well... many, many years before I saddled myself forever with another being. And if anything were to happen to you, I'd be doomed to *pine* forever. Do you see it, darling? Do you see the curse?

"You're a baby, Megan, an infant. Don't dare to love until you are very, very, very grown-up. Don't even let yourself love me. You may love what I do to you, and the gifts I give. You may love my incredible beauty and the luster of my skin and the sweetness of my kisses. But do not put them all together and love this entire creature. If you do, you'll never escape me, and I certainly will never let you go."

Albie called the next day, which was Saturday, and I told him to come. "I don't want to go out, though," I said. "Why don't you rent us a movie on your way here."

"Have you seen 'Underworld II'," he asked.

"Don't you dare!" I told him. "Stories about werewolves frighten me!" Believe it or not, that's true. Thank goodness there's no such thing! "Rent something nice, something lovely and romantic."

"Have you really thought about this?" he asked me.

"The movie?" I said, playing dumb.

"You know what I mean."

"I know what you mean, Albie," I said. "Rent me something

romantic."

I loved him, and if you could see me you'd know that I'm pretty easy to love back (or at least to look at). So I don't have to tell you what started to happen halfway through that movie. And there's probably no reason to mention that it kept on happening all over the house for the rest of that weekend. But early Monday morning, just after Albie left, the phone rang. When I picked it up, she said, "I'm on my way back, you foolish girl." She hung up before I could even gasp.

I feigned illness when Albie called that day, and again the following night. "You're feeling guilty or something, aren't you?" he finally asked.

"No! I love you, Albie," I insisted as I actually began to cry. "I'm really sick. Don't you believe me?"

"Then I'm coming over to take care of you."

"NO!" I practically yelled. "I can't let you catch what I have. I really do love you, and if you love me you'll give me a couple of days to get well. Do you promise?"

For a moment he was silent, but he finally said, "I'll call tomorrow, okay?"

Okay.

How Dahlia got back so quickly I can only guess, but no sooner did I hang up the phone than she was at the door. She didn't come in in a huff, or hysterically—she didn't even seem to be mad. All I could think to say was, "How did you know?"

"I turned you, darling," she said, taking me into her arms. "We have the same blood. Our hearts beat in unison. I felt the little twinge first, and I blame myself for not being here to stop it right then. But there is no stopping it now, is there? Unless, of course, I tear him to shreds."

When I started crying, Dahlia seemed to lose her balance. She let me out of her arms and went to a chair to sit. "I love," was all I could think to say to her.

"I know," she said with a terrible, pitiful look on her face. "It's too late for me even to kill him, isn't it? So, instead I'll try just once to reach you through this fog you're in. In order to have this boy there are three things you are going to have to do. First, you will have to break my heart—which is far more violent a thing than reaching in and tearing it out. Then you will have to break your own, because, though you're too young to know it yet, you *do* love me. Finally, you will have to take your boy's human life away from him and condemn him to love you forever, as you condemn yourself to the same fate. Listen to me closely now, my sweetest dear—the reason we never mate, never let ourselves fall in love male to female, is because our love is addictive and never leaves, even when violent hate begins accompanying it. You'll not be able to stand that boy for even a thousand years, much less forever, but your love will always be so strong that the two of you can never part. Eventually, your final act of love will be to rip each others' hearts from your chests. That or you'll stand together and watch the sun rise. Or perhaps you'll think of a more novel way to do yourselves in. It's bad enough being damned, Megan, but you're about to damn yourself twice."

I was crying the whole time she was speaking. I was still crying when Albie came through the door. "What's wrong?" he asked, looking over at Dahlia, then back to me.

I ran to him and threw my arms around his neck. I could feel my love hurting me as I slipped my delicately sharp incisors into his jugular vein. I ran my still-sunk teeth up his neck till my tongue was behind his ear. Then I took his blood as if I were inhaling him, and eased him down to the floor to die.

"I'm sorry," Dahlia said. "I never should have left you—you're just a child. But I'm forty-five hundred years old, Megan, and I may be getting senile. Can you forgive me?"

"You don't look a day over thirty," I said through my tears.

"I'll have you know I was twenty-six," she said with a beautiful, but sad, girlish smile.

"I killed him because I loved him," I told her. "I know what you said is true, and I couldn't do it to him."

"I realize that, child. I will punish myself for a long time for leaving such a baby to her own devices. Why, it can't be twenty years since I turned you."

"Thirty," I told her.

"It does fly," she said, her eyes gone distant. Then she seemed to snap out of her reverie and hopped to her feet. "Even so, you're an infant, still. Go to bed now, and cry yourself out. I'll be up in a while to love away your sadness. And don't worry, I'll clean up this mess for you. Remember, darling, you took the best part of him when you drank him, and it will always be with you."

She was right, of course, and I have to admit—I'd have missed Dahlia more than I'll miss poor Albie. She's like a mother and a sister and a lover to me. And she always protects me, even from myself.

II
Joshua's Story
A Night of Tails

The sun was just about to do its chin-up on the horizon, and I was still out and about. Not good. I'd intended to dine at a raunchy little strip-club called Willie's, till I found out it was full of wolves—real ones. I know a lot of Drinkers don't believe werewolves exist (which is kind of dumb, if you think about it), but they do. I admit, they're very rare, damn near extinct, but I sipped one once and am here to tell you—when you've had that taste in your mouth, you can smell one a mile away.

How I came to kill a werewolf (once I started, I felt obliged to drink her dry—despite the taste) is another story. But, trust me, there were at least three of those stinking lobos in Willie's, and I didn't like the odds. They'd probably have scattered as soon as I walked in—they're pretty skittish, and can tell a Drinker when they see one—but I wasn't taking any chances. I really didn't feel like dancing—and with their three to my one, they might could have mussed my hair.

Anyway, passing on Willie's left me pretty thirsty, so I decided to press my luck with old Sol and hunt a bit longer. I ended up with a crack whore in a blind alley. Unfortunately, she was pretty high when I drank her dry as a sucked-flat juice box, and I caught quite a buzz off her. Next thing I knew, the stars were fading and my ass was hanging out too far from the dark sanctuary of home (remind me to rip the throat out of the next lobo I come across—just for G-P's).

Luckily, I knew of an Old World Drinker with a cute little neophyte who lived in the vicinity. I also knew Dahlia (being so Old World) liked to travel, and I was hoping she'd be out of town—maybe having left her little chippie, whose name was Megan, behind. But the sun was starting to breathe down my neck and I could smell both of them in there when I hit the front door with an impatient fist.

"Wadda*you* want?" little Megan called through the door, obviously smelling a fellow Drinker.

"How 'bout some sanctuary?" I answered, pretty loudly. "I'm fresh out of ninety-weight sunscreen!"

Megan opened the door a bit. I'd never met her, but had heard she was cute—which was no-shit an understatement—and said. "Don't you have a home of your own, lost-boy?"

"Got sidetracked by a trio of lobos and didn't make it to my hacienda. Mind if I put up for the day?"

"No such thing as lobos, gringo," she told me. "I oughta let you fry for lame bullshit like that."

"Think you've got the cojones to keep me out?" I said, looking her over and practically smacking my lips. She was too-damned-cute, and I was still buzzed up on that crack whore.

"She probably couldn't," came a strangely accented voice from inside. It was that sultry, Old World accent and I knew it was Dahlia. "But if you don't put your eyes back in your head, I'm going to take your heart out and show it to her."

"Hey! Dahlia!" I called. "Just me, Josh. Didn't mean to ogle your little fuck, here, but I'm kindof in a bind. Mind if I..." The rest of my words became pretty much a gurgle, as Dahlia appeared out of nowhere and clamped her bright red nails around my throat. *Damn*, I wish I could move that fast! "Sorry," I managed to squeak.

"That's better," Dahlia said, releasing my newly crushed Adam's apple. "A little respect might just keep you from getting sunburned all to hell. Come in, little boy. If you like your hands, keep them to yourself. As you so indelicately put it, Megan is *my* little fuck—though, for amusement, I may have her don one of my many appliances and fuck *you*."

"Whatever blows up your skirt, Dahlia, just let me in. I'm starting to smell something burning, and I think it's me!"

Dahlia and Megan stepped aside and let me pass. I really *did* need to start minding my P's and Q's. I'd heard about Dahlia ripping the heart out of an Old World male who had a mind to take Megan's gorgeous little ass without Dahlia's permission. Trust me, you've got to be very high up on the pecking order to do in another Old Worlder. Dahlia was pretty much a *force*. I decided to start my obeisances right away. "Look, Dahlia, I'm sorry about the fresh mouth. I was getting a little nervous out there, what with dawn sneaking up on me and all. Forgive me?"

"Of course, dear boy. You're so cute, how could I not? I still might like to watch Megan fuck you, though—if you don't mind."

I didn't know if she was kidding, but I'd rather take it in the bung than do a crispy bacon impersonation, so I said, "Mi coolie es su coolie."

Dahlia laughed, and I could tell it was a laugh that meant, "Don't worry, I'm really not in the mood."

Megan recognized the laugh, too, and said, "Bummer! I wanted to use that big ten-incher on him. Can't I Dahlia? Pleeeease!"

That had me a little worried, till they both started laughing. I unclenched my ass (which, at that moment, you couldn't have gotten a broom straw up) and laughed with them.

"We were just about to retire," Dahlia said, "but there are a couple of fresh pints in the fridge. If you like, I could warm one for you." If nothing else, Old Worlders are hospitable.

"Actually," I said, "all I had tonight was a crack whore. I could use something to sober me up." That was true, but I was really hoping just to be able to look at Megan a while longer. She really was quite a stunner.

"Megan, darling," Dahlia said, as if addressing a servant (which she was, trust me). "Go warm a little something for our guest. Do it slowly, dear—don't scald."

"I'll make enough for two," Megan said. "I'm feeling a little peckish myself."

"Is the sight of this cute boy making you thirsty, darling?" Dahlia asked her. "If you'd really like to fuck him, or even vice versa, you know all you have to do is ask."

(I was thinking, please say you want to go for a roll! Please please please please please!)

"Oh, I don't know," Megan said with a cute little yawn. "We'd probably have to wash him first. He smells."

"Crack whore," I offered.

"Yes," Dahlia agreed. "You're an olfactory menace, to be sure."

Dahlia and I sat in her parlor, which was probably a national treasure trove of antiques and crystal and bright silver this-and-thats. Megan finally came out of the kitchen with a tray on which sat three china teacups, gently steaming. "I fixed you one, too, Dahlia," she said. "If you don't want it, I'm sure lost-boy here will go for a second cup."

I *was* still thirsty, but made myself sip. I didn't have my pinky in the air or anything, but, like I said, I was minding my P's and Q's. I knew I had to, but it was hard to keep my eyes off Megan—especially when she licked that crimson nectar off her lips. She was making my seat pretty damned uncomfortable. I knew Dahlia could tell, and she started up a conversation—probably to help me get my mind off what could easily get me killed. "I heard you mention to Megan meeting persons of the canine persuasion. Tell me about it."

"I thought you told me there *are* no werewolves!" Megan said in a startled tone.

"There aren't, anymore, dear. Don't worry your pretty head."

"What do you mean, *anymore?*" Megan persisted. "You said they were a myth."

"All myths are based in fact, darling. To most humans, *we* are myth."

"*Fuck,* Dahlia!" Megan said, her pretty complexion gone a lighter shade of pale.

"Why does this upset you so, dear?" Dahlia asked, trying to hide a smile that told me she was enjoying Megan's fear.

"*Why?*" Megan asked in an incredulous tone. "Jeez, Dahlia! I'm still trying to get used to the fact that there's *vampires*—not to mention that I'm all-of-a-sudden one myself! Now you're telling me there's werewolves, too!"

"Were, sweetie—*were* werewolves. I killed the last bitch myself nearly five hundred years ago. She called herself Sadia. And though those hounds *are* long lived, when I took out the last of their females, I doomed them all."

"Five hundred years ago, eh?" I said. "Do you mind if I ask..."

"If you value your teeth," Dahlia interrupted me, "you won't ask my age."

"No, no!" I said, draining that delicate teacup. "I was just wondering if I could get a refill."

"Fill our guest's cup, Megan," Dahlia cordially ordered. "He needs something to occupy his mouth." Then to me, she said, "Tell me, child, how old do I *look?*"

Oh shit. I knew I'd pretty much stepped into this when I almost asked her that question, and she was smiling that smile again that told me she was now enjoying *my* fear. I held my breath and answered, sheepishly (and truthfully, because she'd know if I were trying to flatter), "Maybe twenty-five?"

"Good boy," she said, reaching over and patting my cheek. "And does the thought of a little love-tussle with me excite you as much as Megan does?"

"More!" I said, feeling my blood temp suddenly rise. I hadn't even entertained that idea until just then—concentrating instead on Dahlia's *dangerous* aspects. But when she threw the idea out like that, all the possibilities inherent in a romp with a beautiful Old Worlder flooded my brain (okay, not my brain). Somehow, I managed to calm myself and play it smart. If there was any chance of this dalliance occurring, I didn't want to blow it. I bowed my head toward her and said, "I am at your service, lady—though I'm afraid my youth and inexperience might disappoint you."

"Chivalry!" Dahlia exclaimed. "Did you hear that, Megan? He's trying to be chivalrous."

"Woop-dee doo!" Megan said, rolling her eyes. "What about the damned werewolves?"

For a moment, I thought I saw a flash of anger in Dahlia's eyes and it excited me. If she'd taken Megan over her knee, I wouldn't have been able to keep my hand out of my pants. But that flash turned to something else—maybe pity. On a human it could have been love, but love for vampires is a dangerous thing. We call it "The Most Potent Curse." Finally, Dahlia said, "Go to bed, this instant, dear. Joshua and I will be up in a short while, and we'll all have a tender moment."

"Really!" Megan said enthusiastically—which told me she liked real dick and probably hadn't seen one in a while.

"Don't make your desires so obvious, darling, you'll embarrass Joshua. But, yes—*really*. Now go on up and let the anticipation build. And put on something special for our guest. Perhaps that little red tidbit I brought you from Paris."

I didn't know about *Megan's* anticipation, but mine could just about hear Carly Simon singing. Megan trotted off up the stairs, but locked her eyes to mine as she left. She had a real hungry look on her face, and I heard myself let out an involuntary moan. "Yes," Dahlia said. "She does do that to a body, doesn't she?"

"Never seen a more stunning little Drinker," I said without realizing it. Then I recovered and said, "Except for you, of course, Dahlia."

"Don't start lying now, dear boy. I know she's to die for, and several have. It's why I turned her, after all."

"She does know about 'The Curse,' doesn't she?" I asked.

"I've instructed her, and I believe she understands. In fact, in her own little way she has demonstrated her understanding. Why, dear? You aren't so self-infatuated as to think she'd fall in love with you, are you?"

"My concern was for her, Dahlia," I said, just a little defensively.

"It takes two to do that tango, sonny. She's a mightily gorgeous creature, after all. Not feeling a pang, by any chance, are you?"

"I'm no newbie, Dahlia. But how long has *she* been toothy? Maybe forty years?"

"Thirty, I think," she informed me.

"Shit, she's an *infant*. I've got two hundred years on her."

Dahlia laughed when I revealed my age, and it gave me gooseflesh. Then she said, "She's a fast learner, Joshua—and you, old man, are but a toddling boy. Now tell me about these canines of yours. How can you be so sure of what they were?"

"I'm guessing you've tasted one, since you claim to have killed a bitch," I told her. "If that's so, you know their scent is unmistakable. Nothing else smells like that, or that strongly."

"I did kill Sadia," she said. "But I didn't *drink* her. How repulsive. I broke every bone in her body, one at a time, then sat and watched her whimper till she expired. It is one of my most pleasant memories. And if there *are* still more of those filthy beasts walking the Earth, I shall make it a point to present them each with an encore performance."

"There's something I don't understand, Dahlia. You say you killed the last bitch to end their line. But don't they infect humans, who then become werewolves themselves?"

"That *can* happen," Dahlia told me, "but it's rare—rather like rabies. Actually, more like herpes. The lycanthrope virus has to be extremely active in them at the time, and their saliva must be deep in the wound."

"What if one were to *fuck* a human?" I asked.

"That's quite a disgusting thought, dear boy, though it would probably do the trick. But werewolves, when they're active and in the lunar throes, aren't generally interested in intercourse. Carnality, for them, runs more toward the actual root of the word—as in *meat*. Anyway, only born werewolves can procreate, and turned ones are very short lived. Now what makes you so sure you saw three of them tonight?"

"I smelled them."

"And how do you know what they smell like?"

"I drank a bitch dry not a hundred years ago."

Dahlia was silent for a good minute after I told her that. Finally, she said, "Did you know I'm psychic, Josh?"

"No," I answered. "I've never heard that."

"Well, I am. And I see you and me going on safari in the very near future."

"Where?" I asked her.

"I think we shall begin our expedition at Willie's. But right now, let's not keep little Megan waiting any longer. I'm sure she's all a-twitter up there, contemplating the arrival of a phallus with some real blood in it. Do you think you'll survive the both of us, dear boy?"

When she said that I could feel my blood grow dangerously hot. I felt two hundred years young, and seriously cocky. "I'm going to wear *both* your lovely asses out," I told her.

"Oh my!" Dahlia smiled. "Now *I'm* all a-twitter!"

III
Dahlia's Story
Isiri

Young Joshua quite surprised me, and I'm not one who is easily impressed. His delightfully vulgar little promise to "wear out" my and Megan's tushes was quite well fulfilled—though I felt obliged to wear his out as well in a little game of "role reversal." He took it quite well, actually, and please excuse the double entendre.

That forty-eight hours or so we spent in my waterbed had me looking forward to the hunt I intended we two to embark on. But what *really* surprised me was Megan's insistence upon accompanying us. "I thought you were deathly afraid of werewolves," I said to her.

"I *am!*" she insisted. "And I *know* one of them will come and get me while you two are out hunting them!"

"That's absurd," I told her.

"Not so very," Joshua piped in, no doubt desiring Megan's company for aesthetic purposes. "If they find out you're hunting them, they'll try to hurt you as best they can."

"See!" Megan said, with little pink tears in her eyes. "If I'm with you, you'll protect me, I know. You wouldn't let them eat me, would you?"

"No, I wouldn't," I said, comforting her. Those tears of hers are a weapon, and I hope she never discovers the extent of their power over me. "I reserve that pleasure for myself," I added, giving her a squeeze.

"You could save some for me," Joshua said. I gave him a little scowl to dissuade his growing boldness, but I sometimes forget my *own* looks, and he seemed to quite enjoy it, saying, "I could go for a little two-course snack right now, as a matter of fact."

The night we set out for Willie's was a lovely, crisp autumn eve. The sun was newly set, and still shimmering the sky with the gold and orange colors of fall. "It's hot," Megan said, as we leisurely strolled toward the seedier side of town.

"I'm sorry, darling," I told her. "I forget how fair a baby's skin can be. I should have let the sun go deeper beneath before I brought you out."

"But the colors on your cheeks are really cute," Joshua told her. "You look almost alive."

"I *am* alive," she insisted, to which Josh and I tried to restrain our smiles.

When we arrived at the nasty little dive called Willie's, we found it closed and wrapped in yellow, "Crime Scene" ribbon. I could smell that the inside was soaked in human blood. But there was also a scent I hadn't smelled in nearly five hundred years. "Great Caesar's ghost!" I said. "So you *did* know what you were talking about."

"Smell it?" Joshua said.

"Smell what?" Megan asked. She was beginning to tremble.

"The hounds of Acheton!" I breathed.

"Oh fuck me naked!" Megan said, through her violently chattering teeth.

"Don't even say it," I warned Joshua. "This is no joking matter. Look at her, she's going into pernicious shock!"

"Oh *shit!*" Josh exclaimed, seeing what I was seeing. "We've got to get her home! Do you have any more pints in your fridge?"

"No time," I told him. "Take her down that alley. I'll be with you momentarily."

Though the streets were strangely absent of passers-bye, I found a urine-stained drunk sucking on the dregs of a very cheap bottle of wine. I grabbed him by the collar of his natty jacket, and had him in the alley before he finished swallowing his swill. With a fingernail, I opened his carotid artery and held him over Megan—whose head was in Joshua's lap. "Squeeze him or something!" he said in a panicky voice. "We're losing her!"

When my little darling's mouth was full of that alcohol spiked blood, Joshua pinched her nose closed, and she swallowed. That brought her around enough to reach up and bring the bum's neck to her lips. She drank frantically, and when she was finished, Joshua and I guided her home.

After tucking Megan into bed, Josh and I went downstairs to the parlor. As soon as we entered there, I turned and slapped his face. "What did I do?" he asked.

"You're falling in love with her, you fool!" I told him. "Snap out of it, or so help me I'll put you out of your misery. You *know* what's at stake!"

Josh dropped into a chair and rubbed his jaw. I hadn't meant to hit him that hard, but he'd get over it. I was sorely afraid, however, that he'd *never* get over Megan. "I'm just *fond* of her," he said to me. "I didn't want to see beauty like hers expire. I couldn't bear seeing her go into shock like that. She's so fragile..."

"And you wanted to pro*tect* her, didn't you?" I said.

"I just..." he stammered.

"You're just falling in love!"

"Oh shit," he said, finally admitting it. "How can I stop it?"

"What am I to do with you children?" I said. "Is it television, or what? What makes you fall so easily?"

"I swear, Dahlia, I've never felt this before. I'm not even sure I really..."

"You *really!*" I said, interrupting him. "And you're damned lucky I'm here to help you, and that I don't just erase you and be done with it. What do you despise? What disgusts you?" I asked him.

After thinking a moment, he answered, "Lobos, I guess."

"Good. Look at me."

"What are you going to do?"

"Look into my eyes or I'll bloody well take out your heart and feed it to my little ailing darling upstairs!"

It took me about half a minute to get all the way into his mind, where I would do a little rearranging. As soon as I finished, Joshua would see, hear, and smell Megan as a werewolf ever after. When I released him, he said, "What have you done?"

"I've cured you, dear boy. Now come with me. There's a spare bedroom down the hall. I think we could both use a little something to take our minds off the events of this evening."

"What about Megan?" he asked.

"I think she's a little too frail right now for what I have in mind."

"I mean," he said, "do you think she's going to be fine?"

"For me," I told him. "But never again for you."

Joshua and I remained abed for a couple of days. Occasionally, I went up to check on and feed Megan. Josh wanted to come with me, but I wasn't ready for him to know what I had done. I was enjoying him much too much to spoil things just yet. I was hoping my own beauty would lessen his dismay at my ruining Megan's for him. In fact, I planned on giving him this sort of therapy on a regular basis for a while. I was much too fond of (and good to) that boy, I'm afraid.

We had to wait for Megan to fully recover before we began anew our hunt for those beasts. There was no leaving her behind now, as she would surely worry herself into shock again over this question of the werewolves. I've never been clear on the idea of reincarnation, but Megan's abject terror on the subject of those filthy animals (as well as her enchanting beauty) had me wondering.

"Why do you think they terrify her," Joshua asked me one day in the spare bedroom.

"I don't know," I said, curling tightly into his arms.

"Why do you hate them so?" he asked.

"Isiri," I whispered, unaware that I had.

"Who was Isiri?" he pressed.

"How do you know she's a 'was?'" I said, turning to face him.

"Your voice," he answered. "I've never heard sorrow in it before."

I stayed silent a moment, wondering if it were really in my best interest to reveal so much of myself to this child—this lovely child who impaled me so skillfully. What if the idiot fell in love with *me*? Or what if… no. Not possible. "She was my lover many centuries ago," I told him. "Her beauty was rivaled only, and only *perhaps*, by Megan's. I loved her."

"You mean *loved* loved? Cursed loved?"

"Yes."

"And do you love Megan?"

"Yes. But you should take care with all these questions, Joshua. I really don't know why I answer you, but one day I may decide you know too much."

"Could you really kill me, Dahlia?"

"Do you know where New York is?" I asked him.

"Yes," he answered.

"Do you know how quickly the minutes pass there?"

"I get the message. So, what happened to Isiri?"

"You are a brave lad, I'll say that much. I was a huntress back then, pretty much all the time. The most interesting and challenging game were, and apparently are again, werewolves. I became quite enamored of stalking them. They were rare even then, but not nearly so rare as they are today. Their present nearness to extinction can mostly be attributed to my rage after Sadia caught Isiri—who was an infant, not a decade turned—alone one night. You see, I had killed Sadia's twin sons, whom she'd called Remus and Romulus—the egotistical bitch. She left Isiri's half-eaten body for me to find, with a note that read, 'I stopped dining on her the moment she died.'

"Sadia was truly the queen of those wretched animals, though I hate to dignify her memory with such a title. It took me nearly a century to finally capture her, by which time I'd killed a thousand of her brethren and every other female of their kind. I kept her in a stone vault, and broke a bone every hour till I'd snapped them all. I watched her whimper till she was at death's door, then I bid her farewell and sealed her in."

"Where?" Josh asked.

"In a hilly region of Persia. Why?"

"I've heard tales that true-born werewolves can only be killed in certain ways—with silver or by severe dismemberment. Did you ever go back and view her dead body?"

"Silver does kill them quickly," I told him. "But that rabid bitch did not, I guarantee you, survive what I inflicted on her. Even if she had, which is simply not possible, she couldn't have escaped that imprisonment. I entombed her deep in a towering hill."

"So how do you account for the lobos at Willie's? he asked.

"As I once old you, the true-born are very long lived. I know I didn't get all the males. There must be a few still alive and occasionally infecting men. Those beasts at Willie's were most probably turned humans. They'll live no longer than a human life-span, unless, of course, I get my hands on them first."

"What about the female I drank a hundred years ago?"

"Damn you and all your questions, child! I have no more answers for you! Now shut up and close your eyes! Relax!" I insisted, making my way down his body to put him into my mouth. I needed to shut *me* up as well.

It was the fifth night after Megan's episode that I heard her making her way down the stairs. Joshua and I had just come from the spare bedroom, and were sitting in the parlor sipping sustenance. We were both still naked, and I was fondling his lovely lance—which was once again hard in my hand. The moment Megan came into view, he lost that erection and recoiled in his chair. "She's infected!" he said, in a terrified and pitiful voice.

"She's not," I told him. "It's the cure I placed in your mind."

Joshua was not an unintelligent child, and understood immediately what had been done to him. "It's cruel," he said, as he stood and walked off toward the spare room.

"Yes," I smiled. "And effective."

"What's got into *him*?" Megan asked, watching his pretty behind trot off down the hall.

Me, mostly, and vice versa, I was thinking. "Feeling better?" I said to Megan.

"A little weak, maybe. How do I look?"

"Delectable. Sit and let me warm you a cup. Then it's back up to bed. I'll come with you and gently massage you into ecstasy."

"That's a good idea, 'cause I'm god-awful horny, Dahlia. Why don't you grab Mister Thick-Dick and bring him up, too?"

"Such a mouth on you, child. Can you not strive toward the refinement I try to instill in you?"

"How's this?" she asked. "Could you also fetch your erstwhile paramour to fill my quinny with a gout of hot semen?"

I had to laugh. She was so cute in her frail condition. "Where, darling, on Earth did you hear that word?"

"What word?"

"Quinny!"

"I heard it in a movie. It was called *Elizabeth*, I think."

"As in the queen?"

"Yes. I think, Elizabeth the First."

"I knew her," I said. "And, yes, she was quite a 'quinny.'"

"So what do you think? Do I get a little dick, or what?" Megan persisted.

"Not a real one, I'm afraid. I fear young Joshua has contracted a carnal ailment. I was tending to it when you came down. He's quite embarrassed, so mum is the word. It also affects the temperament, so you're likely to see a change in him for some time to come—till he's completely cured. Do you understand?"

"What kind of ailment? You mean like VD? I thought we were immune to everything."

"Not everything, darling, as you yourself experienced just the other night."

"I thought you said that was precocious shock."

"Pernicious, darling," I corrected with a smile. "Now sit while I fix you a nice cup. Then it's upstairs to a little bliss. Okay?"

"Okay," she agreed. "But I need something *in* me. And I want you to warm it up, first."

"Whatever you like, little princess," I told her. Then I caught a glimpse of Joshua, scowling at me from the shadows down the hall.

It took but another day for Megan to completely get over "pernicious" and return to "precocious." I immediately began preparations anew for the hunt. Joshua tried his best to ignore the suggestions I'd placed in his mind, but I could see his hackles rise whenever Megan came close to him. Unfortunately, she could see it, too, and I could tell it bothered her tremendously. I was beginning to fear the curse had been a mutual affliction upon them. But my little spell was working quite well, perhaps even too much so. One night as we were sitting in the parlor, Megan walked in and lightly ran her fingers across Joshua's back. He recoiled at her touch, and Megan said, "Well fuck you, too, you stuck-up prick. I guess only Old World quinny is good enough for you now!"

When she stuck her tongue out at him, I heard him growl deep in his chest—and tense as if to spring at her.

"Now, Megan," I told her. "Remember our talk. And you, Joshua, should go fetch those knives I told you about. Remember? In the spare room? Tonight we hunt."

"But what if I go all pre-nishissed again?" Megan asked, paling a bit (if that's possible).

"I have lovely drugs for you to swallow," I told her.

"Human drugs?" she asked. "I thought they didn't work on us."

"They will work, though you'll have to take quite a handful."

"What are you giving her?" Joshua asked, his eyes conspicuously turned away from Megan's visage.

"Oh, some Valium and Seconal and Thorazine. All together they should calm her a bit."

"I hope you know what you're doing," he said.

"Relax, dear boy. I've slept with Florence Nightingale and Clara Barton and Marie Curie—though I don't think Marie really applies in this instance. I was concocting herbals while your ancestors were sleeping in caves—and, of course, I'm joking. I'm nowhere near that old."

"I don't know," Megan began, "but you're pretty damn..."

"Megan!" I shushed her. "I'll scald your bottom if you betray our secrets!"

"I was *gonna* say, pretty damn good lookin' for a middle-age Drinker."

"Yes. Middle-aged I'll accept."

When Joshua headed off to the spare room, I followed. The knives

I'd spoken of were in a chest in the closet. They were four, in all, eighteen-inch daggers made of an alloy rich in silver. I hadn't had them out since I killed Sadia, and the sight of them again—as well as thoughts of putting them to use—gave me quite a thrill. "See here," I told Joshua. "They have sheathes that go on the belt. You carry two and I shall do the same. If you wound one enough to have your way with him, the edges of these blades are sharp enough to peel the beast like an apple. Their screams are sufficient to excite the dead!"

"There's three of them that I'm sure of," Joshua told me, staring at me with his eyes gone an aroused shade of red. "When those are dead, I'm gone. I'll help you kill them for Megan's sake, then I want nothing further to do with you. I could have killed her tonight when she touched me, Dahlia. I can barely control my instincts."

"You wouldn't have made it out of your chair, dear boy, so keep that in mind. I'd hate for Megan to have to see you all opened up and spilled. Do I make myself clear?"

"I'm trying, Dahlia. I admit that I was falling in love with her, but you made me despise her. Don't you think you could have done this thing with a little moderation?"

"I'm a vampire, Joshua, in the oldest sense of the word. Moderation is not my strong suit. Expecting moderation from me is like asking a hurricane to tone it down. I am elemental, dear boy. But you have enjoyed playing in my fire, have you not? Could you resist me if I wanted you this instant?"

"If I could, Dahlia—if I were able—I'd love you to *death*, this instant."

"Death is a peer of mine, Joshua. We have an understanding. Sometimes we argue about who has been around the longest. You've been with death, been in her and had her in you. You can bring me no closer to myself than I already am. Try to remember this, as I would decry the world without you in it."

Young Joshua's wrath was a lovely thing to behold, and he growled—barely audibly and continuously—as I spoke. Almost as if he were purring. The thought of him loosing this wrath on those foul creatures nearly caused me to slip into a state of orgasm. I was feverish with the hunt, once more. I felt a thousand years younger, and longed for the stench of dying canine flesh.

When we left the house to begin our hunt, I searched the skies for Diana. Megan, at my side like a gorgeous puppy, wore a placid, drug-stained smile. I was in such a state of ardor that I was tempted to strip her naked and place her on a leash. Joshua was tensed into a crouch and sniffing the air. Both our senses were heightened by our confrontation in the spare room. Then he turned to me and I could see his teeth flash in the moonlight. His eyes were crimson and glowing. "I have their scent!" he hissed.

"Yes," I answered, inhaling deeply. "I have it as well! Take us to them, my darling boy! Lead the way! Cry havoc into mother night's sweet embrace!"

IV
Megan's Ending
Sadia's Revenge

It seemed like I was floating when we left the house to go on that hunt. Dahlia had fed me a handful of pills, and I was so fucked up I didn't really know *how* I felt. I knew we were going after werewolves, and I knew I should be, *wanted* to be, scared. I wanted to be *something*. And the way Dahlia kept looking at me had me thinking she just might throw me down in the dirt and start having me right there under the stars. I doubt I could even have felt an orgasm, if she had, over all those drugs. I was dumbstruck and grinning, I knew, to beat all hell.

"Mmm, I should have brought you nude," I heard Dahlia whisper. She was some kind of fucked up herself, like *heightened* or something. Then I heard Josh say, "I have their scent!" and Dahlia saying something about "havoc."

Then we began moving fast. Dahlia had me gripped by the front of my jeans, dragging me along. The backs of her fingers felt hot on my belly. "If I had Joshua's accoutrements," Dahlia said at one point, "I'd *ride* you to this battle!"

"What?" I said. "How the fuck..."

"Quiet now," Dahlia said, slowing us. "They're near."

"There's a pasture two miles west!" Joshua called, his voice gone feral. "They've rustled a calf and are feasting!"

"I'm thirsty," I said, feeling a little faint.

Dahlia took my face in her hands and looked me over. Then she put her wrist to her mouth and gashed it open. "Drink," she said, putting it to my lips.

I hadn't had Dahlia's blood since the night she turned me. I had no idea why she was giving it to me now, but I really couldn't have cared less. *Forty* handfuls of pills couldn't have gotten me as high as those few mouthfuls of Dahlia's ancient blood. Suddenly, everything around me came alive. My senses were gone minutely acute. Dahlia had to slap me to get me to stop drinking her. When she pulled her wrist away, I moaned loudly and cried out, "More!"

"That's it!" Joshua said out loud. "They know we're here!"

"Will they run? Are they running?" Dahlia asked in a frantic tone.

"Not yet. They're loath to leave their kill," Joshua said. "But we'd better take them now!"

"Stay here!" Dahlia said to me.

"NO!" I cried, snatching one of those long, bright blades from her belt. "I'll kill them before I'll be eaten again!" I screamed, making no sense at all.

"That's the spirit, Isiri!" Dahlia said, her eyes glazed and glowing red. "Flay their hides, bleed them dry!"

With that, both Joshua and Dahlia let out screams—no, not screams, *wails*. Then they pointed their sharp daggers west and seemed to vanish, so fast did they move! I took a more cautious approach, and vampire-crept toward the fray.

There were no more wails, at least for a while, but I could hear violent actions in that field of tall grass. Finally, I came upon the scene just as some *really* hideous screaming started. Dahlia and Joshua were hovering over a dark creature, slashing him and cutting away his skin as he howled. When they heard me arrive, they looked up at me, and their faces held no sign of anything resembling sanity. Then I saw fear in Dahlia's eyes as something grabbed me from behind and held me with its arm across my throat. "Let him go, or I'll snap her neck and suck the marrow from her bones," it said to Dahlia.

What happened next I know *did* happen, but I don't know *how*. In a move that made me feel like I was lightning or fire, I spun out of that creature's grasp. In the same fluid motion I buried my blade between his eyes till the point of it protruded from the back of his skull. Then I slid my dagger back out of his head. As he crumbled into a heap, I said, "And the motherfucking horse you rode in on!"

Dahlia and Joshua laughed hideously, then went back to skinning their wolf alive. "There were *three*!" I yelled at them. "Where's the third?"

"She's there!" Joshua screamed, jumping to his feet and pointing his blades at me. When he did that, Dahlia backhanded him and he flew twenty yards through the air if he went an inch!

"Snap out of it," she yelled at him. "That's Megan. Where's the third?"

Suddenly, we heard a howl off to the south, maybe a mile or two away. "There's a little barn out there," I said, looking into that distance. "The howl came from the barn."

"I see it," Dahlia said, looking toward the horizon.

"One more," I said, "and we're rid of them!"

"No," Joshua breathed. "I smell a bitch!"

"Oh for fuck sake!" I told him. "How many of these things are there?"

"Enough for our pleasure," Dahlia answered. "Let's go!"

Dahlia kept herself between me and Joshua. I didn't know why then, I do now. Now I know everything. And I'm here to tell you, everything is a lot when you're dealing with the likes of Dahlia, or even Josh. I know now he was a baby to Dahlia's eyes, but a couple of centuries of living is nothing to sneeze at. People—or *creatures*, anyway—get complicated by all that time.

When we got to the little barn, even I could smell that there were more than one or two of those things hanging around there. "They've got a whole club thing going on in this barn," I said to Dahlia.

"Slaughterhouse," she told me, grinning. "It's about to become a slaughterhouse. Ready for some slaughter, Joshua?" she asked.

Josh just made a growling noise, then the two of them started to move in those amazingly quick fits and starts that look so surreal. I concentrated on the barn, looking for doors and windows. Then I saw a door *over* the big, front door, and I guess that was the hayloft. There was a creature up there looking down directly at me, and I can't tell you how much that pissed me off! Well, believe it or not, without even getting a running start, I just *jumped* all the way up there. I cut his head completely off before he could so much as squeal. Then I pushed his body out and threw his head down at Dahlia and Josh's feet. "Isn't she cute?" I could hear Dahlia say.

"She's killing her own," was Josh's less-than-sane reply. I saw Dahlia slap him again, after which he shook his head and said, "Remove this spell, Dahlia, before it's too late!"

Just then, those things started coming out of the barn. I could also hear them clamoring up to where I was, so I jumped back down to Dahlia and Josh. "What spell?" I asked Dahlia. "What did you do to him?"

"Saved him from himself, and you from yours." she told me. "There's no time for this. Slash for the throat, kill them quickly! There's too many for fun!" she said.

"No shit!" I told her. "I think we're surrounded."

Then a female voice cried out, "Dahlia al Akira! I'd have a word with you!"

"Five minutes peace!" Dahlia called back. "Then you all die!"

"One old woman and a couple of children will kill us all?" said the bitch, as she made her way toward us.

"Fuck," I said, really feeling my oats and Dahlia's blood. "I'll kill you all myself!"

Dahlia laughed, and placed her palm on my cheek. "Give her five minutes, dear. Let's see what she looks like with her skin still on." But when that she-wolf came within sight, Dahlia's knees seemed to buckle. Then she hissed, "Sadia! But how?"

"Sadiin," the bitch corrected. "Though they say I do look just like my mother. You can call me Sadie. I like to keep up with the times."

"But I *killed* her!" Dahlia said. "And she had no she-pups!"

"She didn't die," Sadie said. "Though she never again left that vault where you entombed her. My fathers burrowed in and found her lying in a heap, unable to move. And though they fed her and cared for her, she never moved again. But she insisted they mate with her, over and over, though it caused her great pain—until finally she conceived and bore a fine bitch in her image. She died as they pulled me from her broken body. And I've been fucking like a toothy rabbit ever since. We've been keeping a low profile, Dahlia. We're still fairly few, but we're all over the world again. And we've been looking for *you* for quite some time. We located you in Africa, apparently engaged in some kind of bizarre zoological taste test. Then you suddenly disappeared again, though we picked up a trail that led us to this little corner of the world. We decided to risk our anonymity with a few small, but provocative, appearances—to see if we could draw you out. Our plan worked surprisingly well, as that little blood-letting at Willie's was our very first calling card."

"Not so well as you think, puppy-girl," Dahlia told her. "In fact, it was pretty much blind luck."

"Either way, Dahlia, You're here and we have you!"

"Well shit fire to save matches!" I said.

"What?" Dahlia laughed.

"Something a nun back at the orphanage used to say. It seemed appropriate."

"How many of you are here right now?" Dahlia asked Sadie.

"Enough to kill three suck-faces," she answered.

"Not nearly," Dahlia told her. "It's what your kind never did understand. If every last one of you were here right now, we'd kill you all—it would simply take more time. But I want you to know, Sadiin, that I'll do my best to save you for last so that you can get a truer idea of how your mother was broken, and broken, and broken. But I think that, in your case, after I break your bones I shall take them out and show them to you."

"You *can't* kill us all," Sadie said, but there was a definite note of doubt in her voice.

"Five minutes are up," I told Dahlia. "Let's do this thing so we can go home and screw."

No sooner had I said that than Sadie let out a howl, and werewolves started coming out of the woodwork. The flashing of our silver blades, moving so fast in the moonlight, became almost blinding. It was exhausting and exhilarating and seemed to go on forever. But neither Dahlia nor I nor Josh took so much as a scratch. Then I realized the few we hadn't killed were starting to flee. Sadie was one of them. She wasn't but ten or twelve yards away from me when I pitched my knife through the back of her neck. Then I turned and found Josh coming at me. His eyes were practically rolled up into his head, and he had a knife in each of his hands. At first I smiled, then I realized I was about to die. But at the last moment, Dahlia came up behind him and spun him around to face her. "Look in my eyes!" she screamed.

Josh did, then fell to his knees, just as Sadie came up behind Dahlia.

She reached back and pulled my blade out of her neck, then ran it directly through Dahlia's heart. Through my tears I watched my hands tear Sadie's head from her shoulders. Then I turned and caught Dahlia before she hit the ground. I wanted to pull that dagger out of her, but she wouldn't let me. "I'll live a few minutes longer with it in," she told me. "Now, quickly, drink while my heart still beats."

"No!" I cried.

"Drink," she begged, blood beginning to froth from her mouth. "Take as much of me as you can, Megan. It will always be with you."

I took Dahlia's wrist in my hand and brought it to my lips. I could taste my own tears falling into the blood I was taking. Even as sorrow punished my heart, I felt power flowing through me. I even started remembering things I couldn't be remembering. Then there was simply no more blood to take—no pulse. "Good-bye, dear," Dahlia said. "Joshua will take care of you now. He loves you, you know. Live as long together as you can." Then she closed her eyes and died in my arms.

Joshua and I are cursed. Doubly so, I guess. We even got married, one night, at a little drive-thru wedding joint in Vegas. I don't know how long it will be till we can't stand each other anymore—and can't survive without one another either—but neither of us thinks too much about that. Vampire love is *intense*! And, hey, we've got something to keep us busy for a very long time to come. As the old song goes, "We're on safari to stay!"

V
Joshua's Ending
Lost and Found

Had we stayed alone together in that spare room a minute longer, I'd have fought Dahlia to the death—my death. The fight might have lasted ten seconds if I'd fought with every ounce of my skill and strength. Dahlia knew that, of course. As she'd said herself one day, while I was holding her naked in my arms, she'd have killed me in a New York minute if it served her purposes. In fact, the only reason I was still alive, after she discovered my love for Megan, was because *that* served her purposes—though, at the time, I didn't know what those were. You cannot unravel the mind of a creature who has lived for thousands of years, not when you've only lived a couple of hundred yourself.

Not a moment too soon to suit me, we left the house for the embrace of Mother Night—which is the true home of every vampire. Dahlia was in the throes of the hunt's fever, as was I. Both those fevers had arisen earlier, back in that room. At Dahlia's side was a small, bitch werewolf grinning evilly. I still knew it was Megan, but I was losing that knowledge rapidly.

I may have been two hundred years young, but I wasn't stupid. I knew Dahlia didn't have to take that spell of hers so far. She *wanted* me to despise Megan, so that Megan couldn't help but despise me back. First and foremost, she wanted Megan to herself. Secondly, and this she would live without if she had to, she wanted *me* to herself. She not only wanted her cake, and to eat it, she wanted everyone else's cake as well.

When I caught the werewolves' scent, and Dahlia exhorted me to beckon into Mother Night's sweet embrace, my fever became a siren in my ears. I had to keep my eyes off Megan, whom Dahlia was dragging around like a rag-doll, or I'd have attacked her (and been killed before I could lay one finger on her). "They're in that field," I called to Dahlia, "feasting on a calf."

Then I looked and saw that little werewolf drinking from Dahlia's wrist. I could see, even beyond the tampering Dahlia had done in my mind, the power and confidence flowing into her lover/apprentice. Then I heard the little wolf howl, "More!" and I knew her brothers in the field had heard her warning.

Killing for sport becomes a blur of fever and heat and scents and tiny sounds—all roiling together. When Dahlia and I descended on that trio of lobos, they scattered. By poor luck we both chose the same victim to pursue, and the other two escaped. The blood-lust was so needy in us that we forgot those other two, and playfully ravaged the one we had. Then the most incredible thing (to *my* eyes) occurred. A great male wolf had the small bitch by the throat and was threatening to kill her. This made no sense at all to me, and then—even more bizarrely—the little bitch moved like ball-lightning and killed the larger male. I aimed my blades at the tiny lobo and started for her, screaming something I can't even remember now. Then I heard and felt an incredible *crack* to the side of my head, and found myself flying across the field. When I lifted my head off the ground, I momentarily saw Megan—as incredibly beautiful as ever—but she began to transform once more into a foul beast.

Dahlia and her bitch stood conversing in the field. They had located the escaped lobo, but I could smell another bitch—in addition to the one at Dahlia's side. Between my fever and blood-lust, Dahlia's spell, and the blow she'd inflicted on my skull, very little was making sense to me anymore. I needed the simplicity of killing to keep me sane, so I concentrated on the hunt. I needed quarry—I needed to slash and tear.

After covering a mile or two in a minute's time, we came to a barn and I could smell wolves all around and inside. The intensity of that scent had me grinding my teeth and breathing what felt like flame. Then the little wolf leapt away and killed one of her own, throwing its head at us like an obscene mace. For some reason Dahlia slapped me again, and I could once more see Megan in her vampire form—made even more stunning by the blood she'd taken from Dahlia. "Please," I begged, "remove your spell before I harm her!" But my moment of clarity was quickly over, and I was lost again—totally lost.

What took place after that is unclear to me. Some sort of parley occurred, during which I tried to gather my strength and wits—as I knew the final battle would ensue shortly. When it started with a howl, I simply allowed the instinct for survival (which is the unstoppable force behind every vampire) to do my killing for me. This was no longer sport, this was mechanical—like a frenzy of sharks or an overwhelming legion of assassins. Those werewolves, who outnumbered us by factors of tens, were doomed when we left the house to hunt them.

My confused fever would not allow me to stop until all were dead. The little bitch was the last, and I went for her—blades up—intent to dice her to pulp. But the next thing I knew I was staring into Dahlia's eyes. I could feel her removing things from, and placing others into, my mind. I could also hear things in hers that I'm sure she did not intend for me to hear. All the mayhem (not to mention feeding Megan) had thinned her mental barriers. Then I heard the thing that dropped me to my knees. "I could never kill you, Joshua. I love you, as I love Megan. My great age has cursed me, and I can no longer fight my love."

I remember nothing after hearing the confessions of Dahlia's mind. I awoke days later in Megan's bed, with her—once more radiant and beautiful—bending over me. I could also see the gash on her wrist, and knew she'd been feeding me her own strength.

The Most Potent Curse is on us now, in its most virulent and wonderful form. Our addiction to one another is complete. I would do *anything* for Megan now (including marry her in a bizarre and beautiful ceremony), and she would (and does) do anything for (and to) me.

Our honeymoon will last the rest of our lives, which, if vampire history indicates correctly, will be shortened by The Curse. According to dictate, we will become so close that we'll begin to despise the sight of one another, but not be able to survive apart. Our love, and hate, will consume us. But it could be worse—we could be mortal and trapped in just such a relationship, with no werewolves to hunt, or sweet Mother Night to embrace us.

Contributor Biographies

Amy Sterling Casil

Amy Sterling Casil is a 2002 Nebula Award nominee and recipient of other awards and recognition for her short science fiction and fantasy which has appeared in publications ranging from *The Magazine of Fantasy & Science Fiction* to *Zoetrope*. She is the author of 21 nonfiction books, 100 short stories, primarily science fiction and fantasy, one fiction and poetry collection, and two novels. She lives in Playa del Rey, California with her daughter Meredith and a Jack Russell Terrier named Badger. Amy has worked since 2005 as the Vice President for Development for Beyond Shelter in Los Angeles, and she currently teaches writing and composition at Saddleback College in Mission Viejo, CA. She is currently the Treasurer of the Science Fiction and Fantasy Writers of America and a co-founding member of internet author cooperative Book View Cafe.

J. Kathleen Cheney

J. Kathleen Cheney is a former teacher and has taught mathematics ranging from 7th grade to Calculus, with a brief stint as a Gifted and Talented Specialist. She is a member of SFWA, RWA, and Broad Universe. Her works have been published in *Jim Baen's Universe, Writers of the Future XXIV, Beneath Ceaseless Skies,* and *Fantasy Magazine,* among others. Her website can be found at www.jkathleencheney.com

J. Michael Shell

Southern writer J. Michael Shell is a serious and dedicated artist. At the University of South Carolina (B.A. in English) he studied under the great American poet and novelist James Dickey. Internationally published, Shell's fiction has appeared in *Tropic: The Sunday Magazine of the Miami Herald, Space and Time Magazine,* Hadley/Rille Books' *Footprints* anthology, Spectrum Fantastic Arts Award winning *Polluto* magazine, and the Shirley Jackson Award nominated *Bound for Evil* anthology (Dead Letter Press), to name just a few. His fiction has also been audio produced for MP3 download by Sniplits (www.sniplits.com)

Alan Smale

Alan Smale grew up in Yorkshire, England, but is now in America to stay. By day he labors as a research scientist for a well-known US Government Agency; by night he sings bass with high-energy vocal band The Chromatics and performs occasionally in community theater. His tales of fantasy and horror, alternate and twisted history have appeared in many magazines, including *Realms of Fantasy, Paradox, Abyss & Apex* and *Dark Regions,* and original anthologies *Panverse One, Book of Dead Things, Writers of the Future XIII, Low Port, A Wizard's Dozen* and *A Nightmare's Dozen.* Check out his website (including free fiction) at www.alansmale.com

Michael D. Winkle

Michael D. Winkle was born in Tulsa, Oklahoma, and has lived in the same general area ever since. He received a B.A. in English from Oklahoma State University and is now working on an Associate's in Accounting. He has worked in institutions such as the University Center at Tulsa and Tulsa Community College. He has had over two dozen shorts stories and articles published, including "Wolfhead" (*Tales of the Witch World 3*) and "Typo" (*Cthulhu's Heirs*). He has also written several novels which slowly creep toward publication. Michael's website is at: www.fantasyworldproject.com

Susan McKivergan
(*Cover Artist*)

Susan studied Fine Arts at St. Petersburg College in Florida, and is a self-taught Digital Artist and the mother of two beautiful children. Susan accepts commissions, including backgrounds for greeting cards, websets, artworks, photography, etc. All Susan's designs are original, created by combining 3D elements, brushwork, and hand painted details. She also offers image licensing for CD covers, magazines, book covers, etc. You can find Susan's website at www.thedigitalmuse.net

Dmitri Sled
(*Layout Artist*)

An erstwhile resident of Moscow's rain-drenched outskirts, Dmitri has lived in the United States for over a decade and a half. A relatively recent graduate of Bennington College, young Dmitri cannot yet claim any significant achievements in his chosen fields of science fiction writing and metal music (though he finally does have his own band—Kulak). To compensate for this scant info, he invites the interested reader to fill in the mysteries of his persona with their own conjectures and imaginings.

Breinigsville, PA USA
13 September 2010
245255BV00003B/5/P

9 780615 377360